Also by Gwen Cooper

Homer's Odyssey: A Fearless Feline Tale

Homer: The Ninth Life of a Blind Wonder Cat

Love Saves the Day: A Novel

Spray Anything: More True Tales of Homer & the Gang

PAWSOME! Head Bonks, Raspy Tongues, & 101 Reasons
Why Cats Make Us So, So Happy

<u>YOU</u> are PAWSOME! 75 Reasons Why Your Cats Love You,
and Why Loving Them Back Makes You a Better Human

YOU ONLY LIVE NINE TIMES

A HOMER WHODUNIT

GWEN COOPER

interrobang

New York

For my grandfather David Berkowitz (not *that* David Berkowitz).

For my grandmother Claire Moskowitz Berkowitz, one in a long
line of women in our family who never lost their "witz."

For all the cats I've loved before.

And for Laurence, always

For my grandfather David Berkowitz (not *that* David Berkowitz).

For my grandmother Claire Moskowitz Berkowitz, one in a long
line of women in our family who never lost their "witz."

For all the cats I've loved before.

And for Laurence, always

FOREWORD

It took me an absurdly long time to begin writing this book. What can I say? I was incredibly intimidated at the thought of writing a mystery novel. This now strikes me as particularly foolish, given that writing this book has been the most fun I've ever had in my entire writing career.

I'm so excited for you to begin solving mysteries alongside Homer and his crew!

You'll notice that while the cats—Scarlett, Vashti, and Homer—are the same cats you already know and love, their human friends have different names and faces than the ones you're used to. I wrestled for months with the decision of whether to write myself directly into this fictional series, or to create a character who my readers don't already know, but who would be free to make her own mistakes, solve her own mysteries, and live her own life.

It's pretty obvious which side I came down on. But in order to ease the transition, you'll notice that the protagonist and I do share a few superficial similarities. ;)

As for the other characters in the book, there are no direct one-to-one corollaries. No character in this book is anybody other than themselves.

This novel has been a great, great joy to work on. If you're one of those readers who's been with me since *Homer's Odyssey*, please know that I wrote this with *you* in mind. There's love for you on every single page of the book you're about to read.

PEOPLE & PLACES

Coacoochee, Florida, A SMALL South Florida coastal town only ten minutes up A1A from South Beach, which it resembles in many ways. Tourists flock to Coacoochee for its iconic Art Deco buildings, pristine shoreline, and vibrant nightlife. But beneath the glamorous veneer of celebrity hotspots and sun-drenched beaches lies an intimate community, where locals navigate exclusive enclaves and whispered secrets the travel brochures never reveal.

Rachel Baum, the thirty-year-old manager of Coacoochee's only bookstore, Title Wave Books; Rachel recently moved to town following a breakup.

Homer, Rachel's one-year-old blind, black cat who gets into more trouble than is entirely good for him.

Vashti, Rachel's two-year-old white cat, an acknowledged beauty and cleverer than most people give her credit for.

Scarlett, Rachel's three-year-old, imperious gray tabby who sees it as her job to keep her two siblings in line.

Tommy "Mr. Nightlife" Duvall, originally from Savannah, GA and the gossip/nightlife reporter for glossy *Palm* magazine; Tommy is Rachel's closest friend in Coacoochee

Daisy Locarro, a twenty-something scenester who's worked as a part-time assistant for numerous Coacoochee notables (including Natalie Dunbar and Julian Singer-Adams), and who seems to know the entire town's secrets.

Natalie Dunbar, an Australian investigative journalist, now living in Coacoochee, who tracked Australia's most-wanted criminal to South America.

Hot Mike, Natalie's eighty-pound German Shepherd who flunked out of police training but still views himself as a "working dog."

Isabella Stuart, known around town as the "Queen of the Scene;" Isabella is about to leave her prestigious columnist position at the *Miami Daily News* to start her own PR business.

Marc Gottsegen, ambitious nightlife authority who writes the annual *Coacoochee After Dark* guidebook and views Tommy Duvall as his chief professional rival.

Danny Elliott, celebrity chef and owner of Sabrosa, one of Coacoochee's hottest restaurants.

Griselda Carderas, the strikingly beautiful hostess at Sabrosa.

Laurie Castillo, one of the original Coacoochee "pioneers" and owner of Laurie's Closet, a trendy boutique on Hibiscus Road.

Kotik, Laurie Castillo's one-year-old tuxedo cat who has a tremendous crush on Vashti.

Dahlia Delgado, Director of Community Outreach for the Coacoochee Department of Tourism and an enthusiastic supporter of Title Wave Books.

Dorothea Wilson, owner of Title Wave Books, a former elementary school teacher, and a friend of Rachel's mom.

Julian Singer-Adams, a high-profile real estate developer and philanthropist who owns half of Hibiscus Road.

Brock Winfield, an aspiring author and former manager of Title Wave Books, who resents both Dorothea for firing him and Rachel for being hired as his replacement.

Samkhat, a feral "tortie" cat of indeterminate age who lives in and around the alley and loading dock behind Title Wave Books.

Nick Torres, Coacoochee's Chief of Police.

Jessica Martinez, a Coacoochee beat cop, relatively new to the force.

Dr. Edwidge Michel, Coacoochee's Medical Examiner

Evan Kirschner, sales rep for Daydouble Books who frequently does business with Rachel.

Nadia, a University of Miami graduate student and part-time clerk at Title Wave Books.

Stewie, a local mockingbird who frequently bedevils the five cats.

Title Wave Books, Coacoochee's only bookstore, and the setting for much of this novel!

CHAPTER 1

IT WAS TEN-THIRTY A.M. exactly as Rachel Baum descended the wrought-iron staircase leading from the front door of her apartment to the back-office storeroom of Title Wave Books. Racing ahead of her were three cats—Scarlett, a plump and imperious gray tabby with a white chest and yellow-green eyes; Vashti, an emerald-eyed beauty with long, silky white fur and a gentle disposition; and, darting out in front of them all despite his blindness, a small and slender black cat named Homer.

"Stop pushing, Vashti!" Scarlett aimed a warning swipe at Vashti's head with one white paw. *"You'll knock Homer down!"*

Scarlett didn't like to move fast. But that was only because, as far as she was concerned, Scarlett didn't have to move for anybody. (It's possible that Rachel and Scarlett had watched *Goodfellas* together one too many times.) Nevertheless, she hated being passed by her younger sister, and so perpetuated the fiction—despite all available evidence to the contrary—that Homer was apt to lose his balance if Vashti rushed ahead too quickly.

"As if!" Homer scoffed. To prove his point, he leapt from the step up to the staircase's handrail. Balancing there for a precarious moment, he propelled himself upward once again and smoothly glided through the air, landing neatly in the precise center of Rachel's desk in the shop's back room, located several feet to the right of the staircase.

"HA!" Homer crowed triumphantly. *"Nobody's ever knocked me down, and nobody ever will!"* He twitched his ears in Scarlett's direction, to hear whether she'd been impressed by this latest feat of derring-do.

Rachel had rescued both Scarlett and Vashti when they were less than two months old. She'd adopted Scarlett three years earlier at her mechanic's garage, out of a cardboard box on which someone had scrawled *Found Kittens*. Vashti had been discovered a year after that in pitiable condition, wandering alone on the playground of the elementary school where Rachel's mother worked.

Dr. Andi, the kindly veterinarian who'd treated Scarlett and Vashti, was the one who'd performed the emergency surgery a year ago when Homer was only two weeks old—surgery that had saved his life but left him permanently blind. The couple who'd first brought Homer to the vet decided they no longer wanted the tiny black foundling. After a week of posting flyers and making increasingly desperate phone calls, Dr. Andi had been unable to find anybody else who did.

Until she'd called Rachel.

Homer had always been blind. He didn't know what colors were, or what it meant to picture something in your mind. (He could *smell* and *hear* things in his mind, but he knew that wasn't the same thing.) He had no frame of reference when humans remarked on how much smaller he was than other cats, or how much curlier Rachel's dark hair was than most people's, or how well the new cut she'd recently gotten showcased her dark-brown eyes. He'd never seen a face and had no idea what Rachel's or anybody else's might look like.

Nevertheless, Homer's other senses were so finely honed, it was like he had his own kind of vision. Even Scarlett was impressed that Homer could smell the difference between a sealed can of tuna and a sealed can of tomato soup. When they'd still been living in Coral Gables—where Rachel had run a nonprofit dedicated to Everglades wildlife preservation—Homer had been able to pick out the sound of Rachel's car heading home at the end of the day from among the hundreds of others whizzing down LeJeune Road, five whole blocks away.

And even though Homer himself couldn't have told anyone exactly how he did it, he had a way of sensing the walls and objects even in an unfamiliar room, and mapping it all out in his mind, that usually kept him from bumping into things.

"Look at him go!" Title Wave customers would exclaim upon watching Homer leap from floor to counter without knocking anything over, or thread his way seamlessly through bookshelves and disappear like a shadow into the back storeroom.

"It's sad how easily humans are impressed," Scarlett often observed.

"You shouldn't goad Homer like that," Vashti chided Scarlett now, swishing her glorious white plume of a tail—like an Arctic fox's—in mild reproach.

"Don't worry about me," Homer said. *"Anything Scarlett can do, I can do better!"* With that, he sprang effortlessly from the desktop to the back of Rachel's computer chair. He perched there for a moment, with the jaunty air of a parrot on a pirate's shoulder, before jumping to the floor. Rachel had just reached the foot of the stairs, and Homer strolled over casually to rub his head against her shins.

To Rachel, all the meowing and feline acrobatics conveyed nothing more than three cats who were impatient to start their day. "Take it easy, guys," she told them. "I'm moving as fast as I can." Pulling a keyring from the pocket of her jeans, she opened the locked storeroom door, and all four of them entered Title Wave Books.

As always, Rachel paused to savor the quiet peacefulness of the store before it opened. Sunlight streamed through tall, south-facing Art Deco windows, and the wave-patterned terrazzo floor that had given Title Wave its name seemed to undulate in varying shades of blue and sand. The faint smell of salt from the nearby ocean permeated everything.

The cheerful cat calendar tacked to the wall behind the register declared that it was Friday, October 2nd, 1998. Tonight Rachel was hosting a book signing for Danny Elliott, the owner and head chef at Sabrosa, which was located only three blocks down trendy Hibiscus Road from Title Wave. His new cookbook, *Miami Spice*, had come out a week earlier, and copies were selling briskly thanks to a relentless round of local and national publicity.

Rachel knelt to give Homer a scritch under the chin. "Remind me to look for our black Sharpies later," she told him, wishing as she so often did that her cats could actually talk to her.

Homer was delighted with the attention and pressed his face into Rachel's hand. *"I will!"* he promised. He didn't know why Rachel couldn't understand him when he talked, when all three cats had no problem understanding each other or the humans around them. *"Humans are slow,"* was what Scarlett always said, although sometimes she'd grudgingly concede that Rachel was better than most of them.

As she flipped on the central AC, Rachel was grateful, not for the first time, that her apartment upstairs had its own separate unit. It would have been hard to justify air conditioning the entire building twenty-four hours a day in the blistering Miami heat, and Rachel didn't want to get on the wrong side of her mom's friend Dorothea. A retired teacher who'd once taught sixth grade at the elementary school where Rachel's mother still taught first, Dorothea Wilson had had the foresight to invest her pension in Coacoochee real estate back when it was still cheap. She owned Title Wave Books, along with the building that housed it, and she'd come through with a new job and a new home just when Rachel had desperately needed both.

Rachel was a thirty-year-old Miami native who'd never lived anywhere else. It was only six months since she'd moved east to Coacoochee from Miami's Coral Gables, where she'd shared a home with the fiancé she was now no longer engaged to. A ten-minute drive up A1A from South Beach (assuming no traffic, which in Miami was never a safe assumption), and a world away from Coral Gables, Coacoochee was a sun-swept spot right on the Atlantic Ocean.

Measuring two square miles in its entirety, Coacoochee was the very definition of a small town, albeit one that could hardly be described as "sleepy." For most of Rachel's youth, Coacoochee had been nothing more than a collection of dilapidated Art Deco buildings where, some thirty years earlier, entertainers who'd been famous during her mother's youth had put on extravagant shows at the big hotels. Changing tastes and decades of neglect had left the town moldering into decay, its once-gorgeous Deco apartments mostly occupied by recent immigrants and broke retirees who couldn't afford anything fancier.

Then the Eighties TV show *Miami Vice* had persuaded the rest of America there was still a hint of glamour to be found in South Florida. Artists and adventure seekers had flocked to Coacoochee, lovingly restored its shops and hotels, opened restaurants and nightclubs, and put the town back on the celebrity radar. These days, Coacoochee was practically overrun by the beautiful crowd. As Isabella Stuart, Coacoochee's best-known gossip columnist, liked to say, it had become a playground for the genetically blessed.

It was also filled with plenty of the workaday types, like Rachel, who kept the whole thing running.

Rachel switched on the overhead track lights and got a pot of coffee started in the small café, carefully arranging muffins, scones, and croissants—delivered fresh that morning from Butterflake Bakery—in the display case. Homer, in the meantime, positioned himself atop the Local Authors display table, which was closest to the front entrance. The moment when the first customer of the day entered, and Title Wave's front door opened onto Hibiscus Road, was always Homer's favorite moment of the morning. He waited for it now—tail flicking, ears pricked, every ounce of him straining at attention.

Hibiscus Road was an open-air pedestrian mall that stretched twelve blocks east to west, from the Oceanside Drive boardwalk at one end all the way down to apartment-lined Jacaranda Drive at the other. It was a vibrant blend of Mediterranean Revival, Midcentury Modern, and Nautical Moderne architecture, lined with restaurants, art galleries, eclectic shops, jazz clubs, nightclubs, a performance theater, and Coacoochee's last remaining cigar store, where elderly Cuban men in colorful *guayaberas* gathered to sit outside and play dominoes over medianoche sandwiches.

Minutes after Rachel had unbolted the front door and flipped the *Closed* sign to *Open,* the door swung wide with the day's first customer and a cacophony of aromas from Hibiscus Road tumbled in. Homer smelled the tang of seaweed and salt water mingled with the sweetness of citrus blossoms from sidewalk planters; the woodsy fragrance of the royal palms that lined Hibiscus Road and the heady touch-up paint that city workers dabbed as needed on curbs and benches every morning; the fake-coconut smell of tourists drenched in sunscreen on their way to the beach; a profusion of exotic spices spilling from the back doors of trendy restaurants that wouldn't open their front doors until later in the day.

Threading through it all: the aroma of the books around him, the fresh coffee brewing in the store's café—and, most importantly, the reassuringly familiar scent of Rachel herself.

The day's first customer turned out to be Daisy Locarro, looking slightly the worse for wear but still undeniably stunning in what was clearly last night's party dress. Originally from Palm Beach, Daisy had arrived in Coacoochee five years earlier for vaguely defined reasons. "Palm Beach was *dull*," was all she was apt to say when anybody asked. Daisy always seemed to be working as a part-time assistant for this or that celebrity or Coacoochee notable, collecting gossip wherever she went. But the gigs never lasted long, and nobody was quite sure where she got the cash to finance her "party all night, sleep all day" lifestyle.

"Here comes trouble," Vashti observed from her favorite overstuffed armchair in New Fiction.

"Look at that dress she's not wearing," Scarlett added from her sunny spot in the front display window, one of two that flanked the store's recessed entrance.

"Hello, gorgeous!" Daisy threw herself into Rachel's arms. "I need coffee as black as my soul—preferably in an IV drip, if you have it."

Homer twitched his ears at Daisy's familiar voice, recognizing the faint trace of cigarette smoke and the remnants of a sultry perfume wafting from her disheveled blond hair. There was also the barest whiff of something else, something maddeningly elusive, that he couldn't identify.

Rachel laughed and disentangled herself from Daisy's arms, heading for the café. "Morning, stranger," she said. "Salvation awaits right this way." She pulled an aqua-blue cup and matching saucer from the stack next to the coffee maker and poured generously. "You look like you had fun last night."

"If by fun you mean dancing until I practically passed out, then yes." Daisy breezed over to the counter and collapsed onto a stool. Rachel watched, amused, as she took a deep gulp from the coffee cup, looking grateful for the jolt of heat and caffeine. Nevertheless, her complexion paled slightly, and she pressed a hand to her forehead as if willing away a bout of queasiness.

"Late night?" Rachel posed the question mostly out of habit—she could guess the answer from Daisy's smudged eyeliner and the body glitter still clinging to her skin.

Daisy exhaled a playful groan. "I think my night actually started *two* nights ago. I have this vague recollection of closing the bar at Sabrosa after that *Palm* party and heading down to the Marlin on South Beach." Rachel herself had attended the party at Sabrosa to celebrate glossy *Palm* magazine's fifth anniversary. She'd stayed late enough to feel it the next day—although clearly she'd still gotten home at a much more reasonable hour than Daisy had. "Then an after-hours," Daisy continued, "then home for a disco nap." She sipped again at her cup. "Mmmmm, you really do make the best coffee in Coacoochee. Anyway, *last* night a friend scored us an invite to a celeb party out on Mercury Island that didn't end until about an hour ago."

Mercury Island was an exclusive, manmade island nestled in Biscayne Bay off the coast of Coacoochee. Infamous for its privacy, its over-the-top decadence, and the occasionally off-color hijinks of its famous denizens, it was a difficult place for paparazzi to access—which made it an eminently good place to be bad.

"Julian Singer-Adams himself gave me a ride back," she added, name-checking a well-known philanthropist and real-estate developer who owned half of Hibiscus Road. Julian divided his time between Los Angeles and Coacoochee, and a few years back Daisy had been his part-time assistant. "I always forget he knows actual movie stars like—" Rachel raised an intrigued eyebrow, but Daisy caught herself and shook her head. "I can't give away all my secrets. Yet. But trust me, you'd recognize them if they walked in here right now."

Rachel smiled. "I'll have to pry it out of you later. At Danny Elliott's book-signing tonight?"

"Deal." Daisy drained the last of her coffee in two gulps and set down the empty cup. "You're the best. Thanks, babe!"

With that, she fished a couple of crumpled bills from her sparkly evening bag, set them on the counter, and started for the door. She paused long enough to blow an airy kiss toward Rachel—then she was gone, the clang of the bell announcing her exit.

Calm descended on Title Wave once again. Rachel began her morning walk-through of the store, re-shelving stray titles and straightening display tables, as she made mental notes about what would have to be adjusted or pushed out of the way to accommodate the expected crowd that night. She'd already hosted smaller author events for local writers, but so far nothing as well-attended as the Danny Elliott signing looked to be.

Title Wave was divided into intimate reading nooks and browsing areas by tall maple bookshelves, with plushly comfortable vintage armchairs scattered throughout. Rachel noted with amusement that Vashti had wasted no time in claiming her favorite, distinguishable by its thick white coat of marshmallow-soft fur. That same fur speckled Rachel's own furniture and about two-thirds of her wardrobe, no matter how diligently she deployed the lint brush.

"Rich people may have designer labels on their clothes," she often said, "but happy people have cat fur on theirs."

Amusement now turned to dismay, however, as Rachel observed the deep claw marks Vashti had gouged into the chair's back. Groaning slightly, she maneuvered the chair—which was heavier than it looked—so its scarred back was pushed up against a wall, rendering Vashti's handiwork invisible to the casual observer. Still, it was only a matter of time before Dorothea discovered it. Even though Dorothea herself was proudly owned by two enormous Maine Coons, Rachel didn't want to test the limits of her tolerance.

"Stop clawing up the chair, Vashti," Rachel admonished breathlessly, as she finished shoving it into place and Vashti leapt delicately to the ground. "I mean it."

Vashti regarded her with innocent green eyes. *"But how will everyone know it's mine?"*

As Rachel continued her morning walk-though, Homer began his own daily inspection. He'd long-since memorized the store's layout, mapping in his mind exactly where the bookshelves stood, where the aisles turned, and where chairs and display tables had been set up. Brushing his body and whiskers gently along floorboards and shelves helped orient him, as did the scent markers he'd thoroughly rubbed into every inch of the place over the past six months.

Despite Homer's intimate familiarity with Title Wave at ground level, subtle things were apt to change from day to day. Without consciously thinking about it, he now adjusted his mental map of the shop to account for the wounded chair Rachel had just moved, his hyper-sensitive ears acting as a kind of sonar that told him it was now over by Caribbean Travel. Right next to the earthy aroma of coffee brewing in the small café.

Skimming his whiskers lightly against the lower shelves of New Fiction and Beach Reads, Homer made a sharp left into Latin American & Caribbean Literature. One of the store's speakers was directly overhead, piping the low-level thrum of jazz and Spanish guitar Rachel had mostly stopped hearing. This told Homer it was time to make a right through Tropical Gardening & Landscaping. Another right brought him into Biographies, and from here it was one left and a straight shot past Memoirs, Self Help, and Florida History all the way to the back of the shop. A final right turn took Homer past colorful arrangements of calendars and greeting cards until he arrived at the cash register.

With practiced ease, Homer leapt gracefully from floor to countertop, deftly wending his way around stacks of bookmarks, pens, journals, and prominently displayed copies of *Palm*. The closest friend Rachel had made since moving to Coacoochee—Tommy "Mr. Nightlife" Duvall, who'd recently broken up with a long-term boyfriend of his own—wrote a weekly column for *Palm*, which accounted for its pride of place.

Homer gave the stack of glossy magazines a cursory sniff, satisfied that nothing in his immediate surroundings required further investigation. Then he hopped lightly from the countertop to the floor. He'd just begun to examine an intriguing bit of tile, which still bore the trace aroma of a fish taco dropped by a careless tourist the day before, when a familiar sound caused him to raise his head.

"Natalie's coming," he announced to Scarlett and Vashti. The recognizable human stride, still a few blocks away, was confident yet measured, its soft thuds on the pavement accompanied by the faint swish of denim. Alongside this familiar sound, Homer also caught the gentle jingle of a metal leash and the distinct panting of a large German Shepherd.

"I doubt it." Scarlett, still sprawled in the front display window, stretched lazily and flipped onto her back, exposing the fluffy white mound of her belly. This front-window perch was, to her way of thinking, the best in the whole shop. It allowed her to keep an eye on the store's goings-on—a

queen surveying her realm—while basking in the hot Miami sun. All from a spot that was agreeably inaccessible to the humans who filtered in and out over the course of the day. *"If she were coming, I'd be able to see her."*

"Your eyes are closed," Vashti pointed out.

"Homer doesn't have eyes at all, and you never question him,*"* Scarlett retorted.

Vashti didn't bother responding; everybody knew that when Homer said he'd heard something, you could stake your last can of tuna on it.

Only a few minutes later, the bell above the door jingled merrily once again. "Hello, swee-tie!" Natalie's brassy voice filled the shop, her Australian accent making *sweetie* sound like two separate and distinct words. "How's my favorite bookseller on this fine Miami morning?"

A large, auburn-haired woman in her late thirties, Natalie Dunbar was an investigative journalist and a field producer for Australian *60 Minutes*. Her claim to fame was having tracked Australia's most-wanted criminal to South America and capturing him there. Uniformly cheerful and endlessly resourceful, Natalie lived in a coral-colored stucco house only a few blocks from Title Wave.

Rachel set down the stack of new paperbacks she'd been shelving and smiled as she headed back to the café. "So far, so good. How are you?"

"Can't complain. Hot Mike and I are out for our morning constitutional." She paused to pat the enormous head of the eighty-pound German Shepherd by her side. Gesturing to the small board propped on the café's counter, which announced daily specials in colored chalk, she added, "A café con leche with coconut milk would hit the spot."

Homer was already headed for the clean-dog smell of Hot Mike, which was accompanied by a gruff, *"Morning, Homer."* Hot Mike turned his muzzle toward Vashti, now balanced casually atop the Hardcover Best-sellers front table, and added a respectful, *"Ma'am."*

"Miss," Vashti corrected gently, and commenced grooming the lustrous fur of her back. Scarlett rolled her eyes for what would undoubtedly be the first of many times that day.

Natalie was always accompanied on her morning coffee runs by her two-and-a-half-year-old German Shepherd, Hot Mike. As a puppy, Hot Mike was in training to be a police dog, but a tendency to hesitate when given a direct command made him unsuited for service. Natalie happened to be friendly with the K9 officer looking to rehome the six-month-old, and a tight bond between woman and dog had instantly formed.

The day she'd adopted Hot Mike, Natalie had asked Daisy, then working as her part-time assistant, to do two things: call the veterinarian to make an appointment for the puppy, and then transcribe a recording taken from a "hot mic," i.e. a microphone left on after an interview had concluded. Daisy had dutifully booked a vet appointment later that same afternoon for one "Hot Mike."

Nobody had laughed harder than Natalie at the inaptly bestowed moniker, and two years later it still made her chuckle. Despite this—or perhaps because of it—Hot Mike was an exceptionally serious dog. He never chased his tail or barked at squirrels or rolled around on his back in the grassy dog park. Natalie's attempt to alleviate his seriousness a *tiny* bit by dressing him as a hot dog last year for Coacoochee's annual Halloween parade had been, as she'd observed dryly, rather like putting Christmas antlers on Sam the Eagle.

Hot Mike's commitment to Natalie was absolute and his guiding North Star. Deep down, though, he had the nagging sense he'd failed at fulfilling his life's true purpose, and he secretly hoped for an opportunity to prove himself.

For his part, Homer liked Hot Mike immensely. He knew Hot Mike would have protected Natalie with his life, if it ever came down to it. Which was exactly how Homer felt about Rachel.

Natalie unhooked Hot Mike's leash from his collar and perched on one of the café stools. "I don't know how you do it," she said, "but you make the best café con leche in Coacoochee."

"Daisy Locarro said the same thing not one hour ago. Ironic, since I never touch the stuff." Having finished steaming the coconut milk, Rachel combined milk and coffee in a wide, shallow white coffee cup, which she slid across the counter to Natalie.

"You don't know what you're missing." Natalie took an appreciative sip. "How is it possible for a Miami native to reach the age of thirty without developing a taste for coffee?"

"I know, right? I lived with a Cuban man for three years, and even that didn't…"

A darting pain shot through Rachel unexpectedly, cracking her voice and bringing a sudden dampness to her eyes. It had been six months, and most days Rachel was mostly okay. But there were still moments, like now, when even an oblique reference to Henry was enough to derail her. Natalie gave her a moment, sipping coffee and reaching down to pat Hot Mike's head.

Rachel took a deep, steadying breath. "You'd think six months would be long enough to get over it." Gesturing at the shelved books all around her, she added, "Working here, you realize it's the oldest story in the world: Girl meets boy, girl and boy plan a future together, boy breaks girl's heart by sleeping with other women."

Natalie grimaced sympathetically. "I could write a chapter or two of that book myself. How'd you figure it out?"

"I found a piece of paper with another woman's name and phone number." Rachel paused to shoo away Vashti, who had leapt onto the counter and was sniffing a small pitcher of cream with interest. "And then it was like everything clicked into place at once—all the late nights 'at work,' all the excuses for suddenly not being around." Rachel laughed ruefully and brushed a lock of curly hair—impossible to tame in Coacoochee's seaside humidity—from her forehead. "Having my nonprofit lose its funding a week later was the cherry on the sundae."

Homer had instinctively moved closer to Rachel and was now rubbing his head furiously against the backs of her legs. An unpleasant sort of feeling bloomed in his belly. If he'd been a human instead of a cat, he might have called the feeling guilt.

Even though he'd only been six months old at the time, it was Homer who'd first detected the scent of a female human who wasn't Rachel clinging too closely to Henry's skin to be explained by casual contact. It was Homer who'd been able to hear the tiniest pauses in Henry's speech—indiscernible even by Vashti and Scarlett—when he'd smoothly explained why he was working longer and coming home later.

And Homer had been the one who'd nosed a small, discarded scrap of paper out of Henry's coat pocket. Scarlett and Vashti hadn't noticed anything amiss at first, but to Homer it had reeked of this mystery woman's scent.

Although all three cats were perfectly capable of understanding human speech, none of them had ever even tried to decipher the gobbledygook humans were forever writing down. Nevertheless, Vashti had sensed something damning about this particular piece of paper. Its very brevity was incriminating. Some woman had wanted to tell Henry something sharp and urgent. Something he'd deliberately kept hidden from Rachel. And even though she'd liked Henry just fine (*"You* always *like men,"* Scarlett pointed out waspishly), Vashti had been the one who'd left the incriminating slip of paper conspicuously placed on the couch.

"If Henry isn't doing anything wrong," she'd reasoned, *"there's no harm in Rachel finding it."*

Scarlett had never had the smallest particle of use for Henry, who'd refused to acknowledge that the spot on the sofa closest to the lamp was reserved by rights for Scarlett's exclusive use, and who never cleaned the litterbox to Scarlett's exacting (but entirely reasonable!) standards, and who acted as if typing things into the computer on his desk was more important than crumpling up a ball of paper for Scarlett to play with.

But even Scarlett had grieved for Rachel's obvious heartbreak during those first few post-Henry weeks. Surprisingly, it was Scarlett who'd spent the most time curled up reassuringly on Rachel's chest while she'd cried. *"We'll be all right,"* she'd purred, nuzzling deeper into the crook of Rachel's neck. *"You'll see."*

Rachel bent down to grab a plastic bottle of water from the café's small refrigerator, rubbing Homer behind the ears as she did so. When she stood again, she was smiling. "Still, I can't say I'm sorry to have ended up here." Her eyes slid appreciatively over what had to be one of the finest sights life had to offer: a sunny, beautiful room filled with books. Then she sighed. "Now I just need to get through tonight."

"The big shindig with Danny Elliott!" Natalie's eyes lit up. "Got a case of the jitters?"

"Maybe a little," Rachel confessed. "Press and photographers and an actual VIP guest list make it a bit more complicated than I'm used to. Plus, I've been looking for our black Sharpies for two days now. I can't have Danny autographing books with a blue ballpoint."

Homer's ears flicked. It was the second time this morning Rachel had mentioned the Sharpies. Feeling a sudden need to do something nice for her, he crept quietly over to where Hot Mike still sat attentively next to Natalie, using his nose and whiskers to guide him toward Hot Mike's sturdy paws.

"Hey, Hot Mike! Did you catch that about the Sharpies? Do you know what they smell like?"

Hot Mike gave an affirmative dip of his head. *"Natalie uses them to label all her tapes. I know the scent."*

"What do you say we try to find Rachel's before she drives herself crazy?"

"Copy that." With a clatter of well-trimmed claws, Hot Mike hoisted himself to his feet.

"I'll help too," Vashti announced, and leapt gracefully from the hardcover display table.

"Great!" Homer replied. *"Let's fan out."*

Scarlett, half-dozing in the warmth of the front window, opened one eye. *"I saw her writing up shelf talkers the other day for some Agatha Christies that just came in. The ones on the top shelf of the bookcase toward the back of the store."* Scarlett heaved a mighty yawn. *"She got distracted when the phone rang. Maybe she left them up there?"*

Rachel and Natalie found themselves highly entertained, if somewhat bemused, by what sounded like a sudden clamor of meows from the cats and low rumblings from Hot Mike.

"They're certainly chatty this morning!" Natalie noted. "It's amazing how Homer isn't intimidated by Hot Mike. Most cats see all that bulk and run for the hills."

Rachel cast a fond glance in Homer's direction. "Homer's never been intimidated by anyone. Maybe it's because he's blind. He can't see how big the other guy is, so it doesn't faze him."

"We could all take a page from Homer's book," Natalie said. "By the way—do you have that copy of *Midnight in the Garden of Good and Evil* I ordered? I want to take it on the plane with me to Argentina tonight."

"Argentina!" Rachel's eyebrows lifted. "Sounds exciting!"

"Just a work thing." Natalie shrugged. "Although it's kind of a funny story..."

While Rachel and Natalie talked, the three cats and Hot Mike plotted their next move, trying to keep their voices down.

"Vashti, can you show Hot Mike and me which shelf Scarlett's talking about?" So Vashti went first, and Homer and Hot Mike followed one by one a moment later, trying to make their collective departure from the café area inconspicuous. When they arrived at the bookcase where Vashti stood in wait, Homer cocked his head, whiskers twitching as he sniffed the air and recognized faint traces of the pungent, acrid odor the Sharpies gave

off. *"They're definitely up there."* He turned his head in the dog's direction. *"What do you think, Hot Mike?"*

Hot Mike arched his neck, nostrils flaring. *"I smell it, too,"* he confirmed. *"But I don't see how we can get to them."*

"I can think of a way, but we'll need a distraction."

"I'll take care of that." Her magnificent tail held high, Vashti strutted across the bookstore with the poise of a runway model. A fluid leap brought her to the countertop beside the cash register. She paused for a moment, waiting until she was sure Rachel's eyes were on her. With a casual flick of one dainty white paw, she batted a stack of Title Wave bookmarks from the edge of the counter, sending them fluttering to the floor like confetti. She swished her tail again and scattered a neat pile of postcards onto the ground, then sent a pencil holder brimming with Title Wave–branded pens after them in a clattering cascade. A colorful heap of palm cards promoting the Danny Elliott book signing quickly followed.

"Vashti!" Rachel hurried over from the café. "What's gotten into you?"

Vashti once again regarded Rachel with wide, innocent eyes. *"Who, me?"*

Natalie, observing Vashti's antics from across the store, couldn't help but laugh. "I think she wanted some attention." She rose from her stool. "Here, let me help."

Vashti leapt down from the countertop to join Rachel and Natalie, who had now both knelt on the floor to gather the detritus she'd strewn about. *"I'm sorry."* She rubbed her head along Rachel's arm. *"But it's for your own good."*

Rachel had never been able to resist an affectionate Vashti (or any affectionate animal, really) and chose to interpret her soft *mew*s as contrition. She stroked Vashti's back with one hand as she gathered up pens and postcards with the other. "There are easier ways to get my attention, you know," she told the cat. To Natalie she added, "Thanks for giving me a hand. Clearly I need three of them." Both women laughed, while Vashti purred and nuzzled her head into Rachel's palm for all she was worth.

In the meantime, Homer had crept closer to Hot Mike. *"Ready?"* Homer asked. *"If you can give me a boost, I should be able to jump the rest of the way."*

"On my signal," Hot Mike agreed. He lowered his body, bracing his weight on muscled forelegs. Though towering in stature, he always took care to move gently around Homer.

Homer hopped neatly onto Hot Mike's back, sniffing the air to judge distance. Then Hot Mike rose upon his hind legs, giving Homer just enough extra height to leap onto the top shelf of the bookcase. For a precarious moment, it looked as if he might lose his footing. Scarlett and Vashti, both watching from their respective spots across the store, held their breath. Homer's back paws scrabbled against the wood's smooth finish, but he steadied himself, his keen nose detecting the sharp, chemical odor of permanent ink.

"Got 'em!" Homer declared triumphantly.

Working quickly, he nudged one Sharpie at a time off the edge. Hot Mike, waiting below, caught each marker in his mouth. He made a face at the unpleasant smell but said nothing.

"Now," Vashti said, *"we just need to put them someplace where Rachel will think she found them herself."*

"I'm *petting* you." Rachel, still gathering loose pens with one hand while stroking Vashti with the other, assumed the cat was meowing at her. "It's not *my* fault my other hand is occupied."

Scarlett flicked her tail languidly. *"Slide them near the café register. Where she keeps her notepads."*

Nodding, Hot Mike trotted around the shelves back in the direction of the café, setting the markers down where Scarlett had indicated. Then he padded calmly back to the stool Natalie had abandoned, just in time for Natalie and Rachel to return. Natalie was holding the book Rachel had rung up for her.

"Well," she said, draining the last of her café con leche, "time for me and Hot Mike to finish our walk. Thanks for the coffee and the chat, love." The bell above the door jingled merrily as Natalie and Hot Mike left, the dog's nails clicking on the terrazzo floor.

LATE MORNING DRIFTED INTO early afternoon as the sun climbed higher over Coacoochee, streaming through the tall Art Deco windows of Title Wave Books. A woman came in looking for a birthday gift for her father, something that captured the charm of 1950s Miami, and Rachel led her to a neat row of vintage photography books. She sold a couple of breezy romance novels to a pair of tourists who wanted recommendations on beach reads, and served coffee and pastries to a few of her regulars, who liked to spend a leisurely hour with their newspapers in the small café. Homer—fulfilling his role as what Rachel often described as "Title Wave's unofficial greeter"—made sure each visitor was met at the door with a hearty *"Howdy, friend!"* and welcoming head-bonk to the shin. The comforting scent of coffee and sugar hung in the air, mingling with the briny ocean breezes drifting in from Hibiscus Road.

With the mini rush winding down and her coffee regulars settled into quiet reading, Rachel turned her attention to Title Wave's two front display windows. One of them, naturally, was devoted to copies of *Miami Spice* and the upcoming author signing. Scarlett continued to snooze in the other, sprawled regally atop a hardcover copy of *Oceanfront Empire*, the autobiography-slash-business advice book "written" (almost certainly ghostwritten, Rachel thought) by Julian Singer-Adams. Scarlett's plump posterior obscured his book almost completely, while the placement of her white front paws seemed to call special attention to *The No. 1 Ladies' Detective Agency*, which rested next to it.

Rachel leaned into the display window to place the newly updated version of *Coacoochee After Dark*, written by local nightlife authority Marc Gottsegen, which had been delivered by his publisher the day before. She paused in her work to rub Scarlett affectionately behind the ears, dropping a kiss on the black tiger-stripe "M" on Scarlett's forehead.

"You have good taste!" Rachel whispered in her ear.

"I know." Scarlett purred contentedly, closing her eyes and turning her face toward the sun.

Rachel knew her friend Tommy would be dismayed to see Marc Gottsegen's new book displayed so conspicuously in the shop's front window. While pretending at least superficial friendship whenever they ran into each other (which was often; Coacoochee was a *very* small town), Tommy and Marc not-so-secretly detested each other, and their professional rivalry went back years.

Marc was at pains to let all and sundry know that while Tommy wrote a silly little nightlife *column,* Marc wrote actual *books*. Marc's updated guidebook appeared like clockwork every October and was distributed to bookstores, tourists, and travel agents around the globe—which *obviously* made its publication a much bigger deal (here Marc would sneer almost imperceptibly) than a thousand weekly words in some local rag.

Then again, Coacoochee locals looked for Tommy's thousand words in *Palm* every Friday, eager to learn in real-time which people and places were *hot* and which were definitively *not*—which meant Tommy enjoyed higher year-round visibility than Marc. Perhaps this was why Marc had lately taken to mocking Tommy's (admittedly self-appointed) moniker of "Mr. Nightlife" behind Tommy's back. *Mr. Nightlight? Never heard of him.*

"He's just jealous he didn't think of it first," Tommy coolly informed anyone who reported this bit of cattiness back to him—although privately, with Rachel as a sympathetic audience, he seethed.

Rachel was Team Tommy all the way—as was Vashti. Men were always admiring Vashti for her beauty, which made her prone to liking men more than women as a general rule. But Tommy was an especially enthusiastic admirer. "She's so glamorous!" he always exclaimed. Vashti would preen and press the top of her head into Tommy's hand as he petted her, while Scarlett rolled her eyes and Rachel chuckled, remembering the scraggly, woebegone kitten she'd rescued. "She looks like a movie star!"

Rachel was happy (and so was Vashti!) to do Tommy a favor if and when she could. But Coacoochee's only nightlife guidebook certainly warranted the attention of Coacoochee's only bookstore.

"Tommy's not going to be happy when he sees that," Vashti predicted, having resumed her perch on her favorite scratched-up armchair.

"Maybe he won't notice." Homer brought up one hind paw to scratch furiously at his itchy right ear—grateful, as he sometimes was, that he never had to worry about seeing things that made him unhappy.

Rachel had barely finished positioning the last copy of Marc Gottsegen's updated nightlife guide when in swept Tommy himself, all effortless style and brimming energy in a sleek linen blazer that perfectly complemented his dark jeans. Far more interested in fashion than football, Tommy never-theless had the tall, broad-shouldered build of a natural athlete. His black eyes were several shades darker than his light-brown hair, and they sparkled in a devilish, perpetually amused way that never failed to lift Rachel's spirits. A thirty-two-year-old Savannah transplant who'd arrived on the Coacoochee scene a few years earlier, Tommy had a knack for slipping seamlessly among its many social circles and scoring A-list invites to its most exclusive VIP rooms. Despite the success of his current gig, he'd made no secret of his bigger ambitions. Now, from the gleam in his eyes, Rachel could tell he had news to share.

"Hello, my darling!" He warmly bussed Rachel on both cheeks—although not before he threw a scathing look at the updated window display. "I see we've done some redecorating."

"Don't you know frowning causes wrinkles?" Rachel laughed as Tommy's forehead instantly smoothed out. "Come and get a cup of coffee," she said. "I can tell you've got news, and I can't wait to hear it."

"Neither can I!" Vashti hurried across the store and leapt onto the café counter next to Tommy, who patted her head more absentmindedly than usual. Even Scarlett—feeling a bit overwarm after more than three hours in the sun—left the front display window and edged closer to the café with studied nonchalance.

Only Homer kept his distance, choosing to remain in one of the reading chairs closer to the back storeroom, where he snoozed on and off. Truth be told, he wasn't as fond of Tommy as everyone else seemed to be. Homer's favorite moments in life were spent curled up in the warmth of Rachel's lap, upstairs in their apartment. Ever since Rachel had met Tommy—who insisted on taking her to this nightclub or that cocktail party three or four nights a week (*you can't mourn Hunter or Hendrix or whatever his name was* forever, *darling*)—those evenings had become fewer and further between.

Tommy tried, and failed, to dial down a broad grin. "Isabella Stuart's leaving the *Miami Daily News*," he announced. "She's decided to start her own PR firm, and she's going to recommend *me* to be her replacement!"

Isabella Stuart wrote the "Queen of the Scene" column for the *Miami Daily News*—South Florida's largest and most prestigious newspaper. Her signature blend of charm and savvy allowed her to float seamlessly from rooftop parties to exclusive dinners to gala fundraisers, gathering scoops without ever ruffling the wrong feathers. She was tall, poised, and polished, with sleek chestnut hair and a couture wardrobe that had left many an after-dark doyenne weeping with envy. Isabella could command a room with a smile or a flash of her discerning green eyes, and insiders whispered that half the city's social scene owed its rise—or downfall—to her strategic coverage.

Tommy often described Isabella as his mentor and one of his closest friends. But to Rachel, it seemed as if Isabella sometimes treated Tommy more like a sidekick (*be a love and fetch me another glass of champagne*) than a colleague. She was thus genuinely delighted to see Isabella come through for him at last. "That's *amazing!*" she told him with sincere enthusiasm. "I'm so happy for you!"

Tommy beamed. "Right? I mean, I've dreamt of this for years, but I never thought she'd actually leave the *Daily News*." His black eyes gleamed, as if already seeing his new byline and photo in print. "She's more attached to that column than I am to my weekly manicures."

Rachel laughed. "Maybe she was getting bored at the top."

"Or ambitious. You know Isabella. If she's decided to start her own PR firm, it'll be the talk of Miami." A shadow flitted across Tommy's face. "I hate leaving an opening for Marc Gottsegen at *Palm*, though. He can run me down all he wants, but I hear he's been looking for his own weekly column. Apparently he's tired of writing that glorified Yellow Pages for nightclubs once a year and wants to get into the bold-face name business."

"Who cares? You'll be at the *Daily News!*" Rachel wiped some stray crumbs from the café counter with a cleaning rag. "Stop worrying about Marc. Think about ways to make the column your own after Isabella leaves."

They chatted about it for another few minutes—angles he could take that would differentiate his own version of the column from Isabella Stuart's—and then Isabella herself arrived, dressed in a crisp white sheath dress that perfectly showcased her trim-yet-curvy figure and the glossy curtain of hair that fell down her back. Every inch of her radiated poise, from the sharp click of her white Christian Louboutin heels on the terrazzo floor to the tilt of her prominent chin, one of her distinguishing trademarks.

Scarlett, who'd been standing behind the café counter near Rachel, now leapt to the countertop to sit next to Vashti. *"All hail Her Majesty,"* she whispered in Vashti's ear. Vashti snorted before she remembered herself and attempted to look disapproving.

"Darlings!" Isabella's smile was brilliant. "I hope I'm not interrupting anything important?"

"Never too important for you, lovely." Tommy hopped down from his stool to plant a light kiss on Isabella's cheek. "I was just telling Rachel your big news."

Isabella was a woman who'd been photographed sitting down hundreds, if not thousands, of times. She'd been filmed and photographed in the plush velvet banquettes of exclusive nightclubs, in box seats at the ballet, in uncomfortable cross-back chairs at $20,000-a-table charity galas, and in any number of chaise lounges, wingbacks, ottomans, poufs, and loveseats in her own beachfront home—all to provide fodder for South Florida's bottomless trough of lifestyle magazines and TV shows. Isabella seated herself now at the café counter with the air of someone who believed every moment of her life to be a documentable event, smiling once again as Rachel placed a steaming cup of coffee before her.

"I'm meeting Julian Singer-Adams here so we can go together to the groundbreaking today." Julian's plan to finally build Coacoochee a first-run multiplex, down at the westernmost end of Hibiscus Road, was the talk of the town—as was his announced intention of donating the entirety of the theater's first-week earnings to the Coacoochee Historical Society. "Is he not here yet?" Isabella glanced at her watch with the tiniest flicker of annoyance. As a columnist, she'd never waited for anyone and never had to.

Like everyone else in Coacoochee, the bell above the door seemed to hate being left out of the conversation. It rang again, this time to announce the arrival of Julian Singer-Adams. His lean frame carried an aura of understated elegance, each movement reflecting the disciplined lifestyle that kept him fit into his fifties. His suit hovered in a shade somewhere between sand and champagne and was exquisitely tailored. Julian moved with the easy confidence of someone who owns every inch of the land he walks on—which he essentially did.

Isabella smoothed her expression back into a smile. "Julian! Perfect timing."

"Sorry to keep you waiting," Julian said, his own smile suggesting he wasn't particularly sorry at all. His name at birth had been Julio Santos Aguilar, but whatever traces of an accent he still retained were barely detectable. His smile cooled as he looked at Tommy—only a degree or two, but Rachel noted it. "Tommy, always good to see you." His gaze settled on Rachel. "And, Rachel—the place looks even better than the last time I was here. Dorothea must be pleased."

"Thank you," Rachel replied, a touch warily. She knew Julian was itching to get his hands on the building Title Wave occupied, and suspected he'd made more than one offer to Dorothea.

"We should get going." Isabella glanced at her watch. "The ground-breaking is at two, and you need to be fresh for the cameras."

"You look a lot fresher than Daisy Locarro did this morning," Rachel noted, then flushed as she caught the look Tommy threw her way. Had she unwittingly breached etiquette?

But Julian chuckled. "I ran into her at a party last night and drove her home this morning—poor kid could barely keep her eyes open."

"She's lucky you were there to be her knight in shining armor." There was, perhaps, the tiniest edge to Isabella's voice, although her smile was blinding. It was equally bright when she turned it once again on Rachel. "I almost forgot! I'm also representing Danny Elliott now, and I have a few more names to give you for tonight's VIP list."

"Ah, yes. The big soiree for the boy genius." Julian's tone was withering. "You'll all forgive me if I take a pass tonight."

"Your presence will be missed at every moment," Tommy assured him.

"Let me just grab my notepad," Rachel said to Isabella, and hastily slid her hand into the space next to the café register where she kept her pads and pens. With immense satisfaction, all three cats heard the exclamation they'd been waiting for since that morning:

"My black Sharpies!" Rachel shook her head in wonder. "They must have been here the whole time!"

THE AFTERNOON PASSED UNEVENTFULLY after Isabella's departure. With Tommy's help, Rachel brought the folding tables out of the storeroom and pushed aside bookcases—which had been built with wheels for this exact purpose—to make room for them. Tommy eventually headed back to his office at *Palm*, and Rachel divided her time between answering phone calls about the event, fretting over arrangements (Isabella had said Danny was sending over hot hors d'oeuvres and wine, and where was she supposed to set *that* up?), and alternately worrying that the outfit she planned to change into would be too dressy or not dressy enough. The cats tried to find out-of-the-way spots where they could snooze undisturbed by all the hubbub, and were mostly unsuccessful in their efforts.

Beyond Title Wave's doors, sun-dazed tourists stumbled back from the hot beach to chilled hotel rooms. Office workers gathered for happy hour at trendy-chic Sabrosa, or over at the 710 Bar, dark and intimate, where Hibiscus Road intersected with Seventh Street. Families in nearby homes started dinner preparations, sending intoxicating aromas into the air that made Homer's mouth water. Scenesters stood before their mirrors to rehearse off-the-cuff witticisms they planned to dazzle fellow partygoers with later that night. The sun set on another perfect Coacoochee day, drifting into what gave every promise of being a perfect Coacoochee night.

Had Rachel, or Homer, or any of their new friends known what was coming, they might have appreciated it more.

CHAPTER 2

RACHEL ALWAYS SAID SHE loved her three cats equally but had differ-ent relationships with each of them. While this was undoubtedly true, it was probably more accurate to say that a single core truth—one that was unique to each individual cat—lay at the heart of each of the three intense bonds. Not many humans would have intuited the fierce love radiating through Scarlett beneath the brittle crust of her independence. Vashti was absolutely convinced that Rachel was the only reason she was alive today—and, moreover, that Rachel was her own true blood mother. (Vashti wasn't entirely sure how this was possible, but nevertheless knew it was so.)

It was different with Homer. Something had happened when he was only a few weeks old, and Rachel's hand had first reached out to him in the darkness. Dr. Andi—noting the way Homer's little face always turned toward Rachel, like the black heart of a sunflower following the sun—said that Homer had "imprinted" on her in that moment. It was as if they had become symbiotes. When Homer—as a kitten still figuring out how to get around—would bump headfirst into a wall, it was Rachel who exclaimed, "Oof!"

So it was no surprise that Homer was full of restless energy as the hour for the book signing drew near. All the unusual activity at Title Wave—the moving aside of bookcases, the hanging of signs, Rachel's running back and forth to the endlessly ringing store phone—left him feeling itchy under his skin. Mostly, though, Homer's tension was a reflection of Rachel's own in the same way Homer always seemed to mirror Rachel's feelings—following cheerfully in Rachel's wake when she was in a good mood, and curling up glumly beside her on the couch when she spent too much time thinking about Henry or her derailed career.

This tendency of Homer's could be trying because, as Scarlett loved to point out, humans were far moodier than cats. They were forever worried about foolish things like money (little scraps of paper you couldn't even *eat!*), or what clothes to wear (better to grow an attractive coat of fur and be done with it), or what other humans thought of them. When Scarlett tried to imagine being a human and devoting even a second to worrying about other humans' opinions on things, it left her chortling so helplessly she'd have to fake a string of sneezes. Otherwise, Rachel might suspect she was being laughed at—and everybody knew how much easier it was to wound a human's feelings than those of a cat.

Scarlett had her paws full with Homer as the sun sank deeper into the western sky. He tried to dispel some of his excess energy by springing upon her in mock Hide and Pounce attacks, which was excruciatingly annoying for two reasons. The first was that Homer refused to play the game of Hide and Pounce by the *correct* set of rules established long before he'd ever come to live with them. Those rules very clearly dictated that Scarlett—and *only* Scarlett—was the pounce-er, never the pounce-ee.

Then there was the fact that Homer—despite his well-honed ability to walk so silently that even he could barely hear himself—had no innate understanding of the "hide" component of Hide and Pounce. He'd creep in a noiseless crouch toward Scarlett across the wide-open middle of the Title Wave floor, his black fur gleaming in dark contrast to the sand and pale-blue of the terrazzo—and he was only slightly less conspicuous than a blinking neon arrow would have been. Homer would scurry forward a few steps, pause to sweep his head and ears from side to side, then crouch even lower and scurry forward again. This was repeated until he was mere inches from Scarlett—at which point he'd crouch directly in front of her, wiggling his backside in gleeful anticipation of the "surprise" attack he was about to launch.

"I can see you, genius." Scarlett's tone was a mix of disdain and irritation as—for the umpteenth time—she brought down a none-too-gentle paw upon Homer's head.

"It wouldn't hurt you to let him win sometimes," Vashti murmured to Scarlett once, as Homer shook his head and tried to recover from Scarlett's latest blow. Vashti always let Homer succeed in his mock attacks upon her, and didn't try to defend herself from the playful bites that quickly followed. Which was precisely why Homer secretly thought playing with Vashti was deadly dull, and why he lived in the hope Scarlett would some-day deem him a worthy adversary.

Just as Scarlett was beginning to wonder whether Rachel would *really* mind if she, Scarlett, were to murder Homer in his sleep some sunny afternoon, he abruptly skidded to a stop and turned his head halfway around, ears pricked in the direction of the storeroom. *"Samkhat's out back,"* he announced.

Scarlett looked over at Vashti. *"What do you think?"*

Vashti cast a surreptitious glance at Rachel, who was installing a **MEET THE AUTHOR TONIGHT!** sign in the *Miami Spice* front-window display. *"She's so distracted, I don't think she'll notice if the three of us disap-pear for a minute or two."*

Scarlett brushed past Homer, nudging him slightly in the direction of the door to the back storeroom. Vashti quickly followed and all three cats slipped out, leaving Rachel—and preparations for the evening's festivi-ties—behind for the moment.

Like most of Hibiscus Road, the building that housed Title Wave had been built in the 1950s and gone through countless owners in the ensuing decades. It had, at various times, been apartments, shops, offices, a restaurant, and now was two of the four. With such a long and varied history, it was no surprise the building contained any number of disused, long-forgotten, and otherwise unnoticed nooks and crannies, which Homer had devoted long and loving hours to cataloging with his sensitive nose.

The best discovery by far had been the ancient—but still functional—cat door somebody had installed in a dusty corner of the back storeroom, in what had once been a side door leading to the alley next to the shop.

Some previous owner had decided to build the larger, steel-reinforced door leading directly out to the back loading dock, and this was the door now used by Dorothea and Rachel. The newer door was located clear on the other side of the storeroom from the old, alley-adjacent exit. As the years had passed, and with the coming and going of owners, all manner of metal storage racks, old paint cans, and other junk had accumulated around the rusted-shut alley door, until it was unlikely any human would notice it.

Yet it had taken less than twelve hours for Homer to detect the faint sound of air whistling through the infinitesimal spaces between the rubber cat door and its plastic frame, which had disturbed his slumber all the way upstairs on his first night in their new apartment. Further investigation had commenced the very next morning.

As soon as he realized what he'd discovered—poking through a funny kind of soft wall, which had given way suddenly and left his head and chest exposed *outside*—Homer had brought the news directly to Scarlett. Even Scarlett had realized something of this magnitude couldn't be arbitrated by her alone, and she'd quickly pulled Vashti into conference.

The three of them had discussed the matter from a variety of angles over the next few days. They were intensely curious—of *course* they were curious—to explore the outside world on their own. But did the mere existence of this door make them less safe? Did it make *Rachel* less safe? By concealing that there was a way out, were they unwittingly giving vermin or maybe even other cats a way in? On this point, at least, Homer had been able to reassure them. His nose couldn't detect even the faintest trace of cats, rats, or strange humans anywhere in the vicinity of the inside of the door. Eventually, the three cats had decided there was no need for Rachel to know anything...for now.

So Rachel remained in blissful ignorance of the old cat door, as well as the abandoned dumbwaiter shaft located behind a panel in the upstairs apartment's small pantry—complete with a thick, sturdy length of old rope—that connected apartment and storeroom. Needless to say, Rachel was equally unaware of the excursions into Coacoochee after dark that her three cats occasionally made while she slept. They'd even started to make a few acquaintances among Coacoochee's outdoor feline community, who'd displayed varying degrees of approachability.

Samkhat, a one-eyed black-and-brown tortie, was one of the first and best friends they'd made so far, and they'd come to enjoy her sporadic visits with news of what was happening in the wide world beyond Title Wave. The one thing Samkhat absolutely refused to do, however, was set so much as a single whisker indoors. Despite Rachel's cats' insistence that she was more trustworthy than a typical human, Samkhat remained highly skeptical about the merits of humanity as a whole. *Four legs good, two legs bad,* she frequently opined, having once overheard someone standing outside this very bookstore quoting from *Animal Farm.*

The fading daylight was golden as the three cats squeezed through the old cat door as gracefully as they could. (Although she hotly denied it later, for a worrying moment it seemed as if Scarlett's hindquarters had gotten stuck.) As they walked around the corner to the back loading dock—a far more comfortable spot for a social call than the dark and dank alley—they saw that Samkhat had brought company.

Kotik was a young tuxedo cat with one green eye and one amber, who lived with a human named Laurie Castillo down at the other end of Hibiscus Road. Known for her eclectic and eye-catching style, Laurie owned a popular boutique called Laurie's Closet, which had played a pivotal role in transforming Hibiscus Road into a trendy shopping destination. The shop had been particularly popular among Russian tourists just over a year ago, when she'd adopted Kotik from Coacoochee Humane. They'd *ooh*ed and *aah*ed over the shop's adorable new addition, and the Russian word for a male kitten, "kotik," had stuck as his name.

There was a minor flurry of head bunts and nose taps as the friends all greeted each other. *"Hi, Vashti."* Kotik made a point of greeting her separately. With a valiant, if unsuccessful, attempt at assuming a Russian accent, he added shyly, *"It looks like it will be a beautiful night, yes?"* Kotik thought Vashti was far and away the prettiest cat he'd ever seen, and also the sweetest. While he knew deep down he didn't have a shot with her (being the exact same age as her little brother didn't help), he hoped a Russian accent might make him appear mysterious and sophisticated.

"Are you getting a cold, Kotik?" Vashti inquired with genuine concern. *"You sound funny."*

Scarlett turned her head to one side and pretended to cough. Even Homer snickered, despite himself.

Samkhat steadfastly refused to disclose her age, but she was a few years older than the rest of them and, consequently, a bit more tolerant of feline foibles. She briefly turned a single, indulgent eye on young Kotik, then tactfully changed the subject. *"I hear you're in for a big night at Title Wave. It's all anybody's been talking about up and down Hibiscus Road today. I bet half the town will try to squeeze in."*

Kotik nodded enthusiastically, fluffing up his black-and-white bottlebrush tail—arguably his handsomest feature, aside from his unusual eyes—in a way he thought Vashti couldn't fail to appreciate. *"Laurie's been talking about it all week. Every customer got an earful. Daisy Locarro even stopped by looking for something 'fabulous' to wear tonight."*

"Daisy loves her drama." Scarlett's tail flicked from side to side. *"Did Laurie suggest a neon tutu?"*

"I don't know what they decided on." Kotik was a trifle sorry he'd brought up an unmanly topic like women's clothing in front of Vashti. *"But she seemed set on making an entrance."*

"I know Rachel will be happy to see her, whatever she's wearing," Homer said absently, distracted as he so often was by a sound only he could hear. Something was headed their way. He just wasn't sure what it was.

Samkhat's left ear turned halfway around. Her hearing wasn't quite as sharp as Homer's, but it was nevertheless more acute than the other three cats'. She, too, thought she heard the faint approach of something in the air. Unlike Homer, however, she had a pretty good idea of what they were in for—though with luck she'd turn out to be wrong and they'd all be spared the annoyance. *"Speaking of Daisy,"* she said, *"I saw her with Marc Gottsegen a few days ago, having coffee at that outdoor café on Allamanda Avenue."*

"Daisy and Marc were drinking coffee together?" Vashti's own ears perked up. Daisy was a reliable source of gossip, and she always seemed to know which new clubs and restaurants would be wildly popular before anyone else did. Typically she saved her choicest tidbits for Tommy—which made the prospect of her possibly switching allegiances a cause for concern. *"Could you hear what they were talking about?"*

"I didn't catch much," Samkhat admitted. *"But Daisy seemed angry."*

Samkhat had known Tommy, Marc, and Daisy years longer than Vashti had, so the constant waxing and waning of friendliness versus competition among the three of them came as no surprise to her. What *had* been a little surprising, however, was Daisy's unconcealed anger. She carried more secrets about half of Coacoochee than probably even she realized—but whenever somebody managed to guess one of them, her air was generally one of coy amusement, not raw fury.

She'd been good and mad at Marc, though. She'd stood abruptly and slammed her chair so hard against the table, it had drawn the attention of the café's other patrons. "You don't know what you're talking about," she'd fumed, "so just leave it—and *me*—alone!"

Marc, by contrast, had remained cool as a saucer of ice-cold milk. "C'mon Daisy," he'd said. "You know I'll dig it up anyway. Tommy Duvall's secrets can't be *that* hard to figure out."

"Let me know if you hear anything else about this?" Vashti asked Samkhat, and Samkhat nodded her assent.

Kotik, in the meantime, was weighing his advantages. He wasn't at all pleased to see how much interest Vashti took in Tommy—but maybe he still had a chance to impress her. Unlike Rachel, Kotik's human allowed him a certain amount of freedom to come and go as he pleased. Of course, Allamanda Avenue was a lot farther away than Laurie would be comfortable with him traveling. But what she didn't know wouldn't hurt her, right?

"If you want," he started to offer Vashti, "I could try to follow Marc and see if he—"

Without warning, Homer sprang straight up and was airborne. He pawed furiously at the mockingbird who'd appeared above his head as if out of nowhere. *"Can't catch me! Can't catch me!"* the mockingbird jeered at the cats assembled below. He dove down to within inches of Homer's head, then flew back up just beyond Homer's reach—only to turn around and gleefully dive bomb him again. *"You'll never catch me!"*

For a moment Vashti and Kotik froze, haunches taut and ready to leap heavenward after the tempting, taunting bird. Scarlett was the only one whose attitude didn't change. In Scarlett's considered opinion, there was nothing more working-class—nothing more downright *plebian*—than scrounging after some measly, mangy bird as if an ample supply of gourmet food weren't thoughtfully provided for one at home by one's dedicated human servant.

Samkhat was the only one of them who actually did need to rely on her wits for her evening meal. (Although Rachel, having noticed Samkhat hanging around Title Wave's loading dock, left a full bowl of kibble for her every day.) But she relaxed as soon as she recognized the bird in question. *"It's just Stewie,"* she said dismissively. She knew from long experience that Stewie was essentially impossible to catch—and meaner than an angry hornet if you did manage to corner him. She'd almost lost her one good eye to Stewie the previous summer, and for the life of her couldn't imagine why Rachel had insisted on hanging a birdfeeder in the royal poinciana that grew only twenty feet from Title Wave's entrance. Stewie was a perfect example of why it didn't pay to be nice to birds.

"No blind cat will ever catch me!" Stewie now dived close to Homer's head, although his tone sounded a little less mocking as one of Homer's claws tore right through a loose tuft of feathers.

"Wanna bet?" Homer challenged. *"I don't need eyes to catch anything as loud and annoying as you are!"*

"We should go inside," Vashti said. *"Rachel might start wondering where we are."* She turned back toward the side alley. *"And you should get to your nest before dark,"* she added to Stewie. *"We're not the only cats on Hibiscus Road."*

"Dasvidanya, Kotik!" Stewie screeched in a flawless Russian accent. *"Sayanora! Auf wiedersehen! Ciao! Adios, amigo!"* He cycled through a series of foreign farewells, each accent sounding entirely authentic. *"Let me know if you ever need language lessons so you can impress your little girlfriend!"* With a final heckling squawk, Stewie soared higher and disappeared into the purpling sky.

"Stupid jerk," Kotik muttered, ducking his head in embarrassment. What would Vashti think of him now?

But Kotik had nothing to worry about. Vashti had already disappeared into the gloom of the alley next to Title Wave, visible only by the faint glow her white fur cast in the darkness. Homer and Scarlett were close behind.

CHAPTER 3

Brock Winfield was a great writer.

Not just good. Not merely talented. Brock was *great*. A man of unique gifts. Destined to be remembered long after he'd shuffled off this mortal coil. The voice of a generation—even if that generation didn't know it yet.

Proof positive of his greatness, as Brock often reflected, was the fact that absolutely nobody appreciated him.

This was nothing new for Brock, who'd been great at any number of things and equally unappreciated for all of them. He'd been a great personal trainer in California, a great children's talent agent in New York, a great publicist in Orlando. Nobody at that marketing firm in Atlanta had ever seen an account executive like him, which was particularly impressive considering Brock didn't even know what an "account executive" did.

But the thing he'd been the very best at—nearly as good as he was at writing—was running Title Wave Books. Brock had been an *amazing* bookseller: dedicated, responsible, hardworking. Until Dorothea, in a blatant act of nepotism, had fired him so she could hire her friend's daughter to take his place.

Okay, so he'd shown up late for work a few times. But attending all the town's chicest parties night after night, just so he could talk up Title Wave and give it a little cachet, made it hard to be at work by ten-thirty a.m. What was even the point of opening a store at eleven o'clock anyway in a town that barely got going before noon? If *he'd* been allowed to use the apartment upstairs like the new girl did, maybe he could've been punctual, too.

And he'd been expected to stand on his feet all day! When there were so many chairs scattered all over the store! Like it was such a big deal for Brock to sit in just *one* of them for two or three hours at a stretch, plugging away at his novel *Borrowed Glory* (a soon-to-be bestseller, Brock just knew it). How could a bookstore owner, of all people, not appreciate the importance of supporting those who actually wrote the books she was so gung-ho on selling?

Fortunately, he'd been able to finish a first draft of the entire manuscript before Dorothea fired him. And just to prove he harbored no bitterness, he'd offered Title Wave the opportunity to sell the very first copies of *Borrowed Glory*. Just as soon as he got them back from the vanity press he was paying to print up a couple thousand for him. (No way was Brock entrusting his masterpiece to any of the big corporate publishers—not when they'd never bothered to answer even one of his many query letters.)

He'd generously offered Rachel one of only three advance copies he had at the moment. Rachel had dutifully taken it upstairs that night and read it for as long as she could. One of the characters had a habit of referring to people by dessert-y epithets (*Hey there, cupcake! See you later, honeybun!*) and exclaimed at one point: "Come in and sit down this *instant*, pudding!" That was when Rachel had given up.

"Maybe he's never heard of instant pudding," she said doubtfully to Tommy, when he called later that evening.

"Of course he's heard of instant pudding," Tommy replied. "This is America, isn't it?"

Dorothea had been rather relieved at Rachel's assessment that the book probably didn't merit taking shelf space from another author. "Just tell him I said we're not accepting any more self-published titles right now," she'd advised Rachel cheerfully.

Which was exactly what Rachel had told Brock the next day, trying hard to assume a regretful tone and thus soften the rejection. She was doing a pretty good job of it, too. But then Brock had asked what she'd thought of the novel personally, and before she could get a word out her face had flamed an incriminating red. It was all over after that.

Not that it came as any surprise to Brock; Rachel was hardly the first to be threatened by his talents.

It pained Brock, it really did, to see what Title Wave had come to under its new management. Maybe all Rachel's colorful shelf talkers, and all the little tables she'd set up near the front of the store—with cutesy signs like "Blind Date With A Book" and "Authors We'd Love To Grab A Drink With"—and the way she always seemed to be right there to answer customer questions the second they had one, *maybe* all that was selling a *few* more books. Brock couldn't say.

But what about the air of cool inaccessibility he'd spent so many months cultivating for Title Wave? Everybody knew you couldn't put a price tag on cool.

As if anything could be *less* cool than the three cats Rachel brought to the store every day! The skinny black one gave him the creeps, the way it slunk around with no eyes, yet somehow not bumping into anything—like it was the haunted cat from some schlocky horror film. Brock snickered as he wondered whether Rachel planned to enter it in this year's Coacoochee Halloween parade.

He'd tried to warn Danny Elliott—a dear, personal friend—to avoid Title Wave for his book signing at all costs. Books & Books on South Beach would be a better option, or even a Borders over the causeway. (Coacoochee, like all of Miami Beach, was located on a barrier island accessible to the rest of Miami only via a system of causeways and bridges.)

"There's nobody I'd trust more with my first book than Rachel and Dorothea," Danny had said firmly, when Brock broached the subject.

Which only went to show, Brock mused sadly, how chivalrous and self-sacrificing Danny Elliott could be.

He'd been tempted to skip the whole thing, but in the end too many people he knew were planning to go. He'd even arrived early, so he could have the enjoyment of seeing Rachel flail chaotically in the runup to seven-thirty, and he settled unobtrusively at an empty café table to watch it unfold.

Rachel was calmer than he'd expected. She wore a narrow, black-fringed skirt in purple taffeta that fell asymmetrically from just above her left knee to just below her right. An embroidered silver dragon twisted its way up the front of it. Her black silk top was simple, sleeveless, and high-necked, and her feet were clad in a pair of open-toed black kitten heels. Somebody had dressed her well.

Even more unexpected: she actually looked like she was having fun! It was still too early for Danny to have arrived, but Rachel's face glowed a warm, welcoming pink as she greeted Dahlia Delgado, who was Director of Community Outreach for the Coacoochee Department of Tourism. Tommy Duvall hovered nearby in a peacock-blue jacket. He was deep in conversation with Laurie Castillo and her husband, Robert, who was a prominent local attorney. Isabella Stuart swanned in a few minutes later and touched Rachel's arm. Kisses were exchanged all around—and since when was *Rachel* so chummy with Coacoochee's best and brightest?

Not that it mattered. Any day now, Rachel Baum was going to fall flat on her face like the causeway crawler she was. And Brock—although he routinely told anyone who would listen how much *freer* he felt ever since he'd gotten rid of the *negative energy* that had been holding him back all these years—couldn't wait to see it happen.

CHAPTER 4

Streetlights cast a warm glow onto the darkened sidewalks of Hibiscus Road, and strings of fairy lights twinkled in its royal palms and bougainvillea. The breeze carried the aromas of Coacoochee after sundown, salt-laden air from the Atlantic mingling with the subtle, sweet fragrance of night-blooming jasmine. Live music drifted from the open doors of the 710 Bar, while farther down Hibiscus the steady rhythm of bass from Club Yucca thumped through the chests of all who entered, like an echo of their own heartbeat.

Rachel stood in the front entrance of Title Wave, taking a moment to cast a final, critical eye over the transformation she'd orchestrated over the course of the day. The wave-patterned terrazzo floor glowed under the carefully adjusted track lighting, which had been dimmed to create an intimate atmosphere while still ensuring guests could browse comfortably. The bookstore's normally cozy arrangement had been reconfigured to create a central space where Danny would sign books. The signing table itself was draped in a sea-blue cloth that echoed the wave motif of the terrazzo floor, with stacks of *Miami Spice* arranged in a gentle curve alongside black Sharpies and a pitcher of water with a single glass. Rachel had locked all three cats into her apartment upstairs, and while she missed their always-enlivening presence, it was a relief to have one less thing (or, more accurately, three less things) to worry about.

She had just greeted Isabella, who'd moved inside to schmooze reporters and await Danny's arrival, when a flurry of activity caught her attention. A small battalion of photographers had arrived. One carried the familiar logo of *Palm* magazine, while another sported credentials from *Ocean Drive*. The *Daily News* was represented, as were the *Miami Herald*, the *Sun Post*, the *Sentinel*, and a handful of the local 'zines that seemed to exist for no other purpose than endlessly documenting Coacoochee after dark.

"Let's set you up outside," Rachel suggested, gesturing toward *Miami Spice*'s front display window. "That way you can catch the VIPs as they arrive."

Tommy appeared at her elbow, resplendent in his peacock-blue jacket. "Have you seen the crowd gathering? It's like Studio 54 out there!"

"Don't exaggerate," Rachel laughed, although she had noticed the sidewalk becoming increasingly crowded. "Is Danny here yet?"

"He'll make his grand entrance in..." Tommy checked his watch, "exactly fifteen minutes. Isabella always times these things perfectly so the TV crews get full coverage."

"Rachel! The place looks wonderful!" Dahlia Delgado's cheerful voice carried farther than would have seemed possible, coming from someone of her diminutive height. Her chartreuse dress set off her silver-streaked black hair, and she clasped Rachel's hand in a warm shake while simultaneously kissing Tommy on the cheek. "And it wouldn't be a night out in Coacoochee without Mr. Nightlife!"

Rachel and Tommy greeted Dahlia with enthusiasm, but Rachel was almost immediately pulled away by another band of photographers looking for spots. Tommy steered Dahlia into Title Wave just as a white van marked with the local Fox affiliate's logo pulled up. The reporter who emerged—a slender woman with a choppy black pixie cut and impossibly high heels—approached Rachel with a determined stride, followed by a cameraman.

"Rachel Baum?" the reporter asked, extending her hand. "Belkys Nerey with *Deco Drive*. Could we get a quick statement from you?"

"From me?" Rachel blinked, momentarily taken aback. "I'm just the manager—"

"You're the face of Title Wave Books," Belkys interrupted, gesturing for her cameraman to begin recording. "And this is shaping up to be the biggest pre-Season event on Hibiscus Road." Season, with a capital "S," was how locals referred to Coacoochee's annual peak tourist season—which kicked off officially on Thanksgiving weekend and ran through Easter.

Before Rachel could even smooth down her always-rebellious curls, a microphone was thrust before her and Belkys was firing questions. Rachel found herself speaking about Danny Elliott's meteoric rise in the culinary world and Title Wave's commitment to showcasing local talent.

"And how do you spell your name?" Belkys asked as the camera light dimmed.

"R-A-C-H-E-L B-A-U-M," Tommy's voice answered as he materialized at Rachel's side yet again, sliding a protective arm around her shoulders. "Make sure they get that right," he told Rachel in a stage whisper. "Nothing worse than seeing your name misspelled on the lower third of the screen." He gave Belkys a thousand-watt smile. "Always a pleasure to see you, Belkys."

"Tommy! I didn't realize you'd be here." Belkys' professional demeanor warmed by several degrees. "I'd love to get a quote from you as well."

"Of course you would," Tommy drawled with a wink. He turned toward the camera with practiced ease.

Rachel slipped away, leaving Tommy to bask in the limelight. She thought fleetingly of Henry. What would he think if he saw her on *Deco Drive*? Most likely, he'd simply flip the channel without recognizing her. Her life did look awfully different these days.

Inside, the store buzzed with anticipation. Nadia, a University of Miami grad student who helped out on weekends, manned the register with cheerful efficiency. Curious browsers fingered the spines of books while

Coacoochee's cognoscenti greeted each other with air kisses and enthusiastic exclamations of "Darling!" By the signing table, a small cluster of food enthusiasts flipped through display copies of *Miami Spice*, pointing out recipes and exchanging animated commentary about which dishes they planned to attempt first.

"Rachel!" Laurie called, waving her over. "You look fabulous! That skirt is perfect on you."

"Thanks to you," Rachel replied with real gratitude. "I never could have afforded it without the discount you gave me."

"Just one of the many perks you now enjoy as a fellow Hibiscus Road retailer." Laurie looked striking in a skin-tight maxi dress that featured a bold geometric print in burnt orange and cobalt blue—colors that highlighted her warm complexion and the natural highlights in her shoulder-length brown hair, which she wore in loose waves. A collection of mixed-metal bangles clinked merrily up her arm as she turned to Robert. "Doesn't she look wonderful?"

Robert Castillo presented a polished, understated counterpoint to his wife. He wore slim-fit chinos in a soft sand color and a tailored navy blazer over a crisp white button-down. His salt-and-pepper beard was neatly trimmed, framing a warm smile that appeared frequently as he stood at Laurie's side.

"Very professional." Robert nodded cordially. "Dorothea made an excellent choice when she hired you."

"Indeed she did!" Dorothea, who'd been giving Nadia a few last-minute instructions, joined the group. She was clad in a pair of black jeans, paired with a brown cotton turtleneck and low-heeled black boots. A large turquoise necklace was her only nod to Coacoochee ostentation. In her late sixties, with a cloud of silver hair and the erect posture of someone who'd spent decades commanding the attention of unruly sixth graders, Dorothea radiated a comfortable authority.

"You've done a wonderful job," she said, causing Rachel to blush with pleasure. "I don't think Brock could have ever pulled off anything like this."

"Speaking of Brock." Rachel lowered her voice. "He showed up early and has been lurking in the café. I think he's waiting for the whole thing to go up in flames."

Dorothea's laugh carried clear across the store. "Well, he's going to be terribly disappointed, isn't he?"

The bell above the door jangled nonstop as Title Wave continued to fill with a mix of regular customers, local celebrities, and curious onlookers. Rachel left Dorothea with Laurie and Robert and moved through the crowd, greeting guests and pointing out the restroom to those who asked. A small commotion near the entrance announced the arrival of Griselda Cardenas, Sabrosa's strikingly beautiful hostess, and a team of white-jacketed servers carrying trays of hors d'oeuvres. Griselda's glossy black hair was swept into an elegant updo, and she moved with the confident precision of someone accustomed to orchestrating complex events.

"Rachel!" Griselda air-kissed both her cheeks. "Where should we set up, *mami*?"

"The café counter would be perfect for the wine," Rachel replied, grateful for the professional help. "And maybe your servers could circulate with the hors d'oeuvres?"

"Already on it." Griselda snapped her fingers, and the servers dispersed into the crowd with silver trays of bite-sized delicacies that showcased Danny's culinary prowess and the cookbook's Miami-Caribbean fusion theme. There were miniature Cuban sandwiches made with delicate portions of roasted pork, ham, Swiss cheese, and pickles, pressed between buttery bread with a whisper of mustard. Alongside these were stone crab claws, their shells cracked just so, served with a citrus-infused mustard sauce that perfectly balanced tang and sweetness. There were also bite-sized arepas topped with slow-roasted pulled chicken and avocado crema, garnished with tiny edible flowers. For those with a more adventurous palate, Danny had included plantain cups filled with bacalao salad, brightened with red pepper, olive oil, and tiny capers. Small ceramic spoons held ceviche featuring the day's freshest catch, "cooked" in lime juice and accented with diced red onion, jalapeño, and slivers of fresh coconut—a creative interpretation of a South Florida classic.

To Homer, who had just emerged from the dumbwaiter into the back storage room followed closely by Vashti and Scarlett, it smelled the way he might have imagined heaven would smell—if cats ever imagined that such a thing as heaven existed.

"Stay close to me," Vashti instructed Homer. *"We'll keep to the shadows and under the furniture."*

"Homer doesn't know what a shadow is." Scarlett was feeling even snippier than usual, on account of the extreme indignity of having to squeeze herself into the narrow dumbwaiter and then shimmy her way down an old rope. She wasn't sure she'd ever forgive Rachel for the insult of being forced to gatecrash a party taking place in her own home.

"I do, too, know what a shadow is!" Homer retorted hotly. *"Just because I can't see something doesn't mean I don't know what it is."*

"Just make sure you're with one of us at all times." Scarlett was still a trifle harrumph-y. *"We can't spend the whole night worrying about you wandering around in plain sight. And please,"* she added, *"do try to refrain from your annoying habit of greeting every single person as they walk in."*

"Maybe you *should refrain from your annoying habit of...being annoying."* Homer knew the insult didn't quite land, but he wasn't as good at trading barbs as Scarlett was.

"Come on, you two. I could have stayed upstairs to listen to you bicker." Vashti used her paw to gently push the storage-room door open a scooch further, creating just enough space for them to slip through one at a time into a back corner of Title Wave.

"There are so many people," Homer whispered, momentarily disoriented by the sensory onslaught. The familiar landscape of Title Wave had been transformed into a maze of oddly placed bookcases and unfamiliar feet. His whiskers detected air currents shifting in a dozen different directions as bodies moved about the shop.

Keeping low to the ground, the three cats threaded their way through the forest of human legs. Homer relied on his whiskers and sense of smell to navigate, along with the occasional cue from Vashti. *"Turn right,"* she whispered urgently as Rachel suddenly appeared only a few feet away. *"This way—hurry!"* With a gentle nip to his neck, Vashti guided Homer to safety beneath the white cloth draped over one of the high-top tables Rachel had placed strategically around the room.

Scarlett deftly avoided the treacherous path of a waiter balancing a tray of ceviche-filled ceramic spoons, her nimble paws carrying her between polished loafers and stiletto heels. A boisterous laugh from Tommy momentarily disoriented her, causing her to hesitate as a woman in impractical gold sandals nearly stepped on her tail. *"For the love of—"* Scarlett muttered, making a desperate dive toward the tablecloth beneath which her siblings were hiding. She landed with a soft thump beside them, her yellow-green eyes narrowed in annoyance as she began fastidiously grooming her ruffled fur. *"The things I do for you two,"* she huffed, as if her presence at the party were a favor she had conferred upon Homer and Vashti, rather than the result of her flat refusal to be the only one left out.

For once, Homer refused to be provoked by Scarlett. His sensitive ears were attuned to the crowd, and he picked up fragments of dozens of conversations at once.

"—already made the *New York Times* bestseller list—"

"—absolute best ceviche I've ever tasted—"

"—said Danny's found backers to open Sabrosas in L.A. and Vegas—"

As if summoned by the mention of his name, Danny Elliott himself finally appeared in the doorway.

When he'd first moved to Coacoochee a few years earlier, he'd been nothing more than one of the private chefs who toiled in obscurity in the Mercury Island kitchens of people like Julian Singer-Adams. Tonight, however, Danny Elliott was very much a public figure and clearly a star on the rise. Tall and lean, with the powerful forearms that came from years of professional cooking, Danny embraced his celebrity chef status with bold style. His black chef's jacket, which perfectly matched his black chef's hat, was embroidered with Sabrosa's logo in colorful thread. Instead of traditional chef's pants, he wore dark jeans and polished boots. Barely thirty years old, he possessed an undeniable charisma. His sandy blond hair was fashionably tousled, and he smiled with relaxed charm as Isabella Stuart escorted him inside, cameras flashing around them.

Rachel had been chatting with Daisy Locarro, who was considerably more composed than she had been that morning in a shimmering gold dress that caught the light with every movement. Still, Rachel thought she detected a thin sheen of perspiration on Daisy's forehead. She'd just made a mental note to check whether the AC needed to be turned up a notch when the crowd parted, and Danny and Isabella were standing before her.

"Rachel!" Isabella's voice carried a practiced blend of warmth and command. "The store looks absolutely stunning tonight." Her smile was particularly brilliant as her light-green eyes took in the crowd, the photographers, and the artfully arranged shop. "I told you," she said to Danny, "that Rachel's events are the talk of the town."

"That's an exaggeration," Scarlett muttered from their hiding place. *"Rachel's only done three events so far, and one was just that old man reading poetry to his five friends."*

"Shh!" Vashti nudged her sister. *"It's called marketing."*

"You were right, Isabella." Danny's easy smile crinkled the corners of his eyes. "Great to see you again, Rachel. You've done amazing work here."

"Thanks for trusting Title Wave with your first author signing." Rachel felt a flutter of professional pride. "We're honored to host you."

"Daisy!" Danny exclaimed, noticing her beside Rachel. "I didn't realize you were a regular at Title Wave."

"One of my favorite spots in Coacoochee," Daisy replied with a grin. "Rachel's coffee is even better than Sabrosa's." She managed a small wink that momentarily recaptured her usual sparkle.

Rachel smiled inwardly as Daisy's wink made Danny flush. Apparently, not even celebrity chefs were immune to her charms. "Let me show you where you'll be signing," she told him, smoothing over the moment.

"Thank you." Danny's gratitude seemed genuine. "I'll head over as soon as I've said a few hellos. And save me a Sauvignon Blanc, will you?" he added, looking at Daisy. "Griselda brought the good stuff."

Daisy beamed at him and turned her wine glass, which was already empty, upside down. "I can't make any promises," she said.

THE LINE IN FRONT of the signing table had grown steadily throughout the evening, snaking between bookshelves and curving past the café. An excited murmur floated above the crowd as readers clutched their copies of *Miami Spice,* each one eager for a moment with Coacoochee's celebrity chef. Danny sat beneath soft amber lighting, his pen moving across title pages with practiced flourishes as he offered each guest a warm smile and a few personalized words.

Isabella hovered nearby, her vintage Pucci dress an attraction in its own right as she masterfully managed the flow of people approaching the table. She knew exactly when to usher someone forward, and precisely how long to let them chat with Danny, before subtly indicating their time was up with nothing more than a lift or tilt of her distinctive chin. Rachel watched this ballet of social orchestration with quiet admiration.

The overall effect was elegant, convivial, and exactly the atmosphere Rachel had hoped to create—a perfect blend of literary gathering and social event that showcased Title Wave at its finest. Even Dorothea, observing from near the Paperback Bestsellers table, nodded her approval as she chatted with a group of longtime customers.

"It's going so well!" Tommy whispered in her ear as they maneuvered past each other in the crowd. He briefly caught her hand in one of his own and squeezed. "I'm so proud of you!"

"Thank you!" Rachel whispered back, giving his hand a heartfelt squeeze in return before releasing it.

"Tommy!" a familiar voice behind him called, and Tommy groaned inwardly as he turned to face Marc Gottsegen with a wide smile.

The two men made a show of kissing amiably on both cheeks. "I love that jacket on you, Tommy," Marc said. "I love it *every* time you wear it."

Tommy had to fight to keep from wincing. His salary at *Palm* wasn't exactly exorbitant, and he'd learned to stretch it by practicing certain economies—like re-wearing outfits during the pre-Season, for instance. On the other hand, Marc's great-great-great-great-great-great-grandfather had held one of the original charters from the King of England to found a cotton plantation in the Bahamas. Marc's trust fund afforded him a cushy Coacoochee lifestyle, which included an adorable little house right next door to Natalie Dunbar.

Tommy's laughter rippled through the air, musical but with an edge. "Marc! I didn't expect to see you here. I always think October must be such a sad month for you. I mean, the very instant an updated version of your little guidebook is published, it's already so...last year." Tommy snapped his fingers. "Poof! It really makes you think about how *irrelevant* so many of life's pursuits are, you know?" He took a glass of champagne from the tray of a passing waiter, then lifted it in Marc's direction in a mocking toast.

A muscle in Marc's jaw tightened momentarily, but he nevertheless managed a small, cool smile. "You're absolutely right about how fleeting this all is.'" He nonchalantly inspected his perfectly manicured fingernails. "Why, I've even heard you might not be at *Palm* much longer."

Marc was gratified to see something flicker in Tommy's eyes—the briefest shadow of confusion. But his heart sank as Tommy's confident grin quickly returned with, if anything, even more satisfaction than a moment ago.

"Word really does travel fast, doesn't it?" Tommy looked positively glee-ful. "I can't say I'm completely surprised you've heard. But honestly, Marc, don't tell me you've already given up on landing the *Daily News* position for yourself."

"The *Daily News*?" Marc looked momentarily nonplussed, then cursed himself for having allowed his face to reveal an inconvenient truth: He hadn't the faintest idea what Tommy was talking about.

Tommy's boisterous laugh was genuine this time. "Did you not know? Isabella's leaving to start her own PR firm, and she's recommended me as her replacement." He tilted his head sympathetically, eyes wide with counterfeit concern. "You really should stay better informed, Marc. It's embarrassing for someone in your position to always be the last to know."

It was almost possible to hear the wheels in Marc's brain spin as he processed this nugget of information. "But I know so much more than you realize." Marc was about to say more than he'd intended, but he couldn't resist the impulse to knock Tommy down a peg or two. "I know, for instance, how difficult it can be to get a story *just* right when your source is unreliable." He made his own face look concerned. "Some of your early blind items make for particularly interesting reading."

"It's sad enough that somebody your age is still an up-and-comer." Tommy's grin was taut now. "I'd hate to see you waste even more of your time chasing phantoms."

Marc's shrug was extravagantly casual. "I'm not worried about wasting my time. But maybe don't waste yours measuring for new drapes at the *Daily News* just yet."

With that, Marc glided away, leaving the faintest trail of expensive cologne behind him. He moved through the crowd with the easy confi-dence of someone who believed the last word was his.

Which, of course, it had been.

RACHEL HAD PAUSED ONLY a few feet away from Tommy, having spot-ted a familiar face in the crowd. Evan Kirschner, the local sales rep for Daydouble Publishing, was studying her new "Blind Date With A Book" display table with interest. Rachel was so used to seeing him laden with sales catalogs and advance copies that she almost didn't recognize him unencumbered. As if sensing her attention, he looked up and smiled.

"This is a great idea." He gestured to books wrapped in plain brown paper and festooned with colorful stickers and handwritten descriptions in red, purple, and black ink. He picked one up and balanced it in his hand for a moment, as if testing its weight. *"Read this if you like: moonlit gardens, everyday enchantment hiding in plain sight, and love stories complicated by ancient curses. A sensory feast where magic feels as natural as breathing and as complicated as family."* Evan's brow furrowed in thought. "*Practical Magic*?" he guessed.

"Bulls-eye!" Rachel laughed. "I probably shouldn't have made it *so* easy to guess by using the word 'magic' in the description."

"Nothing wrong with throwing in a few easy ones. It makes people like me feel smart." He placed the book back in the display and picked up another. "Now here's one that has the right dimensions to be a Penguin Classic."

"No fair!" Rachel protested. "You're a professional. You're practically a ringer."

Evan smiled as he placed the book back on the display table, his blue eyes crinkling at the corners. A light dusting of silver in his dark hair contrasted with an otherwise youthful face. "I really love what you've done here." His hand gestured around the store. "I don't just mean tonight. Title Wave feels like a different place since you took over. It feels like…"

"Like…?" Rachel prompted when he paused.

"Like a bookstore run by people who love books," he finished. "Not by people who think of books as 'product.' When you spend as much time in bookstores as I do, you can spot the difference."

"Thank you." Rachel felt a flush of pleasure at the compliment. "Though I'm surprised to see you here tonight. Don't you get enough of bookstores at work?"

"Danny Elliott's a Daydouble author," Evan reminded her.

"Oh, of course." Rachel reddened slightly, surprised by the brief pang of disappointment she felt in realizing Evan hadn't come specifically to see her. She was about to say something else when a sharp, sudden cry from across the store caught her attention.

At this precise moment, Homer was all the way over by the café, struggling manfully to ford a sea of human legs. The event had become a sensory labyrinth for him—each step bringing new smells, sounds, and air currents that constantly rearranged his mental map of the space. He froze suddenly, lifting his head and widening his nostrils.

A distinctive odor tickled his sensitive nose—the exact same strange smell that had clung to Daisy that morning. But Homer could hear Daisy way at the opposite side of the room. This identical aroma was emanating from someone else in the crowd, someone only a few feet from Homer now. The mystery scent was not quite floral, not exactly medicinal, but definitely unique.

Homer swiveled his head, trying to determine who might be carrying the telltale odor, but the press of bodies around him created a confusing vortex of competing smells—perfumes, aftershaves, and the lingering aromas of Sabrosa's exquisite hors d'oeuvres.

"Homer!" Vashti hissed from beneath a nearby table. *"You're way too visible! Come toward me—hurry!"*

Homer reluctantly abandoned his olfactory investigation and scurried toward his sister's voice, his whiskers brushing against a pair of trousers just before he made it to safety. Above him, Brock Winfield paused mid-stride.

It wasn't in Homer's nature to actively dislike anybody. Nevertheless, he actively disliked Brock Winfield. It was just about the only subject upon which he, Vashti, and Scarlett were in perfect agreement. It wasn't only that Brock disliked cats with an intensity even Samkhat could sense—Samkhat who customarily avoided all humans, yet still gave Brock Winfield an even wider berth whenever their paths happened to cross.

Brock's dislike of Rachel was, to Homer's ears, so conspicuous in every oily, unctuous, fake-friendly word he said to her that Homer could feel the fur rise on his back whenever he was in Brock's presence.

Although he knew how imperative it was that he and his sisters remain completely invisible to the humans around him, Homer instinctively recoiled with an audible hiss when his nose encountered Brock's leg. Brock heard the sound and looked down to see what its source was. Then his face twisted into a scowl as he deliberately swung his foot hard, directly into Homer's side. The impact sent Homer tumbling across the floor with a surprised yelp.

Across the room, Rachel's head snapped up, her full attention suddenly captured by an unmistakable sound—the distinctive cry Homer made when startled or hurt. But that was impossible. She'd locked all three cats safely in her apartment upstairs. Still, there was an almost physical imperative to be obeyed when she heard that sound—the swift tension in her legs and sudden pounding of her heart forcing her into action.

"I'm so sorry," she said hastily to Evan. "I need to check on…" She didn't know how to conclude the sentence (because Homer—along with Vashti and Scarlett—was safely locked upstairs, *wasn't he?!?*). "I have to go," she concluded hastily. "Excuse me!" Pushing her way through what was now an almost impenetrably thick crowd, she moved as quickly as she could toward the source of the sound, her eyes scanning the crowded floor.

There was no sign of a small black cat, naturally. She was being ridiculous. Perhaps the sound had come from outside, or maybe she'd imagined it entirely.

She was about to turn back when she nearly collided with Brock. He wore a suit made of raw silk in a shade of mustard that did nothing for his complexion. His smile had all the warmth of a January dip in Biscayne Bay.

"Rachel!" he exclaimed, his voice pitched slightly louder than necessary. "What a smashing success!" He leaned in for air kisses that Rachel reluctantly accepted.

"Thank you." Rachel was still distracted as she cast one more glance around their feet. Nothing.

Brock puffed out his chest slightly. "I've been meaning to tell you—*Borrowed Glory* has attracted some attention lately. Mitch Kaplan's planning to stock it as soon as it comes back from the printer." Mitch Kaplan was the owner of Books & Books, and he was emphatically *not* planning to sell *Borrowed Glory* in either of his stores. Primarily this was because he didn't know it existed, having yet to open the package Brock had sent him weeks ago.

But Brock was the only one who knew that. Besides, it was a given that Mitch Kaplan would be so captivated by the end of page one, he'd *beg* for more copies of *Borrowed Glory*. "I'm sure Dorothea will regret that 'no self-published titles' policy when she sees the reviews," he added.

"I'm glad to hear you've found other outlets," Rachel said diplomatically.

"And *I'm* glad to see what a nice job you and this little store did for Danny tonight." The condescension in his tone was deliberate. "He and I go way back, you know."

Rachel resisted the urge to roll her eyes. "Well, don't let me keep you from enjoying the party," she said, stepping aside.

"Certainly not." Brock's hand lingered on Rachel's arm a beat too long. "I'm sure Danny appreciates what you're doing here, even if it's not quite the scale he's used to."

With that parting shot, he drifted back into the crowd, followed by a trail of aftershave so heavy it seemed to leave a visible wake. Rachel shook her head, still puzzled by the sound she'd heard but too busy to dwell on it.

Meanwhile, Vashti had darted from her hiding place, her white fur momentarily visible through the crowd as she rushed to Homer's side. *"Are you hurt?"* she asked anxiously, nudging him with her nose.

"Just my dignity." Homer scrambled back to his feet. His ribs smarted where Brock's shoe had connected, but nothing seemed broken.

Homer wasn't the only one for whom the party had taken a sudden and unpleasant turn. As Rachel pressed through the crowd, heading back to the signing table to check in with Danny and make sure he still had everything he needed, she spotted Tommy huddled in serious conversation with Daisy not far from the cash register. She couldn't hear what they were saying, but Tommy seemed to have lost some of the swagger he'd started out the evening with.

I should ask him about that later, Rachel thought, watching as Daisy laid a hand on Tommy's arm with what looked like a mix of reassurance and concern. Parties were Tommy's natural element; it was unlike him to look so agitated in a big public gathering like this one.

Vashti noticed the exchange as well. She helped Homer to the spot where she'd been hiding, noting an unusual stiffness to his gait. *"Will you be okay here for a minute?"* she asked him. At his nod—and with firm instructions not to move until she returned (*"Not one inch, Homer!"*)—Vashti slipped beneath display tables and around guests' feet, her white fur allowing her to blend with the luminous terrazzo floor in the dimmed lighting. She paused beneath a small reading table draped with a promotional tablecloth for *Miami Spice*, positioning herself perfectly to overhear Tommy and Daisy's heated exchange. From her vantage point, she could see the paleness of Daisy's pallor beneath her makeup, and the tight set of Tommy's jaw.

"—always *knew* there was something off." Tommy's low-pitched voice was irate. "But I didn't ask too many questions because—"

"Because you were looking for a quick way up the ladder," Daisy interrupted. "If we're being honest."

"I paid you good money," Tommy fumed. "It was nearly all the money I had back then."

"And you got your money's worth, didn't you?" Daisy gestured at the room around them, at the way those closest to where they stood were subtly paying attention to what Tommy Duvall was doing, even while they carried on their own conversations—straining their ears to hear what "Mr. Nightlife" was saying to Daisy Locarro with so much energy.

Tommy plastered a beaming smile across his face, but from close up it resembled nothing so much as the artificial rictus of a comedy mask. "I do not need this right now, Daisy. Isabella Stuart is about to hand me my dream job."

"Relax." Daisy sounded tired. "It was five years ago, and anyway it's impossible to prove a negative. The only two people who know the whole story are me and you, and my lips are sealed."

"How did Marc even get on the scent in the first place?" Tommy's voice was accusing now.

For the first time, Daisy couldn't find an answer. How could she explain in a way that made sense? She'd found herself at the bar at 710 late one Tuesday night—so late it was officially early. Sitting next to her had been Marc Gottsegen, of all people. Someone she'd known for years, in the way one knew people in a town like Coacoochee without knowing them well. It had been near closing time, and they were the only two customers left in the place—both of them waiting for a sudden thunderstorm to pass before venturing out to find cabs. The 710 Bar was always dimly lit and private. But that night, with just the two of them there and the rain falling outside, it had felt even more so—as if they'd been cocooned together in some little side pocket of time, outside the normal flow of things.

Marc had been unexpectedly entertaining to talk to. They'd swapped Coacoochee war stories—trying to one-up each other with tales of the craziest things they'd gotten away with since moving to this crazy town. Daisy had told Marc about the time she'd sneaked into a private party Madonna had thrown in her Coconut Grove home. Marc had once started a rumor that Prince was going to make a surprise appearance at Yucca; it had worked so well that nearly a thousand people showed up and the fire marshal had to shut it down. "I *remember* that!" Daisy howled with laughter. And then, still laughing as tears streamed down her face, she'd delivered her own coup de grace—a story so outrageous that it had set the entire town of Coacoochee to talking for weeks, and changed Tommy Duvall's life forever. It wasn't until she'd noticed Marc falling silent, the amusement in his eyes swiftly sharpening into keen interest, that she realized what she'd done.

Now, Daisy broke off in telling her tale and looked at Tommy helplessly. "It was all the way out of my mouth before I remembered I was talking about both of us." She laid a hand on Tommy's arm. "I'm sorry. I really am. I promise, I won't so much as whisper to Marc again until this has all blown over. Maybe not even then."

"Yeah, well…" Tommy didn't sound convinced, but there was clearly nothing else to be said at the moment. Then he heaved a big sigh. "You're the first friend I made in this town, Daze." He placed his hand over hers. "We have to look out for each other, right?"

Daisy raised a small fist to playfully punch his shoulder. "Don't worry about me, Tommy Boy." She swayed in her high heels, her wan face more serious than usual as she looked into his. "I've always got your back."

THE SIGNING LINE HAD finally begun to thin, and only a handful of people still awaited their moment with Coacoochee's culinary star. Danny remained unfailingly gracious, his energy seemingly undiminished despite having signed well over a hundred books. Isabella continued her expert crowd management, somehow making each person feel special while keeping the line moving efficiently.

The photographers and Coacoochee scenesters had also begun to depart, decamping for the fashionable bars and nightclubs that never got going before eleven o'clock. Rachel bade a hasty farewell to Daisy, who had just emerged from the bathroom and now looked unquestionably ill.

"Just a stomach bug." Daisy waved away Rachel's concerned look. "Too much time clubbing this week and not enough resting."

"You should go straight home and get into bed." Rachel knew there was nothing cool about clucking like a mother hen, but she couldn't help it. "And come by tomorrow for some tea and toast, if you're feeling up to it. On the house."

"Love you." Daisy pulled Rachel into a spontaneous hug before disappearing out the door and into the night.

With the thinning crowd, the open spaces on the bookstore floor grew wider, making it increasingly difficult for Scarlett to slip through unnoticed. The sea of ankles that had provided perfect cover earlier in the evening was now more like a scattered archipelago, leaving fewer shadows for a plump-ish gray tabby to disappear into.

Scarlett had never wanted to be a big sister. Although the memories faded with each passing day, she could still recall a blissful Golden Age when she'd been Rachel's one and only, basking in undivided attention and affection. The arrival of Vashti had been, in Scarlett's considered opinion, entirely unnecessary—a disruption of perfect harmony. But even Scarlett, stubborn as the Florida humidity, wasn't immune to the slow thaw of sisterly affection. She'd grudgingly come to acknowledge that Vashti—despite her vanity and occasional bouts of theatrical sensitivity—possessed qualities that, when tallied with fairness, made her a rather worthwhile addition to their family.

Homer was another matter entirely. When Rachel had first brought him home—a scrawny, helpless thing that reeked of antiseptic and weeks spent at the vet's office—Scarlett had been deeply suspicious. A kitten who couldn't even see? What possible use could such a creature be?

And, in this case, Scarlett's suspicions had been entirely borne out. If Rachel had sat down for a month of Sundays, and done nothing but think of ways to make Scarlett's life as miserable as possible, she couldn't have hit on a better idea than adopting Homer. He pounced on Scarlett's head when she was trying to nap. He insisted on curling up next to her on the bed when the whole reason she'd gone into the bedroom was because she wanted to be alone. If Scarlett was trying to play a dignified game of Slap The Paper Ball with Rachel, Homer insisted on hurrying over and horning in, immediately turning a beloved two-player tradition into a three-way free-for-all. He ate as much as he wanted of whatever he wanted—even stealing bits from Scarlett's own personal bowl!—without gaining an ounce.

Worst of all, Homer possessed an inexhaustible energy that seemed specifically designed to shatter the tranquility Scarlett held dear. Homer was, without question, the absolute worst thing that had ever happened to Scarlett.

And she was going to make Brock pay for having kicked him.

"What are you doing?" Vashti whispered, having spotted her sister's unusual behavior from beneath a display table. *"We have to head back to the storeroom before somebody sees us."*

"Go ahead without me." Scarlett's voice was low and determined. *"I'll catch up."*

Brock stood near the Local Authors table, regaling a captive audience of two politely nodding strangers with tales of his soon-to-be-published literary masterpiece. Scarlett could see them surreptitiously check their watches and gaze longingly in the direction of the door. But Brock was completely oblivious to their quiet desperation, continuing his monologue with a self-assured confidence that was difficult to account for. He shifted his weight, momentarily presenting his back to the rest of the room as he gestured widely at the nearby shelf.

"Perfect," Scarlett thought.

With remarkable agility, and a speed even she hadn't known she possessed, Scarlett darted from her hiding spot, streaking across the terrazzo floor like a gray-and-white torpedo. In one fluid motion, she extended her claws to their full length, reared up on her hind legs, and delivered a vicious swipe across the back of Brock's calf.

The raw silk of his mustard-colored pants offered no resistance to Scarlett's razor-sharp claws. They sliced through the fabric and into the tender flesh beneath, leaving four perfect parallel lines of crimson that immediately began to seep through the torn material.

Brock yelped in surprise and pain, spinning around to confront whatever had assailed him. "What the—!"

But Scarlett was already gone, having executed a perfect tactical retreat. All Brock saw was a flash of something gray disappearing behind a distant bookcase.

"Are you all right?" one of his reluctant listeners asked, noticing his sudden distress.

Brock twisted awkwardly, trying to see the damage to the back of his leg. "Something just—" He felt the wetness on his calf and pulled his hand away to find his fingertips stained with blood. "I've been attacked!"

The cruel irony of it! Brock finally had something unequivocally interesting to say—and yet the drama of his announcement was wasted; his two listeners had already seized upon the opportunity presented by his momentary distraction to beat a hasty retreat.

In the shadows behind the bookcase, Scarlett paused just long enough to admire her handiwork. With one final glance at the chaos she'd created, she slipped silently away to rejoin Homer and Vashti under one of the cloth-covered high-top tables near the storeroom entrance.

"I didn't know you had it in you." There was admiration in Vashti's voice as she butted her head affectionately against Scarlett's.

"I wish I could have seen his face!" Homer chortled. In a more serious tone, he added, *"Thank you."* Then he, too, tapped his forehead to Scarlett's.

"Whatever." Scarlett rolled her eyes. *"Don't make a thing of it."*

The three cats made their way cautiously toward the back storeroom, weaving through the thinning crowd. With practiced stealth, they managed to avoid Rachel's gaze altogether, as she stood near the register and watched Danny greet the very last fan waiting to get a book signed with the same enthusiasm he'd shown for the first. His smile never dimmed, though Rachel noticed a certain tightness around his eyes that suggested the evening's performance had taken its toll.

Rachel glanced at her watch, surprised to find it was after eleven. The night had flown by in a blur of introductions, conversations, and the constant hum of a successful event. The stacks of *Miami Spice* that had towered on display tables earlier were now nearly gone, and a satisfying pile of sales receipts sat beside the register.

"I think we can call this an unqualified triumph." Isabella materialized beside Rachel in a waft of expensive perfume. "You've outdone yourself, darling. Title Wave has never looked more enchanting."

"Thank you," Rachel said, meaning it. Coming from Isabella Stuart, such praise carried real weight. "Though I think Danny deserves most of the credit."

Isabella's smile was enigmatic." A good host creates the stage upon which the star can shine. Don't undersell your contribution." She glanced toward the door where a photographer from *Ocean Drive* was packing up his equipment. "Every picture they publish will showcase this space you've created."

Danny approached them, his chef's jacket somehow still pristine despite the long evening. "Ladies," he said, "I can't thank you enough. This was everything I'd hoped for and more." He took Rachel's hand between both of his. "Isabella told me you were the real deal, and she was right. When my next book comes out, Title Wave gets first dibs on the launch."

"I'll hold you to that," Rachel replied, smiling. She was about to say more when Tommy appeared, looking uncharacteristically distracted.

"Rachel, honey." He kissed her cheek. "I hate to be the first to abandon ship, but I need to chase down a lead tonight. Raincheck on our celebration?"

"Of course," she assured him, hiding her disappointment. She'd been looking forward to dissecting the evening with him over late-night cocktails at the 710 Bar. "Everything okay?"

"Just the usual nightlife columnist drama." Tommy's wavering smile didn't quite reach his eyes. "I'll call you tomorrow with all the juicy details."

Rachel watched him weave through the remaining guests and slip out the front door, his peacock-blue jacket vanishing into the night. Something in his manner left her vaguely unsettled, but before she could dwell on it, Dorothea appeared.

"I haven't seen a signing this successful in all my years owning this place." Her silver hair shone under the track lighting. "Not even when that mystery writer who wintered here got nominated for the Edgar."

Rachel felt a flush of pleasure at the praise. "Thank you for taking a chance on me."

"Best decision I ever made," Dorothea replied matter-of-factly. "Don't let me keep you from saying your goodbyes. We'll have our post-mortem next week."

The next half-hour passed in a whirl of farewells as the crowd dwindled even further and Griselda organized Sabrosa's servers into a cleanup crew. Laurie and Robert thanked Rachel effusively before departing, and Dahlia embraced her warmly, declaring they must have lunch soon.

Finally, only Rachel and Nadia remained, surveying the aftermath of literary celebration. "I think we broke a sales record tonight," Nadia said, as she tallied the final receipts. Despite the late hour, her eyes remained bright with enthusiasm.

"We definitely did." Rachel plucked an abandoned napkin from the space between the register and the counter. "Thanks for staying late."

Together they moved through the store, restoring Title Wave to its usual ordered tranquility. Sabrosa's staff had efficiently cleared away the remnants of food and drink, leaving only minor evidence of the festivities—a forgotten shawl draped over a chair, a few napkins that had escaped notice, the occasional empty wine glass tucked between books.

Rachel and Nadia worked in companionable silence, straightening shelves and returning bookcases to their usual positions. The wave-patterned terrazzo floor reappeared as they folded and stored tables, and the space gradually transformed from glamorous party venue back to comfortable—and thoroughly beloved—bookstore.

When the last chair was stacked and the last book straightened, Rachel locked the register and walked her young assistant to the door. "Get home safe," she said. "And thanks again."

"Are you kidding? This was the most exciting night at Title Wave since I started working here. Who knew books could be so glamorous?" Nadia's laugh was light as she stepped out into the soft night air.

Rachel stood in the doorway for a moment, watching Nadia disappear down the faintly lit stretch of Hibiscus Road. The night had cooled slightly, and a gentle breeze carried a sweet citrus aroma from nearby orange trees. The shops were dark now, though light and music still spilled from Club Yucca down the block. Even at this hour, Coacoochee refused to surrender to sleep.

Turning back to the empty store, Rachel closed the shutters and switched off all but the security lights, casting the familiar space in pools of blue-tinged shadow. The silence felt profound after the hours of chatter and laughter. She ran her hand along a shelf of books as she made her way to the back storeroom, pleased by the sensation of spines beneath her fingertips.

Rachel had arrived in Coacoochee six months earlier, but tonight was the first time she'd felt like she truly belonged here.

UPSTAIRS IN RACHEL'S APARTMENT, the three cats settled in after their adventure. They'd tumbled out of the dumbwaiter in a furry heap, relieved to have made their escape before the crowd had thinned enough for Rachel to notice their presence.

"I think we deserve a round of applause." Homer's whiskers still shivered with excitement as he washed his face with one paw. *"We were there for the whole party and nobody suspected a thing."* Except for stupid Brock, Homer

thought, as he gingerly licked his bruised side. It would probably be a day or two before he was completely agile again.

Scarlett snorted, arranging herself into a perfect circle on the center cushion of the couch. *The real accomplishment was my restraint. I only clawed one human.*

"The look on Brock's face," Vashti giggled from the windowsill where moonlight silvered her white fur.

Homer's tail swished against the floor. *"Did you smell the hors d'oeuvres? I'd risk it all again for one bite of those stone crabs."*

"I thought it was kind of boring." Scarlett stretched comfortably. *"Just a lot of people talking about themselves, mostly."*

"I almost forgot to tell you." Vashti's tone turned serious as she jumped down from the windowsill. *"I caught part of a conversation Tommy and Daisy were having. They seemed worried about something."* Vashti quickly filled the other two in on the exchange she'd overheard.

"Humans and their ridiculous secrets," Scarlett scoffed, but her eyes glinted with interest. *"Whatever it is, it must be important if they're both so worked up about it."*

"I hope Tommy will be all right." The concern in Vashti's voice was genuine.

"Maybe we should keep an ear out for—" Homer began, but stopped abruptly at the sound of Rachel's footsteps on the wrought-iron staircase.

"Act natural!" Scarlett hissed.

By the time Rachel opened the door, Scarlett had arranged herself into a convincing portrait of feline slumber, Homer had (to Scarlett's annoyance) curled up not far from her on the couch, and Vashti was perched elegantly on the windowsill as if she'd been watching the night sky for hours.

Rachel entered with a weary but satisfied sigh. She kicked off her kitten heels and sank onto the couch beside Scarlett, who gave an Oscar-worthy performance of having been deeply asleep until that very moment.

"What a night," Rachel murmured, scratching Scarlett behind the ears. "I wish you guys could have seen it."

Scarlett purred innocently and butted her head against Rachel's hand. Homer padded over and jumped into her lap, his nose twitching at the symphony of scents that clung to Rachel—dozens of perfumes and colognes, the paper and ink of newly signed books, lingering notes of wine and Danny's culinary creations. He pressed his head against her chest, feeling the steady rhythm of her heartbeat. Vashti stretched languorously on the windowsill before leaping down to join them, settling against Rachel's side with elegant grace.

"Dorothea was thrilled," Rachel told them. "Said it was the most successful event Title Wave has ever hosted." She yawned and rubbed Homer affectionately behind the ears. "Tommy and I were supposed to go out and celebrate, but honestly, I'm kind of glad to be home with you three."

Homer purred in response, kneading Rachel's thigh gently with his paws. Her triumph was their triumph, after all.

Hours later, long after Rachel had gone to bed, Homer found himself suddenly awake. His ears swiveled toward the bedroom window, detecting something on the quiet pre-dawn street below. A shuffling sound, then silence. Then more shuffling.

Carefully extracting himself from Rachel's side, Homer made his way to the window where Vashti had been sleeping earlier. He pressed his face against the glass, his whiskers detecting the slightest vibrations from outside.

Someone was down there, moving slowly, erratically. A familiar scent drifted up through the partially opened window—Daisy's perfume, mingled with that strange, elusive smell he'd noticed earlier. Homer heard a soft thump, then nothing more.

He stayed at the window for a long time, waiting for more sounds, more movement. But there was nothing, even as the first hints of morning light began to filter through the darkness.

Whatever—or whoever—was down there had gone completely still.

CHAPTER 5

Nᴉᴄᴋ Tᴏʀʀᴇs sᴛᴀʀᴇᴅ ᴏᴜᴛ the window of his office, where morning light glinted off the tawny façade of the Spanish-style apartment building that faced him across Allamanda Avenue. At forty-five, the salt-and-pepper at his temples had started creeping further into his dark hair, and the laugh lines around his eyes had deepened—evidence of twenty years with the Coacoochee Police Department and five as Chief.

Spread in front of him was Isabella Stuart's latest column in the weekend edition of the *Miami Daily News*, which contained a detailed write-up of the previous night's book-signing for Danny Elliott over at Title Wave. An untidy pile on Nick's desk also contained *Palm* and a sampling of the other local papers and 'zines that covered Coacoochee's social scene. His wife, Elena, teased him about reading "the society pages," but in a town as small as Coacoochee it never hurt to know who the players were and what they looked like.

Nick sipped his coffee, grimacing at how quickly it had cooled despite the mug's alleged insulating properties. On his desk, framed photos caught the sunlight: eight-year-old Hanna with her science fair trophy, six-year-old Lucas in his Little League uniform, both kids flanking him and Elena at last year's Halloween parade. Thinking about his family always made Nick smile, but the coffee was truly irredeemable. With a sigh, he set down the mug and decided to treat himself to a fresh cup and maybe even a bear claw (what Elena didn't know wouldn't hurt her) over at Beachy Beans, only a block down Allamanda Avenue from police headquarters.

It never failed to astonish him how quiet Allamanda was on a Saturday morning. All Nick could hear now were soft ocean breezes sweeping through the royal palms and riotous yellow allamandas that grew in the medians of the four-lane road. By sundown, Allamanda Avenue would be a carnival of club kids in outrageous getups, high schoolers with shoddy fake IDs trying to sneak into nightclubs owned by Prince or patronized by Madonna, the stop-and-go gridlock of rented convertibles blaring dance music from their radios next to cabs containing locals who knew better than to try to find parking on Allamanda after dark.

The Coacoochee Police Department headquarters, located at the intersection of Allamanda and Eleventh Street, was an enormous, gleaming-white, Art Deco relic. The portion of the exterior façade that faced the street was a profusion of curved walls and round porthole windows. Back in the wild and woolly Eighties—when cocaine and cash had flowed so freely, corruption on the force had been more common than colds—there was a joke that the Coacoochee Police Department was so crooked, even the building that housed it couldn't manage a straight line.

But Chief Nick Torres had always played by the rules. The corrupt cops he'd come up with had, for the most part, been rounded up in sting operations by the time the early Nineties rolled around. Nick had been among the scrupulous core that remained, and it had formed the nucleus of the spotless police department he oversaw today.

Nick had just made it to the front of the line at Beachy Beans when a call came in over his handheld transceiver. "Chief, it's Martinez." Officer Jessica

Martinez's normally calm voice held a note of tension. "We've got a body on Hibiscus Road. Found just outside the entrance to Title Wave Books."

Nick reluctantly turned away from the counter and stepped outside. As he did so he held the door open for Mrs. Hernandez, one of Allamanda Avenue's last remaining elderly residents, who came in every morning for coffee and *pastelitos*. "Accident? Homicide?"

"Can't tell yet, sir. No obvious signs of violence, but..." Jessica paused. "It's Daisy Locarro. The jogger who found her knew her socially."

Fifteen minutes later, Nick ducked under the yellow tape cordoning off the area in front of Title Wave Books. Morning tourists clustered at the perimeter, their faces wearing that particular mix of morbid fascination and discomfort that the proximity of death always seemed to inspire.

Martinez met him halfway to the body. "ME's on her way," she said. "Scene's undisturbed."

Nick's eyes scanned the crowd. "Who found her?"

"Early morning jogger. Tends bar at the Tenth Street Diner at night. He's over there, pretty shaken up." Martinez gestured toward a man wrapped in a shock blanket, sitting on a bench.

"Any signs of a struggle?"

"None. No visible injuries. Nothing that looks like foul play."

Nick nodded, his instincts already prickling. Something felt wrong. Daisy was young—mid-twenties at most. People that age didn't typically drop dead on sidewalks for no reason.

He noticed movement at Title Wave's entrance. Rachel Baum, the new manager Dorothea Wilson had brought in a few months ago, stood in the doorway. Her olive-complected face was drained of color, looking even paler next to the tousled brown-black curls that framed it. Beside her stood Tommy Duvall, who wrote for *Palm* magazine, with an arm wrapped protectively around her shoulders. His usually animated face was unnaturally still.

"Has anyone notified next of kin?" Nick asked.

Martinez shook her head. "We're working on it. She has a mother in Palm Beach, but they weren't close according to the neighbors we've spoken with."

"Keep me posted," Nick said, his eyes still on Rachel and Tommy. "I'll talk to them after the ME's done here."

By late afternoon, Nick sat at his desk reviewing the Medical Examiner's preliminary report. Dr. Edwidge Michel sat across from him, her white lab coat immaculate despite the morning's work.

"Cardiac arrest," she said, tapping a manila folder containing her notes. "Unusual in someone her age, but not unheard of. No external trauma, no defensive wounds, no signs of sexual assault."

"Toxicology?" Nick asked.

"Preliminary results show no common recreational drugs, nothing unusual." She adjusted her glasses. "If I had to guess, I'd say undiagnosed congenital heart defect. It happens."

"Anything else?"

"Nothing that would point to homicide." Dr. Michel closed her folder. "I know it feels wrong, Nick. A young, healthy-looking woman found dead. But sometimes nature just has bad timing."

Nick nodded, though he wasn't entirely convinced. He was about to ask another question when Commissioner Carpenter appeared in the doorway—a bearish man in his sixties with bushy white eyebrows that seemed perpetually furrowed.

"Dr. Michel," he acknowledged with a nod, before turning his attention to Nick. "Torres, a word?"

Dr. Michel gathered her materials and made a graceful exit. The Commissioner didn't bother sitting down.

"Please tell me this isn't going to be a problem," he said. "We're six weeks from Season. The last thing Coacoochee needs is tourists thinking there's a killer on the loose."

"The ME's preliminary finding is natural causes," Nick replied carefully. "Cardiac arrest. Possibly an undiagnosed heart condition."

Relief flashed across Commissioner Carpenter's face. "That's good. Sign off on it and let's move on. We've got the Halloween parade coming up in a few weeks. City Hall's breathing down my neck about keeping Coacoochee's image squeaky clean."

After the Commissioner left, Nick stared at the preliminary death certificate on his desk. The official cause of death read "Cardiac Arrest—Natural Causes." All he had to do was sign it, and the case would be officially closed.

He thought about Daisy, of her age and apparent health. He thought about how lively and vivacious she'd always seemed every time their paths had crossed.

With a sigh, he signed the certificate. Officially, Daisy Locarro had died of natural causes.

Mentally, though, Nick filed it under "not quite closed"—a special category he'd maintained for years, reserved for cases that technically met all the requirements for closure but still left that persistent, nagging itch of doubt in the back of his mind.

As he packed up to head home, Nick glanced at his desk calendar. It would be a couple more weeks before the third Sunday of the month rolled around—Title Wave's Story Time, which he never missed with Hanna and Lucas. Maybe Nick would find a reason to pop in before then. It might give him a chance to observe Rachel Baum and the other bookstore regulars more closely. Not as Chief of Police investigating a case, which he absolutely wasn't doing. He was simply a customer with a healthy curiosity about the place where a young woman had spent her final evening before dying unexpectedly on the sidewalk outside.

He closed his office door, locking it behind him. Maybe Daisy Locarro really had died of natural causes. But in Nick's twenty years of police work, he'd learned that coincidences often weren't coincidences at all—and timing was rarely just bad luck.

CHAPTER 6

THE PAPERBACK THRILLER THE customer handed Rachel had a lurid cover featuring a red-headed woman with shockingly white skin. The woman was spilling out of a low-cut dress and appeared to be dead, although maybe she was just unconscious.

Looking at the cover now, Rachel felt sick. She couldn't help wondering what she'd been thinking when she'd decided to stock it.

It was Tuesday, and Rachel's hands still trembled whenever something reminded her of Daisy's pale, lifeless face as she'd last seen it on Saturday morning. She silently willed them to steady themselves as she fished change out of the register (she could only hope it was the correct amount) and handed it over to the customer.

"Terrible thing that happened," the woman said in a hushed tone. "And right outside your front door, too."

Rachel nodded, not trusting herself to speak. It had been like this for nearly four days now—well-meaning strangers offering condolences as if she'd lost a close relative, curious locals fishing for details she didn't want to share, and tourists who'd heard rumors of "a body on Hibiscus Road" peering through the windows with morbid fascination.

Scarlett observed it all from her sunny perch in the front display window, her yellow-green eyes narrowed thoughtfully. Her gray-and-white tail twitched against a display copy of *The Secret History* as she watched Rachel's shoulders tense with each new interaction. Even Homer, who couldn't see the dark circles under Rachel's eyes, heard the weariness in her voice and the heaviness in her usually brisk footsteps.

Her downcast mood was at odds with the gorgeous October day. The sky was the pure, crystalline blue they tried hard to showcase in Coacoochee travel brochures, and the late-afternoon sun beamed down with the exaggerated golden sweetness that was only seen in the fall. All up and down Hibiscus Road, people basked in the beautiful weather, eating at outdoor tables or sitting on benches in small groups while they carried on lively conversations. It struck Rachel as slightly obscene, somehow—as if the weather itself, in refusing to cloud over or offer up a teary drizzle of rain, were mocking Daisy's loss rather than mourning it.

The jingle of the bell above the door cut into Rachel's thoughts, announcing Griselda's arrival. The hostess from Sabrosa entered with her usual poise, although she was noticeably subdued. She was dressed in a simple black sheath dress that accentuated her slender figure, her glossy black hair pulled back in an unfussy ponytail. Even the click of her heels against the terrazzo floor seemed muted, as if she were trying not to disturb the heavy quiet that had settled over the bookstore.

"I thought you might need company." Griselda slid onto a café stool. Her dark eyes, usually sparkling with warmth, were soft with sympathy. "It's been a hell of a few days."

Rachel nodded, grateful for the presence of another human who wasn't asking for details about "the body." She poured Griselda a cup of coffee from the freshly brewed pot, the rich dark liquid streaming into one of

Title Wave's signature aqua-blue cups. She added a splash of cream without being asked, the warm, milky aroma curling upward with the steam.

"I still can't believe it." Rachel's voice caught as she remembered Daisy's pale complexion on Friday night, the way she'd seemed unsteady in her gold stilettos. The image of a laughing Daisy in her shimmering dress was impossible to reconcile with the knowledge that she'd died on the sidewalk just outside.

"I know." Griselda wrapped her elegant fingers around the coffee cup. A delicate silver bracelet slid down her wrist, catching the light. "Danny's completely shaken up."

"Was Daisy close with Danny?" Rachel realized how little she knew about Daisy's connections beyond Tommy. For all her lively presence and seemingly endless stories about Coacoochee's elite, Daisy had revealed surprisingly little about her own life.

Griselda hesitated, her dark eyes flicking around the empty store as if to confirm they were alone. The afternoon sunlight streaming through the windows cast dappled patterns across her face as she leaned forward, lowering her voice. "Not particularly, but..." She traced the rim of her coffee cup with one perfectly manicured finger. "She came by Sabrosa a few nights before she died. She was upset—really upset. Danny was talking to her at the bar after closing."

"About what?" Rachel was intrigued despite herself.

"I couldn't hear everything, but it sounded like something involving Tommy," Griselda said. "I figured they'd had a little spat or something—you know the two of them have been friends for years. Danny had the bartender comp her a couple of drinks until she calmed down," Griselda concluded. "When she came back a few days later for the *Palm* party, it was like nothing had happened."

Vashti, who was fastidiously washing her face with her front paws over in Florida History, felt her ears perk up. She remembered that *Palm* party—Tommy had taken Rachel, and he'd kept her out so late that the cats had to meow and meow directly into her ear the next morning to wake her. She'd ended up feeding them ten whole minutes past their usual time, which had put Scarlett into a snit for the rest of the morning.

The bell above the door jingled again, and Rachel looked up to see Natalie entering with Hot Mike at her side. "G'day, all." Natalie unclipped Hot Mike's leash as she approached the café counter. "I just got back from

Buenos Aires and heard about Daisy." She settled onto a stool next to Griselda. "Heart attack, they're saying?"

"That's what the police told me," Rachel confirmed. She reached for another cup to prepare Natalie's usual café con leche. The metal steaming wand hissed as she submerged it in milk. "Though it seems strange in someone so young."

Homer had positioned himself near Rachel's feet. He recalled the mysterious smell that had clung to Daisy that night—subtle, but distinctive, unlike anything he'd encountered before.

"She seemed ill at the book signing." Rachel poured the steamed milk over the espresso and handed it to Natalie, who accepted it with a grateful nod. "I thought it was just too much partying, but now I wonder if she was already experiencing symptoms."

"Nausea can be a precursor to heart attacks," Natalie noted. She took a sip of her coffee, leaving a faint trace of lipstick on the rim. "Still, it's odd in someone her age without any health issues—at least, none we know about."

Vashti abandoned her grooming and made her way to the café counter. She leapt onto it in a single fluid motion, positioning herself delicately between Griselda and Natalie despite Rachel's half-hearted attempt to shoo her away. Her emerald eyes fixed on the women with unmistakable interest.

Hot Mike, after greeting the cats, had settled himself beneath the café counter with his broad head resting on his paws. His ears remained at attention, shifting subtly as he followed what the humans were saying.

"I saw Tommy arguing with Daisy that night." Rachel admitted this reluctantly and kept her voice low, even though there were no other customers in the store.

Natalie raised an eyebrow, the gesture accentuating the fine lines at the corners of her eyes. "Interesting timing, isn't it?"

"Are you suggesting—" Rachel began.

"I'm not suggesting anything," Natalie clarified quickly. "Just noting that coincidences make me curious. Occupational hazard of being an investigative journalist."

As the women continued their discussion, Scarlett abandoned her spot in the front window entirely, the lure of gossip proving stronger even than the warmth of her sunbeam. She seated herself at the edge of the café area, her tail wrapped primly around her paws, the white tip twitching occasionally with interest.

Hot Mike shifted his weight, the soft jingle of his collar tags nearly imperceptible as he inched closer to the trio of cats. *"Marc Gottsegen lives next door to Natalie and me,"* he confided. *"I heard him talking to Daisy on the phone last week. It sounded like they were arguing about something."*

"Samkhat also said she saw Marc and Daisy arguing last week," Vashti corroborated.

"Somebody at the party had that same weird smell Daisy did," Homer said. *"But there were too many people for me to tell who it was."*

"You always think you smell something weird." Scarlett's tone was dismissive. *"Remember how you got all riled up last month, saying Rachel had some fatal disease, and it turned out she was just trying that new face cream made with sheep placenta?"*

Above them, the humans continued their conversation, oblivious to the discussion happening at their feet. The scent of coffee grew stronger as Rachel brewed a fresh pot, the rich aroma filling the café area.

"I can't believe how quickly word spread." Griselda shook her head. "Half of Sabrosa's customers last night were talking about it. Death by natural causes shouldn't be gossip fodder."

"People can't resist a mystery," Natalie replied. "Young, healthy woman dies suddenly? It breaks the narrative we all tell ourselves about being safe."

Rachel nodded, thinking of her own shattered sense of security. Title Wave had always felt like a safe place, a peaceful sanctuary after the upheaval of her break-up with Henry. Now, whenever the bell above the door jingled, she couldn't help glancing toward the spot where Daisy had been found.

Griselda looked at her watch and stood up. "I should get to Sabrosa. Pre-dinner prep starts soon." She drained the last of her coffee and set the cup down with a soft clink. "Thanks for the coffee, *mamí*."

"Anytime," Rachel replied, taking the empty cup. Their fingers brushed in a small moment of human connection. "And thanks for stopping by."

Griselda smiled gently, her dark eyes full of understanding. The bell jingled softly as she exited, a flash of blinding sunlight dazzling the store before the door swung shut behind her.

Natalie stayed behind, absently stroking Hot Mike's head. His fur was smooth beneath her fingers, the contact comforting both woman and dog.

"Are you really okay, Rachel?" she asked once they were alone, her accent softening the words.

Rachel sighed, leaning against the counter. "I don't know. I keep thinking about that night, wondering if there was something I missed. Some sign Daisy was in trouble."

"Don't do that to yourself." Natalie's eyes were kind but serious. "Second-guessing doesn't help anyone, least of all you."

"But what if she came here for help?" The question that had been haunting Rachel since Saturday morning finally escaped her lips.

Natalie reached across the counter to grasp Rachel's hand, her palm warm and lightly calloused. "Listen to me. There's no way you could have known what was happening with Daisy, and nothing you could have done for her."

Rachel nodded, not entirely convinced but grateful for the support.

Natalie finished her coffee and departed with Hot Mike ("Call me if you need to," she said on her way out the door), and Rachel was left alone with her cats and her thoughts. She watched as Vashti crossed the store to curl up in her favorite armchair, her white fur almost translucent where the sun hit it directly. Scarlett returned to her sun puddle in the window display, arranging herself among the books. Homer rubbed his head on Rachel's legs, his black fur silky against her skin.

The bell above the door announced the arrival of new customers—a pair of women browsing the stacks with the unhurried air of locals rather than tourists. Rachel recognized one of them; she came in every couple of weeks to pick up a new legal thriller. The other woman was unfamiliar—petite with honey-blonde hair pulled back in a practical ponytail, wearing sensible shoes and a lanyard with an ID badge from Coacoochee General Hospital tucked into her purse.

As Rachel reorganized the café counter, their conversation drifted toward her.

"I work in cardiology," the hospital worker was saying. Her voice was low, but it nevertheless carried in the quiet store. "Twenty-six-year-olds don't just drop dead from heart failure."

"But the medical examiner said—"

"Natural causes, I know. But in someone that young? With no warning signs?" She shook her head. "In my twelve years at Coacoochee General, we've had maybe two cases of sudden cardiac death in people under thirty. Both had documented congenital conditions."

"You think it was something else?"

"I'm not saying that. It's just..." The woman selected a paperback from the shelf. "Unusual. Very unusual."

Rachel's eyes drifted to the front door, to the spot just outside where Daisy had been found. What had she been doing there so late at night? Had she come seeking Rachel's help? And, if so, what kind of help had she needed?

There was no way of knowing now. The one person who could have told her was gone. Rachel reached down to stroke Homer's back, finding comfort in the warmth of his fur amid all the unsettling questions that seemed to have no answers.

CHAPTER 7

SNEAKING OUT OF THE apartment to use the secret cat door was always a risky proposition. Those risks were actually heightened when Rachel was out and Nadia was minding the shop—as she was now, having insisted on giving Rachel the afternoon off to relax with a novel and a cup of tea over at Beachy Beans.

Rachel never left home without first confirming that all three cats were safely tucked away upstairs. (She'd once nearly exhausted the patience of a waiting cabbie because Vashti was snoozing invisibly under a pile of laundry in the back of a closet, too zonked out to hear Rachel's increasingly frantic calls of "Vashti? *Vashti, where are you?!?*") So if Nadia were to catch them skulking around the back storeroom while Rachel not only wasn't working, but wasn't even at home, it was hard to imagine how she would account for this anomaly without launching a thorough investigation into potential escape routes.

Nothing good could come of that.

Nevertheless, the series of clipped meows from Samkhat—deafening from Homer's perspective, barely audible from Vashti's—meant she was waiting for them outside. All three cats were anxious to learn whether Samkhat had seen or heard anything of interest out in the wider realm of Coacoochee—perhaps something about the strange circumstances sur-rounding Daisy's death that hadn't yet been hashed over by chattering humans at Title Wave's café counter.

A whole group of them had come in the previous morning for coffee, following the sunrise memorial for Daisy that Tommy had put together at Coacoochee Beach. It was like an inverse version of the celebratory gathering in that very same space for Danny Elliott only six days earlier. Rachel had thought the cats' antics might be unseemly for such a somber occasion, and she'd left them upstairs until the store had opened for regular business a few hours later. People had been speaking in such hushed tones that even Homer, eavesdropping from upstairs, hadn't been able to make out anything interesting—except to note Tommy's conspicuous absence.

Homer and Vashti now debated whether it was worth waking Scarlett, who was sacked out in Rachel's favorite armchair, all four paws in the air and blissfully unaware of Samkhat's cries. Her paws twitched occasionally, and her whiskers fluttered with each breath.

"Let her sleep," Vashti finally decreed. She could tell by the satisfied expression on Scarlett's face that she was in the midst of a pleasant dream. Besides, they'd heard Rachel earlier in the afternoon on the phone, inviting what had sounded like a veritable army of human adolescents to visit the store tomorrow after closing. She'd been struck by some kind of inspira-tion—an idea she'd had to re-enliven Title Wave after the sad events of the past week. Best to let Scarlett enjoy the peace and quiet while it lasted.

As it happened, at that precise moment Scarlett was dreaming that Brock Winfield had shrunk down to the size of a mouse. She was batting him from paw to paw with a pitiless playfulness, while Brock shrieked and cowered before her perfectly manicured claws.

The two cats crept to the panel in the pantry that concealed the dumb-waiter shaft. Homer's whiskers guided them in the darkness as they made their careful descent, the thick, ancient rope sturdy beneath their paws. The faint scent of paper, dust, and the previous day's delivery of new hardcovers drifted up to meet them, and the muffled sound of Nadia's voice carried from the front of the store as she spoke with a customer. "Chef Elliott's new cookbook has this incredible mango-habanero salsa recipe," she was saying. "It's basically foolproof, even for beginners."

They paused once they reached the storeroom, alert for any sign they'd been detected. Then Homer led the way to the ancient cat door, nudging it open with his head. The humid, salty air of Coacoochee washed over them as they slipped into the alley.

Samkhat waited in the shadows, her tortoiseshell fur a patchwork of browns and blacks that melted into the darkness of the cement wall behind her. Her single amber eye gleamed as she greeted them with a gentle nose touch.

"*You just missed Stewie,*" she said by way of greeting. Her wry tone implied that having missed out on Stewie's grating conversational style wasn't much of a loss.

"*Ugh.*" Vashti's delicate pink nose wrinkled with distaste. "*He passed by our bedroom window yesterday morning and made a ruckus for at least twenty minutes.*"

"*He was just being a pest.*" Under his breath, Homer added a muttered, "*One of these days...*" He imagined the profound satisfaction of feeling Stewie's feathers clutched firmly within his claws.

The corner of Samkhat's mouth twitched with amusement. She knew exactly what Homer was imagining—and also how unlikely it was that even he, with all the prowess of his heightened senses, would ever nab Stewie. "*Let's move over to the loading dock,*" she said. "*It's got a better vantage point, and I can keep watch while we talk.*"

Homer and Vashti acknowledged Samkhat's well-known wariness without saying anything further, and the three cats moved silently along the alley until they reached the loading dock. Homer's keen nose detected the mingled scents of nearby restaurants—fresh fish from the seafood place over on Jacaranda, and baking bread from the Cuban café on tiny Lantana Lane, one block to the north of Hibiscus Road.

"I'm sorry about your friend," Samkhat told them once they were all settled. She didn't care much for humans beyond the one or two, like Rachel, who fed her. But she knew her indoor friends felt differently. *"How are your humans doing?"*

"Rachel's sadder than she lets on," Vashti replied. *"So is Tommy. At least, I think he is. He hasn't been around much lately."* Vashti's green eyes were full of sorrow. *"I think he still feels bad because he and Daisy argued at the book signing. That was probably the last time he talked to her."*

Samkhat bowed her head. Even she could appreciate how hurtful it would be to have angry words be the last words you ever got to exchange with someone you cared about. *"I overheard Daisy talking to Danny at Sabrosa a few days before she died. She was really upset. She kept saying how she'd 'betrayed Tommy' by telling Marc something she shouldn't have."*

Vashti's ears swiveled in Samkhat's direction. *"Did she say what it was?"*

"I'm not sure. I was hanging around the back door, waiting for one of the bussers to put out the trash for the night." Samkhat's expression was mildly contrite, but her tone was pragmatic. *"Once he came out I had to follow him, or some other cat would have beaten me to the good scraps."*

Vashti felt a pang as she realized, not for the first time, how much harder her friend's life was than her own.

"Kotik's been following Marc Gottsegen around when he gets the chance to slip away from Laurie's store," Samkhat added. *"He told me the other day that Marc's been going around trying to track down old issues of Tommy's magazine."*

"Kotik is following Marc?" Vashti seemed genuinely surprised. *"Why would he do that?"*

Samkhat rolled her one eye, but said nothing.

"Did you see Tommy at that memorial they had for Daisy yesterday at the beach?" Homer chimed in. Having been deprived of the opportunity to overhear people talking about it, he was curious to know what it had been like.

"Rachel says Tommy's the one who put it together," Vashti added. Her tone was admiring; she thought it was a wonderfully kind and thoughtful thing for Tommy to have done.

"Did he?" Samkhat seemed surprised to hear this. But as she thought about it, her one good eye drifting upward as she recalled what she'd seen the day before, she nodded slowly. *"I guess that makes sense. He was the first*

human to make a speech about Daisy. But still..." Her eye fixed on Vashti. *"He was acting very strangely."*

"What do you mean?"

"Little things," Samkhat replied. *"He kept fidgeting with his tie and his jacket, like he needed something to do with his hands. And he wouldn't look anybody in the eye. After he gave his big speech about how much he missed Daisy, when nobody was watching him, he looked relieved."*

Vashti and Homer were silent for a moment. Neither of them had ever been to a funeral, but even they knew relief wasn't an appropriate emotion to express at one.

It was Vashti who eventually broke the silence. *"Is that all?"* Her voice was cold. *"You came all the way over here just to tell us that Tommy seemed sad at a memorial for a human he was friends with, and then relieved when the speech he had to give was over?"* Vashti didn't know why it was happening, but it seemed to her that everybody was suddenly talking about her friend Tommy as if they suspected him of something—and thought she should suspect him, too.

"No, that's not why I came." Samkhat spoke with a quiet dignity that instantly made Vashti ashamed of her rudeness. *"I came to give you my sympathy."*

Homer sat quietly as he connected Samkhat's report with what they already knew: the mysterious smell he'd detected on Daisy and someone else at the book signing; the argument between Tommy and Daisy; the suspicious behavior at the memorial service; and Marc's sudden interest in tracking down old issues of Tommy's magazine.

"We need to find out more," Homer finally said. *"I think we should—"*

His sentence was cut short by the distant sound of the back storeroom door opening. They froze, and Samkhat quickly moved toward the shadows.

"We should go," Vashti said. *"We don't know how long Rachel's planning to be gone. She could be on her way home already."*

Homer cocked an ear in the general eastward direction of Allamanda Avenue. *"I don't hear her coming yet,"* he said. *"But if she decides to take a cab home instead of walking, we might not get much of a heads-up. Anyway,"* he added, *"I think it's going to rain soon."*

Vashti and Samkhat looked up in surprise—the day had seemed perfectly sunny so far. But a quick glance to the east confirmed Homer's suspicion: a thick mass of black thunderheads was moving quickly in their direction. A moment later the wind picked up, noticeably cooler than the warm breeze that had been gently ruffling their fur until now.

"I'll let you know if I hear anything else," Samkhat promised. Vashti quickly touched her nose in farewell and guided Homer back to the cat door in the alley.

Samkhat was anxious to get to her favorite hiding spot beneath the picnic tables on Hibiscus and Eighth before the rain got too bad. But she also wanted to grab a few bites of the kibble Rachel had left for her and hastily gulped down half the bowl. Her stomach full for the moment, the tortie then slipped silently over the edge of the loading dock. She disappeared into the tangle of bougainvillea growing alongside the building just as the first drops began to fall.

CHAPTER 8

RACHEL SANK DEEPER INTO her comfortable chair in a quiet corner of Beachy Beans, one hand rising unconsciously to smooth down the tangle of curls that were even unrulier when it rained. The other hand cradled a steaming mug of Earl Grey. She was grateful for its warmth as the air conditioning, calibrated for Coacoochee's typical sunshine, sent an unexpected chill through the room. The café hummed with gentle activity—the hiss of the espresso machine, the clink of spoons against ceramic, the murmured conversations of locals and tourists alike. From her corner table, Rachel could observe it all while she flipped absentmindedly through the novel in front of her.

The streak of flawless beach weather had finally broken. A sudden squall descended on Coacoochee, turning what had promised to be a postcard-perfect afternoon into something mercurial and moody. The café's soft amber lighting glowed through its windows, reflecting in the puddles that had begun to form on the sidewalk outside. Rachel watched palm trees bend and sway against the gunmetal sky, their fronds thrashing like the tails of angry cats. Thunder rolled in the distance, a bass note punctuating the percussion of fat raindrops as they struck the awning above the entrance.

Though Sunday and Monday were her usual days off, Nadia had offered to cover the after-lunch shift at Title Wave, giving Rachel an unexpected respite. "I don't have class on Thursday afternoons, anyway," she'd insisted. "Go. You look like you could use a break." Rachel hadn't argued. After the events of the past week, any moment away from the bookstore felt like coming up for air after too long underwater.

The memorial service for Daisy yesterday morning still lingered in her mind. The sunrise gathering at Coacoochee Beach had drawn a surprisingly large crowd, a living map of Coacoochee's social landscape—nightclub promoters and party regulars Rachel had met during Tommy's late-night tours, boutique and gallery owners whose shops flanked Title Wave on Hibiscus. Laurie and Robert Castillo had stood near the shoreline, Laurie's normally colorful demeanor subdued in a simple black dress. Danny Elliott and Griselda had huddled with several of the Sabrosa bartenders and waitstaff Rachel now knew by name. Natalie had been there, looking less formidable, somehow, without Hot Mike by her side. Tommy's colleagues from *Palm* magazine formed a tight cluster, their expressions solemn and professional even in grief. Glenn Albin, editor-in-chief of *Ocean Drive*, had driven up from South Beach with a couple of off-duty photographers.

Rachel had even spotted the wary, one-eyed tortie who hung around Title Wave's loading dock, keeping a respectful distance at the edge of the gathering. Rachel hadn't realized she covered so much distance in her roamings; the thought of a one-eyed cat crossing so many streets unattended troubled her briefly, before Tommy drew her attention away.

It was Tommy who'd arranged the memorial service and gotten a stack of beautifully turned-out programs printed, having spent hours selecting the photos—Daisy laughing in the VIP room at Yucca; Daisy posed dramatically in front of an art gallery on Hibiscus Road; Daisy and a group of bikini-clad friends lounging on some long-ago sunny afternoon, right here on Coacoochee Beach.

Gone was Tommy's usual charismatic exuberance, replaced by a quiet dignity that Rachel found both touching and disconcerting. He'd delivered a beautiful eulogy, his voice steady and clear, yet something in his demeanor bothered Rachel. Several times throughout the service, she'd caught him staring out at the horizon, his expression distant and troubled when he thought no one was watching. He'd been meticulous—almost obsessive—about every detail of the memorial. After everyone who'd wanted to speak had gotten their chance, and the crowd had quietly recited the Twenty-third Psalm, Tommy had made a quick exit while murmuring half-formed apologies. Rachel had suspected he simply couldn't bear to accept any more condolences or share any more reminiscences.

Julian Singer-Adams had made an appearance, arriving just as the service began and positioning himself apart from the main gathering. Dressed impeccably in a black Armani suit, he'd kept his distance, acknowledging few and speaking to fewer. Rachel had caught him watching Tommy more than once, his expression unreadable.

The one bright moment for Rachel had been her brief conversation with Isabella Stuart, who'd arrived in a black Chanel suit that had made Rachel long to go home and burn everything in her own closet. "How are you holding up?" Isabella had asked, her voice low and intimate with what appeared to be sincere concern. "This can't have been an easy week for you."

Rachel had found herself confessing how difficult it had become to walk through Title Wave's doors each morning, how the space that had once felt like sanctuary now seemed haunted.

Isabella's expression had softened, the calculated poise momentarily giving way to something warmer. "You didn't work as hard as you did on Danny's event last week just because it was your job," she'd said. "Anyone can see how much you love that store. Try reconnecting with whatever it was that made you love Title Wave in the first place."

What was it that had drawn Rachel to Title Wave? The books, obviously. But also its place in the community, its potential to bring people together. For weeks she'd been toying with an idea that might bring a dash of communal, seasonal fun to the shop. She'd initially told herself she'd get to work on it as soon as the event with Danny Elliott was over—and after that, the whole thing had felt wrong, as if it might somehow be an insult to Daisy's memory.

Suddenly, though, she felt certain that Daisy would have approved. Before leaving Title Wave that afternoon, she'd called the art teacher at Coacoochee High and explained what she was thinking. He'd enthusiastically agreed to solicit his students for ideas and volunteers. For her part, Dorothea had been so impressed with the initiative that she'd already committed to donating ten percent of October's earnings to the school's art department.

Rachel took another sip of her tea, feeling a spark of excitement kindling within her for the first time since Daisy's death. Tomorrow after school, the students would arrive with sketches and supplies. Maybe Isabella was right—maybe the path forward lay in remembering why she'd fallen in love with Title Wave to begin with.

The café door opened with a gentle chime, pulling Rachel from her thoughts. Marc Gottsegen paused just inside the doorway, surveying the café with an assessing gaze that reminded Rachel of a photographer framing a shot. When his eyes landed on her, a flicker of recognition crossed his face, followed by the briefest hesitation before he approached the counter.

Rachel watched him order, wondering if she should acknowledge him or pretend she hadn't seen him. Before she could decide, Marc had paid for his coffee and was walking directly toward her table.

"Mind if I join you?" His voice carried a hint of amusement, as if aware of her dilemma. "Or would Tommy consider it fraternizing with the enemy?"

Rachel smiled. "I've never considered myself a Shark *or* a Jet." She gestured at the empty chair across from her. "Please, sit."

Marc settled into the seat and pulled two packets of artificial sweetener from the caddy on the table. "Of course not," he agreed easily, as he dumped the sweetener into his coffee cup and stirred methodically. "But loyalties in this town tend to run deep and exclusive."

He took a sip of his coffee, studying her over the rim of his cup. His eyes—a shade of hazel that shifted between green and light brown—were remarkably observant, missing nothing.

"I didn't see you at the memorial service yesterday," Rachel said, the remark slipping out before she'd fully considered it.

If Marc was surprised by her directness, he didn't show it. "No, I was on the other side of the causeway. Following a lead."

"A lead?" Rachel echoed.

"Just a story I'm working on." Marc's expression remained neutral. "And to be honest, I wasn't sure my presence at an event organized by Tommy would be welcome."

"It wasn't Tommy's event," Rachel countered. "It was for Daisy."

"Did you know her well?" he asked.

"Not as well as I would have liked to." Speaking of Daisy in the past tense still made Rachel wince internally. "She was one of the first people I met in Coacoochee. She made me laugh every time I saw her, and I saw her nearly every morning." Rachel lifted her teacup. "Now I wish I'd gotten to know her better before…"

"Before she died," Marc finished for her, his tone matter-of-fact rather than unkind. "It's strange how death transforms acquaintances into something weightier in retrospect."

Rachel was initially inclined to resent this remark, which seemed to make light of the relationship she'd had with Daisy. Then again, the enormous turnout at the memorial yesterday testified to just how many others there were like her—people whom Daisy had made laugh, and who now wished they'd had the chance to get to know her better.

She took a sip of her tea. "Did *you* know her well?" she asked, turning his question back on him.

Marc considered this, his fingers tracing an idle pattern on the tabletop. "I knew her in the way journalists know useful people," he finally said. "She had excellent instincts about Coacoochee—who was up, who was down, what mattered and what didn't."

"So she was a source." Rachel felt a twinge of disappointment at the transactional nature of the relationship.

"Initially, yes," Marc acknowledged. "But over time…" He paused, one corner of his mouth lifting in a half smile of reminiscence. "Daisy was hard not to like."

There was a note in his voice Rachel couldn't quite identify—regret, perhaps, or a more complicated emotion. She found herself studying him more carefully, noticing details she'd previously overlooked—the faint shadows beneath his eyes, the slight tension in his shoulders. He looked like a man carrying a weight he couldn't put down.

"You know," she said slowly, following an intuition she hadn't realized was forming, "I keep thinking about how strange it is that someone Daisy's age would just...collapse from heart failure."

Marc's gaze sharpened, his attention now fully focused on her. "What do you mean?"

Rachel leaned forward slightly. "I overheard someone from Coacoochee General the other day saying cardiac events in people her age are extremely rare."

"The medical examiner ruled it natural causes." Marc's tone was neutral, but his eyes were watchful.

"Yes," Rachel agreed. "But still...doesn't it strike you as odd?"

Marc set his coffee cup down with deliberate precision. "Odd how, exactly?"

Rachel hesitated. "I'm not sure. But the night of the book signing, she seemed off. Pale. Nervous, maybe." She studied Marc's face. "You knew her better than I did. Did she mention anything to you? Was she worried about something? Or someone?"

"Probably just too much partying the night before." Now Marc sounded dismissive.

"I don't know." Rachel was abruptly aware that she'd backed herself into a corner—not entirely sure what she hoped to hear Marc say, yet unwilling to drop the subject entirely. "It's probably nothing. Just my imagination working overtime after seeing her...like that."

"The mind does seek patterns," Marc agreed. "Especially after trauma." He studied her for a long moment. "Has Tommy seemed different to you lately? Since Daisy died?"

The question caught Rachel off-guard. "Different how?"

Marc shrugged, the gesture casual yet somehow deliberate. "Anxious. Distracted. Perhaps overly concerned with appearances?"

Rachel thought of Tommy at the memorial—his careful composure, his hasty departure. "He's grieving," she said defensively, but heard an undercurrent of uncertainty in her own voice.

"Has it ever occurred to you," Marc asked, his voice gentle but direct, "that you might not know Tommy Duvall as well as you think you do?"

The question hung in the air between them. Rachel felt a flash of irritation. "What is that supposed to mean?"

"Just that people in this town often show others exactly what they want them to see." He met her gaze directly. "Tommy's very good at curating how others perceive him."

"And you're not?" Rachel's tone was sharper than she'd intended.

Marc's smile widened slightly, as if pleased by her pushback. "Touché," he acknowledged. "We're all guilty of it to some degree. But some performances are more elaborate than others."

Before Rachel could respond, Marc glanced at his watch. "I should be going." He gathered his messenger bag. The smile on his face suddenly seemed inordinately pleased with itself. "I've got a call scheduled this afternoon with the *Daily News*."

Rachel absorbed the import of that—knowing Tommy would hate it if he knew, and also hate it if *she* knew and didn't tell him. As Marc stood to leave, he hesitated. "For what it's worth, I think Daisy would have appreciated the memorial Tommy arranged," he finally said.

With that parting remark, Marc made his way to the door. The storm outside had passed, and the afternoon light caught his profile for a moment, turning him into a golden silhouette before the door closed behind him.

Rachel remained at her table, their conversation replaying in her mind. She thought about Tommy's behavior at the memorial, his uncharacteristic intensity about getting every detail perfect. She thought about Marc's pointed questions and cryptic advice.

Both men had built careers on knowing things others didn't, on navigating the complex social currents of Coacoochee with practiced skill. But which one was showing her his true face?

Was either of them?

CHAPTER 9

Brock Winfield adjusted the collar of his lime-green blazer—a bold choice he was certain made him look both literary and tropical—as he approached Title Wave Books. He'd dutifully paid his respects at Tommy Duvall's beachside memorial service for Daisy Locarro three days earlier, and although Daisy had been notoriously well-liked, Brock had still been surprised by the size of the turnout. Would the crowd have been this large, he couldn't help wondering, if it had been *his* sunrise memorial instead of Daisy's?

It was an unusually solemn thought for Brock, one that was quickly dispelled by the prospect of thorough enjoyment that now lay before him.

As he imagined the effect that Daisy's death and its discovery had had upon Title Wave Books, he nearly quivered with schadenfreude. Surely business would be suffering. Death was bad for commerce; everyone knew that.

Brock had become a trifle near-sighted with the advancing years (more than once, he'd pulled a bewildered stranger into a damp, enthusiastic hug while exclaiming, "How lovely to see you again!")—plus, his attention to the world around him tended to wane when he was lost in his own daydreams of grandeur. He was therefore nearly at Title Wave's entrance before he noticed the eye-catching Halloween displays that now dominated its front windows.

In the display window to the left of the front door, a backdrop of black fabric was adorned with cut-out orange pumpkins and white ghosts that seemed to dance across its surface. Classic horror novels—paperbacks by Stephen King, Anne Rice, Shirley Jackson, and others—were arranged into the shape of a haunted house, complete with a construction paper roof and tiny windows cut from index cards. Cotton cobwebs stretched across the corners, dusted with glitter that caught the light. A life-sized plastic skeleton—with a "Property of Coacoochee High" sticker visible on its femur—lounged in a beach chair with sunglasses and a gaudy tropical shirt, a paperback mystery novel open in its bony hands.

The other window, which had previously showcased Danny Elliott's cookbook, had been transformed into "Literary Nightmares"—a playful homage to scary stories down through the ages. At the center stood a vintage typewriter with a half-finished manuscript page still in the roller, the visible text reading: *It was a dark and stormy night in Coacoochee...* In a semicircle behind and around the typewriter, DayGlo-colored cutouts of famous literary monsters—from Dracula to Frankenstein's creation—were arranged to look as if they were emerging from the pages of open books. A black light tucked discreetly behind the display made the monsters and the white paper of the manuscript glow eerily against a backdrop of black fabric studded with glow-in-the-dark stars.

The windows, assembled over the course of the previous afternoon and evening, were a loving testament to the collaborative magic between Rachel and the Coacoochee High art students. What began as empty frames had blossomed into vivid Halloween tableaux, thanks to a heaping helping of teenage laughter and boundless creativity.

Mia Puccino, whose father "Joey Pooch" owned Coacoochee's favorite pizza joint over on Rollins Avenue and Eighth, had arrived with paint on her jeans and a tower of pizza boxes. The store had hummed with newfound energy—scissors snipping, glue guns hissing, construction paper crinkling—as students perched on ladders and sprawled across the floor. Even the handful of customers still lingering in the store as closing time drew near found themselves drafted into service. One elderly gentleman proudly cut out a perfect paper bat, while a young mother with twins helped arrange tiny pumpkin lights along the edges of the windows. Homer had weaved between busy feet, occasionally presenting himself for petting to paint-stained hands, while Vashti supervised benevolently from atop a bookshelf. (Scarlett, of course, had disapproved entirely of having so many boisterous teenagers in the store at one time, and had remained adamantly upstairs.)

Brock looked at the windows now and saw nothing unifying, alluring, or even seasonally amusing. The tackiness of it all made his upper lip curl. How utterly tasteless to decorate so festively when a real death had occurred right outside! It was no skin off his nose, but still...it was disrespectful to Daisy's memory, that's what it was.

With a disapproving sniff, Brock pushed open the door—and then he stopped short, momentarily stunned by the scene before him.

Instead of the empty, tomb-like atmosphere he'd been counting on, Title Wave was bustling with an unusual level of activity, even considering it was Saturday. It seemed as if the entire town had found a reason to stop by the bookstore—Brock even spotted Nick Torres, Coacoochee's Chief of Police, standing in the long line of customers that snaked out from the café counter, where Nadia efficiently prepared a round of espressos. Across the store, Rachel rang up stacks of paperbacks and cheerfully kept an equally lengthy line moving briskly.

Orange and black paper garlands hung from the ceiling, dangling alongside cardboard bats and ghostly cutouts. The café area featured a display of pumpkin-spiced delicacies, with a hand-lettered sign proclaiming "Treats, No Tricks!" Small cauldrons filled with candy sat at the end of each bookshelf, inviting browsers to help themselves.

As Brock surveyed the transformation with growing disgust, he spotted something that irritated him even more than the decorations: Rachel's gray tabby was lounging atop the New Releases table, sprawled across an edition of the latest Stephen King as if it were her personal throne. Brock's aversion to cats was as passionate as his love of his own unpublished man-uscripts. He viewed felines as nature's most overrated creation—furred ingrates celebrated for the very qualities that would get humans fired: sleeping on the job, knocking things over, and bringing dead animals to important meetings.

As he stood there, silently fuming, the tabby's yellow-green eyes locked onto him. The memory of claws raking across his calf (*hers? were they hers?*) sent a phantom pain shooting up his leg.

"The Halloween windows are absolutely darling." The familiar voice of Laurie Castillo was suddenly right behind him. "Title Wave might have the best Halloween display on Hibiscus Road this year."

Brock twisted his head around and saw that Laurie was talking to Sabine Ackermann, former runway model and founder of ModelHaus Miami, which was headquartered on Oceanside Drive. ModelHaus had earned a reputation for discovering raw talent in Europe and throughout the Americas, and then turning that talent into fashion icons.

"I just love her 'bookstore cats.'" Sabine's throaty voice carried a strong German accent. Her chic black blouse was unbuttoned nearly to her navel, displaying to full advantage the milk-white skin and platinum-blond hair that had made her famous. "I wonder if she ever hires out the white one for photoshoots?"

Normally, Brock would have taken full advantage of the opportuni-ty presented by finding himself in such close proximity to two of Coa-coochee's most influential citizens. He had mastered the art of fawning over his social betters with the sort of fulsome flattery he was certain they loved—it was, in fact, the skill that had gotten him to where he was today. He was sorely tempted now to treat Laurie and Sabine to a hands-on demonstration.

But Brock Winfield had come to Title Wave on a mission, and he was resolved not to be deterred.

He maneuvered himself into the queue for the register, his thin lips pressed into a bloodless line. A teenager nearly backed into him while trying to get a better look at the "Midnight Reads" display table Rachel had created.

"Excuse me," Brock snapped. "Some of us are here on actual business."

The girl gave him a perplexed look before turning back to the display. The white cat, who hovered on a nearby table, fixed Brock with what seemed to him an imperious stare before turning disdainfully away.

After ten excruciating minutes of waiting, during which Brock was forced to listen to customer after customer exclaim over the books Rachel had recommended ("It's like she knows exactly what I like to read!"), he finally managed to position himself at the register counter. Rachel looked up, and her smile dimmed noticeably.

"Brock," she said. "I didn't expect to see you today."

Brock infused his voice with false sympathy while glancing pointedly at the Halloween decorations. "I just had to come by and see how you're holding up. Such a tragedy, and right on your doorstep! But I must say," he added, his voice now dripping with disapproval, "I'm surprised by your festive approach, given the circumstances."

Before Rachel could respond, Nadia appeared with a fresh tray of pumpkin-shaped cookies. "We're almost out of these," she told Rachel. "And Mrs. Applebaum wants to know if that Isabel Allende novel came in yet."

Rachel nodded to Nadia before turning back to Brock. "As you can see, we're actually quite busy. Was there something you needed?"

Brock noticed the blind cat slinking between bookshelves, his ears at full attention as he navigated with unsettling precision. Brock's upper lip curled involuntarily. "That can't be sanitary," he said. "A cat wandering around a place that serves food? I wonder what the health department would make of it."

Rachel's expression hardened slightly. "Is there anything specific I can help you with today, Brock?"

He paused for dramatic effect, savoring the moment despite his deflated expectations. "I've been researching health codes for businesses that serve food. Did you know there are specific regulations about animals on the premises? Fascinating stuff."

A customer approached the counter with a question about regional ghost story collections and Rachel excused herself, leaving Brock standing there with his mouth half-open, his threat dangling, incomplete, in the air.

He wandered toward the Local Authors display and ran his fingers along the spines of books written by others who'd had the connections to secure traditional publishing deals—proving how much more important it was to know the right people than it was to work hard. When Rachel finally returned, he adopted his most benevolent expression. "I was wondering if you'd reconsidered stocking *Borrowed Glory*? I think a few copies would look perfect right here." He tapped the center of the display.

"Our policy on self-published works hasn't changed," Rachel replied evenly. "But I appreciate your interest."

Brock felt the heat rise in his face, and he tried to regain his footing. "Maybe you should think it over. Especially with all these people here today. You wouldn't want them distracted by any...health concerns."

Rachel glanced at him sharply, but before she could respond, her attention was drawn by a crash from the vicinity of Caribbean Travel. The gray tabby had emerged and was now staring at Brock with undisguised hostility, her yellow-green eyes narrowed to slits of contempt. Next to her, a fallen stack of travel guides lay scattered across the floor—clearly knocked over in what Brock, if he hadn't known better, would have sworn was an act of deliberate sabotage.

"I need to take care of that." Rachel was already moving away. "If you'll excuse me."

Brock was suddenly eager to exit before the angry tabby could get any closer. "Just wanted to check in. Good luck with...everything."

As he pushed through the door back onto Hibiscus Road, the warmth of the day engulfed him—a stark contrast to the chill that had run down his spine under the gray cat's unwavering stare. He stood outside, looking back at Title Wave's festive Halloween windows. One day, he thought, Title Wave would beg for the opportunity to stock *Borrowed Glory*. And on that day, he would magnanimously agree.

After Rachel Baum was long gone, of course.

With a final glare at the bustling bookstore, Brock headed for home, his lime-green blazer a garish splash of color against the pastel backdrop of Hibiscus Road. He began mentally drafting his complaint to the health department; Rachel Baum may have charmed everyone else in Coacoochee, but Brock knew better.

Inside, Rachel watched him go with a mixture of relief and annoyance. She turned to find all three cats regarding her with identical expressions of concern—even Homer, who crinkled the muscles of his forehead in a way that perfectly conveyed solidarity.

"Don't worry, guys." Rachel bent to scratch an irritated-looking Scarlett (even by her standards) behind the ears. "It'll take more than Brock Winfield to bring us down."

"You've got that right." Vashti and Homer noted Scarlett's steely tone but didn't add their own thoughts. Scarlett stood there for a long time after the other two cats had left, watching through the window until Brock's receding back was a lime-green speck bobbing in the distance.

CHAPTER 10

Club Yucca pulsed with rhythm and the incandescence of Coacoochee's beautiful people. Isabella Stuart moved through the crowd with practiced ease, her emerald silk dress catching fractured beams of colored light as she paused here and there to accept an air kiss and offer one in return. Conversations hushed momentarily, eyes tracked her movement, postures straightened. It pleased Isabella to observe these subtle ripples of her influence.

Her usual corner banquette awaited, perpetually reserved even on a busy Saturday night. From this vantage point, Isabella could observe both the entrance and the dance floor—the perfect position for someone whose entire career was seeing and being seen. The leather was cool against her skin as she settled in, arranging herself with the graceful self-awareness that came from years of being photographed.

"Miss Stuart." A young server approached. "Your Grey Goose martini, three olives. If there's anything special you need—"

"Everything's perfect, thank you." Isabella cut him off with a smile that was genuine, yet established boundaries. After he departed, she surveyed the club with a practiced eye. DJ Tracy Young's latest mix had the dance floor packed. At the bar, a rising fashion designer laughed too loudly with a group of admirers. Near the VIP entrance, the star of a popular cable series was trying and failing to be inconspicuous, clearly hoping to be recognized. Isabella catalogued it all, reflexively collecting the material that had fueled her column for the past decade.

But the Queen of the Scene's tenure had already ended with her farewell column in this morning's paper. Tomorrow, the *Daily News* planned to run a two-page retrospective of her years as their nightlife columnist. By Monday, Isabella reflected, both papers would be lining birdcages—and she would officially become Isabella Stuart, PR maven. The thought sat a touch uncomfortably, like shoes that had once fit perfectly but now pinched in strange places.

Isabella had arrived alone, but she didn't remain by herself for long. David Brier, who owned the club, slid into the banquette beside her. He was accompanied by Alessandra Vicente, the Brazilian jewelry designer whose handcrafted pieces had become Coacoochee's latest obsession. Her slender wrists and elegant neck were adorned with her own creations, which caught the club's pulsing lights with each animated gesture.

Isabella took a delicate sip of her martini, her mind drifting from the conversation even as she perfunctorily made all the appropriate responses. Danny Elliott had finally sent her his first monthly check, although it had arrived nearly a week late. He'd left her an apologetic message about "temporary cash flow issues related to the L.A. expansion," but Isabella suspected he'd simply forgotten. Danny was brilliant in the kitchen and magnetic in person, but details like bills and due dates seemed to evaporate from his mind almost instantaneously. Isabella had seen this quality in many of the artists and creative types she'd encountered over the years—they possessed extraordinary gifts in some areas yet remained almost childlike in others.

What Danny needed was someone to keep him on track—some down-to-earth wife or girlfriend who could manage his life outside of Sabrosa. Isabella's wandering thoughts landed on Rachel Baum at Title Wave Books, with her warm smile and expressive dark-brown eyes. Rachel was undeniably pretty—not in league with the models who paraded through Coacoochee's nightclubs, of course, but Tommy had worked true wonders with her. She'd looked smashing at Danny's book signing, and Isabella had noticed how Danny's gaze had found Rachel over the course of the evening, lingering appreciatively when she laughed or tucked a wayward curl behind her ear.

Danny could use someone with her work ethic and organizational talents—and Rachel could use somebody charismatic and connected after that unfortunate business with her ex-fiancé. Isabella decided to look for ways to bring the two of them together.

The champagne David had ordered arrived in a silver ice bucket, the bottle glistening with condensation. As the server expertly popped the cork with a discreet hiss, Alessandra leaned across the table, her cascade of dark curls momentarily blocking Isabella's view of the dance floor.

"Before I forget." Alessandra's Portuguese accent was still evident despite her years in Miami. "That journalist from *Vogue* called again about featuring my collection. I told her to speak with you next week." She tapped a blood-red fingernail against Isabella's wrist. "You'll handle it better than I ever could."

Isabella nodded, pleased at the way business for her fledgling firm kept rolling in. At least this new client appeared appropriately appreciative of the services that Isabella—uniquely among all the other (and lesser) publicists in Miami—was able to provide, the victories she was able to rack up on their behalf.

She'd gotten Julian Singer-Adams an utterly beautiful, front-page, above-the-fold story in tomorrow's *Daily News*, filled with glorious photos and fawning praise over the new wing he'd just donated to Coacoochee General. It was as solid a win as any publicist could hope for, yet Julian seemed entirely unimpressed. He'd arrived the previous day for their meeting in her new office suite—a minimalist space of white and chrome at the top of Coacoochee's only office tower—twenty minutes late and decidedly morose. He'd been out of sorts ever since the groundbreaking for the new multiplex, and Isabella was at a loss to account for why.

"Come have a cocktail with me at Sabrosa." It was a spontaneous suggestion, one she hoped might smooth over rough edges. "Danny will prepare something incredible for us, and we can talk about how we're going to capitalize on all this great press."

But Julian had turned and left without another word.

Isabella's reverie was broken by a disturbance at the VIP section's velvet rope. Brock Winfield, wearing a searingly bright lime-green blazer, was attempting to talk his way past security. The doorman glanced in her direction, one eyebrow raised in silent question. Isabella was pleased to note that he looked to her for his cue, even though the owner sat right next to her. She gave a slight, almost imperceptible shake of her head, and Brock was politely but firmly redirected to the main bar area.

Isabella suppressed a smile. Brock was harmless but tedious—a man whose opinion of his own talents exceeded reality. He'd once cornered her at a gallery opening and spent twenty excruciating minutes detailing the plot of some novel he'd written, seemingly oblivious to her complete uninterest.

It had been eleven-thirty when she'd arrived at Club Yucca, and by midnight she was kissing David and his guests goodbye. It never paid to spend too much time at any one club or party—and, besides, she felt a sudden hunger for something more substantial than pulsing dance music and scattered conversations.

Outside, Hibiscus Road glowed under lights spilling from bars and late-night cafes. It was only a three-block walk to Sabrosa, which welcomed her with the rich aromas of saffron and garlic. The restaurant had passed its dinner rush but wasn't yet empty—the sweet spot Isabella preferred.

Danny emerged from the kitchen the moment she entered, his black chef's jacket rolled up to reveal strong forearms dusted with flour. "Isabella!" His smile was warm. "I was hoping you'd swing by." He guided her to her favorite corner table where, to her pleasant surprise, Irina Kahan was already seated. The Persian-born fashion photographer rose to exchange air kisses. Her spiky silver hair was cut close to her head. A fitted velvet suit of midnight blue draped her tall, slender frame. "Darling, what perfect timing. I was just telling Danny about my upcoming show at Gallery Moda." Isabella settled across from her, accepting the glass of champagne Danny poured before disappearing back into the kitchen. "And I want you to handle the publicity."

"Consider it done." Isabella mentally added Irina to her growing client roster. The photographer's thirty-year career had included everyone from Paloma Picasso to Princess Diana. Her gallery show was sure be a highlight of the upcoming Season.

Danny returned minutes later bearing small plates of perfectly composed bites: paper-thin slices of *jamón ibérico* draped over compressed melon, a single perfect shrimp nestled on saffron rice, plantain cups filled with slow-braised beef and topped with microgreens.

"My newest experiments." Danny's boyish enthusiasm was irresistible. "The plantain cup filling is what I'm most excited about—twelve hours at exactly a hundred and eighty degrees, with a spice blend I created just yesterday." He beamed at Isabella again before disappearing back into the kitchen.

The conversation with Irina flowed easily from food to fashion to the perpetual gossip that was Coacoochee's lifeblood. Isabella could feel herself relaxing for the first time in days, the tension of Julian's visit and her impending career change momentarily forgotten in the pleasant cocoon of good food and better company. For all the calculations that drove her professional life, Isabella savored these rare instances of uncomplicated pleasure—the cool fizz of champagne against her lips, the shimmer of candlelight on crystal, and a shared laugh with a genuine equal.

As she prepared to leave, gathering her Louis Vuitton clutch and signaling for the check that Danny would inevitably refuse to bring, a familiar voice intruded.

"Isabella!" Brock Winfield was suddenly beside their table, his lime-green blazer somehow even more offensive under Sabrosa's warmer lighting than it had been at Club Yucca. His smile strained for charm but didn't quite get there. "I've been meaning to ask—once my novel hits the shelves, would you consider representing me? A publicist of your caliber would be perfect to manage my book launch."

Isabella regarded him with the neutral expression she reserved for people she found tiresome. "I'm sorry, Brock, but my client roster is full." The lie slid easily from her lips, smooth as the silk of her dress.

Outside Sabrosa, Isabella kissed Irina goodbye and watched as she turned the corner onto Tenth Street and disappeared. Isabella paused on the sidewalk, taking in the glittering expanse of Hibiscus Road at night. The street stretched before her like a jeweled necklace, each light and storefront a gem she had helped polish. A pang of nostalgia tugged at her, yet she also felt the spark of anticipation. There would be challenges ahead—difficult clients, demanding deadlines, the constant balancing of competing interests—but also opportunities that only someone in her position could leverage.

She had spent a decade chronicling Coacoochee's social scene; now she would help mold it. Only time would tell whether the role of chronicler or builder brought greater satisfaction. But Isabella Stuart had never been one to shy away from reinvention.

CHAPTER 11

Rachel's apartment, perched above Title Wave Books, wasn't much to speak of. It consisted of two square rooms in its entirety—one small square that served as the bedroom, and one larger square that functioned as the combined living and dining rooms. A small Formica counter jutted from the wall toward the back, separating the cramped, galley-style kitchen from the rest of the space and giving it, perhaps, some modest claim to being considered a separate room. Rachel had briefly contemplated placing a couple of tall chairs on the living-room side of the counter and trying to pass it off as a breakfast bar. But then there wouldn't have been sufficient space for a full-sized sofa—and a sofa that could simultaneously accommodate three cats plus one woman with a book was, in Rachel's opinion, a deal-breaking necessity.

Books were everywhere—stacked on the end table, tucked into corners, and arranged on the coffee table in artful disarray. Where most people would have placed a dining table in the small alcove meant for that purpose, Rachel had installed a large and gloriously overstuffed bookcase. Indoor dining generally happened on the couch, anyway, with the coffee table serving as her primary eating surface.

The apartment was comfortable, cheerful enough, and perpetually coated with a fine layer of cat fur. That, Rachel often reflected, was probably all that could be said about it.

What made the place exceptional was the enormous outdoor terrace—a sprawling expanse that was easily bigger than the entire indoor living space. If the size and dimensions of Rachel's apartment corresponded roughly with Title Wave's back storeroom—located directly below it—then the outdoor terrace was approximately the same size as Title Wave itself.

Better even than the terrace's size, however, was its commanding view overlooking Hibiscus Road. Tommy had been relentless in insisting that Rachel needed to transform the space into the perfect backdrop for elegant entertaining it was so clearly destined to be. "Just imagine what your dates will say when they see this place!" His Savannah accent had thickened as his imagination took flight. "Think of all the candlelight dinners and romantic *tête-à-têtes* you'll have here." This had been back in the early days of Rachel's Coacoochee residency, when she was still reeling from her breakup with Henry, and just the thought of dating again left her queasy.

Besides, Rachel had neither the time nor the money to accomplish anything close to Tommy's ambitious vision. She'd managed to collect a couple of battered old chaise lounges—the kind with metal frames and horizontal plastic strips that had been ubiquitous around Miami pools back in the Seventies—and covered them with lively, tropical-print cushions she'd unearthed at a Salvation Army thrift store. She'd also acquired an outdoor table—complete with umbrella and matching chairs—from a moving sale she'd spotted in the *Daily News* classifieds shortly after her arrival in Coacoochee.

She'd positioned the table and chairs close to the low wall that overlooked Hibiscus Road. On the right kind of day, with just the right weather conditions, dining at that table felt like having a private VIP perch above the bustling pedestrian mall below. Any of the upscale restaurants that dotted Hibiscus Road would have killed to be able to offer such a spot to well-heeled patrons.

Rachel was up early this morning, having invited Natalie over for a Sunday bagel brunch. Raised to believe that the only thing God hated worse than a heretic was a stingy bagel brunch and the person who'd thrown it, Rachel had driven at seven a.m. up to Bagel Bar in North Miami Beach—and returned to Coacoochee with a half-dozen assorted bagels, scallion cream cheese, thinly sliced lox, the oily and delicious kippered salmon Rachel and her dad preferred to lox, whitefish salad, potato salad, pickled herring layered delicately with white onions and cream sauce, sliced red onions, ripe tomatoes, Muenster cheese, and a baker's dozen of various rugelach fresh from the oven.

The rich aroma of smoked fish, once it had been set up under the umbrella outside, made the cats restless with anticipation. Even Scarlett—who generally eschewed human food as inherently inferior to the individually canned servings of her preferred flavors—could feel her mouth water. They found it hard to restrain themselves, and several times Scarlett had to stop Homer in the act of "sneaking" (in plain sight) onto the table to gobble down a morsel or two.

"Homer!" Scarlett's paw shot out with lightning speed, catching Homer just as he was about to hoist himself onto the edge of the table. *"What do you think you're doing?"*

"I'm just smelling everything, that's all." Homer's wildly twitching nose belied his air of innocence.

"Get down now." Scarlett's tone brooked no dissent. *"Otherwise I'll start knocking things off the table until Rachel comes out to see what's happening."*

"You wouldn't hurt…" Homer gulped nervously, and his skin paled beneath his fur. *"You wouldn't hurt the* salmon, *would you?"*

"Wouldn't I?" Scarlett raised one front paw in the air and gently waved it back and forth. The sound it made was infinitesimal—nevertheless, Scarlett knew Homer could hear it loud and clear. She watched as he slowly backed away.

"Scarlett! Get down from there!" Both Scarlett's and Homer's heads whipped around as Rachel—who'd spotted Scarlett atop the table through the kitchen window—came rushing out. "I'd expect this from Homer, but

I'm surprised at *you*, Scarlett." Her scolding tone was one Scarlett rarely heard—and never liked.

Scarlett leapt to the ground with an air of wounded dignity that made Rachel smile despite herself. She stalked toward her favorite chaise lounge, head and tail held high, ignoring Homer's barely suppressed laughter and the look of genuine sympathy Vashti threw her way.

"*Some people,*" Scarlett muttered, "*have no gratitude at all.*"

All three cats consoled themselves with the knowledge that they'd get their fair share of leftovers once the human brunch had concluded; it was manifestly impossible for two women alone to consume so much food.

Homer was the first to hear Natalie's approach, his keen ears picking up her familiar footfall before it reached the outdoor metal staircase that ran up the side of the building. It was the one Rachel used when inviting guests to her private home above the shop, or when she herself wanted to come and go without first having to walk through Title Wave. *"Natalie's here,"* he announced to the others. *"And Hot Mike, too."*

Vashti, who had been meticulously grooming her pristine white fur in preparation for company, paused to lift her head. *"I hope she brought those treats again,"* she said. *"Those dried fish bits in the little plastic bag."*

"She didn't," Homer replied with certainty. *"I smell orange juice, though. And champagne."*

"Champagne for them, leftovers for us," Scarlett harrumphed, although secretly she believed she and her feline siblings were getting the better end of the deal.

The sound of footsteps on the stairs outside had grown loud enough to catch Rachel's attention, and she opened the door with an enthusiastic greeting. Natalie entered, carrying a bottle of Mumm in one hand and a carton of fresh-squeezed orange juice in the other. Hot Mike padded in beside her, his posture stiff and correct, but his eyes brightening as he spotted the three cats. *"Morning, all,"* he greeted them, with a courteous dip of his head, as he followed Natalie out onto the terrace.

"You've outdone yourself!" Natalie exclaimed, surveying the spread Rachel had arranged.

The two women settled into their seats, the October sunshine warm but not oppressive against their skin. A gentle breeze carried the mingled scents of the ocean and of the restaurants and cafés below. From their elevated vantage point, they could see outdoor tables bustling with the brunch crowd, and the line outside Butterflake Bakery that stretched down the block as tourists waited patiently for the bakery's famous guava pastries.

Street performers had begun to appear—a busker playing a guitar outside the 710 Bar, a caricature artist who'd set up near the crossing at Eighth Street, and a young woman creating enormous iridescent soap bubbles that drifted up lazily toward Rachel's terrace. Tourists strolled unhurriedly, cameras at the ready, many wearing the telltale pink glow of yesterday's sunburn, while locals moved with more purpose, some walking dogs, others toting their finds from the open-air antiques market that ran every Sunday on Hibiscus Road from Fifth Street to Ninth.

The cats had arranged themselves on the chaise lounges in a sunny corner of the terrace not far from where Rachel and Natalie sat. Hot Mike, ever the professional, had settled himself in a shady spot beneath the table. It was his preferred position—close enough to Natalie to respond instantly if needed, yet unobtrusive so as not to disturb the humans' meal.

Rachel spread cream cheese on her sesame seed bagel as she gestured to the *Daily News* that lay on the table. "Did you see the sendoff they gave Isabella?" She added kippered salmon and a slice of onion. "Two full pages with photos spanning her career."

Natalie nodded appreciatively as she surveyed the newspaper. "She's earned it. Ten years as the voice of Coacoochee nightlife is no small accomplishment." She speared a piece of lox with her fork. "Isabella has a knack for making herself indispensable. Her PR venture will be a success—you can bet on it." Natalie took a sip of her mimosa, the plain jade band she wore on her index finger making a soft *clink* against the glass. "I hear somebody's finally taken over that storefront on Lantana Lane where the souvenir shop used to be."

Rachel spooned a piece of pickled herring onto her plate, careful to get a dollop of cream sauce and onion along with it. "Dahlia mentioned it's going to be some kind of gourmet ice cream place. Apparently they make everything with local ingredients—mango from Homestead, key lime from the Keys."

"I need more ice cream within walking distance like a kangaroo needs a surfboard." Natalie laughed. "But I'll be first in line anyway. There's something about living in a tourist town that makes you act like a tourist."

"I know what you mean. Before I moved here, I hadn't been to the beach in years. Now I'm there with a book at least once a week."

A breeze swept across the terrace, rustling the pages of the newspaper. The sun had climbed higher, casting the terrace in a brilliant light that fell through the prism of the water pitcher to throw rainbows onto the terrace floor. Rachel looked out over Hibiscus Road, her thoughts clearly elsewhere.

"You seem distracted," Natalie observed. "Everything all right?"

Rachel sighed, setting down her bagel. "I've been worried about Tommy," she admitted. "I left him at least three messages to join us today. But he never called back." She bit her lower lip. "He hasn't been himself since...well, since what happened to Daisy."

The name hung in the air between them. Rachel's voice had grown quieter, as if merely speaking of Daisy might disturb her rest.

"It's affected all of us," Natalie agreed, her tone somber. "But Tommy arranged such a beautiful memorial service. Maybe he just needs time alone to process everything."

Rachel nodded slowly. "Maybe. But there's something off about the way he's been acting." She hesitated. "I saw him and Daisy arguing during the book signing. I meant to ask him about it later, but then..."She gestured vaguely. "And now I keep wondering if it was important."

"What were they arguing about?"

"I couldn't hear. But they both looked upset. And then there was this woman in the store the other day—she works in cardiology at Coacoochee General." Rachel's hands picked restlessly at the paper napkin in her lap. "She was saying how unusual it is for someone Daisy's age to have heart failure with no warning signs."

Natalie's expression sharpened. "Medical professionals tend to notice when things don't add up."

"I know it probably doesn't mean anything," Rachel said. "But I ran into Marc Gottsegen at Beachy Beans." She met Natalie's eyes. "He asked me how well I really know Tommy."

The cats, despite appearing to lounge in the sun with complete uninterest in what the humans were doing, had perked up at the mention of Tommy's name. Vashti's ears swiveled in the direction of the conversation, twitching as she listened. Even Hot Mike, resting near Natalie's feet, tensed slightly.

"How well *do* you know Tommy?" Natalie asked. "Your friendship is barely six months old."

"I know him better than I know Marc." A touch of defensiveness crept into Rachel's voice as she asked, "How well do *you* know Marc? I know you live next door to him, but you hardly seem like tight friends."

Natalie didn't appear offended. Instead, she nodded thoughtfully, her auburn hair catching the sunlight. "I've lived next door to Marc for years," she said. "We may not be the closest of friends, but we have each other's spare keys. We get together socially now and then—we had lunch yesterday, as a matter of fact." She paused, considering her next words carefully. "The one thing I can say about Marc with absolute certainty is that I've never known him to lie."

Rachel fell silent. Part of her wanted to defend Tommy outright, to dismiss Marc's insinuations entirely. But, despite herself, another part of her kept circling back to the argument she'd witnessed, to Tommy's behavior at the memorial, to the cardiology worker's comments about how unusual Daisy's death was.

Hot Mike crept as discreetly from beneath the table as an eighty-pound German Shepherd could and loped over to the chaise the cats occupied. Settling down nearby, he joined their whispered conversation.

"Rachel doesn't seem as sure about Tommy as she'd like to be," Hot Mike said.

"No, she doesn't." Homer's tail jerked anxiously. *"Maybe we should try to discourage him from coming around Title Wave so often."*

"I've spent more time watching Tommy than any of you," Vashti said staunchly. *"I don't know how to explain everything, but I know he has a good heart."*

"Humans are always full of secrets," Scarlett said. *"Even the nice ones."*

"Even Rachel?" Vashti challenged.

Scarlett rolled onto her back and closed her eyes—indicating that, as far as she was concerned, the conversation was over.

The sun had risen higher in the sky. The initial tension between the two women dissipated as they continued to eat, but the subject of Tommy hadn't been abandoned entirely.

"I'm not a fool, Natalie," Rachel finally said. "I understand why Tommy's behavior might seem suspicious to you. But I can't believe he'd ever hurt anybody—especially not Daisy."

Natalie's expression softened. "You're probably right," she conceded, reaching for a piece of rugelach. "The odds are still in favor of natural causes, like the ME said." She popped the pastry into her mouth, then smiled. "Maybe we should put it all behind us and enjoy this beautiful day." She glanced around, taking in the bright sunshine and gentle breeze. "Do you know what you're dressing as for Halloween?"

Rachel's eyes danced mischievously. "The real question is, what will the *cats* dress as for Halloween?"

Scarlett's entire body instantly stiffened, her yellow-green eyes flying open in horror. Vashti, by contrast, looked intrigued by the possibility, mentally sorting through costumes that might showcase her angelic white fur to best advantage. Homer cocked his head to one side.

"What's the point of a costume anyway?" he wondered aloud. *"Looking different doesn't make you smell or sound any different. That's all anybody needs to figure out who you really are."*

"Don't ask me," Hot Mike said stiffly. *"Natalie made me wear a costume last year, and I felt ridiculous."*

"Let's hope she doesn't give Rachel any ideas," Scarlett muttered darkly.

Back at the table, Rachel and Natalie had moved on to lighter topics—the upcoming Coacoochee Halloween parade, a new vintage store that had just opened on Allamanda Avenue, the rumor that a famous actress was house-hunting on Mercury Island. The breeze picked up, carrying with it the faint strains of music from a café below.

Rachel raised her mimosa glass, letting the sunlight filter through the pale orange liquid. Homer stood and arched his back in a stretch, then padded over drowsily to jump into Rachel's lap. He kneaded her leg with his paws before lying down and sinking into a purring half-nap beneath Rachel's gentle, stroking hand.

Hot Mike and the other two cats dozed as well, all of them content in the certainty that a bounty of whitefish and salmon would soon be theirs. Whatever mysteries and concerns might lie beyond this terrace, whatever secrets Tommy Duvall might be keeping, could wait for another day.

CHAPTER 12

Monday started out with promise. Rachel had to come in on her day off so Nadia could drive her grandmother to the doctor, which was kind of a bummer. Nevertheless, she opened Title Wave promptly at eleven and business flowed in a steady, pleasant rhythm. Morning thunderstorms gave way to an afternoon of sunshine, which fell through the shop's windows and made the wave-patterned terrazzo floor sparkle like the surface of the ocean. Rachel called Evan Kirschner about holiday titles and got his voice mail, noting the way that hearing his voice on the other end of the line gave her day a lift.

Homer, as always, took up his post near the front door, greeting each customer with an enthusiastic head-bonk to the shin. Vashti claimed her new favorite spot—a small stuffed pouf Rachel had installed near Self Help—and her white fur shone like platinum in the afternoon sun. Scarlett, temporarily ousted by the Halloween decorations from her beloved display window, settled regally atop a stack of coastal-themed coffee table books, where she undertook a thorough grooming of her face and whiskers.

It wasn't until a little after three that the bell above the door announced Evan. He was lugging a cardboard box filled with advance copies, the muscles in his forearms visibly working beneath rolled-up sleeves as he set the heavy load on the counter.

"I know Monday's usually your day off. But when I got your message I figured I'd take a chance." A smile crinkled the corners of his dark-blue eyes. "Thought you might want to get your hands on some of these before they officially hit shelves."

"You certainly know the way to a girl's heart." Rachel rifled through the books with undisguised excitement. "Is this the new Haruki Murakami?"

"Out in paperback this month," Evan confirmed. His dark hair fell across his forehead in a way that suggested he'd forgotten to get it cut rather than deliberately styled it that way. "I had a feeling you'd appreciate that one—and not just because there's a cat in it."

Rachel rewarded him with a beaming smile. "I've been waiting for this since I finished his last book." Her eyes met his. "Thank you. This is incredibly thoughtful."

"He's been saving that one especially for her," Homer observed from his spot near their feet. His sensitive ears had picked up the slight quickening of Evan's heartbeat when Rachel expressed her excitement.

Vashti had abandoned her pouf to join the conversation, her snow-white paws moving silently across the terrazzo as she approached. Now she leapt smoothly onto the counter beside the books, settling herself with perfect calm.

"Look how big Rachel's smile is," she noted. *"She used to smile at Henry like that sometimes."*

Homer had begun to weave between Evan's ankles, his active black nose mapping every scent: coffee, books, the faint trace of cologne, and something else that piqued his interest.

"He brought treats!" Homer announced to his siblings. *"The good kind with real chicken."*

As if on cue, Evan reached into his pocket. "Almost forgot." He produced a small bag of gourmet cat treats. "These are for the famous Title Wave bookstore cats. The lady at the Coacoochee Pet Spa assured me they're the caviar of cat treats."

Rachel laughed, the sound warm and genuine. "You're about to make yourself three friends for life," she told him.

"I'm hoping to make four friends, actually." Evan's voice took on a more serious tone as he placed three treats in his palm, offering them to the cats. Homer lunged for his while Vashti took her treat delicately between perfect white teeth.

Even Scarlett had been drawn from her sunny perch by Evan's arrival, although now she hesitated, looking at the treat in his hand with displeasure. *"I don't eat from human palms like a trained monkey,"* Scarlett informed him, casting a withering look at her less-discerning siblings. All Evan heard was a low growl of disapproval, but he seemed to get the message and placed Scarlett's treat on the ground. She waited until he'd stood up straight again, then approached at a measured, dignified pace to claim it.

"I was wondering," Evan continued, once the treats had been distributed, "if maybe you'd like to—"

The bell above the door interrupted whatever Evan had been about to say. Dahlia Delgado swept in, her teal pantsuit a splash of vivid color against the bookstore's more subdued palette.

"Rachel, *mi amor*!" Her voice filled the space with its characteristic warmth and energy. "I've had the most wonderful idea, and I couldn't wait to talk it over with you!"

Evan stepped back from the counter, recognizing that the moment for private conversation was gone. "I should head out." His voice was tinged with what Rachel thought might be disappointment. "I have to get down to the Borders in Kendall before rush hour."

"Thanks again for the books," Rachel said, reluctant to see him go. "And the treats."

"My pleasure." Evan hesitated, as if wanting to say more, then simply smiled and nodded. "I'll see you soon."

Dahlia watched him go with a knowing look. "That man is smitten," she observed, once the door had closed behind him. "And he's pretty easy on the eyes."

Rachel felt warmth creep into her cheeks. "He's just good at his job," she said, though her heart wasn't in the denial. "Now, what's this wonderful idea you couldn't wait to share?"

Dahlia beamed as she placed her leather satchel on the counter. "I had brunch with Isabella Stuart yesterday," she began, her hands moving animatedly as she spoke. "We were discussing the upcoming Halloween parade, and something she said sparked absolute genius. The Department of Tourism wants to sponsor a special Halloween event here at Title Wave!"

"Here?" Rachel repeated.

"Think about it," Dahlia continued enthusiastically. "A dual event—family-friendly activities during the day for children and parents before the Hibiscus Road trick-or-treating begins. Then it'll transition into a gathering for adults in the evening, right before the parade starts." She gestured expansively around the bookstore. "Your Halloween decorations are already the talk of Hibiscus Road! The Coacoochee High art students did a magnificent job."

Rachel looked around at the displays she and the students had created. The black-light monsters glowing in the front window, the skeleton lounging in a beach chair with a mystery novel, the carefully crafted paper bats suspended from the ceiling—it had all come together in a way that still took her pleasantly by surprise when she first entered the store every morning.

Nevertheless, a full-scale event sponsored by the Department of Tourism was a significantly more ambitious undertaking. "I'm not sure Title Wave is equipped to handle something that large." She absently stroked Vashti, who had returned to the counter and had her large green eyes fixed on Dahlia.

"Nonsense!" Dahlia dismissed Rachel's concerns with a wave of her bejeweled hand. "After how brilliantly you managed Danny Elliott's book signing, I have complete confidence in you. And speaking of Danny," her smile widened, "I've already spoken to him. The Department has a budget for these kinds of things, and he's extremely enthusiastic about providing themed food for both portions of the event."

Rachel raised her eyebrows. "You've already talked to Danny?"

"Just preliminarily," Dahlia assured her. "Nothing's set in stone. But he seemed quite excited by the prospect."

Despite her initial hesitation, Rachel found herself warming to the idea. The Halloween decorations had brought new customers into the shop, and an official event might introduce even more readers to Title Wave.

Aloud she said, "I'd need to get approval from Dorothea."

"Of course, of course," Dahlia readily agreed. "But between you and me, I already mentioned it to her when I ran into her at the Sunday farmers market. She thought it was a marvelous idea."

Rachel laughed. "You've really covered all the bases, haven't you?"

"When you've been in government service as long as I have, you learn to anticipate objections," Dahlia replied with a wink. "So, what do you say? Will Title Wave be Coacoochee's Halloween hotspot this year?"

"Tommy and I are having dinner at Sabrosa tonight," Rachel said. "I could talk to Danny in person about the details."

"Perfect!" Dahlia clapped her hands together. "I'll messenger over an outline of what we're thinking, and you can discuss the specifics with Danny." She gathered her satchel and tucked it under her arm. "This is going to be wonderful, Rachel. I'm so excited!"

With that, she stood on tiptoes to lean across the counter and buss Rachel's cheek. Then she disappeared through Title Wave's door, the merry jingle of the bell an echo of her own perpetual enthusiasm.

RACHEL DIDN'T LIKE TO admit how relieved she'd been to get Tommy's phone call, suggesting they have dinner at Sabrosa that night. Tommy had been so elusive since Daisy's memorial that she'd begun to wonder if maybe she'd done something to offend him. But on the phone, he'd sounded almost like his old self—insistent that a night out together was long overdue.

"I know I've been MIA lately." His voice became huskier. "I'm still coming to terms with Daisy being gone."

Rachel had readily accepted both the explanation and the dinner invitation, relieved to hear Tommy sounding more like his usual self. And if he still seemed closed off to her in some way—as if there were something in the events that had unspooled since the night of Danny Elliott's book signing that she still didn't quite understand—well, grief affected everyone differently.

The evening air at Sabrosa was infused with the aromas of *sofrito*, toasted coconut, and the fresh herbs that Danny grew in the restaurant's lush planters. The massive wooden containers, strategically placed under sky-lights to receive full daylight, overflowed with greenery: basil with leaves the size of Rachel's palm, mint that threatened to cascade onto diners' shoulders, and the delicate cilantro Danny harvested daily for his signature ceviches. Tropical flowers grew in extravagant clusters of white and red, creating partitions between tables that gave each setting an intimate feel while maintaining the open, airy atmosphere that had made Sabrosa Coacoochee's most sought-after reservation.

Griselda had seated them in Tommy's favorite spot, a conspicuous center table that afforded an excellent view of the restaurant's comings and goings. Sabrosa was busy even on a Monday night, filled with the pleasant hum of conversation and occasional bursts of laughter. The candlelight caught amber highlights in the glass of sangria Griselda had brought Rachel, and she breathed in the rich scent of wine-soaked fruit.

Tommy looked good, though perhaps a shade thinner than when she'd last seen him. His jacket, a deep aubergine that paired well with his dark eyes and the lighter brown of his hair, hung looser on his frame. Still, his smile was as bright as ever, and the hand he placed over hers was warm and steady.

"I've missed this." He gestured between them. "Just the two of us, hanging out."

"Me too." The sincerity of the sentiment shone in Rachel's dark-brown eyes. "And you picked the perfect night for dinner—I need your advice on something."

Tommy's eyebrows rose with interest. "Do tell," he said, and Rachel realized how much she'd missed his familiar drawl.

As Rachel recounted Dahlia's visit and the proposed Halloween event, she caught snippets of conversations happening around her—business deals closing, romantic whispers exchanged, laughter bursting in bright bubbles above the Latin jazz that spilled from discreetly hidden speakers. Through the restaurant's floor-to-ceiling windows, Rachel could see the fairy lights along Hibiscus Road begin to twinkle as dusk settled.

"—and so I thought, since we're here anyway, I could talk to Danny about the food for both parts of the event," she concluded. "What do you think? Am I crazy to consider doing this?"

"Not at all," Tommy assured her. "You've proven you can handle it. And the Department of Tourism's backing means you'll have resources. Plus," his smile widened, "you know I'll help. I'm the Halloween parade's unofficial documentarian, after all."

Rachel was about to respond when she caught sight of something across the room. Marc Gottsegen sat at the corner table he usually occupied on Monday nights, but he wasn't alone. Isabella Stuart and Julian Singer-Adams flanked him, creating a striking power triangle. Isabella wore a floor-length midnight-blue dress, slit dangerously high up one side. Julian cut an imposing figure in a tailored charcoal suit that emphasized his lean frame.

A now-empty plate sat before Marc, fork and knife neatly crossed face-down upon it—although in front of Isabella was nothing more than a half-empty glass of champagne. A tumbler of scotch, untouched, rested on the table near Julian's left hand. It was clear that Isabella and Julian hadn't dined with Marc, and probably hadn't been at his table for very long.

Marc's leather-bound reporter's notebook sat beside his own left hand. The capped pen lying atop it seemed to indicate that, whatever the three of them were discussing, it wasn't a formal interview, since Marc wasn't taking any notes. Isabella leaned forward across the table to speak to him in a low, intimate tone. She occasionally turned to cast a glance at Julian, or lightly touch his right hand, while he gazed impassively at Marc without saying a word.

Tommy turned to follow Rachel's gaze, and his jaw tightened. "What an interesting threesome," he observed coolly, but Rachel could hear the thin wire of nerves that ran through his voice. She was suddenly glad she hadn't yet gotten the chance to tell him about Marc's phone call with the *Daily News*'s editor the other day.

"Isabella's here with Julian—which means Julian's probably all they're talking about." Rachel tried to sound reassuring. "Isabella's on good terms with everybody. She has to be. Her sitting with Marc for a minute or two doesn't mean anything."

Tommy nodded, and Rachel was glad to see his jaw relax. "You're right," he acknowledged. "Besides, I can't imagine Isabella would suddenly decide to back Marc over me at the *Daily News*."

Nevertheless, Tommy's watchful eyes remained fixed on Marc's table, where the conversation appeared to have reached its conclusion. Isabella gathered her small silver clutch—made from metal and shaped like a clamshell—while Julian stood and adjusted his jacket. Marc remained seated, watching them depart with an enigmatic smile.

Tommy hastily turned to face Rachel once again. "They're coming this way," she warned him in a low murmur, although Isabella and Julian's progress was slowed as Isabella paused every few feet to receive gestures of obeisance from well-wishers and supplicants, each of whom hoped she'd remember them the next time some small crumb of media attention—the kind that could make or break an entire enterprise—was hers to bestow.

Tommy grinned with genuine warmth as the two finally reached their table. "Isabella!" He rose to plant a kiss on her cheek. "Always a vision."

Isabella's smile was dazzling. "Tommy, darling! And Rachel—lovely to see you both." She leaned down to press her cheek against Rachel's, her perfume enveloping Rachel in notes of gardenia. Turning to Tommy, Isabella added, "Have you heard? Club Nebula is finally reopening next month."

"Really." Tommy's eyes widened with interest. "After the fire last year, I thought Marcel had given up on the place entirely."

"Julian's investment group stepped in at the last minute." One of Isabella's perfectly shaped eyebrows arched meaningfully. "We were just talking it over with Marc."

Julian remained slightly apart, his gaze sweeping over the restaurant with a vaguely proprietary air. At the sound of his name, his attention shifted back to them. "Rachel," he acknowledged with a slight nod. "Tommy," he added, his expression cold.

"Julian." Tommy's tone was cordial but cautious. "How's the multiplex coming along?"

"The usual delays with permits and contractors. Nothing unexpected." Julian adjusted the French cuff of his shirt, revealing cufflinks that glinted in the candlelight.

Isabella's expertly lined eyes settled on Rachel. "Dahlia tells me you and Danny will be working together on a Halloween event. I think it's a wonderful idea."

"Word really does travel fast," Rachel noted dryly. "We haven't even started figuring out the details ourselves yet."

Just then, Danny Elliott emerged from the kitchen, his black jacket and matching black chef's hat still immaculate three hours into the dinner service. His smile grew as he made his way over to Rachel and Tommy's table.

"Isabella! Julian!" Danny's voice carried the confident warmth of someone in his natural element. "I didn't realize you were here tonight."

Isabella turned, her own smile widening. "Danny, what perfect timing. Rachel and I were just discussing your upcoming Halloween collaboration."

Danny nodded enthusiastically, resting one hand on the back of Rachel's chair. "I've been brainstorming already—monster-eye cake pops and 'spooky' edible bookmarks for the kids. And for the adults, maybe literary-themed cocktails and appetizers?"

"That sounds perfect." Despite her earlier apprehension, Rachel found herself warming to his enthusiasm. "Could you come by Title Wave after hours sometime? We can work out the specifics."

"I'll bring samples." Danny's eyes sparkled with creative energy. "I've been looking for an excuse to experiment with Halloween flavors. Black garlic aioli, squid ink risotto. Maybe a blood orange panna cotta with activated charcoal crumble?"

"Well, I'll leave the two of you to it." Isabella seemed pleased as her eyes shifted between Rachel and Danny. "And be sure to send me a writeup once you've ironed out the specifics," she added. "I'd be happy to donate PR assistance to help you get the turnout you deserve."

"Thank you!" Rachel hoped her voice reflected only sincere gratitude—and none of the surprise she also felt. "That's a very generous offer."

The casual wave of Isabella's hand assured Rachel that nothing could be of less consequence than one of Miami's most in-demand publicists donating her services free of charge...to promote an indie bookstore's Halloween party. "We want to make sure Title Wave shines as brightly as it was meant to." She turned to Julian. "Shall we?"

Julian's roaming gaze returned to them one last time before they departed, his hand resting lightly on the small of Isabella's back. Rachel watched them go, noting how Isabella paused to say something to Griselda, eliciting a smile and nod from the hostess, before they disappeared out onto Hibiscus Road.

"I should say hi to a few more people." Danny squeezed Rachel's shoulder lightly. "Give me a call and let me know when's a good day to come by."

With one last smile, Danny moved onto greet other diners. Marc remained alone at his table, sipping a glass of wine and jotting something in his notebook, which now lay open before him. If he'd been paying attention to the small gathering that had just broken up at Rachel and Tommy's table, he gave no sign of it.

"That was interesting," Rachel observed, turning to face Tommy as he sat back down.

Tommy's expression had become thoughtful. "You know what? Marc and I have been at each other's throats for too long." He exhaled slowly, his shoulders relaxing. "Maybe it's time we called a truce. This town's too small for constant feuds."

"Maybe," Rachel said dubiously. Something had surfaced between Tommy and Marc in the days since Daisy's death—something more serious than the garden-variety cattiness of two competing nightlife writers. Rachel didn't know exactly what it was, but she sensed that Marc wasn't as ready to bury it as Tommy now seemed to be. "Just keep it simple, okay?"

"Of course," Tommy assured her. His customary easy smile was firmly in place. "Back in a minute."

He rose from his seat, straightening his blazer as he made his way to Marc's table. Rachel watched him go—skeptical that any lasting good could be attained, but hopeful that perhaps some basic public courtesy might be restored between the two nightlife chroniclers.

As she watched Tommy and Marc across the restaurant, Rachel's thoughts drifted to Evan Kirschner's visit earlier in the day. There had been something in his eyes when he'd handed her that advance copy of Murakami—something warm and interested that had nothing to do with sales quotas or professional courtesy. Even now, hours later, she could recall the way his fingers had brushed against hers as he'd passed her the book. She was almost certain he'd been about to ask her out when Dahlia interrupted them. The realization sent a surprising flutter through her stomach.

Not that flutters necessarily meant all that much. Her bare shoulder still tingled where Danny had squeezed it before leaving their table. Danny was unquestionably attractive (and he knew it, Rachel reflected). He was charming, too, with his easy manner and creative enthusiasm, and the instinctive way he seemed to know how to work a room. His charisma was likely just as responsible for his rapid rise in the culinary world as his indisputable cooking talents. But still...

Rachel had thought precious little about dating since her split from Henry. Now, however, and despite all her reservations, she found she couldn't stop thinking about Evan. Maybe it was their shared love of books, or the unassuming way Evan had connected with her cats. Maybe it was the way his deep-blue eyes seemed to smile into hers whenever they spoke.

Whatever it was, Rachel hoped Evan would come back to Title Wave. Soon.

Her attention shifted back to Tommy and Marc, their heads bent close together in what appeared to be an intensely private conversation. What had Isabella and Julian really been discussing with Marc earlier? Isabella's ready explanation had been breezy enough, but Rachel couldn't help wondering what had held their attention so intently.

Rachel sipped her sangria, watching as Marc leaned back in his chair, saying something that made Tommy's shoulders tense. The restaurant seemed to recede around her, the ambient noise fading as she focused on the scene unfolding at Marc's table. Something in Marc's expression had changed—a subtle hardening around his eyes, perhaps, or a tilt of his head that spoke of calculation rather than conciliation.

Tommy shifted in his seat, his posture becoming more rigid. Then Marc stood abruptly, pushing his chair back with a scrape that carried even to where Rachel sat. Tommy rose as well, his movement more deliberate, as if giving himself time to regain control.

The two men faced each other, Marc's lips moving rapidly, his expression now openly mocking. Tommy's hands clenched at his sides, then relaxed, then clenched again. Rachel began to rise, sensing disaster. If she got to Marc's table quickly enough, perhaps she could defuse the tension and draw Tommy back to their own table. They could calmly discuss whatever it was Marc had said to anger him, and then they'd find a way to laugh it off and enjoy the rest of their evening.

But she was too late.

Whatever Marc said next caused Tommy's face to contort with sudden rage. His fist connected with Marc's face, the crack of the blow silencing the entire restaurant. Marc reeled backward, clutching his nose.

Sabrosa erupted in chaos. Diners gasped and pushed back their chairs. Servers rushed forward, unsure how to intervene. Griselda appeared from the direction of the hostess stand, moving with surprising speed for someone in four-inch heels.

Rachel sat frozen for a second, not entirely able to believe she'd actually seen what she just saw. Then instinct took over and she was on her feet, weaving through the maze of tables toward Tommy. He stood over Marc, fist still clenched. His expression was equal parts shocked and gloating.

Danny emerged from the kitchen, immediately taking charge with calm authority. He helped Marc to his feet, efficiently directing Griselda to bring ice and towels. Then he turned to Tommy and politely, but firmly, asked him to step outside.

"Let's go," Rachel murmured, taking Tommy's arm. His right hand was already swelling, his knuckles reddening where they'd connected with Marc's face. "What happened?" she asked as she led him toward the door.

"I can't talk about it," Tommy said tersely. "Not here, anyway."

Outside, the balmy night air did little to cool Tommy's anger. He paced the sidewalk beneath the string lights illuminating Hibiscus Road, flexing his injured hand. "He called me a hack, Rachel. He said I'm the kind of 'journalist'," Tommy's fingers made scare quotes in the air, "who prints whatever story gets handed to me whether it's true or not." Tommy's voice was tight with a mixture of anger and what sounded like fear. He continued pacing, his steps quick and agitated on the smooth white pavement. "He said Isabella's only backing me for the *Daily News* job because she needs a dupe like me in that position."

Before Rachel could respond, Griselda emerged from Sabrosa. Her expression was composed, but Rachel could see the tension in her slender frame. "One of the bussers is taking Marc over to Coacoochee General," she informed them. "Danny convinced him not to call the police right now, but..." She shrugged expressively. "No promises about tomorrow."

Tommy cursed under his breath, running his uninjured hand through his hair. "I really messed up, didn't I?"

"Danny smoothed things over." Griselda's voice was professional, although not unkind. "But I wouldn't plan on dining at Sabrosa for a while if I were you." She glanced back at the restaurant. "I need to get back inside. We've comped everyone's dessert to make up for the...entertainment."

As Griselda disappeared back into the restaurant, Rachel noticed a few photographers hovering nearby. No doubt they recognized "Mr. Nightlife" and were hoping to document the aftermath of the restaurant drama for their various 'zines and fledgling websites.

"We should go," Rachel said gently. "Unless you want to be tomorrow's sole topic of conversation from here to South Beach."

Tommy nodded grimly, and they turned in the direction of Title Wave. Hibiscus Road bustled with its usual evening vitality. An overcrowded party spilled from Gallery Moda out onto the sidewalk, and every so often a bar would open its doors to pour live salsa or throbbing techno into the night air. Amber streetlights cast alternating bands of light and shadow across Tommy's face as they walked. Rachel noted how he cradled his injured hand against his chest, the knuckles already darkening with bruises.

They'd barely made it a block when Rachel spotted a familiar figure approaching from the opposite direction. Brock Winfield strolled toward them. He wore a jacket in a particularly unflattering shade of brown that made his complexion appear sallow in the streetlight, and his face contorted into a grimace of practiced enthusiasm when he saw them.

"If it isn't Mr. Nightlife himself!" Brock lifted a hand in greeting. He pointedly refused to look at Rachel, clearly hoping he could ingratiate himself with Tommy while not deigning to acknowledge her presence. "What a delightful—"

He stopped mid-sentence as they drew closer, his gaze dropping to Tommy's swollen knuckles, then traveling up to take in Tommy's disheveled appearance and tightly controlled expression. Brock's eyebrows shot up with a theatrical surprise that couldn't quite mask the gleam of satisfaction in his eyes.

"What in the world happened to your—" Brock suddenly stopped himself, then stepped aside to let them pass. "Please," he said, "don't let me keep you."

Rachel felt Tommy stiffen beside her but kept walking, her hand firmly on his arm as they moved past Brock without another word. She deliberately kept her eyes down, to lessen the risk of being recognized again, and didn't lift them until Sabrosa was well behind them.

"What was Marc talking about?" Rachel finally asked when they were far enough from prying eyes and ears.

Tommy shook his head, his usual smooth confidence fractured. "I don't know. Or maybe I do, but..." He stopped to lean against a wrought-iron railing that separated the sidewalk from a small tropical garden. The yellow glow from a nearby tiki torch caught the worried lines around his eyes, making him look older than his thirty-two years. "Look, it's complicated. And not a conversation for tonight. Right now, I just want to ice my hand and pretend this whole night never happened."

They reached the front of Title Wave, the bookstore dark but for the blue security light winking through the closed shutters. Rachel stood on the sidewalk, the same spot where Daisy's body had been found just days before.

"Call me tomorrow?" she asked.

"Yeah," Tommy replied, but his tone lacked conviction. Rachel watched as he continued down Hibiscus Road, his usual confident stride almost hesitant now. He didn't look back, and Rachel waited until he turned the corner before retrieving her keys from her purse.

A troubling thought surfaced in Rachel's memory: Tommy had argued with Daisy at the book signing, too. Rachel recalled seeing them huddled near the cash register, their expressions tense, their conversation urgent and heated. And then, the very next morning, Daisy had died unexpectedly on the sidewalk outside Title Wave.

Now Tommy had lost control with somebody else.

Stop it, Rachel told herself firmly. *This is Tommy we're talking about.* Tommy, who'd sat at her bedside and made her laugh for hours when she had the flu. Tommy, who'd spent a whole day helping her paint her living room walls in dove gray. Tommy, who Vashti had taken a liking to faster than Rachel had ever seen with any new person.

She remembered the April day when Tommy had first wandered into Title Wave, barely a week after she'd started. She'd been entering a stack of newly arrived books into the store's inventory system, her fingers unfamiliar with the register, her heart still raw from her breakup with Henry.

"Whatever that is, I'll have one, too," he'd said, nodding at the steaming mug of chamomile tea she'd made herself.

Their conversation had flowed so easily. They'd commiserated over mutual heartbreak—Tommy had just broken up with the man he'd been living with for two years—but talk had quickly turned to their shared love of Cajun food (and the complete lack of it anywhere in South Florida), the transformation of Coacoochee from forgotten outpost to world-famous hotspot, the way they'd both ended up there feeling slightly out of place among the glam crowd.

Something about Tommy's presence had made her shed the armor she'd been wearing since the breakup—the reflexive shrug, the studied indifference. She hadn't expected to see him again after that first day; there was, after all, no good reason for someone like Tommy to take an interest in Rachel. She wasn't cool or connected, certainly not the type who could help advance the career of an ambitious social columnist.

But Tommy had shown up only a few days later with an invite to a gallery opening, insisting it would be "tragic" for her to miss it. She'd protested on the grounds of having nothing remotely chic or stylish enough to wear, and Tommy had laughed.

"Everyone there will be too busy looking at themselves to notice what you're wearing," he'd assured her.

He'd been right, of course. That night had become the first of many when Tommy would guide her through Coacoochee's sparkling nightscape, introducing her as "my brilliant friend Rachel" to people whose faces she recognized from magazines, treating her opinions as if they carried weight in a world where she'd felt weightless.

In the darkest days right after Henry, Rachel had sometimes wondered if there was something fundamentally uninteresting about her, some essential dullness that had driven him to seek excitement elsewhere. Tommy had swept away those doubts simply by treating her like someone worth knowing—even when her life had seemed to be in ruins.

Rachel now had the sinking feeling that Tommy's life was the one falling apart. His impulsive action tonight had only made matters worse, creating a public spectacle from what had previously been subtle whispers and private threats.

Rachel hurried up Title Wave's side staircase. She found herself suddenly eager for the comfort of her own bed and the uncomplicated affection of her three cats.

CHAPTER 13

Vashti couldn't remember the last time she'd seen the sunrise. Waking up early was something she associated with worrying—and what was there for Vashti to worry about? True, she had unsettling memories of intense suffering when she was very young. In the earliest days after her rescue, she'd worried constantly that something might separate her from Rachel and send her back to that place of starvation and loneliness. She'd stay awake until dawn, perched on Rachel's pillow, watching the rise and fall of her human's chest to reassure herself that Rachel was still there, still breathing, still hers.

That was a long time ago. Vashti had known for a while that Rachel wasn't going anywhere—that she was the firm rock upon which Vashti would build the rest of her life. But now, as she watched the first rays of daylight brush the living room in golden hues, Vashti reflected that perhaps it didn't pay to get too comfortable. You forgot what it felt like—that tight, uncomfortable sensation in your chest and belly. You forgot how it felt to worry.

And worry she did. About Brock and his thinly veiled threats. About Tommy's uncharacteristic violence at Sabrosa the night before. "I wouldn't have believed it if I hadn't seen it myself," Rachel had confided to the cats when she got home. Then she'd washed her face and gotten into bed, where she'd tossed and turned all night. Vashti's green eyes had remained open, gleaming in the darkness, hours longer than they usually did—before she, too, had drifted into a restless, too-brief sleep.

"You're up early." Scarlett emerged from the bedroom and padded across the living room to join her sister at the window. *"Thinking about your boyfriend?"*

"Tommy's not my boyfriend," Vashti replied automatically, though without her usual indignation at Scarlett's teasing.

Scarlett settled beside her, their reflections a study in contrasts against the window glass. *"Tommy can take care of himself, you know."*

"Like he did at Sabrosa last night?" Vashti countered. *"Breaking Marc's nose was hardly in his own best interests."*

"Depends how you look at it, I guess. I'd have given Marc a good slap in the face ages ago." Scarlett brought up her right front paw and chewed at an itchy spot. *"Remember back in July when Homer attacked those three vet techs just for trying to take a blood sample?"*

The memory drew a reluctant purr of amusement from Vashti. Homer—small, blind, seemingly defenseless Homer—had transformed into a tiny tornado of claws and teeth when the vet technicians attempted to stick him with a needle. It had taken all three of them, plus Dr. Andi, to subdue him, and they'd still emerged with impressive scratches.

"He was so small they thought it would be easy," Vashti recalled. *"They never saw him coming."*

"Exactly," Scarlett said. *"Everyone has their limits."*

A flutter of movement outside caught the cats' attention. Stewie the mockingbird had landed on the windowsill, his beady eyes fixed on Vashti through the glass.

"*Why so glum, princess?*" he squawked. "*Didn't get your beauty sleep? Or were you too busy thinking about—*" he shifted into an uncannily accurate impression of Vashti's own voice: "*Tommy! My precious Tommy!*"

Vashti's ears flattened against her head. "*Go away, Stewie.*"

"*Make me!*" The mockingbird preened, secure in the knowledge that a closed window separated them. "*I hear things, you know. People talk right in front of me all the time. The things I could tell you about this town...*"

"*So tell us something useful for once,*" Scarlett snapped.

But Stewie just cackled and flew away, his mocking laughter lingering in the morning air.

Homer appeared from the bedroom, stretching languorously as he navigated the familiar path toward his sisters. "*Was that Stewie I heard?*" He moved more slowly than usual as he began his morning face-grooming ritual. Clearly, Vashti thought, Homer had slept as badly as she and Rachel had.

"*Just being his usual irritating self,*" Scarlett replied.

Homer laid down next to them, his sensitive ears picking up the slightly faster beating of Vashti's heart. "*You're worried,*" he observed. "*Rachel's worried about Tommy, too.*"

It would be another two hours before Rachel finally emerged from the bedroom. Her eyes were shadowed, her movements sluggish as she prepared for the day ahead. The usual morning ritual of tea and breakfast was performed in distracted silence. Homer had to nudge his empty bowl meaningfully toward her with his nose—twice!—before she remembered to feed them.

"Come on, guys," she finally said, gathering her keys. "Let's go open up."

The morning passed slowly. Rachel spent most of her time restocking shelves, while the three cats settled into comfortable spots and fell into deeper naps than they usually did during their "working" hours.

Shortly after noon, Tommy arrived, looking as haggard as the rest of them felt. Dark circles beneath his eyes contrasted sharply with the bright blue of his shirt. The knuckles of his right hand were puffy and discolored.

"*Tommy!*" Vashti abandoned her pouf in Self Help and hurried toward him, rubbing against his legs in greeting.

"Hello, beautiful." Tommy's voice lacked its usual energy as he bent to stroke her back. "At least somebody's happy to see me."

Rachel emerged from between the bookshelves. "How's the hand?"

"Hurts like hell," Tommy admitted. "And Isabella's been calling all morning. Apparently, breaking someone's nose in public is bad for my image." His attempt at humor fell flat.

Tommy's arrival had awakened Homer, who was drowsier than usual—so it took him longer than it normally would to realize that something about the woman browsing nearby had changed subtly with Tommy's entrance. Her breathing had become more controlled and purposeful—not the relaxed inhales and exhales of a casual browser, but the measured breaths of someone paying close attention while pretending not to.

"Hey! Psst!" Homer called to Scarlett, who had found a secluded catnap spot over in Florida History. When Homer could tell by the change in Scarlett's own breathing that she was awake and alert, he said, *"Something's off about that woman in Mysteries. Can you see what she's doing?"*

"She's not actually looking at the books," Scarlett confirmed. *"She's watching Tommy."*

Vashti had most of her attention focused on Tommy, but she too had noticed the browser. The woman wore jeans and a simple white blouse, appearing casual enough, but her feet were planted in what Vashti recognized as a ready stance. It reminded her of Hot Mike—the quiet alertness of someone trained to respond quickly.

"We should get Rachel's attention," Vashti said. *"Something about this woman doesn't seem right."*

"Let Homer do it." Scarlett liked Tommy more than Homer did, but ultimately she didn't care all that much about anybody except for Rachel, herself, and (albeit reluctantly) her two feline siblings. Sometimes she imagined how deliciously quiet the world would be if everyone else in it disappeared. Scarlett's mouth opened wide in a yawn as she added, *"Homer loves attention, anyway."*

"Oh, fine." Homer was uncharacteristically cranky; he, too, was feeling the effects of a sleepless night. *"You two always make me do everything just because I'm the youngest."* With an annoyed sigh, Homer stalked across the store to the Staff Picks table at the end of the Mysteries aisle. Then, with a precisely calibrated leap, he jumped toward the top of the table—only

to encounter a stack of books taller than his jump. Books and Homer promptly tumbled to the ground in a series of audible thumps.

"Oh no, look at the mess I made," Homer deadpanned. *"Because I'm so blind and clumsy."*

Rachel had been pouring Tommy a cup of coffee in the café when the sound caught her attention. "I'll be right back," she told him, and hastened over to the Staff Picks table. The mystery woman knelt on the ground, gathering the toppled books and stroking the back of a "startled" Homer.

"You okay, buddy?" Concern was evident in Rachel's voice. "It's not like you to miss a jump." Homer hated worrying Rachel (the one flaw in this plan), and, as she knelt down beside him, he quickly reassured her with loud purrs as he pressed his face into the palm of her hand. *"I'm fine,"* he told her. *"I promise."*

Satisfied that no lasting damage had been done to Homer or to the books, Rachel turned her attention to the customer. "Thank you," she said, as the woman handed her the stack of books collected from the floor, and Rachel placed them back on the Staff Picks table. "Homer almost never bumps into things."

"It's amazing how well he gets around." The woman regarded Homer with friendly curiosity. "Has he always been blind?"

"Since the day he was born," Rachel confirmed—which was true; Homer's eyes had been badly infected from birth, and had never properly opened at two weeks the way most cats' did. "Let me buy you a cup of coffee," she told the woman. "It's the least I can do."

"There's no need," the woman protested, but she nevertheless followed Rachel over to the café and took up a seat a few feet away from Tommy's chair.

Rachel eyed the woman more closely as she poured, a quizzical expression on her face. "I'm sorry, but have we met before? You look so familiar."

"I'm Officer Jessica Martinez. With the Coacoochee PD. I was first on the scene when…" She paused, dropping her voice. "When your friend was found outside." Her eyes flicked to Tommy. "My sister and her husband happened to be having dinner at Sabrosa last night."

The room seemed to freeze mid-breath. Tommy's posture stiffened, and Rachel's hand that was pouring the coffee wobbled just enough to send a few drops spilling from the cup onto the saucer. None of the humans was paying attention to the cats in that moment—but if they had been, they'd have noticed that all three were holding their ears at rigid attention.

"Of course." Rachel's expression shifted from smiling to wary, and she set the coffee pot down carefully. "That's where I remember you from." She glanced at Tommy, then back to Officer Martinez. "Are you here because of what happened at Sabrosa, or...?"

"Just browsing. It's my day off." Officer Martinez accepted the coffee with a nod of thanks. "Though when I recognized Mr. Duvall here, I thought he should know that Marc Gottsegen filed a police report this morning about last night's incident."

Tommy's face paled. "He did?"

"Nobody's made a decision about pressing charges yet," she hastened to assure Tommy. "A lot of times, these things blow over. But it wouldn't surprise me if Mr. Gottsegen were to pursue civil damages, aside from anything the DA might decide to do criminally."

"A lawsuit?" Tommy's knuckles whitened as he gripped the edge of the counter. "For one punch?"

Officer Martinez turned her eyes away from Tommy, giving him a moment to absorb what she'd said. She looked around the bookstore, taking in the Halloween displays and the three bookstore cats, who seemed—to Jessica Martinez's fanciful imagination—to be following the conversation as closely as the humans were.

"Off the record," she added, in a softer tone, "I've been reading your column for a while now, Mr. Duvall. Whatever's going on, I hope you can sort it out."

Over Rachel's protests, Officer Martinez placed a five-dollar bill on the café counter. "The Chief doesn't like us taking freebies," she explained, almost apologetically. "Thank you, though." She collected her purse and leaned down to give a decidedly unenthusiastic Vashti—still standing by Tommy's café chair—a scritch on the head before walking out.

Rachel watched as Tommy slumped forward. The sunlight that had been warming his shoulders now highlighted every line of worry etched into his face.

"This could ruin me, Rachel." His voice was barely above a whisper. "If I'm facing legal troubles, the *Daily News* will never hire me."

Rachel reached across the counter to squeeze his uninjured hand. "Is there anything I can do to help?"

Tommy's smile was strained. "Not unless you can make the last twenty-four hours disappear."

"Tommy—" Rachel began, but he was already pulling his hand away and checking his watch.

"I should go. I have a column due by five, and apparently I need to add finding a lawyer to my list of things to do today." He stood and slipped his wallet into the back pocket of his jeans, wincing as the movement jarred his injured hand. "I'll call you later, okay?"

"Promise?"

"Promise," Tommy replied, though something in his eyes suggested his mind was already elsewhere. He dropped a quick, distracted peck on her cheek and headed for the door just as it swung open to announce a new arrival.

Laurie Castillo stood in the doorway. On any other day, she and Tommy would have greeted each other with enthusiastic air kisses and a rapid exchange of gossip—two of Coacoochee's most-social butterflies colliding in a flutter of animated conversation.

Today, they barely registered each other's presence.

"Hey, Laurie," Tommy muttered distractedly, stepping aside to let her pass.

Laurie nodded automatically, but her eyes were already scanning the store for Rachel. She and Tommy brushed past each other like strangers, each lost in their own private worries.

"Rachel." Laurie hurried over to the café counter. "Have you seen Kotik? He didn't come home last night."

"Kotik is missing?" Vashti, still standing next to Tommy's abandoned café chair, felt her fur bristle with concern.

"I'm sorry, I haven't." Rachel's heart instantly went out to her friend. "Could he have gotten locked into your storeroom at the boutique?"

"I've checked everywhere." There were unshed tears in Laurie's voice. "He's never stayed out all night before."

Rachel came around from behind the café counter to give Laurie a sympathetic hug. "He's probably just exploring. Cats do that sometimes."

"But he always comes home for dinner," Laurie protested. "Always."

Rachel used Title Wave's computer and photo scanner to help Laurie design a "Missing Cat" flyer, printing a stack of them to distribute along Hibiscus Road. While Rachel gathered tape and pushpins, Vashti slipped over to the back of the store, where Homer and Scarlett were already huddled in conference.

"Kotik wouldn't just disappear," she whispered. *"Something must have happened to him."*

"Maybe he found a new girlfriend." Scarlett said this with an arch look at Vashti—but if Vashti had caught Scarlett's implication, she didn't let on.

"We should look for him tonight," Homer suggested. *"After Rachel falls asleep."*

"Yes," Vashti readily agreed, although she'd been looking forward to catching up on the sleep she'd missed the night before. *"We can search the loading dock and alley first, then check Samkhat's usual spots. She might have seen him."*

Rachel took the unusual step of flipping the sign on Title Wave's front door to *Closed* during regular business hours. Then she locked up and left to help Laurie hang the "Missing Cat" signs up and down Hibiscus Road. She was slightly uneasy about leaving the cats alone in the store—so many unusual things had been happening lately!—but when she returned an hour later, perspiring from having walked up and down the entire length of Hibiscus Road in the heat of midday, everything was exactly as she'd left it.

The rest of the afternoon was uneventful, and the hours crawled until closing. It had been a draining day, filled with uncomfortable conversations and too few customers. As Rachel performed her closing routine—counting the register, straightening shelves, wiping down the café counter—the three cats watched her with unusual attentiveness. Rachel barely noticed, lost in her own thoughts.

"I think I'll turn in early tonight, guys," she said with a yawn as she locked up the store. "I'm completely wiped."

True to her word, Rachel went to bed almost immediately after consuming half a stale bagel, left over from Sunday's brunch. Her eyes were closing before she'd swallowed the last bite, and she fell into a deep sleep as soon as her head hit the pillow. She placed the phone next to her ear in case Tommy decided to call as he'd said he would—but the phone didn't ring all night.

The three cats regarded the comfortable bed with longing. How wonderful it would be to slip in beside Rachel and fall into a warm, dreamless sleep together!

One by one, they slipped through the concealed panel in the pantry and into the dumbwaiter shaft. The darkness enveloped them as they made their way carefully down the old rope, their paws finding the familiar handholds with practiced ease. The storeroom below was silent and still, illuminated only by the faint glow of the security light.

Homer's sensitive ears picked up no sound as they approached the hidden cat door, but his whiskers detected the subtle shift in air currents that told him it was unblocked. He pushed through first, emerging into the warm night air of the alley beside Title Wave.

"Let's try behind Sabrosa," Vashti suggested. *"Kotik likes to hunt for scraps there."*

The night air was heavy with humidity, carrying the mingled scents of the ocean and yesterday's cooking. The alleys and loading docks of Hibiscus Road were so silent, the cats could hear waves crashing on the beach that was blocks away.

"Nothing," Homer announced, after thoroughly investigating every corner and crevice of Sabrosa's back alley. They checked the loading dock of Laurie's Closet next, then behind the Cuban bakery where Kotik sometimes hunted mice. With each empty location, Vashti's anxiety grew. Even Scarlett's usual nonchalance gave way to concern.

"Maybe we should try near Marc's house," Homer suggested. *"Samkhat said Kotik's been following him around."*

"How would we even find Marc's house?" Scarlett sounded exasperated. *"We've never been there."*

"He lives next door to Natalie and Hot Mike, and I know both their scents," Homer argued stubbornly. *"It's worth a try. Unless you have any better ideas?"*

"Literally any idea would be better than watching you parade around town with your nose in the air."

"We could ask Samkhat." Vashti—at least as irritable as both her siblings from worry and lack of sleep—interjected before Homer could respond. *"She knows every inch of Coacoochee."*

"Fine," Homer and Scarlett both muttered. *"Let's not be all night about it,"* Scarlett added grumpily.

They were heading toward Samkhat's usual evening haunt—a covered bus stop on Rollins Avenue—when a rustling sound from behind a row of garbage cans caught their attention. The three cats froze, their senses on high alert.

"Who's there?" Homer called out, his whiskers fanned forward to detect movement. A small puff of breeze blew his way, carrying a scent he recognized. *"Kotik? Is that you?"*

A familiar black-and-white figure emerged from the shadows, his fur disheveled and his mismatched eyes wide. Vashti and Scarlett noted how enlarged his pupils were—so large that his eyes appeared to be all pupil.

"Kotik!" Vashti's relief was evident in her voice as she hurried toward him. *"Laurie's been worried sick about you!"*

"I was just coming to look for the three of you."

Homer could hear the faster-than-normal beat of Kotik's heart. Something extraordinary must have happened if it had kept Kotik out all night. Something that had left him so rattled, his heart was still pounding about it.

So it almost didn't come as a surprise when, after hesitating for only a second, Kotik told them what he'd come to tell them:

"Marc Gottsegen is dead."

CHAPTER 14

The alleyway fell silent. A distant rumba from one of the party boats out on Biscayne Bay pulsed faintly in the background, incongruously festive.

Homer spoke first, his voice quavering only slightly. *"Dead? Are you sure?"*

Kotik nodded. He'd seen dead things before, having killed a few mice in his day—something he wasn't particularly proud of now. Laurie's reaction when he'd left one on her pillow as a well-intended gift had been decidedly unenthusiastic.

Vashti moved closer to Kotik, her white fur almost luminous in the dim light of the alley. *"Tell us everything,"* she urged gently. *"Start from the beginning."*

"I've been following Marc for days because—" Kotik hesitated, his eyes moving involuntarily toward Vashti.

Scarlett, ever practical and always impatient, filled the awkward pause. *"Never mind why. Tell us what you saw."*

"Yesterday," he continued, sounding relieved, *"I followed Marc to Sabrosa. I planned to watch him for a while before heading home. But then Isabella Stuart walked in with Julian."*

"Rachel mentioned that," Vashti said. *"They were talking to Marc just before she and Tommy got there."*

Kotik nodded vigorously. *"They sat with Marc for a while. I couldn't hear what they said—I was outside, watching through the window—but after they left, he wrote something in his notebook."* Kotik's gaze dropped to his paws. *"Then Tommy came over, and..."* He glanced hesitantly at Vashti.

"We know what happened," Scarlett interjected matter-of-factly. *"Tommy punched Marc in the face. Rachel told us all about it."*

"Right." Kotik seemed grateful to be allowed to skip over that part. *"After that, I heard Griselda say she was sending Marc to Coacoochee General. I thought about following him, but I don't know how to get to the hospital. So I decided to go to Marc's house and wait for him there."*

The scent of the ocean grew stronger as the breeze shifted, carrying with it the faint aromas of fried fish and garlic from a nearby restaurant. Homer's stomach growled, reminding him they'd been out longer than anticipated.

"How long did it take Marc to get home?" Homer asked.

"Hours," Kotik replied. *"It was very late when he finally got back. He looked terrible—his nose was all bandaged up, and he seemed unsteady."*

"Drunk?" Scarlett suggested.

"No," Kotik shook his head. *"Sick. He went straight to the bathroom and threw up. A bunch of times. I could hear him through the window. But afterward he seemed okay. He made himself tea and sat at his desk looking through papers."*

Vashti's tail swished anxiously behind her. *"And then what happened?"*

"I must have fallen asleep in his backyard," Kotik admitted, looking ashamed. *"It was dark already by the time I woke up. I was worried Laurie*

would be looking for me, but I wanted to check on Marc before leaving." His voice grew quieter. *"That's when I saw him through the window. He was lying on the floor of his living room, not moving. His eyes were open, but...empty."*

Homer felt a chill run through him despite the warm night air. He knew the emptiness Kotik described—that blank spot in his sensory field where sound and movement were supposed to be, but weren't. He'd sensed it around Daisy's body the morning she'd been found.

"Does anybody know yet?" Vashti asked. *"The police? Neighbors?"*

Kotik shook his head. *"No. At least, nobody did by the time I left to look for the three of you."*

A heavy silence fell over the four cats. Homer wondered if the others were thinking the same thing he was.

"We should go now," he said. *"Before somebody finds him."*

"Are you crazy?!" Scarlett's tail bristled with alarm. *"We can't just waltz into a dead human's house! What if whoever did this comes back?"*

"That's exactly why we should go." It was Vashti who spoke this time, and the fervor in her voice surprised them all.

"You'd do any stupid thing if there was even half a chance it might clear Tommy's name," Scarlett snapped. The idea of entering a home with a corpse in it clearly unnerved her.

But Vashti's fur remained unruffled, her voice as patient as Rachel's had been back in the long-ago time when she'd first taught a kitten-sized Homer how to find his food bowl and litter box.

"We know Tommy was angry at Marc." Everyone was surprised to hear her admit even this much. *"Maybe somebody else was, too. But half the town walks into our café at least once a week. And that means,"* she concluded, *"we won't know Rachel's safe until we get to the bottom of this."*

Scarlett's expression softened. If there was one thing that could overcome her natural caution, it was her devotion to the human who had rescued her from that cardboard box.

"How far is it to Marc's house?" she asked.

"Only a few blocks." Kotik was reluctant to return—but, after all, it would give him more time with Vashti. *"It won't take us long to get there."*

"Fine," Scarlett relented with a dramatic sigh. *"Let's get going while we still have all nine of our lives left."*

She rose to her feet and arched her back in a deep stretch, grateful to be in motion again after sitting so stiffly while Kotik told his tale. Then she fixed Vashti and Homer with an expression so stern, even Homer could feel it.

"Everybody had better be extra careful, though." Her tail twitched up and down emphatically, as if to punctuate the sentence. *"If we end up dead, too, Rachel will kill us."*

CHAPTER 15

MARC'S HOUSE WAS NESTLED in a quiet residential neighborhood along-side other homes whose well-tended gardens spilled the scent of hibiscus and impatiens into the humid night air. It was trash night, and the smell of refuse waiting in cans in front of each house mingled with that of the flowers in a sour-sweet fug. As the cats drew closer, Homer found that Hot Mike's familiar scent—a distinctive blend of dog, the oatmeal shampoo Natalie used on him, and the metallic smell of his collar tags—served as a comforting beacon, pulling him forward with increasing certainty.

"We're almost there." Kotik attempted to sound manly and reassuring, but his voice cracked on the word "there."

Vashti padded close beside him. *"It's going to be all right,"* she murmured, trying to calm Kotik's evident nerves. *"We'll take a quick look around and get you back to Laurie."*

Kotik nodded, not quite able to meet her eyes. Vashti's white fur caught and reflected the moonlight in a way that made her glow like a goddess. Her proximity, her scent like fresh-washed cotton with the faintest hint of the lavender sachets Rachel kept in her dresser drawers, made Kotik's heart race in a way that had nothing to do with their nighttime investigation.

Scarlett, walking behind them, rolled her eyes. *"This is even worse than when Rachel watches* Felicity,*"* she muttered.

As they turned the corner onto the street where Marc and Natalie lived, all four cats froze. Down at the end of the block, they could see a figure emerging from Marc's backyard, moving silently and with deliberate stealth. He wore dark clothing and what appeared to be a ski mask pulled over his face.

"Look," Scarlett hissed, crouching instinctively lower to the ground.

The masked intruder closed Marc's gate behind him, the soft click of the latch audible in the quiet night. Homer's ears swiveled toward the sound, tracking the man's footsteps as he moved away from the house.

"He's carrying something," Vashti whispered, her green eyes narrowed. *"In his right hand. Something small."*

"Evidence." Kotik's voice was no louder than Vashti's. *"He must have been looking for something in Marc's house."*

"This could be the killer." Scarlett's tail twitched anxiously. *"We can't let him get away."*

"But what are we supposed to do?" Vashti's voice held a note of desperation. *"It's not like we can walk over and ask him what he's doing here."*

Homer's ears were aloft, his head moving evenly from side to side in a way that Rachel always said reminded her of a sonar dish. He catalogued every sound, from the soft scrape of the man's shoes against pavement to the distant rustle of palm fronds in the night breeze. Then he heard something new—the distinctive rubbery flap of a doggie door opening.

"Hot Mike," Homer whispered.

A moment later, Hot Mike burst into his backyard, his powerful form illuminated by the security light that had clicked on at his movement. The German Shepherd's ears were pricked forward, his entire body tense as he detected the intruder. With a deep, resonant bark that shattered the night's stillness, Hot Mike announced his presence.

The masked man started visibly, his head whipping around as he took in the former police dog's massive size. Then he broke into a run.

Homer didn't think—he simply acted. Before Vashti or Scarlett could stop him, he darted after the fleeing figure, his small black body a swift shadow against the pale sidewalk.

"Homer!" Vashti cried out, but he was already gone, guided by the sound of the man's pounding footsteps.

The three remaining cats stared at each other in horror.

"What do we do?" Kotik's voice rose in alarm.

Vashti made a split-second decision. She raced toward Natalie's yard where Hot Mike still barked from behind the chest-high wooden fence that confined him.

"Hot Mike!" she called. *"You have to help Homer!"*

The surprise of hearing Vashti's familiar voice in such an unexpected context silenced Hot Mike. None of his feline friends had ever been to his and Natalie's house before, and nothing he could think of would account for why they were here now.

"We think that man may have killed Daisy and Marc." Vashti was frantic, and she sounded it. *"Who knows what he'll do if Homer actually catches up to him?"*

"Wait…Marc is dead?!" Hot Mike's mind tried to process this new—and astonishing—piece of information.

"Marc is dead, we think that man might have killed him, and Homer's chasing after him." Even Scarlett was beginning to panic. *"Now you know everything we know."*

The German Shepherd hesitated, his training warring with his instinct to protect. *"I can't leave the yard without Natalie,"* he woofed softly. *"Those are the rules."*

"You're a police dog!" Vashti's voice rose an octave. *"Isn't stopping criminals what you were trained for?"*

"Was," Hot Mike corrected stiffly. *"I was a police dog. But I failed."*

"You didn't fail at anything that mattered!" Vashti's white fur bristled. *"Homer needs you! You're the only one who can help him!"*

Hot Mike's ears flattened against his head, his mind roiled by competing loyalties. What would Natalie want him to do? On the one hand, she'd very firmly impressed upon him that he was never, *ever*, to leave the yard without her. But surely Natalie wouldn't want Homer—who was almost comically tiny from Hot Mike's perspective—to chase a possible murderer through the streets of Coacoochee without any backup at all. Hot Mike shifted his feet uncertainly as he tried to decide.

Vashti could read the conflict plainly in his large brown eyes, and her impatience grew until it was unbearable. *"HOT MIKE!"* Her normally elegant voice rose to a sharp, desperate shriek that reverberated off nearby houses to echo through the silent streets. Cats for blocks around—indoor and outdoor alike—woke from naps or paused in the middle of foraging through trash cans to lift their heads in wonder and alarm. Even Kotik gaped at Vashti with open-mouthed astonishment.

"GO GET HOMER!" Vashti yowled at the top of her lungs. ***"GO GET HOMER, HOT MIKE!"***

Hot Mike turned his back on her and galloped away toward the house. For a terrifying heartbeat, Vashti thought he intended to disappear through the doggy door—to go back inside and abandon Homer to whatever fate had in store for him.

But when he reached the opposite side of the yard, Hot Mike turned to face her again. Then he broke into a run. He reached the wooden fence within seconds and, with a single powerful leap, cleared it to land on the other side. Without breaking stride, Hot Mike accelerated to the top speed his legs were capable of, and he raced off in the direction Homer and the intruder had gone.

"He's going after them." Vashti's voice was hoarse and trembling with relief.

Scarlett came up beside her. *"They'll be okay,"* she said, although she sounded less than convinced. *"Remember the vet's office? Homer's a lot tougher than he looks."*

Vashti didn't say what she was thinking—that the only reason Homer had been able to "overpower" all three vet techs was because they were reluctant to take even the smallest risk of hurting him. It was this unwillingness to fight back that had allowed Homer to subdue three humans so easily.

Somehow, Vashti doubted that the man who might have killed Daisy and Marc would show similar restraint.

Homer's paws flew over the pavement as he followed the sound of retreating footsteps. His nose and whiskers mapped every obstacle—parked cars, street lamps, hedges. His heart thrummed against his ribs, and each breath came in a short, sharp pull. Homer had never run this far or this fast before. His ability to mentally map the space around him as he went was less accurate than it normally was, and every so often he'd stumble over an unexpected tree root that pushed up the sidewalk, creating cracks and hillocks.

Nevertheless, Homer felt glorious. The thrill of the chase brought with it a crystalline feeling of elation, and everything contributed to it—the wind in his face, the sound of his own blood pounding in his ears. Even the uncertainty of what would happen when he finally caught the man (Homer refused to think in terms of "if") was more exhilarating than otherwise.

Yet Homer could feel his strength beginning to flag. He tripped over a child's roller skate that had been left in the middle of the sidewalk, and in the time it took him to recover, he could hear the masked man widen his lead. He'd been nearly a full block ahead when Homer had begun chasing him—and even though Homer had closed much of that gap, if the man didn't slow down soon, Homer might actually lose him.

But the man was tiring, too. The jagged rasp of his breath made clear he was winded. The sound of it became louder in Homer's ears as the man turned his head to look behind him. It was doubtful he even realized that a small black cat was chasing him, and he might have stopped running altogether.

If not for what he saw coming up fast on Homer's tail.

Homer heard it at the same moment the man saw it—the steady four-beat cadence of a large dog running at full tilt. The sound grew rapidly closer.

The intruder took a deep breath and lunged forward in a desperate increase of speed just as something gripped Homer by the scruff of his neck. He felt his paws leave the ground as Hot Mike's teeth gently but firmly lifted him.

For a disorienting moment, Homer was airborne. Then he landed on Hot Mike's broad back, instinctively digging his claws into the German Shepherd's thick fur to secure himself.

"Don't let him get away, Hot Mike!" Homer pleaded, afraid the oversized dog would take him straight back to Marc's house.

But Hot Mike was now in full pursuit mode. *"Hold on tight,"* he growled through clenched teeth, never breaking stride.

Homer flattened himself against Hot Mike's back, feeling the powerful muscles working beneath him as the two of them—cat and dog—raced through the night. The sensation was like flying, but safer, anchored to Hot Mike's steady strength.

"He's turning left," Homer directed, his acute hearing tracking their quarry.

Hot Mike adjusted course, his nails clicking against the pavement as they hurtled through the night. The wind rushed past them, carrying a kaleidoscope of scents: flowering jasmine, the chlorine from a nearby pool, the lingering exhaust from parked cars.

Occasionally, when the wind shifted, Homer caught tantalizingly familiar traces of the man they were pursuing—something that tugged at his memory, a scent he knew but couldn't place. But these moments were fleeting, disrupted by the overpowering aromas of garbage night in Coacoochee. The trash cans awaiting morning pickup created an olfactory obstacle course that confounded even Homer's exceptional nose.

"Can you smell him?" Hot Mike asked between breaths.

"Not clearly," Homer admitted. *"There's something familiar, but the garbage is getting in the way. Plus, we're upwind. I keep getting hints of something I've smelled before, but I can't place it."*

They raced down a side street and through a narrow passage. Homer realized they were heading into a more commercial area—he could smell the restaurants and shops of Hibiscus Road drawing nearer.

"He's slowing," Homer whispered as the footsteps ahead grew more hesitant. *"I think he's trying to figure out where to go."*

Suddenly, the footsteps quickened again, then turned sharply. The echoing quality of the sounds told Homer they'd entered a narrow space—an alley, perhaps.

"Blind alley off Hibiscus Road," Hot Mike confirmed, his pace slowing as they approached. *"He's trapped."*

They rounded the corner to find the masked figure facing a tall, chain link fence. The man whirled around when he heard them enter, his breath coming in quick gasps. For a tense moment, predator and prey regarded one another.

Then the man turned and leaped for the fence, scrabbling for handholds. As he did, something slipped from his grasp, fluttering to the ground like a fallen leaf.

The man froze, one leg already hooked over the fence top. He hesitated, clearly torn between escaping and retrieving whatever he'd dropped.

Hot Mike stepped forward, his posture alert but controlled. With a precision that spoke of his training, he placed one large paw directly over the fallen object and fixed the intruder with a steady gaze. A low, rumbling growl rose from his chest—not aggressive, but unmistakably a warning.

The man made his choice. With a final glance at what he'd lost, he hauled himself over the fence and disappeared.

Hot Mike's growl faded to silence as the sound of retreating footsteps grew fainter. Homer slid from the dog's back, landing softly on the alley floor.

"We lost him." Frustration and exhaustion were evident in Homer's breathless voice. *"I can't believe we ran all this way for nothing."*

"He did get away," Hot Mike admitted, *"but he dropped what he was carrying."* Hot Mike was also winded, and he panted as he sniffed at the object the masked man had left behind. *"It looks like a photograph—that instant kind, with the white border around it."*

"What's in the picture?" Homer sat on his haunches and bent his head forward to sniff at the Polaroid photo still pinned beneath Hot Mike's enormous front paw.

Hot Mike cautiously lifted his paw and studied the image. *"It shows two people at what looks like a party,"* he finally said. *"There's a woman I don't recognize—dark hair, younger than Natalie."*

"And?" Homer prompted. *"Is there anybody else in the picture with her?"*

"There's a man standing next to her with his arm around her shoulders." Hot Mike brought down his head to examine the picture more closely. *"It looks like Julian Singer-Adams."*

CHAPTER 16

Vashti's eyes remained fixed on the shadowy street where Homer and Hot Mike had disappeared. *"They should have been back by now."* Her tail swished with uncharacteristic impatience.

Kotik paced between two ornamental palms, his black-and-white tuxedo fur blending with the shadows. Every few moments, he paused to glance at Vashti, then quickly looked away when she turned in his direction.

Scarlett had made the reluctant decision to lie down in the grass, her exhaustion after two near-sleepless nights overruling her innate distaste for the outdoors. The grass was damp with dew and tickled the fur of her belly uncomfortably. *"I'll bet they never even catch up to him,"* she asserted calmly.

Nevertheless, her yellow-green eyes flicked repeatedly toward the empty street.

The sound of a large dog barking softly made all three cats perk up their ears. Relief washed over them as, a moment later, the duo appeared around the corner of Marc's yard—Hot Mike's powerful form moving with surprising grace, Homer perched triumphantly atop his broad back.

"Oh, thank goodness!" Vashti bounded forward to meet them. *"Don't you ever do anything like that again, Homer!"* she scolded. *"That was unbelievably stupid! You could have gotten yourself lost or even killed!"*

Homer leapt nimbly to the ground, where Vashti immediately and aggressively began grooming the top of his head with her tongue. *"I'm fine. Leave me alone,"* he grumbled, pulling away irritably. He didn't at all appreciate the way Vashti was treating him like a little kid, even though he'd just returned unharmed from a daring mission with Hot Mike—the manliest man Homer knew.

Scarlett rarely found herself in the role of peacemaker, but she was anxious to get on with the investigation so they could all return as quickly as possible to the safety and comfort of their own homes. *"All's well that ends well,"* she said with inarguable finality. *"Did you catch him or not?*

"No, but we got this." Homer tilted his head in Hot Mike's direction, and the dog set down the Polaroid he'd been carrying in his mouth.

The four cats and one dog formed a curious circle around the photograph. Even in the moonlight, they could clearly see Julian Singer-Adams, his arm draped casually over the shoulders of a pretty, dark-haired young woman. A man's hand—likely the hand of the person who'd taken the picture—was just visible in the lower left-hand corner of the photo, pointing at Julian and the woman as if directing them into a pose. Both Julian and the mysterious woman were smiling broadly.

"That's Julian," Vashti mused, her delicate head tilted thoughtfully. *"But who's the woman with him?"*

Kotik hovered at the edge of their circle. *"I should get home,"* he said reluctantly.

Vashti's expression softened as she turned to him. *"Thank you for your help, Kotik. You were very brave."*

The compliment sent a visible thrill through the young tuxedo cat. He stood a little taller, and his bottle-brush tail fluffed out handsomely. *"I'd do anything to help you—all of you, I mean,"* he added hastily.

Scarlett graciously pretended to examine a nearby garden gnome. *"We should check inside the house,"* she said, as Kotik padded off in the direction of Hibiscus Road. *"The back window is still open where that man broke in."*

The partially opened window provided just enough space for the cats to slip through one by one, with Homer navigating by sound and scent. Once inside, Scarlett stood on her hind legs atop a kitchen chair, her front paws manipulating the doorknob until the back door swung open to admit Hot Mike. Her agility with doors and drawers was a skill Scarlett had honed purely as a matter of principle; the very idea of being locked out of, or away from, anything she might happen to want was an intolerable affront to her dignity.

"Impressive." The German Shepherd padded inside and surveyed the kitchen with professional interest.

The darkness of Marc's house enveloped the four of them like velvet, shadows pooling in corners and stretching between furniture in ways that would have left humans fumbling and disoriented. But to Vashti and Scarlett, the nighttime gloom merely transformed the colors around them into various shades of silver and blue—the outlines of furniture, picture frames, and household objects all perfectly distinct to their nocturnal vision, as if the house had been redrawn in a moonlit palette specifically for feline eyes.

To Homer, of course, the lack of lighting made no difference at all. *"Let me know if you need help finding your way around,"* he whispered to Hot Mike, whose nighttime vision was much better than a human's—but still nothing compared to Homer's keen senses.

The kitchen felt still and uncluttered, with few interesting smells. A mug holding tea sat half-empty on the counter, a paperback lay splayed open on the table, and a jacket hung carelessly over a chair back—all evidence of a life interrupted mid-sentence.

Their exploration led inevitably to the living room, where Marc Gottsegen lay on the polished hardwood floor, motionless in the moonlight that dappled the room around him. His nose was heavily bandaged, the skin around it swelling in a way that indicated he would likely have woken up with two black eyes in the morning.

Now he would never wake up at all.

Homer began a thorough sensory investigation, his nose working to catalog the information a sighted cat might miss. He detected the same unusual smell he'd first noticed on Daisy—something bitter and floral with medicinal undertones.

"Poison," Vashti breathed, when Homer reported his findings. *"It must be. First Daisy just days ago, and now Marc."*

Hot Mike circled Marc's body, his trained nose detecting additional information. *"There are hospital smells, too,"* he observed. *"Antiseptic, bandages."*

"From his emergency room visit," Homer said. *"After Tommy hit him."*

Vashti drew in a deep breath and sighed. *"Let's see what else we can find."*

Their investigation continued into Marc's small home office, where a computer sat dormant on a wooden desk, flanked by tidy stacks of reporter's notebooks. One of them lay open beside the computer, and Vashti leapt to the top of the desk to examine it more closely. *"It looks like something was attached here."* She noted the rectangular depression impressed into the paper, which was the exact size of the Polaroid photo Homer and Hot Mike had recovered. A hastily bent paperclip discarded beside it confirmed Vashti's guess.

"What do you think, Homer?" Vashti's quiet voice as she turned to her little brother gave no hint of the way she'd screeched like a howler monkey on his behalf not one hour ago. Homer leapt up beside her and sniffed at the notebook. *"The last person to hold this was wearing the same kind of gloves they wear at the vet's office."* His nose wrinkled with distaste *"That's all I can smell."*

Three drawers lined the desk's left side, promising additional secrets. Scarlett tackled them systematically, slipping her left front paw beneath each in turn to pull it open. *"Office supplies,"* she reported of the first drawer. *"Boring human stuff,"* she said of the second, which contained clipped bundles of the same kinds of credit card bills and bank statements Rachel got at home, along with an assortment of takeout menus. The third and largest drawer at the bottom yielded only a few back issues of *Palm* magazine.

"Nothing helpful." The obvious disappointment in Scarlett's voice reflected what all of them felt.

They were about to move on when Homer paused, his head tilted in concentration. Something about the bottom drawer had captured his attention.

"It smells more like Marc's hands than the other drawers. He must have spent a lot of time in it." Homer pawed at the drawer. *"And there's something else here. Something that sounds...hidden."*

Hot Mike used his greater strength to pull the drawer open wider and scanned the contents with his keen eyes. *"Nothing looks unusual."*

"No, there's more," Homer insisted. He reached a paw into the drawer again and gently tapped against the wood. *"The bottom isn't flat—it feels like there's a gap. And it sounds hollow. Can't you hear it?"*

Scarlett joined him, her yellow-green eyes narrowing as she, too, pawed at the inside of the drawer, feeling along its edges. *"He's right. There's something beneath the bottom."*

Hot Mike used his mouth to remove the stack of *Palm* magazines, then stood back as Scarlett and Homer—working together cooperatively for once—patted their paws gently along the bottom of the drawer, jiggling it until Scarlett was finally able to work the top left corner of the bottom free from the drawer's frame. She slipped a single sharp claw beneath the corner and kept working until she was finally able to slide her entire paw beneath it.

After that, Hot Mike was able to pry the false bottom out of the drawer altogether. It lifted away to reveal a hidden compartment, inside which lay a thick file folder with a photograph taped to the front—a picture of Tommy Duvall.

"So Marc was investigating Tommy." Vashti's voice was tinged with disappointment.

Hot Mike carefully lifted the file folder from the bottom drawer and deposited it on the floor. Vashti flipped it open and rifled through the papers on top. There were newspaper clippings, handwritten notes, and magazine articles featuring small, identical photos of Tommy near the top—clearly some of his columns from *Palm.*

"We can't just shove everything back in the desk drawer," Vashti said. *"Rachel needs to know what we found."*

Hot Mike twitched his ears thoughtfully. *"What if we put it all on the coffee table where it's sure to be noticed? I'll leave the back door slightly open. When Natalie walks me in the morning, I'll bring her here."*

"And then Natalie will tell Rachel what she found." Vashti dipped her head once to indicate her approval.

Hot Mike carried everything over to the coffee table, where he and Vashti arranged the complete collection of evidence conspicuously enough that it couldn't be missed—the file folder with Tommy's picture, the Polaroid of Julian with the unknown woman, and Marc's open notebook with its telling impression and mysterious writing that might hold answers the cats couldn't decipher, but that Natalie and Rachel hopefully could.

"We should head back." Scarlett eyed the gradually lightening sky visible through the blinds. *"It would be a disaster if Rachel woke up and found all of us missing."*

They made their way back through the kitchen and out the door, which they left slightly ajar according to their plan. The night air felt cool and refreshing after the stillness of Marc's house, carrying with it the promise of morning. The first birds were beginning to stir, their drowsy chirps punctuating the pre-dawn stillness, but all three cats were too exhausted to be tempted into a hunt as they made their way through the quiet morning streets of Coacoochee. Shop windows along Hibiscus Road reflected the first hints of the coming sunrise, while sprinklers twitched to life on manicured lawns.

As they approached Title Wave Books, Homer reflected on the night's discoveries. The photograph of Julian with the unknown woman, the hidden file about Tommy, the strange scent he'd detected on both Daisy and Marc—pieces of a puzzle that didn't quite fit together yet.

"What do you think it all means?" he asked Vashti, as they slipped through the secret cat door.

"I don't know yet," Vashti admitted. Her voice was troubled. *"But I hope Julian Singer-Adams doesn't come back to the store anytime soon."*

CHAPTER 17

POLICE CHIEF NICK TORRES had just settled at his desk with a fresh cup of Beachy Beans coffee when the phone rang. He checked his watch as he lifted the receiver and sighed. Seven-fifteen on a Wednesday morning. This couldn't possibly be good.

"Nick." Natalie Dunbar's Australian accent was more pronounced than usual, her voice tight with urgency. "Marc Gottsegen is dead. I've just found his body."

Nick's hand stilled over the notepad he'd been reaching for. "Where?"

"His house. Hot Mike was acting strangely on our morning walk—practically dragged me to Marc's place. The back door was ajar." Her voice remained steady, though Nick could hear the subtle tremor underneath. Natalie had seen death before—her work as an investigative journalist had taken her to some dark places—but finding it next door to her quiet home in Coacoochee was different.

"Don't touch anything. I'm on my way." Nick was already on his feet, gesturing to Officer Martinez through his office window. "Is anyone else there?"

"No. Just me and Hot Mike. And...Marc."

"Stay outside. We'll be right there."

Nick ended the call and grabbed his jacket. He stepped out of his office as Jessica Martinez approached, her expression shifting from routine alertness to focused concern.

"Marc Gottsegen's been found dead in his home." Nick headed for the exit. "Natalie Dunbar just called it in."

Martinez followed, her stride matching his as they crossed the bullpen. "Natural causes?"

"Unknown. Let's take your cruiser."

The drive to Marc's house took precisely eleven minutes. Coacoochee's morning streets bustled with early rush-hour traffic, which Jessica navigated with practiced efficiency. Nick used the time to make calls from the car's radio to the Medical Examiner's office and to the crime scene unit.

Natalie was waiting at the curb when they arrived, Hot Mike sitting attentively at her feet. Marc's house sat on a quiet street lined with similar Mediterranean-style homes, all sporting terracotta roofs and stucco exteriors in tropical shades. A royal palm stood sentinel in the front yard, its fronds rustling in the morning breeze.

"He's in the living room," Natalie said by way of greeting. The leash tethering Hot Mike to her wrist suggested she'd been taking him for his morning walk when the discovery was made. "The back door was open when we arrived."

Jessica Martinez squinted into the rising sun as her eyes followed in the direction Natalie was pointing. "Any signs of forced entry?"

Natalie shook her head. "None that I could see."

She led the two officers around the side of the house. As promised, the back door stood slightly open, a sliver of darkness visible through the gap. Nick pulled latex gloves from his pocket and slipped them on with practiced ease. "Wait here," he instructed, and Martinez nodded, positioning herself near Natalie.

The kitchen was sleek and impressive—high-end appliances glittering under recessed lighting, Italian marble countertops bare save for a single mug half-filled with cold tea. A paperback lay splayed open on a custom-built breakfast nook, as if its reader had momentarily stepped away.

Original art adorned the walls of the living room—small but clearly valuable pieces that spoke of particular collecting rather than showy display. A leather sofa was positioned to face the lush, well-tended back yard. Marc lay on the hardwood floor, clearly beyond help. Nick knelt beside the body, his experienced gaze confirming what he'd already suspected—no obvious signs of violence except for the bandaged nose from Monday night's altercation.

Nothing appeared disturbed. No signs of a struggle, no overturned furniture, no forced entry. Nick's gaze caught on three items placed conspicuously on a Noguchi coffee table—a file folder with Tommy Duvall's photo attached to the front, a Polaroid photograph of Julian Singer-Adams with his arm around an attractive young woman, and an open reporter's notebook. Nick leaned closer to examine the notebook page. Someone had written *J S-A and Alicia Rodrigue, Dec. 4, 1993* in black ink beneath a rectangular impression where something had been attached—probably the Polaroid.

He heard Martinez's radio crackle outside, followed by her voice confirming the Medical Examiner was en route. Nick finished his methodical assessment of the living room, noting the normal signs of habitation—magazines stacked on an end table, a remote control balanced on the arm of a recliner. Nothing suggested robbery or violence.

When Dr. Edwidge Michel arrived twenty minutes later, Nick had completed his initial survey of the house. The Medical Examiner moved with quiet efficiency, her white lab coat and meticulous manner lending an air of clinical detachment to the proceedings.

"Morning, Nick." She knelt beside Marc's body. "What do we have?"

"Marc Gottsegen, age thirty-eight. Found by a neighbor about an hour ago. No obvious cause of death."

Dr. Michel nodded, her gloved hands already beginning their examination. "You're thinking it's suspicious?"

"I'm reserving judgment." They both knew that meant yes.

Martinez stepped into the room as Dr. Michel worked, her footsteps soft on the hardwood floor. "Canvassing update, Chief. So far, none of the neighbors heard or saw anything unusual last night. One of them mentioned seeing Marc return home from the hospital around midnight Monday, but nothing after that." Martinez consulted her notes. "Though Mrs. Rubio next door did say she heard Hot Mike get into it with a cat late last night."

Nick nodded, unsurprised. This tranquil, tree-lined street seemed like the type of place where unusual activity would have been noticed—if there'd been any to notice.

"Crime scene unit is here," Martinez added, before heading back outside.

Dr. Michel worked in focused silence, her examination thorough and methodical. After several minutes, she looked up at Nick. "No obvious external trauma beyond the nasal fracture. No defensive wounds. Nothing that immediately suggests foul play."

"But?" Nick prompted, hearing the hesitation in her voice.

"But the coloration isn't quite what I'd expect from a standard cardiac event. And the timing is unusual, considering his ER visit. I'll need to run a preliminary tox screen right away, and then order a complete panel."

Nick nodded. "I want whatever you can get me as quickly as possible."

"You'll have the basic screening this afternoon." Dr. Michel rose from beside the body, peeling off latex gloves and signaling to her assistants who waited in the doorway with a gurney. "The full workup will take a week or two. Though I should warn you, from external appearances, this could pass for natural causes—cardiac arrest following physical and emotional stress."

After Dr. Michel finished her preliminary examination, Nick stepped outside to check on the growing crowd. Martinez had done an admirable job maintaining the perimeter, but curiosity was a powerful force in a small town. When he returned to the house, he found Natalie still waiting by the back door, Hot Mike sitting patiently beside her.

"I know you've already seen enough," Nick said, "but would you mind taking another look at the living room?" Nick led Natalie back through the kitchen, Hot Mike padding alongside them. In the living room, Natalie's gaze was drawn immediately to the coffee table.

"I didn't notice those before." She studied the conspicuously placed items. "I was rather focused on..." She gestured toward where Marc had been lying.

Hot Mike moved directly toward the coffee table, his nose twitching as he examined the file and photograph. Nick couldn't help noting how intently the German Shepherd's attention focused on them.

"A file about Tommy Duvall," Nick said, "a photograph of Julian Singer-Adams with a woman I don't recognize, and one of Marc's notebooks with a name and date written on it—*JS-A and Alicia Rodrigue, Dec. 4, 1993*. Were these part of an investigation Marc was working on?"

Natalie's journalistic instincts had clearly kicked in. "I don't know. Marc wasn't really the investigative type." She paused, considering the name. "Alicia Rodrigue...I don't recognize it, but that date's from five years ago. Before my time in Coacoochee."

"The name sounds vaguely familiar." Nick frowned. "But I can't place it. Might be from another jurisdiction."

Hot Mike remained fixated on the items, his tail still, his entire body radiating the alert attention of a dog who'd found something important.

Nick made a mental note to have the crime scene unit photograph everything meticulously before processing. The deliberate placement bothered him more than he cared to admit.

People who died of natural causes didn't typically arrange evidence files before collapsing.

By late Wednesday afternoon, Nick sat at his desk re-reading Dr. Michel's preliminary report. As he'd expected, she'd listed the cause of death as cardiac arrest, though her notes included several observations that warranted further investigation—unusual coloration of the lips and nail beds, the timing relative to his hospital visit and, most significantly, traces of cocaine in his system from the initial toxicology screening.

The first time he'd gone through the report had been with Dr. Michel in her office, and his exclamation of surprise had interrupted her patient recitation of her initial findings. "Cocaine?" Drug use didn't track with what Nick knew of Marc.

"The levels are consistent with medical use," Dr. Michel had explained. "It's a common topical anesthetic for nasal procedures. With his broken nose, I'm guessing it was administered during his ER treatment. I'm still waiting on the comprehensive tox panel—that'll take another week or two."

But now, re-reading the preliminary report alone in his own office, Nick knew the cocaine finding would overshadow everything else. A wealthy nightlife writer with drugs in his system made for a tidy narrative—one that avoided uncomfortable questions about potential murder.

As if summoned by Nick's thoughts, Commissioner Carpenter appeared in the doorway. "Got a minute, Torres?" He entered Nick's office and settled his considerable bulk into the chair across from Nick's desk, the wooden frame creaking beneath his weight.

"Dr. Michel sent over her report," the Commissioner said. "Natural causes."

"Her findings are consistent with cardiac arrest," Nick acknowledged. "Though she's noted several unusual aspects that require further investigation."

"Always more investigating with you." The Commissioner's tone was almost fondly exasperated. "Look, Torres, the man had cocaine in his system. Combined with the stress of a public fight and an ER visit? Heart attack waiting to happen."

"The cocaine was likely from his medical treatment."

"Perhaps. Or perhaps our nightlife columnist had habits the public wasn't aware of."

"And the file on Tommy Duvall? The photograph of Julian Singer-Adams? Those don't strike you as unusual?"

The Commissioner shrugged. "From what I hear, Gottsegen was hoping to take over Isabella Stuart's gossip column." His expression registered distaste for what he clearly regarded as a disreputable line of journalism. "He was probably assembling files on half the notable people in Coacoochee."

"The items were placed deliberately on the coffee table," Nick said. "As if someone wanted them to be found."

"Torres, I've been patient. You've had your investigation, your autopsy, your canvassing. But the medical report says natural causes, and that's what we're going with."

"Commissioner—"

"Season starts in a month." The Commissioner's voice lowered, though his intensity increased. "We've got hotels at record pre-bookings. The Halloween parade is projected to bring in more tourists than ever. What we don't need is a murder investigation suggesting Coacoochee isn't safe."

Nick knew when to pick his battles. "I'll need to formally close the case file."

"Good. Do that." The Commissioner stood. "And, Nick? No press conferences, no public statements about suspicious circumstances. Far as anyone needs to know, Marc Gottsegen died of natural causes. End of story."

After he left, Nick sat in silence. Just like Daisy Locarro's, the death certificate now awaiting his signature also stated, "Cardiac Arrest—Natural Causes." Nick stared at it for several minutes. Then he picked up his phone and dialed Dr. Michel.

"Edwidge? It's Nick Torres. About Marc Gottsegen's comprehensive tox panel..."

"Still processing," she told him. "I should have results early next week."

Nick hesitated. "Cancel it."

A pause. "Nick?"

"Case is closed. Natural causes. No need for further testing."

Another pause, longer this time. "I see." Dr. Michel's tone was neutral, but Nick could hear her disappointment. "I'll stop the panel."

Nick hung up, feeling like he'd just buried evidence. With a sigh that seemed to come from somewhere deep within, he scrawled his signature onto the certificate, making it official. For the second time in less than two weeks, Nick was closing the file on the sudden death of an otherwise-healthy young person before a proper investigation could even begin.

The phone on his desk rang, interrupting his thoughts.

"Nick? It's Natalie." Her voice carried a note of tentative inquiry. "I just got a call from Marc's mother. She's asked me to pack up his personal effects before the family flies his body back to the Bahamas for burial."

"The scene's been released," Nick confirmed. "You're free to go in."

"That's not why I'm calling." She paused. "I was wondering about those items on the coffee table."

Technically, Nick thought, the file, photo, and notepad were evidence. But they were evidence in an investigation that had been shelved at the direct order of the Commissioner of Police. As far as the City of Coacoochee was concerned, Marc Gottsegen had died of natural causes.

"The ME's initial report indicates cardiac arrest," he said finally. "That's what the death certificate says."

"So the case is closed?"

"Officially, yes." Nick let his emphasis on the first word hang in the air between them.

"I see." The shift in Natalie's tone was subtle—the silent acknowledgment of someone who understood what wasn't being said. "So those items on the coffee table?"

"They belonged to Marc. His mother asked you to handle his personal effects." Nick kept his tone professionally detached. "You should be thorough in fulfilling that responsibility."

"Of course." The relief in Natalie's voice was unmistakable. "Thank you, Nick."

As he hung up the phone, Nick looked out his window at the gathering dusk. The setting sun over Allamanda Avenue had painted the sky in the pink and creamsicle shades of vacation postcards. Coacoochee had never looked more picturesque.

Whatever Marc had discovered, whatever had led to his death, Natalie Dunbar was now on its trail.

And Nick Torres would be watching. Unofficially, of course.

CHAPTER 18

RACHEL SET THE TEAKETTLE onto the kitchen counter and knelt to rub Homer behind the ears. "Take it easy, buddy," she told the startled cat, her voice low and soothing. The sound of a car backfiring outside had made Homer jump three feet in the air—something that hadn't happened since he was a kitten.

Counterintuitive though it seemed, Homer was usually the least likely of Rachel's three cats to be afraid of a loud noise. Scarlett and Vashti would hide deep under the bed the moment the vacuum cleaner made an appearance, whereas Homer had a habit of napping on the rug so deeply while the vacuum ran that Rachel was often forced to vacuum in a circle around him.

This morning, however, Homer was every bit as jumpy as Vashti and Scarlett ever were. More so, actually, because even gentle sounds—like Rachel rifling through her sock drawer, or the puffs of breeze blowing gaily through palm fronds outside—echoed in his preternaturally sharp ears like gunshots.

By now, everyone in Coacoochee knew that Natalie Dunbar—accompanied by the ever-faithful Hot Mike—had found Marc Gottsegen's lifeless body lying on the floor of his own home the previous morning. The three cats, however, were among the very few who also knew that a file folder full of evidence—along with a mysterious photo and some cryptic notes—had been found at the scene as well.

At least, they *thought* somebody must have discovered all the clues they'd painstakingly arranged on Marc's coffee table. But which human had ultimately taken possession of them? Natalie, as intended? Someone else? Had they somehow been overlooked? Not knowing was maddening, and all three cats would gladly have given a week's worth of salmon treats for even the smallest update from their intelligence network.

Samkhat had yet to make an appearance. As for Kotik, he was currently under house arrest; Laurie had called Rachel early Wednesday morning to announce Kotik's return, along with her plan to "keep him close and drown him in cuddles" until he'd learned never to worry her like that again.

"Ugh." Scarlett's face contorted into a grimace of distaste when Homer, who'd been able to overhear Laurie's end of the conversation, repeated this to his sisters. *"All that cooing and baby talk and forced snuggling."* With genuine sympathy, she added, *"Poor Kotik."*

"It doesn't sound so *terrible,"* Homer mused, his voice almost wistful.

The cats had taken it for granted that Natalie and Hot Mike would come by Title Wave in the hours following the discovery of Marc's body—as they did every day, rain or shine. *Then* they would hear, straight from the source, what had happened to the Polaroid they'd recovered at such great peril, along with the mysterious note and the folder bearing Tommy's picture.

More importantly, they might finally learn what it all meant.

But Natalie and Hot Mike had never shown up—although, just around the time last night when all three cats had begun to wonder if exploding from pent-up curiosity was a real thing that could actually happen to a cat, Natalie had called Rachel at home.

"How are you holding up?" Rachel had asked sympathetically.

"It was difficult." Natalie's controlled voice suggested emotions held in check. "That's actually why I'm calling. Could I come by the store tomorrow before you open? It's important."

"Of course." Rachel's response was automatic, and she hadn't asked anything further. She was torn between her natural desire to know right away what was behind Natalie's unusual request, yet also grateful for twelve hours' clemency—because what could Natalie possibly want to discuss so urgently, right on the heels of finding Marc's body, if not for Tommy's real or imagined involvement in Marc's death?

So if the cats were edgy on Thursday morning, Rachel was edgier still. Her hands slipped repeatedly as she applied her eyeliner, until finally she was forced to remove it altogether and start from scratch—unless she wanted to go around looking like Pete the Pup from The Little Rascals. She distractedly turned the stove on and off beneath the teakettle without producing a single cup's worth of hot water.

She was supposed to meet Natalie at ten o'clock, and at ten minutes till she grabbed her keys and hustled the cats toward the stairs. "Come on, guys, let's get the day started," she said with forced cheerfulness. "It won't kill us to be a little early for once." Then she winced at her own choice of words.

The list of things that wouldn't get you killed in Coacoochee was getting shorter by the day.

By the time she'd opened the store the previous morning, word of Marc's death had already spread through town like wildfire. It wasn't until early in the evening that the Coacoochee PD had released a terse state-ment saying Marc had died of natural causes—which meant that rumors and speculation had been given the entire workday in which to flourish unchecked.

It had been one of Rachel's weirder days at Title Wave. Her morning coffee crowd was thicker than usual—something that hadn't struck her as odd at first, until she'd noted the strangely anticipatory atmosphere in the café. People spoke to each other in hushed tones, lingered longer over their empty coffee cups, and turned expectantly each time the door opened.

Then it hit Rachel: Everybody knew Tommy stopped by Title Wave for his morning coffee before heading to his office at *Palm*. It hadn't taken Coacoochee long to connect Marc's sudden death with the dramatic fight he and Tommy Duvall had had at Sabrosa on Monday night. How would Tommy act the next time he appeared in public? Would his face wear a look of guilt? Defiance? Maybe Tommy hadn't even heard the news yet, and they would get to witness his first, unfiltered reaction.

But Tommy seemed to have disappeared into the ether; he didn't show up at Title Wave all day, nor at any of his other usual haunts. Equally missing in action were Isabella and Julian, who were also persons of general public interest—everyone knew they'd been sitting with Marc at his table Monday night, just before Tommy had punched Marc in the face.

This left Rachel—who certainly couldn't hide from the general public while also running Title Wave Books—as the only eyewitness people had access to. She'd tried to distract herself with phone calls to potential vendors for the Halloween event, asking for price quotes, but even that simple task was interrupted every few minutes by another "casual" visitor.

Every now and then, somebody would come into the store who Rachel recognized from the pages of *People* or *Vogue*. More frequent, however, were what she thought of as "local celebrities"—people like Tommy who knew everybody in Coacoochee, and who everybody in Coacoochee knew. They were club promoters, underground artists, non-famous models, or simply colorful personalities who were high-profile around town. They went out five or six nights a week and never paid for a single cocktail, cover charge, or the bottle-service champagne delivered to their perpetually reserved VIP tables. Their photos graced the pages of *Ocean Drive*, the *Sentinel*, the *Herald*, the *Sun Times*, and—most prestigiously—Isabella's erstwhile column in the *Daily News*. A lucky few would rise through the ranks, the way Isabella had, to become a bona fide bold-faced name—someone who was written about in *Page Six* and photographed at galas for *Vanity Fair*. This was the lure that had underlain the fierce rivalry between Marc Gottsegen and Tommy Duvall.

The steady trickle of local celebrities into Title Wave the day Marc's body was found was larger enough than usual to be conspicuous. They'd browse Staff Picks or the Paperback Bestsellers table with elaborate casualness, then make their way over to the café for a cup of coffee and an attempt to pry information out of Rachel—some insider-y tidbit they could carry back to their friends and frenemies. With varying degrees of subtlety, they let her know that invitations to certain A-list gatherings and VIP rooms would be forthcoming. And not just as Tommy Duvall's plus-one, but in her own right.

"*Vultures*," Scarlett decreed. With an inward sigh, she realized that the task of giving these humans a much-needed lesson in manners fell to her—although, in truth, she did seem to have a talent for the work. She would leap onto the counter and sit right in front of her tutee, fixing them with a disdainful stare. Then, after looking them slowly up and down, Scarlett would stand, very deliberately turn her back, and stalk away with a single, disapproving flick of her expressive tail.

"Did you *see* that?!" a shiny-haired woman who worked the velvet rope at Groove Jet exclaimed. "That cat just snubbed me!"

"Don't take it too personally." Rachel's tone was sympathetic, but the corners of her lips twitched with amusement. "Scarlett is *very* exclusive."

She had to give credit to Sabine Ackermann of ModelHaus Miami, who took the unusual step of trying to get to Rachel through Vashti. "Such a stunning creature," she pronounced in her heavily accented voice, as Rachel rang up her copy of *The Givenchy Style*—which, at seventy-five dollars, was currently the most expensive book Title Wave had in stock. "That bone structure, and that beautiful coat."

Vashti, who had been listening raptly, leapt down from her favorite armchair in Caribbean Travel and crossed the floor of the bookshop with studied grace. She appeared nonchalant as she circled slowly past the register, pausing to arch her back in a way she knew would accentuate the perfection of her form.

"And look how elegantly she carries herself!" Sabine exclaimed. "She was born for the camera."

"*Rachel should make Sabine stop,*" Vashti protested with a modest, downward glance. "*Her praise is far too generous.*" She then swished her extravagant tail a few times, so her viewers could appreciate its full alabaster glory.

Scarlett, whose eyes were beginning to tire from all the times she'd rolled them over the course of the day, nevertheless managed to produce one more Olympic-caliber eyeroll.

"If you ever consider hiring her out for a photo shoot," Sabine continued, her own eyes still on Vashti, "I would be interested in talking to you."

It was impossible to keep Rachel's heart from melting when somebody praised one of her cats. And it had been, in its way, a particularly lonely day for her. She was feeling just as pent-up as the cats were, and growing rather desperate to talk to someone—anyone—about the doubts and anxieties swirling in her head.

Nevertheless, when the conversation had inevitably turned to Tommy and Marc, Rachel gave Sabine the same reply she'd given everybody else that day.

"Sorry." Whatever Tommy might or might not have done, he deserved better from her than being used as gossip fodder. "I don't know anything more than you do."

NATALIE WAS STANDING IN front of Title Wave the following morning at ten a.m. on the nose. As Rachel unbolted the door to let her and Hot Mike in—re-locking it behind them and checking that the *Closed* sign still faced Hibiscus Road—the thick folder Natalie carried told her that, if nothing else, she was about to receive some fresh intelligence.

"Good morning." Rachel embraced her friend. "I made coffee."

"Perfect." Natalie's smile took some effort, but was grateful nonetheless. "I didn't sleep a wink last night."

They seated themselves at one of the café tables, Hot Mike lying near Natalie's feet. The familiar morning ritual provided a momentary buffer against whatever serious conversation lay ahead. Rachel poured coffee, adding cream for Natalie, then prepared tea for herself in the other. The cats positioned themselves strategically around the café. Vashti settled on a nearby chair where she could observe the proceedings, and Scarlett arranged herself regally atop the Local Authors display. They both observed with satisfaction as Homer claimed Rachel's lap; it was as good as planting a microphone at the table.

Natalie set the manila folder facedown, her hands lingering on its edges. Rachel caught a quick glimpse of what appeared to be a photograph clipped to the front of it, although she couldn't make it out.

"Marc's mother called from the Bahamas yesterday," Natalie began. "She asked me to go through his things before they ship his body home for burial."

Rachel's face reflected her empathy. It made sense for Marc's mother to ask this of his closest neighbor, but it still must have been a difficult task.

"When I found Marc yesterday morning," Natalie continued, "these were on his coffee table." She turned the manila folder in front of her faceup, and Rachel was now able to see Tommy's familiar smile beaming up at her from the photo clipped to the front of it. From the folder, Natalie withdrew two additional items: a Polaroid showing Julian Singer-Adams with his arm around an attractive young woman, and a reporter's notebook opened to a page bearing Marc's handwriting.

Rachel leaned forward, studying the materials spread before her. Something in the Polaroid—something other than Julian's familiar face—tugged at the edges of her memory. "What was Marc investigating?"

"Tommy's blind items," Natalie said.

Rachel's brow furrowed. "I'm not sure I know what a 'blind item' is."

"They're little stories about unnamed celebrities or public figures," Natalie explained. "*Which action star was seen out on the town last night with a woman who definitely wasn't his wife?* That sort of thing. The readers are supposed to guess who it's about, but the columnist doesn't name names directly. Tommy's written maybe ten or fifteen blind items during his time at *Palm*—and according to this file, Marc was working his way through all of them, trying to verify them."

Once again, Rachel's forehead creased. "But why? What was the purpose?"

"I think Marc was trying to prove Tommy was sloppy with his reporting—maybe even making things up."

A spark of understanding flared in Rachel's mind. "That's what Marc meant when he called Tommy a hack," she said slowly, her voice growing more certain as the memory crystallized. "He said Tommy was the kind of 'journalist' who prints whatever story gets handed to him, whether it's true or not."

Natalie nodded as another piece of the puzzle slid into place.

Rachel stared at the file, her mind working to process the implications. Professional rivalry was one thing, but this suggested something far more serious—a systematic investigation that could destroy Tommy's career, his reputation, everything he'd worked for since arriving in Coacoochee.

As if reading her thoughts, Natalie continued, "Marc probably started out hoping to embarrass Tommy, maybe even discredit him badly enough that *Palm* would fire him and give Marc an opening. But he'd been able to verify all of Tommy's blind items—until he got to the very first one Tommy ever published. It was a big story for Tommy," Natalie added. "Before this, he was one of a rotating team of junior writers who covered nightlife for *Palm*. After this blind item came out, Tommy became *Palm*'s fulltime nightlife and gossip reporter."

Natalie pulled out a photocopy of a column from *Palm* magazine, dated five years earlier:

> *Which Mercury Island mogul's "models and bottles" weekend went off the rails (the powdered kind, that is) when a beautiful "party girl" went from dancing on tables at two a.m. to borderline comatose by dawn? Instead of calling 911, we hear our panicked magnate spent hours on the phone with his lawyers and publicist—everybody, it seems, except a doctor or the girl's family. Whispers from the cabana suggest the party favors on offer weren't exactly FDA-approved. Even more interesting? The guest list from that weekend has mysteriously vanished—although our host has been throwing money around like confetti ever since, suddenly making surprise (and surprisingly generous) donations to some of his friends' favorite causes. Guilty conscience much?*

"So Marc expected to find this was fabricated," Rachel said. "Tommy's first big story, and it would turn out to be fake."

"That's what I thought initially," Natalie said. "But this blind item appeared in *Palm* magazine under Tommy's byline on Friday, December 10th, 1993. Now look at this." She turned the notebook to show Marc's handwriting: *J S-A and Alicia Rodrigue, Dec. 4, 1993.* "I believe this Polaroid was taken on that date—six days before Tommy's story ran. If that's accurate, then there really was a party that weekend. Maybe this is the girl the blind item refers to, and maybe Julian was at the party with her."

"So Tommy's story was true after all?" Rachel felt a small surge of relief. "Then why was Marc so interested in investigating it?"

"If something scandalous really did happen five years ago—and if Marc had been able to tie that scandal to Julian Singer-Adams—that's not a column in *Palm*. That's the front page of the *Daily News*. That's CNN. That's a whole different league than Tommy's playing in."

Rachel couldn't help thinking how much Tommy would have hated having indirectly helped Marc attain that level of professional success. The conversation she'd had with Marc at Beachy Beans suddenly made more sense.

Natalie's expression grew more serious. "Rachel, you mentioned at brunch that Tommy's been acting strangely since Daisy died—distracted, elusive, behaving oddly at the memorial service..."

The observation forced Rachel to examine her own words more carefully. Tommy's increasing anxiety, his evasiveness when she'd tried to reach him, his uncharacteristic violence at Sabrosa. She felt a small, cold weight settle in her stomach.

"You think Tommy killed Marc to stop the investigation."

"I think," Natalie said, "that we need to consider all possibilities. Tommy had reason to think Marc was trying to destroy his professional reputation. He had public conflicts with both Daisy and Marc shortly before they died, and both of them died under suspicious circumstances. And neither of us knows where Tommy was in the hours leading up to either of their deaths."

The logical progression was undeniable, but it still felt wrong. No matter how convincing the circumstantial evidence might appear, in her heart Rachel couldn't believe Tommy was a killer.

The three cats, in the meantime, were silently connecting dots on their own. The argument Vashti had overheard between Tommy and Daisy at the book signing now made sense—Daisy must have carelessly let slip to Marc that one of Tommy's blind items was made up. The only way Daisy could know that for certain was if she was the one who had made it up and sold it to Tommy as a true story. The fight between Daisy and Marc that Samkhat overheard must have been Marc pressing Daisy for more details.

That would give Tommy an excellent reason to be angry with Daisy and Marc both. Maybe even angry enough to kill—although the steely look in Vashti's eyes proclaimed she still didn't believe Tommy had murdered anybody.

Besides—the photograph of Julian from only a few days before the blind item was published suggested the party actually did happen. So why would Tommy be mad at Daisy for selling him a true story?

"I wish we could tell Rachel and Natalie everything we know," Homer fretted.

Rachel reached one hand down and reassuringly stroked the top of Homer's head. With the other she picked up the Polaroid, studying Julian's confident smile and the attractive young woman beside him. She looked to be in her early twenties, with long dark hair and bright eyes full of life. "Who is Alicia Rodrigue? What happened to her?"

"I don't know yet," Natalie admitted. "The question is—was she the person who needed medical attention at the party in the blind item? And if so, how serious was it? Did she recover, or..." Natalie's voice trailed off.

"But wait a minute." The story Natalie had been weaving was so compelling, so disturbing in its implications, that Rachel had gotten caught up. "You're talking about all this like it's a murder investigation. The police specifically said Marc and Daisy both died from natural causes."

"That's true. The case has officially been closed." Natalie paused. "But when Marc's mother asked me to go through his effects, Nick Torres encouraged me to be thorough in fulfilling that responsibility."

Rachel's eyes sharpened. "You're saying the Chief of Police has doubts?"

Natalie chose her words with care. "My guess is that the powers that be don't like the idea of an open murder investigation this close to the start of Season. Coacoochee might seem less appealing to tourists if suddenly there's a killer on the loose."

Rachel nodded absently, lost in thought. "There could be other explanations," she finally said. "Besides Tommy, I mean. If Tommy's blind item was true, and if it was about Julian, then Julian would have just as much reason to want Marc silenced. More, even. He has way more to lose than Tommy does."

"That's certainly possible," Natalie agreed. "But, Rachel, if I'm going to investigate this properly—if I'm going to find out what really happened to Marc and Daisy—I need your help."

Homer felt Rachel's muscles tense. She already knew what Natalie was going to say.

"If anyone can get honest answers from Tommy, it's you." Natalie paused, her expression softening with sympathy. "I know it's not fair to ask you to question someone you care about. But if Tommy is innocent, talking to you might be his best chance to clear his name."

Rachel stared at the evidence spread across the table. Morning sunlight streamed through the tall windows, dancing across the swept-clean terrazzo and outlining her head in a fiery gold halo. The familiar comfort of her bookstore surrounded her—the scent of coffee and paper, the colorful shelves of neatly arranged books, the distant sound of the ocean. It all felt so normal, so safe, that the conversation they were having seemed surreal.

"When should I talk to Tommy?" Rachel asked quietly.

"Soon." Natalie's voice was steady. "Before he realizes we have Marc's files. Before he has time to prepare explanations."

Homer rose in Rachel's lap and turned to press the warmth of his face against her chest. He was pleased at the way the comforting gesture slowed the rapid pace of her heart just a bit.

"We'll figure this out." Natalie tried to sound reassuring. "Whatever the truth is, we'll find it."

Outside, Hibiscus Road was waking up. Tourists lined up patiently at Café Rhapsody, which offered a champagne brunch on its lushly landscaped patio every day of the week. Florists delivered fresh bouquets to art galleries and boutiques. Street sweepers cleared the detritus of last night's bar-hopping from the bright pavement. The blue sky above was clear and cloudless, aside from a few cottony white puffballs.

It would be another splendid day in Coacoochee.

Natalie gathered the evidence back into the manila folder and rose to leave. Rachel saw her and Hot Mike to the door, and was just about to close it behind them when Natalie abruptly turned to face her again.

"Rachel?" She paused, clearly struggling with her next words. "I think you should meet Tommy somewhere public," she finally said. "A restaurant, maybe, or a coffee shop with lots of people around."

Rachel opened her mouth as if to speak, but no words came out. She nodded instead, then watched as Natalie and Hot Mike walked down Hibiscus Road before they turned a corner and disappeared from view.

Rachel pulled Title Wave's door shut firmly and turned the bolt to lock it. The shop wouldn't open officially for another half-hour. She wanted to make sure no unexpected visitors came in before then to surprise her.

CHAPTER 19

Isabella Stuart sat at a corner table on the waterfront terrace of Azul, watching pelicans fold their wings and plunge into the marina's sun-dappled water with the precision of silver arrows. The late-afternoon light cast everything in shades of honey and turquoise, while a warm breeze carried the mingled perfume of salt air and grilling seafood from the restaurant's kitchen.

At three-thirty, the place was nearly empty—too late for the lunch crowd, too early for Friday happy hour. Perfect for a conversation that needed privacy without appearing clandestine. Isabella wasn't hiding out, exactly, but this week she'd been even more selective than usual with her daytime appearances, turning down lunch with Dahlia Delgado on Wednesday and an afternoon at White Spa with Alessandra Vicente on Thursday. Marc's death wasn't about *her*, of course, but she and Julian had been at his table, in full view of Sabrosa's packed dining room, just before Tommy Duvall had punched him—which was the last time anyone had publicly seen Marc alive.

Isabella prided herself on being a shrewd crafter of public reputations. But even she had been unprepared for the one-two wallop of having her hand-picked successor violently assault a rival in the middle of Coacoochee's hottest restaurant, and then having that rival turn up dead two days later.

The only reason she'd been at Sabrosa on a Monday night was because everybody knew Marc always ate there on Mondays. When Julian had called her first thing Monday morning, he'd let her know—in his maddeningly vague way—that Marc was on the verge of unleashing a crisis, and that no time could be lost in trying to prevent it.

"Marc Gottsegen's been digging around in my closet for skeletons," Julian said. His voice had been as smooth as it ever was, but Isabella had detected a tightness beneath the surface. Something from years ago, Julian had claimed. Ancient history that could be misconstrued. Nothing illegal, nothing that would hold up to real scrutiny, but damaging enough in the wrong hands.

Isabella had learned that what Julian didn't say often mattered more than what he did—and his omissions on this call had been glaring.

Monday night at Sabrosa had been a calculated gamble. She'd come prepared to offer Marc something irresistible: an exclusive interview with an Oscar-winning, A-list movie star, for whose upcoming film—shot in and around Coacoochee—she was handling local publicity. The star was notoriously reclusive, granting no more than one or two interview requests in any given year, and an exclusive for *Palm* magazine would have been Marc's ticket out of local nightlife coverage and into legitimate entertainment journalism—exactly the kind of career-making opportunity that should make an ambitious writer forget about investigative hit pieces. Isabella had additionally made it clear that the offer was specific to *Palm*—that it wouldn't transfer if Marc were to find himself, for example, writing for the *Daily News* instead.

Technically, she hadn't secured the interview yet; time had been too short to approach the movie star's publicity team before meeting Marc, and doing so would require a significant investment of personal capital. She shuddered to think what kind of favor she might be called upon to grant by the movie star's publicist somewhere down the line. Nevertheless, that hint of tightness in Julian's voice—Julian who usually moved through Coacoochee like a great white shark, barely noticing the smaller fish swimming around him—persuaded her that now was the time to ante up.

Just another day as her own boss, she thought wryly. Making promises she wasn't sure she could keep in order to protect a client who wouldn't tell her what she was protecting him from in the first place.

If she did manage to pull this off, though, she'd be killing two birds with one stone: the hit piece on Julian would be buried, and Tommy would once again have a clear and uncontested path to the *Daily News* position she still intended to place him in. Marc's newfound determination to secure a high-profile byline of his own was all well and good, but Isabella had spent years burnishing her reputation as a king-maker. She wasn't about to let Marc Gottsegen mar her unblemished record.

This, of course, had been before Tommy had punched Marc in full view of half of Coacoochee. (Having her protégé turn violent didn't exactly make Isabella look like a canny power player.) According to the rumor mill, Marc had filed a police report about the incident. She'd heard that a uniformed officer had followed Tommy to Title Wave and accosted him there, throwing him against the café counter and all but reading him his Miranda rights. While she'd acknowledged that some of this had undoubtedly been exaggerated in the retelling, Isabella had nevertheless braced herself for a messy public trial, tabloid coverage, the slow-motion destruction of Tommy's career and maybe even her own.

She had to admit it, if only privately: Marc's death was a relief.

The thought still made her feel guilty, but there was no denying the practical benefits. No trial, no hit piece exposing whatever Julian was hiding, no challenge to Tommy's ascension to the *Daily News*. She'd never have to call the movie star's publicist with the kind of request she most loathed making—one she wasn't already sure would be granted the moment she asked for it.

At first she'd been concerned about the potential impact of the fight and its aftermath on Sabrosa—the scene of the crime. But Danny Elliott continued to be a bright spot in her portfolio (despite having paid his first month's fee late, and already hinting about delays with the second). Isabella had stopped by Sabrosa the previous evening and found the restaurant packed beyond capacity, clearly exerting some kind of morbid fascination as the place where Marc had so conspicuously spent his final public hours. Danny had worked the dining room with characteristic charm, mentioning the upcoming Halloween event with Rachel Baum and seeming genuinely excited about the project.

Isabella was glad she'd facilitated that collaboration before all this unpleasant business with Marc began. While the Coacoochee PD's determination that Marc died of natural causes had quieted much of the speculation around Tommy, it was wise for Rachel to have social connections beyond her friendship with "Mr. Nightlife." Danny's star was rising rapidly, and Rachel seemed like exactly the kind of grounded, intelligent woman who could keep him focused.

Now all Isabella needed was someone similar who could take Tommy in hand and get him back on track. She'd called him twice—twice!—since Marc's death, leaving messages on his voicemail, without hearing back. Isabella literally could not remember the last time a phone call from her hadn't been promptly returned. Tommy's silence was infuriating—not to mention foolish. He should be managing his public image, crafting a response that showed appropriate remorse while defending his character. Instead, he was hiding like a guilty man, which only fueled more speculation.

The sound of Italian leather on porcelain tile pulled her from her thoughts as Julian Singer-Adams approached with a stride that was measured and confident. His silver hair was perfectly styled, his linen blazer crisp despite the humidity. They exchanged a quick kiss on the cheek in greeting, and Julian said, "Thanks for making time on such short notice."

Julian had called that morning, suggesting they meet to "touch base on the waterfront project." His tone—lighter than she'd heard in weeks—had piqued her curiosity. They'd already covered most of the waterfront details in their previous meetings, but she'd agreed immediately, hoping this might finally be her chance to learn what Marc had actually been investigating. Forewarned was forearmed, after all—and just because Marc would soon be buried didn't mean Julian's secrets would be buried with him.

"Of course." She studied his face as he spoke, noting the transformation. His color was better—the gray pallor that had worried her replaced by his usual healthy tan. The lines around his eyes remained, but the brittle quality was gone. "You look well, Julian. Much more like yourself."

"I feel much more like myself." His drink arrived, and he lifted it in acknowledgment to the server before taking an appreciative sip. "I was letting work pile up more than I realized. Sometimes you have to step back and refocus."

For the next twenty minutes, they discussed the waterfront development and the Hibiscus Road multiplex. Isabella, however, found herself increasingly puzzled by the meeting's purpose. They were rehashing details they'd already covered in previous conversations—marketing timelines she'd already finalized, promotional strategies they'd already approved. Their business could have been handled with a brief phone call—if it had needed to be handled at all.

"The press materials look excellent," Julian said, reviewing mock-ups they'd discussed two weeks earlier. "I particularly like the emphasis on Coacoochee as a lifestyle destination."

"Thank you." Isabella waited for him to elaborate, to reveal some new concern or direction that had prompted today's meeting. Instead, Julian simply nodded approvingly and moved on to equally familiar territory about media placement strategies.

She'd hoped this might be her opportunity for some diplomatic probing about Marc's investigation. But whenever she attempted to steer the conversation toward more personal territory, Julian smoothly deflected with renewed focus on business matters. It became clear he had no intention of enlightening her about what Marc had been investigating, which only deepened her curiosity about why he'd arranged this meeting.

"I've been worried about Tommy, with everything that's happened this week," she finally said. Business talk had wound down, and Isabella was trying a subtler approach; perhaps if she could get Julian talking about the events of Monday night, he'd let something slip about what had brought the two of them to Sabrosa to begin with. "People are still talking, despite the medical examiner's ruling. He won't return my calls."

"Understandable, given the circumstances." Julian's expression was sympathetic. "These situations can be overwhelming for everyone involved."

"I keep hoping the speculation will die down naturally, but you know how this town loves its gossip."

"I suspect it will settle, particularly as more context emerges." Julian swirled his scotch thoughtfully. "I was golfing with Commissioner Carpenter yesterday. He mentioned the ME found cocaine in Marc's system." The look Julian gave Isabella was heavy with meaning, managing to convey that Marc's drug use had been neither light nor infrequent.

Isabella didn't bother trying to cover her own expression of shocked disbelief. This didn't track at all with what she'd thought she'd known about Marc—although, if Julian had heard it directly from the Commissioner, it must be true. Still, she couldn't stop herself from asking, "Cocaine? Are you sure?"

"Apparently so." Julian shook his head. "Such a tragedy when someone so young is struggling with those kinds of problems."

The implications had already begun to unfold in Isabella's mind: This was a piece of information that completely reframed the narrative around Marc's confrontation with Tommy. Marc had probably said something cruel and intolerable, provoking Tommy beyond endurance, because that was what addicts did. Like just about everybody in Coacoochee, Isabella had seen the casualties firsthand—people who'd imploded after too many nights on the scene and then viciously blamed everyone around them for their own mistakes and rapid downfalls.

With a dawning realization, Isabella saw that this was the real reason Julian had invited her to meet him today. Julian also benefitted from this new revelation about Marc. Whatever suspicions Marc had been harboring about Julian, whatever wild claims he'd been preparing to make—even if they still came out—could now be dismissed as the typically paranoid delusions of a habitual cocaine user.

Julian had just given her an insurance policy, Isabella saw with uncomfortable clarity. He had no intention of ever telling her what Marc had been digging into. But he'd handed her a weapon to pre-emptively neutralize those claims before they could even surface. All she had to do was ensure that the tidbit of innuendo he'd picked up from the Commissioner found its way into the court of public opinion.

Isabella felt a little queasy. It seemed wrong to use Marc's personal struggles to discredit his work posthumously. But she couldn't deny how neatly this information resolved multiple problems. Julian was off the hook—and as for Tommy, people would understand how someone in Marc's condition might have been more confrontational than usual. Her faith in Tommy as her chosen successor would be vindicated.

And she and Tommy and Julian were still alive, Isabella reasoned; Marc's reputation could hardly matter to him now.

"That certainly provides context for what happened at Sabrosa," she said thoughtfully. She wondered idly whether the Commissioner had sought out Julian, or whether Julian had sought out the Commissioner.

"I thought you should know." Julian finished his scotch, his tone appropriately somber. "You should let Tommy know, too," he added, in an offhand way that confirmed her hunch.

They concluded their meeting with Julian mentioning plans for a trip he planned to take soon—a visit to a vacation home he was thinking of buying in Sardinia. Isabella nodded and smiled, her thoughts elsewhere. As she waited for the valet, she reflected on the strange ways truth sometimes emerged. She'd begun this week managing multiple crises without really knowing what they were about, and she was ending it with a new bit of information that changed everything. Now it was just a question of how to get that information into the appropriate hands.

Up until two weeks ago, Isabella had written the most widely read gossip column in all of South Florida. She was a publicist now instead of a gossip writer, but ultimately that was a distinction without difference. She was still and always the Queen of the Scene. There were at least half a dozen high-profile reporters who would instantly pick this story up the moment she handed it to them, simply because it came from her.

True, some of them might find the sourcing a bit dicey. It wasn't like she'd been the one to speak directly with the Commissioner to get the information firsthand. But that was only a minor snag. She was sure she could get someone to run it as a blind item.

Everyone in Coacoochee would know exactly who was being described.

CHAPTER 20

Rachel's heart pounded as she knocked on the door to Tommy's apartment, situated in a renovated, pastel-yellow Art Deco building down at the quieter end of Jacaranda Drive. She shifted the bakery bag to her other hand, wiping her palm on her jeans. Was this a mistake? Should she have listened to Natalie about meeting Tommy somewhere public? What would happen to her cats if she never came home?

This last thought sent a dart through Rachel's belly, and she paused before knocking again.

For the second Sunday in a row, Rachel was up and out the door before nine a.m. She hadn't been able to reach Tommy since her meeting with

Natalie on Thursday, and had decided the only way to get answers from him once and for all was to ambush him at home. She'd spoken with Natalie again yesterday afternoon, a conversation that had only reinforced her determination. They had arranged to meet at Title Wave for Story Time that afternoon to compare notes.

The weight of Natalie's discoveries—and what they might mean for Tommy—had kept Rachel awake most of the night. Part of her dreaded this conversation, fearing what she might learn. But a larger part needed to know the truth, however painful it might be.

The door swung open to reveal a tousle-haired Tommy in a silk bathrobe. "Caffeine and carbs," Rachel announced brightly as she held up the paper bag and a coffee cup, each of which bore a Butterflake Bakery logo. "The universal cure for what ails you."

Tommy's face shifted from surprise to something like resignation as he stepped aside to let her in. "Fair warning, the place is a disaster."

Tommy's apartment was stylishly furnished with vintage pieces that somehow worked together despite their disparate origins, colorful art on the walls, and a collection of quirky cocktail shakers displayed on open shelving. It was a space that reflected its owner—lively, eclectic, and meticulously curated to appear effortlessly chic.

But Rachel also noticed signs that the chaotic week had taken its toll: unopened mail piled on the side table, two empty vodka bottles that hadn't yet made it into the trash, and the general air of neglect that came of hiding out from the world.

They settled at his small dining table while Tommy investigated the bakery bag. Rachel noted a few lingering scabs and bruises on the knuckles of his right hand.

"Blueberry scones." The corners of Tommy's mouth lifted. "You know my weakness." He pulled a packet of sugar from the Butterflake Bakery bag and stirred it into his coffee. "So how are things at the store? Getting ready for the big Halloween event?"

"It's really coming together." Rachel noted that Tommy's hands were shaking. When had she ever seen his hands shake? "I finally got the palm cards back from the printer, and Danny's supposed to come by to go over the menu once his schedule clears up."

"Good, good." Tommy's voice didn't reflect the enthusiasm of his words as he said, "I can't wait to see what the two of you come up with."

The small talk stalled into an awkward silence. Rachel's heart was hammering so hard she was sure Tommy could hear it. She took a deep breath, gathering her courage.

"Tommy, I have to ask you something," she said, "and I need you to be completely honest with me."

Tommy's hand stilled, a scone suspended in mid-air. "That sounds ominous."

"It's about your first blind item." Rachel watched his face. "The one from five years ago about a multi-millionaire and a wild party."

He set down the scone with a light laugh. "Ancient history, darling. Why the sudden interest?"

"Marc was investigating it," Rachel continued, refusing to let him deflect. "He'd put together a whole file about it."

"How could you possibly know that?" Tommy's voice was suddenly sharp, the false cheer on his face replaced by something like suspicion.

Rachel and Tommy had never had a fight, and Rachel wouldn't allow herself to be goaded into one now by seeming defensive. "Natalie found it when she discovered his body. He suspected the story was fabricated, and that Daisy was your source."

Tommy pushed back from the table and stood, moving to the kitchen counter. "You drink tea, right?" His back was to her as he began opening kitchen cabinets. "I don't usually have any, but I could swear somebody from Azul sent me a gift basket a couple of weeks ago."

"Tommy."

"I should really check my messages." He remained at the counter, opening and closing kitchen drawers. "Isabella's been calling nonstop. And lord knows how many other calls I've missed."

"Tommy, please." Rachel's voice was kind but firm. "Did Daisy make up the story?"

Tommy stood perfectly still, frozen at the counter. The only sound was the distant cry of a seagull and the hum of the refrigerator. Rachel counted her own heartbeats—five, ten, fifteen—before Tommy turned around.

"Yes," he said quietly. "Yes, she made it up."

Rachel waited, giving Tommy space to continue. His gaze drifted to the window, to the floor, to the vintage cocktail shakers on the shelf. He rubbed the back of his neck with one hand. Finally, with a heavy sigh, he returned to the table and sank into his chair.

"It was five years ago," Tommy began. He spoke slowly at first, drawing out each word, as if hoping that something or someone would stop him before he had to say anything more. "I'd just moved to Coacoochee, trying to break into the local scene. I was nobody—just another wannabe lifestyle writer pitching stories that kept getting rejected. I was doing some work for *Palm*, but I was one of a half-dozen stringers they had covering nightlife. None of us even got a byline."

He paused and took a deep gulp of his coffee. "Daisy was one of the first friends I made here. She was working as Julian Singer-Adams' personal assistant, which gave her access to all kinds of events and people I couldn't reach. But she was broke all the time. Like, *all* the time." He laughed mirthlessly. "You think she was short on cash when you knew her, but back then she never had two nickels to rub together."

"She sold you information," Rachel guessed.

Tommy nodded. "She'd tell me who was dating who, which clubs were about to close, which restaurants celebrities were frequenting—little tidbits I could use in my freelance pieces. I paid her for good tips."

"And the blind item?"

"One night she called me. Said she had something big—a wild private party on Mercury Island and some girl who'd partied a little too hard. She wouldn't give names, but the details were juicy enough that I thought it might finally get me noticed. I wrote it up as a blind item and sold it to *Palm*. And it just kind of exploded—everyone was talking, speculating about who it might be. Within a week, I had a regular column."

"But it wasn't true," Rachel said gently.

"I started to have doubts," Tommy admitted. "The fact that there was nobody to corroborate the story because the guest list had mysteriously 'disappeared' was a red flag. I made up my mind to confront Daisy about it a million times, but..." He looked away. "But time passed, and I just...never did."

"And then Marc started digging."

"He said something at Danny Elliott's book signing that made me think he might be looking into it, crazy as it seemed after all this time." Tommy's expression darkened. "When I asked Daisy later, she confirmed it."

"Is that what you two were arguing about?"

Tommy nodded. "She was worried she'd said too much to Marc. I was angry that she might have jeopardized everything I'd worked for."

"But you didn't—" Rachel hesitated, unsure how to phrase the terrible question circling her mind.

"Kill her?" Tommy finished for her, his voice hollow. "No, Rachel. I was furious, but I could never kill anybody. Not even Marc, despite what happened at Sabrosa."

Rachel wanted to believe him—desperately wanted to—but doubt crept in. "The timing is so suspicious. First Daisy dies, then Marc, both of them just as he's investigating a story that could ruin your career."

"Don't you think I know how it looks?" The words burst from Tommy, edged with frustration.

Rachel studied his face, which looked exactly like that of an innocent man sincerely tired of being unfairly suspected. If Tommy was acting, he was doing a better job of it than she would have expected. "Where did you go that night, anyway? After the book signing?"

"Tobacco Road." Located over the causeway in downtown Miami, Tobacco Road was a well-known dive bar touted as Miami's oldest. Tommy would have been unlikely to encounter anybody from the Coacoochee party crowd there on a Friday night. "I didn't feel like going home to an empty apartment. I flirted pretty heavily with a couple of bartenders," Tommy added, the ghost of an impish smile flitting across his face. "I think they'd remember me."

Rachel felt herself relenting as she mentally struck Tommy's lack of an alibi from the checklist of things that had made him look suspicious. And although he'd clearly gone to great lengths to avoid having this particular conversation with anyone, he did seem relieved to finally be having it now, with her.

"What about Julian?" Rachel asked. "Could he be involved in this somehow?"

Tommy frowned. "Julian? Why would he care about an old blind item?"

"Natalie found a photo in Marc's files. It's of Julian at a party with a girl who looks to be in her early twenties. Marc had dated it to the weekend before your blind item was published. Natalie thinks it might have described a real party, and that Julian was there."

The furrow in Tommy's brow deepened. "But Daisy basically admitted she made it up. And she was always so careful back then not to bite the hand that fed her."

"What do you mean?"

"She'd gossip about everyone else—people she knew around town, guests at Julian's parties. But never Julian himself." Tommy shrugged. "It made sense at the time. I figured she didn't want to trash talk the person signing her paychecks."

The phone rang, shrill in the quiet apartment. "I bet that's Isabella again. She's been trying to reach me all weekend." There was a note of defiance in Tommy's voice. "She probably just wants to tell me the police said Marc died from natural causes—like everybody's not still whispering behind my back."

"Come by the store later," Rachel said impulsively. "Story Time's always fun, and you can help me hand out cookies. It'll be the perfect pick-me-up." She stood and gathered her purse. "Natalie will be there, too," she added. "She's been following up on Marc's investigation. We're hoping to get a few minutes with Nick Torres during Story Time."

Tommy's face paled. "Wait—Natalie's still investigating? But I thought the police said Marc died from natural causes."

"Natalie thinks someone killed Marc, and Daisy too. She thinks the blind item connects them both."

Tommy's voice rose. "Rachel, if she tells people that story was a fake, it won't matter that I didn't kill anyone. My career will still be over."

"But I told you—what you wrote might actually have been true."

Tommy was silent for a long moment, trying to reconcile this new information with what he'd believed for five years. Then he said, "If there really was a party, and something really did happen to that girl..."

"Then somebody might be killing to keep it quiet," Rachel finished.

"Be careful, Rachel." The concern in Tommy's voice was unmistakable. "If someone's killing people to keep secrets buried, asking questions could put you in danger, too."

Once again, Rachel had a vision of her three cats alone in the world. A shiver ran through her despite the warmth of Tommy's apartment.

"I'm serious." Tommy's voice cracked. "If anything happened to you because of something stupid I did five years ago—"

"You don't need to worry about me. My only part in the 'investigation,'" Rachel's hands made quote marks in the air, "has been talking to you. Aside from that, I'm basically just offering Natalie moral support while she does her thing." When Tommy continued to look skeptical, Rachel reminded him, "She's pursued criminals before. She knows what she's doing."

Tommy's hand lingered on the doorknob, not quite ready to open it. "Rachel..." He paused, seeming to struggle with the words. "I've been terrified to have this conversation. Terrified you'd look at me differently once you knew the truth."

Rachel studied his face—the dark circles under his eyes, the way his high cheekbones (which she'd always secretly envied) seemed more prominent now than they had only two weeks ago. His stylish silk robe was rumpled and would benefit from a thorough cleaning. He was as different from the polished Tommy who worked every room in Coacoochee as she'd ever seen him appear.

"You were young and ambitious, and someone offered you a shortcut." Rachel couldn't help but think fleetingly of Henry as she added, "We've all made choices we regret."

Tommy's eyes glistened. "Not everyone would see it that way."

"Yeah, but those people are jerks." Rachel pulled Tommy into a hug, and he hugged her back fiercely. "Who cares what they think?"

The two friends held each other, grateful for the moment of physical warmth amid what had been an almost unbearably discomfiting three weeks. Then Tommy kissed Rachel on the cheek and released her.

"I'll try to get to the store this afternoon." He looked down at his bathrobe ruefully. "Just give me a few hours to clean up my act."

"Good!" Rachel made no attempt to hide her pleasure. "You'll have a good time. You'll see."

As she headed back to Title Wave, she found herself thinking about that night at Sabrosa. Tommy's explosion of anger, his fist connecting with Marc's face in full view of the entire restaurant. It had been reckless, impulsive—and utterly lacking in calculation. The same man who couldn't control his temper for five minutes in public seemed unlikely to have planned and executed two careful murders.

Tommy was many things—passionate, ambitious, sometimes rash and impetuous—but he wasn't a cold-blooded killer.

But if not Tommy, then who? And what secret was worth killing for?

CHAPTER 21

Rachel slipped through the back door into Title Wave just as Dorothea was settling into the story chair with a copy of *Higglety Pigglety Pop!*, surrounded by a semicircle of eager children on colorful cushions. The familiar Sunday chaos of Story Time—parents chatting near the café, toddlers wandering between shelves, the rustle of pages turning in picture books—filled the bookstore with a happy energy. Rachel quietly checked the clipboard holding the Halloween volunteer signup sheet she'd asked Nadia to set up on the café counter, grateful to see all the parents who'd already offered to help with craft stations and candy distribution.

Story Time had been one of Rachel's earliest initiatives, and even now, six months later, the sight of those rapt little faces turned toward Dorothea made her chest warm with satisfaction. It was worth coming in on her day off just to see five-year-old Leigh Falconer claim her usual spot right at Dorothea's feet, to watch the Hernandez twins clutch their worn copies of *Goodnight Moon* while listening to something new, to observe how Dorothea transformed back into the teacher and storyteller she'd been before retirement, her silver hair catching the light as she brought tales to life.

Neither Homer, nor Vashti, nor Scarlett had ever attended Story Time, not even "unofficially" by sneaking down the dumbwaiter and through the back room. Vashti had literal nightmares in which a sticky-fingered child smeared blackberry jam all over her beautiful white fur and Rachel, despite her best efforts, was unable to get it out—forcing Vashti to live out the rest of her days with a child's gooey handprint marring the perfection of her snowy white fur. Scarlett, far more concerned with her dignity than her physical appearance, thoroughly agreed with Vashti that any contact with grubby-handed mini-humans was to be avoided at all costs.

Homer was the only one of the three who thought about Story Time with a certain amount of wistfulness. It was out of particular concern for him that Rachel kept the three cats away, and part of him knew he was better off up here with his sisters. But there was another part, the part that still felt kittenish despite his year of age, that wondered what it would be like in the middle of all that glorious roughhousing and excitement.

Rachel caught Nadia's eye. The grad student was already setting up juice boxes and arranging trays of Butterflake Bakery sugar cookies specially crafted to look like books—another of Rachel's additions that had quickly become tradition. "Everything under control?"

"Always," Nadia assured her with a smile, her dark ponytail swaying as she worked. "Dorothea just started. About twenty kids today."

Rachel spotted Natalie near the Caribbean Travel section, seemingly absorbed in a guidebook about the Bahamas. Their eyes met across the store, and Natalie closed the guidebook with deliberate casualness. Rachel nodded toward the café area, weaving between a mother trying to corral a pair of gap-toothed siblings and a father photographing his daughter hugging a stuffed Wild Thing. The café tables were crowded with Story

Time parents nursing Sunday coffees, their quiet conversations creating a comfortable blanket of background noise.

"This one's free," she said as Natalie joined her, and guided her to a small table near the front window. It offered a perfect view of both the entrance and the story circle. "Nick Torres should be here soon. He and his kids never miss Story Time. Can I get you a coffee in the meantime?"

"Please." Natalie sat down at the table, positioning herself to watch the door.

"There must be more to life than having everything," Dorothea read from her chair, her voice taking on the wistful quality of a little dog with big dreams. Several children giggled at her exaggerated sigh.

Rachel returned to the table with a steaming café con leche. "How did it go with Tommy?" Natalie asked. Her face was relaxed, prepared to accept whatever Rachel said, whether or not it jibed with her own hunches.

"It wasn't him." Rachel kept her voice low, aware of the crowd around them. "But he did confirm that Daisy was his original source for the blind item, and that she led him to believe she was making it up."

Natalie nodded, and Rachel breathed a small, inward sigh of relief. "That tracks with what I've found out about Alicia Rodrigue." Natalie took a sip of her coffee. "She's—"

The bell above the door chimed, and both women looked up to see Nick Torres arriving with his children. "I'll tell you once Nick's joined us," Natalie concluded hastily.

Nick's son, Lucas, six years old and boundlessly energetic, could barely conceal his excitement as he tugged his father toward the story circle. Hanna, eight and determined to be too cool for children's books, affected an air of sophisticated boredom that didn't quite hide her interest in Dorothea's animated reading.

Nick got his children settled—Lucas dropping cross-legged onto a cushion while Hanna perched on the edge of hers, ready to spring up at the first sign of anything too juvenile. Rachel watched him scan the store, his gaze pausing when he spotted them at their corner table. A brief nod acknowledged their presence before he turned back to ruffle Lucas's hair and murmur something to Hanna that made her roll her eyes but smile. Once he could tell Dorothea had them fully engrossed in Jennie the dog's theatrical ambitions, Nick made his way toward the café.

"Natalie, Rachel." He pulled out the empty chair and positioned himself where he could keep an eye on his children. "Mind if I sit with you for a minute while the kids are occupied?"

"Please do." Natalie's tone was friendly and offhand, but there was an expectant light in her eyes as they settled on Nick.

Nick sat down, his own expression shifting from casual to quietly alert. "How are you both doing?"

"Managing." Natalie took a sip of coffee. "It's been a tough week."

"That it has," Nick agreed. On his desk back at the office was the latest *Coacoochee Wire*—a weekly rag devoted to nightclub events and the people who attended them, pored over religiously by the Coacoochee nightlife crowd. The gossip column in this week's edition, which had come out just yesterday, included what was clearly a hurriedly appended blind item about a recently deceased nightlife writer with a secret cocaine habit. The Commissioner certainly hadn't wasted any time in spreading the word about Marc's "drug problem," Nick thought dryly.

"Nick? Would you like some coffee?" At his nod, Rachel made her way to the counter, taking her time with the simple task. A burst of laughter from the story circle made Rachel smile—Dorothea must have done one of her silly voices. She poured Nick's coffee slowly, adding the splash of cream and single packet of sugar she knew he liked, then paused to straighten a display of coffee mugs emblazoned with literary quotes. When she judged enough time had passed for Natalie to cover the basics, Rachel headed back. She arrived just as Natalie was saying, "...which brings us to what I've learned so far about the girl in the photo."

Rachel set Nick's coffee in front of him and reclaimed her seat. Nick nodded his thanks, wrapping his hands around the warm cup.

"I think the girl in the picture is the Alicia Rodrigue from Marc's notes." Natalie's voice was low enough that Rachel had to lean in slightly. "Alicia Rodrigue was a University of Miami senior who died of an apparent overdose on December 4th, 1993. She was found abandoned outside the Jackson Memorial ER."

At the word "abandoned," Rachel felt her stomach twist. Somebody had dumped her there. Jackson was located over the causeway in Miami proper. If Alicia had been at a party on one of the private islands—like Mercury Island—that dotted Biscayne Bay, it wouldn't have made sense to bring her all the way out there.

Unless whoever had brought her wanted to be sure he couldn't be connected to her.

"That's all I could find in the newspaper archives," Natalie continued. "Just a brief mention in the *Daily News'* metro section. No follow-up stories, no investigation. Nothing more than her name, age, and where and when she was found."

Nick's expression hardened almost imperceptibly. "The same time frame as Tommy's blind item."

"Exactly." Natalie nodded. "Rachel and I think the 'fabricated' blind item might have described a real event. Something that may connect Julian Singer-Adams and Alicia Rodrigue's death."

Nick took a sip of his coffee, using the moment to scan the nearby tables. The surrounding parents remained absorbed in their own conversations—discussions about Halloween costumes, the upcoming school bake sale, whose turn it was to host a playdate.

Behind them, Dorothea's voice rose and fell with dramatic flair. *"To be leading lady of The World Mother Goose Theatre you must have experience."*

"If Marc was close to proving that connection..." Nick said quietly.

"It gives Julian a motive," Natalie finished.

"It gives him a motive in Daisy's death, too," Rachel added. "She was the original source for Tommy's blind item."

Nick glanced toward his children—Lucas was completely absorbed, leaning forward with his mouth slightly open. Hanna was pretending to examine her nails but clearly listening to the story. "This is all speculation," he finally said, though his tone suggested he found their speculation compelling. "The ME ruled both deaths as natural causes—heart attacks."

"Two healthy people dying of heart attacks within days of each other?" Rachel challenged, forgetting to keep her voice down. A nearby parent glanced their way, and she quickly moderated her tone. "Both connected to the same investigation?"

"I share your suspicions," Nick admitted, his voice barely above a murmur. He shifted in his chair, angling his body to block their conversation from curious eyes. "But without evidence, my hands are tied. Commissioner Carpenter has made it clear he doesn't want a murder investigation disrupting the tourist season."

The way he said it—flat, factual, with just a hint of frustration—told Rachel everything about how Nick felt about those orders.

"Politics," she said dismissively.

"Reality," Nick countered. "Without proof of foul play, I can't justify the resources for a full investigation, especially against the commissioner's direct orders."

Natalie's voice dropped. "What if we found evidence? Something conclusive?"

"Then I'd have grounds to proceed officially." Nick's voice carried the weight of both warning and possibility. "But I need to caution both of you—if someone is willing to kill to protect this secret, asking questions puts you at risk."

"I understand." Natalie's voice was subdued. "But Marc was onto something important, and now he's dead." She glanced at Rachel before continuing. "I have a contact at the UM registrar's office who might be able to help. If I can track down some of Alicia's professors or classmates, I can confirm that she's the one in this photo with Julian. Maybe someone will remember if she mentioned going to a party that weekend, or who invited her."

"Just keep your eyes open." Nick's expression was grave. "And if you find anything—anything at all—come to me first. Not the press, not anyone else."

The sound of enthusiastic applause from the story circle made all three adults turn. Dorothea was taking an exaggerated bow from her chair, having reached the story's triumphant conclusion. "Now then," her voice carried clearly across the store, "who would like a cookie?"

"Me!" several children announced in unison, already bouncing to their feet.

Nick drained the last of his coffee and stood. "That's my cue. Lucas will expect me to help him choose between vanilla and chocolate. It's a very important decision when you're six." He paused, his expression growing serious again. "Be careful, both of you. Please."

With that, he moved back toward the story circle, where his children were already joining the stream of excited kids heading for the café counter. Rachel and Natalie remained at their table in silence for a moment, both apparently lost in thought. Then Rachel spotted Tommy hovering near the entrance, looking uncertain about venturing into the family-friendly chaos. He wore pressed chinos and a light blue button-down—cleaned up from this morning, but the strain still showed in the shadows under his eyes.

"Is that Tommy?" Natalie followed Rachel's gaze.

"Yes. He said he might stop by."

Natalie gathered her purse and stood. "Good timing, actually—I want to call my contact at UM while I'm thinking of it. See if she's in the office tomorrow." She glanced toward the café counter, where parents and children were waiting for cookies. "I'm glad we got to speak with Nick. It helps to know he's on our side, even if his hands are tied."

"Let me know what you find out about Alicia's classmates?"

"I will." Natalie headed for the door. As she passed Tommy, she said, "Tommy, good to see you out and about."

"Hey, Natalie." They paused just long enough to buss each other's cheeks, although both sets of shoulders were slightly tense. "Yeah, Rachel convinced me I needed to rejoin the land of the living."

"She's good at that." Natalie's tone was warm enough, but she kept moving. "Take care."

Rachel waved Tommy over. "You made it."

"I promised I would." He managed a small smile. "Though I feel a bit out of place without a toddler in tow."

"Come help with cookie distribution. You'll be knee-deep in toddlers."

They moved to the café where Nadia was unveiling trays of sugar cookies shaped like books, complete with colorful icing spines and titles. Children formed a surprisingly orderly line, their excitement humming in the air.

"One each," Rachel reminded them automatically, while Tommy helped pass out napkins. "And what do we say?"

"Thank you!" a gap-toothed girl chirped, clutching her cookie like treasure.

The crowd was thinning now, families drifting out into the bright afternoon, many heading for late lunches on Hibiscus Road. Through the windows, Rachel could see tourists wandering past with beach bags and sun hats. She felt a sudden, sharp longing to be outdoors with them.

"I need pizza," Tommy said. "And somewhere to talk. Your terrace?"

Rachel grinned. "It's like you're reading my mind."

"Pucci's?"

"Perfect."

Rachel hugged Dorothea goodbye, thanking her for another wonderful Story Time. Outside, the October afternoon wrapped around them like a warm blanket. The fairy lights strung between palms wouldn't turn on for hours yet, but Hibiscus Road still sparkled in its daylight glamour—bright awnings, cheerful crowds, the distant sound of live music from one of the beachfront hotels.

They reached Pucci's to the familiar scents of garlic and baking dough. Joey Pooch himself was working the counter, his thick Brooklyn accent unchanged despite fifteen years in Florida.

"Rachel! And Mr. Nightlife!" He beamed at them. "What can I get for you?"

They ordered a large pizza—half mushroom for Rachel, half pepperoni for Tommy—and Joey promised to have it ready in twenty minutes. "You want to wait, or should I send Mia over with it?"

Mia Puccino sat at a nearby table with a biology textbook propped open in front of her. Tommy smiled at her and she blushed prettily, decidedly shyer in her father's restaurant than she was standing behind an easel and canvas.

"We'll take it to go," Rachel decided.

Outside, Tommy glanced toward the beach, visible just a block from Rollins Avenue. "Twenty minutes to kill?"

"Let's walk," Rachel agreed.

They crossed to the beach access, their shoes sinking into the soft sand at the entrance, and sat next to each other on an empty bench facing the water. They watched as a family packed up their umbrellas and beach toys. "But it's not even dark yet!" one of the children protested.

"So," Tommy said. "What did Natalie find out about the girl in the photograph?"

Rachel kept her gaze on the ocean. "Her name was Alicia Rodrigue. She was a UM senior. She died the night that picture was taken—December 4th, 1993."

"Died?" Tommy turned to look at her.

"She overdosed. Somebody left her outside the Jackson Memorial ER."

"Jesus." Tommy ran a hand through his hair. "So Daisy's made-up story..."

"Might not have been made up after all," Rachel finished.

Tommy was quiet for a moment. "I don't really like myself right now for having written it up the way I did. Like it was some silly gossip item. Party games and rich people behaving badly." He shook his head. "And someone actually died."

"You couldn't have known."

He watched a pelican dive for fish. "So you think whoever was involved in her death is now killing people to keep it quiet?"

"That's what Natalie and I are thinking. First Daisy, who was the source. Then Marc, who was investigating."

"Do *I* need to worry?" Tommy sounded alarmed.

"I think the killer will figure if you knew anything more about it, you would've written it five years ago," Rachel pointed out. "Still, it couldn't hurt to be cautious until we know more."

Tommy stood, brushing sand from his pants. "Come on, the pizza should be ready. I need to process this with carbs."

The boxed pizza was warm between them as they walked back to Title Wave in companionable silence. Rachel led the way up the exterior staircase, keys jangling as she unlocked her apartment door. Homer bounded forward immediately, nose twitching.

"See?" he exclaimed to his sisters with an air of triumph. *"I told you they were bringing a pizza!"* Pizza cheese was, in Homer's estimation, by far the best of all possible cheeses. Rachel and Tommy had still been blocks away when Homer caught the scent, and his tummy had been rumbling since.

"Yes, it's very impressive how you can smell a pizza all the way from the far end of Hibiscus Road," said Scarlett, who didn't care much for pizza. *"And yet you can't hear an important conversation when it's happening right downstairs."*

Homer looked uncharacteristically crestfallen. All three cats had been anxious to learn what Natalie had discovered about the mysterious photograph and file folder, and Homer knew Vashti and Scarlett were counting on him to listen in on her conversation with Rachel and report back. But between the chaotic cacophony of the children at Story Time and their chitchatting parents in the café, it had been impossible even for Homer to single out one specific conversation.

"Come on, Scarlett." Vashti cast a sympathetic look in Homer's direction, which of course he couldn't see. *"Even Homer's hearing has its limits."*

"Hello, my patient darlings," Rachel said, interpreting their chorus of meows as complaints. "Yes, I know. Story Time is off limits. But look! We brought pizza!"

"As if that makes up for locking us in here." Like a lot of cats, Scarlett resented being locked behind a closed door, even when she had no actual interest in being on the other side of it.

The two humans and three cats headed out to the terrace, the afternoon sun welcoming them with its perfect October warmth—neither too hot nor too humid. Rachel set the pizza box on the outdoor table while Tommy collapsed into one of the chaise lounges, kicking off his shoes.

"God, what a week," he said, closing his eyes against the sun.

The cats followed them outside. Homer angled himself as close to the pizza as was possible, while Vashti perched on the low wall overlooking Hibiscus Road and Scarlett commandeered the second chaise lounge before either of the humans could.

"So what happens next?" Tommy asked as Rachel handed him a slice on one of the paper plates Joey Pooch had packed up with their order. "With the investigation, I mean."

"Natalie's going down to UM this week." Rachel settled with her own paper plate on the chaise lounge next to Scarlett—who had rather liked the idea of having the entire thing to herself, but was secretly pleased to find Rachel sitting next to *her* rather than one of her needier siblings. "Try to find people who knew Alicia, confirm she's the girl in the photo. If she really is the girl who overdosed the night it was taken, then we know Julian was with her the night she died. Maybe he's even the one who threw the party."

Homer was sitting next to the pizza with his ears pricked at rigid attention, waiting for the slightest hint that either Rachel or Tommy was on their way to get another slice and maybe—just maybe—pull off a warm, gooey fragment of cheese for him. But his ears drooped as he heard Rachel's words, and he could sense the deflated looks that passed between Scarlett and Vashti. It shouldn't have come as a complete surprise that something bad had happened to the young girl in the picture—two people connected to it were dead already—but hearing it still hurt.

The five of them sat in silence, Rachel and Tommy continuing to eat in the sunshine. The faint pulse of electronica drifted up from Hibiscus Road, and Tommy looked at his watch. "Tea dance at 710 started twenty minutes ago." Once a week, the 710 Bar pushed aside its intimate table settings and threw a Sunday afternoon dance party. "Should we check it out?

"Really?" Rachel looked around at the half-eaten pizza, the peaceful terrace, the three cats blinking drowsily in the sunlight. "This feels pretty perfect to me. Don't you want to finish your pizza?"

"Pizza is always better than going out dancing!" Homer voted immediately.

Tommy laughed at Homer's insistent meow. "I think someone agrees with you."

"He wants cheese," Rachel said, pulling a small piece of mozzarella from her slice and tossing it toward the table where Homer waited. He immediately leapt down, nose close to the concrete floor of the terrace, and found the aromatic tidbit within seconds.

Below them, Hibiscus Road buzzed with Sunday afternoon activity—tourists with shopping bags, locals heading to early dinners, the distant sound of a steel drum from the beach. The contrast between the peaceful terrace and the busy pedestrian mall below made their perch feel like a private oasis.

"Thank you," Tommy said suddenly.

"For what?" Rachel smiled as Scarlett, seemingly apropos of nothing, stood and walked across the chaise to settle in Rachel's lap. It was something she didn't do often—and, somehow, Rachel correctly intuited that it was her way of voting they all remain together here on the terrace, rather than going to the 710 Bar or anywhere else.

Tommy turned to look at her. "Let's just say it's been the kind of week where you find out who your friends are."

Rachel's cheeks pinked with pleasure as she reached over and squeezed Tommy's hand. "I'm always in your corner," she told him. "That's what friends are for."

"And also cheese." Homer swallowed the last bit of the mozzarella and licked his chops with satisfaction. Then he scampered over to sit on his haunches before Rachel, turning his face up hopefully toward hers. *"Friends are also for cheese."*

CHAPTER 22

Natalie Dunbar sat on a weathered bench beneath one of the University of Miami's sprawling banyan trees, its aerial roots creating a natural cathedral around her. Hot Mike lay at her feet, his enormous head resting on his paws but his ears alert to every passing student. The campus was a hive of midweek activity, buzzing with students who'd survived Monday and Tuesday but weren't yet ready to coast toward the weekend.

Watching the stream of backpacked students hurrying between classes, Natalie studied the Polaroid in her hands. A young woman smiled at the camera, Julian Singer-Adams' arm draped casually around her shoulders, her hand touching a distinctive shell necklace at her throat. Natalie had spent the early part of the week making calls, navigating the delicate dance of academic bureaucracy and five-year-old memories. Professor Nina Reyes had been surprisingly easy to track down—still teaching in the Marine Science department, still advising the students who reminded her of Alicia Rodrigue.

Natalie glanced at her watch—Professor Reyes' office hours started in ten minutes. She'd deliberately arrived early, wanting a moment to collect her thoughts before what promised to be a difficult conversation.

The building itself was a modern structure of glass and white concrete, designed to catch the ocean breezes. Inside, the halls smelled of salt water from the specimen tanks and the sharp scent of preserved samples. Natalie found Professor Reyes' office easily—third floor, corner office with a view of the green campus below. The door was ajar, and Natalie could see the professor at her desk grading papers. She knocked gently.

"Come in," Professor Reyes called without looking up. "If this is about the midterm extension—" She stopped mid-sentence as she registered Natalie and Hot Mike. "Oh. You're not a student."

"I'm Natalie Dunbar. I called yesterday about Alicia Rodrigue?"

The change in the professor's demeanor was immediate—a closing off, a protective wariness. She set down her pen. "Yes. I remember." She studied Natalie for a long moment. "I don't usually discuss former students with journalists."

"I understand," Natalie said. "May we come in? This is Hot Mike—he's very well-behaved."

Something in Natalie's tone—or perhaps Hot Mike's steady, dignified presence—seemed to soften the professor slightly. She nodded. "Close the door, please."

Professor Nina Reyes's office was a comfortable chaos of marine charts, student papers, and photographs of coral reefs in impossibly bright colors. The professor herself—late fifties, steel-gray hair pulled back in a practical bun, kind eyes behind horn-rimmed glasses—gestured to a chair across from her desk.

"Ms. Dunbar." Her handshake was firm, her gaze direct but cautious. "I must admit, your request to discuss Alicia after all this time was unexpected."

"I appreciate your willingness to see me. I know this must be difficult." Natalie took the offered chair while Hot Mike positioned himself beside her.

"She was a good student," Professor Reyes said, "hoping for an internship with the Coral Restoration Foundation. She used to stay after class with questions all the time, always excited about the next research project." Professor Reyes raised her glasses to rub at her eyes, her face momentarily fragile and almost birdlike in their absence. Then she sighed and resettled the glasses on her nose. "When Alicia died, it felt like such a waste."

"The official cause was accidental overdose," Natalie said. "But I understand there were unusual circumstances."

Professor Reyes' shoulders tensed, and there was old anger in her eyes now. "She was abandoned outside the Jackson Memorial emergency room. Someone—whoever was with her when she overdosed—simply tossed her out and drove away. By the time someone found her and got her inside..." She trailed off, composing herself.

"Did Alicia ever mention Julian Singer-Adams?"

The change in the professor's expression was subtle but unmistakable—a tightening around the mouth, a sharpening of the gaze. "Why do you ask about him specifically?"

Natalie withdrew the Polaroid from her bag and placed it on the desk. "Is that Alicia with him in this photo?"

Professor Reyes's hand reached toward the photo, stopping just short of touching it. "Yes, that's Alicia. That's her shell necklace—she made it herself and wore it everywhere." The professor's eyes glistened. "Where did you get this?"

"It's part of an ongoing investigation," Natalie told her. "This was taken at a party the weekend Alicia died."

The silence stretched between them. Hot Mike shifted, pressing closer to Natalie's leg.

"Alicia mentioned being invited to a party at Julian Singer-Adams' home," Professor Reyes finally said. "She was excited—networking opportunities, yes, but also..." A sad smile touched her lips. "She was twenty-one. The idea of a glamorous party on Mercury Island appealed to her. I advised caution, but..." She spread her hands in a gesture of helpless regret.

Natalie noted that Professor Reyes had confirmed what she'd already suspected: Not just that Alicia had been with Julian Singer-Adams on the night she died, but that Julian's own home had been the scene of the party.

They talked for another few minutes, Professor Reyes telling Natalie about a beach cleanup Alicia had once organized. Her grief for the once-promising student was palpable. Hot Mike rose and padded over to her side of the desk, resting his head near her hand—not quite touching, just offering his presence. Professor Reyes's fingers briefly touched his fur.

"If I find out more about that night—about what really happened—I'll let you know." Natalie rose to leave, picking up Hot Mike's leash as he dutifully returned to her side.

"I'd appreciate that." The professor straightened, composing herself. "Thank you," she added. "For still caring about what happened to her."

Natalie nodded, closing the door softly behind her as she and Hot Mike left.

CHAPTER 23

"No, WE DON'T HAVE records going back that far." The receptionist's voice crackled through the phone. "Have you tried Beacon Staffing?"

With a sigh, Rachel crossed another agency off her list, the yellow legal pad now covered in scratched-out names and dead ends. Homer, sitting nearby with one ear cocked, shook his head subtly in a silent *no* for the benefit of his sisters across the store. But it was unnecessary; they could hear the back-and-forth scratching sound the pen made on the pad, and by now they knew what it meant.

Rachel hadn't expected the work to be exciting when she'd first volunteered to do it, and had said as much at the time. "I was always the kid who helped the other kids do their homework," she'd told Natalie cheerfully, drawing a reluctant chuckle.

"It'll just be a lot of background research and phone calls," Natalie had warned, her hesitation apparent even as she'd acknowledged there was only so much ground she could cover alone. Even with Rachel's help, she still faced the prospect of days spent making fruitless phone calls before maybe—*maybe*—turning up a single useable lead. It was the kind of grunt work she would normally have hired an assistant to help out with—work, she reflected now, that Daisy herself had done for her, once upon a time. "At least ninety percent of it'll be dead-ends and hang-ups."

"My whole life is on the phone these days." Title Wave's phone line had been rather busier of late with back-and-forth calls to vendors for the Halloween party. "Please let me help," Rachel added earnestly. "At least with this little part of it." She couldn't have said why, but Rachel was almost as invested in uncovering what had happened to Alicia Rodrigue as she was in finding the truth about Daisy. The smiling girl in the photograph with Julian had deserved better than what she'd gotten.

Natalie, understanding everything Rachel wasn't saying, had nodded. "Say you're researching Coacoochee social history for a book project. Don't mention my name or the investigation."

The cats had been delighted by this turn of events. Nobody, they'd told each other, was more organized and determined than Rachel was, once she'd made up her mind to do something. New information about Daisy and Marc's killer was bound to start rolling in the moment she picked up the phone.

The cats, of course, had never done homework of any kind—their own or anybody else's. So they had no idea what days of research for a group project—taking notes, making calls, looking things up in old newspapers—actually looked like. Their own part in the investigation thus far had been dangerous and terrifying and more exciting than anything else they'd ever done. They didn't expect Rachel to break into private homes or chase bad guys through the streets of Coacoochee the way they had. Still, the reality of investigative work—dull, repetitive, and frequently pointless—was far from what they'd anticipated.

Rachel had been more prepared, but even she was starting to get discouraged. Between helping customers, she'd spent hours calling every employment agency in the phone book, starting with the large firms and working her way down to smaller specialty services. Now it was Thursday, and so far all she had to show for her efforts were sore ears, a stiff neck, and a growing pile of dead ends. Homer had been by her side the entire time, occasionally offering commentary in the form of small chirps and meows that Rachel interpreted as encouragement.

"I don't understand why humans make everything so complicated," Scarlett groused. *"When we investigated Marc's house, we just went there and looked around."*

"How would Rachel walking into all these employment agencies instead of calling them be easier?" Vashti asked—a fair point for which Scarlett had no response.

"I know, I know," Rachel said to Homer as he meowed plaintively. "It's boring for you too, isn't it?" She reached over to scratch behind his ears before dialing the next number. One of her regulars, Mrs. Richter, approached the register with her Thursday selections, and Rachel quickly tucked the phone between her shoulder and ear while ringing up the purchases.

"Maven Staffing Solutions, how may I direct your call?"

"Hi, I'm trying to reach former employees who worked events for Julian Singer-Adams on Mercury Island in the early Nineties. I'm researching the social history of Coacoochee for a book project," she added, the lie now smooth as sea glass after days of use.

Homer's ears perked up as the woman on the other end laid the phone down with a thunk. His sensitive hearing picked up her muffled conversation in the background: "—asking about the Singer-Adams parties—" and then, more clearly, "—Maria needs to hear this—"

Homer let out a sharp chirp of excitement. *"This one's different!"* he announced to his sisters. *"They're actually getting someone!"*

The cats pressed closer, and Mrs. Richter had to sidestep them carefully on her way out with her shopping bag. Homer's ears swiveled forward with intense focus, trying to hear more. Vashti abandoned her perch in Caribbean Travel to sit near the phone, and even Scarlett stopped pretending to be uninterested. *"Move over, Homer,"* she said imperiously, walking over and batting at his head with her upraised paw as she jostled for position. *"I can't hear anything."*

A new voice came on the line, older and more cautious. "This is Maria. You're asking about the Singer-Adams estate?"

"Yes." Rachel felt her pulse quicken. "I'm particularly interested in anyone who might have worked security or—"

"You move over." Homer gave Scarlett a good shove with his shoulder. *"I was here first! It's not my fault you're practically deaf."*

Their mutual sniping and meows of complaint had gotten so loud, they were audible over the phone. Rachel placed one hand over the receiver and angrily whispered, "Both of you, stop it now! I'm sorry about that," she added to Maria automatically. "My cats are being vocal today."

"Oh, you work from home?" Maria's tone warmed slightly.

"Actually, I manage a bookstore. They come to work with me."

"They? You have more than one?"

"Three." Rachel found herself smiling, despite her momentary irritation. "They think they run the place."

"Wait—" Maria's voice changed completely. "Do you mean Title Wave on Hibiscus Road? Are you the one with the little blind cat who greets everyone?"

"That's Homer, yes."

"Oh my goodness! My granddaughter is obsessed with him. She makes these little toys for him out of yarn—brings them every time we visit. She must have given him a dozen by now."

"The fuzzy mice?" Rachel laughed. "He loves those! Your granddaughter is very sweet."

"Hey." Vashti pawed at the leg of Rachel's jeans for attention. *"Did she say anything about me?"* It seemed improbable that any cat-loving little girl could spend time at Title Wave yet fail to notice the beautiful white feline who looked just like a fairy-tale princess.

"What is *with* you guys today?" Rachel once again covered the receiver and shooed Vashti away. "Can't you see I'm on the phone?"

"She'll be thrilled to know I talked to you." Maria was still talking about her granddaughter. Then she paused, and when she spoke again, her tone had shifted. "You know, my daughter thinks I'm crazy, but I always say you can tell a lot about a person by how they treat animals. Especially animals that need extra care."

"Homer doesn't need extra care," Rachel replied. "He's pretty convinced he's invincible."

Maria chuckled, then grew quiet. Rachel could almost hear her making a decision. "Listen...I shouldn't be talking about former clients. But that

Singer-Adams contract..." She paused. "We had good people working security at those parties. One of them—Eddie Torrino—he was one of our best. Honest, reliable, never missed a shift."

"Was?" Rachel prompted.

"December of '93, something happened at one of those parties. Eddie came into our office the next Monday, turned in his uniform, and quit. No explanation, no notice. Just said he was done."

Rachel's pen hovered over her notepad. "Did he ever say why?"

"Never. And then, maybe a week later, Julian Singer-Adams called personally to cancel our contract. Said he was 'going in a different direction' with his security needs." Maria snorted softly. "Five years of business, gone just like that."

There was a long pause. Then Rachel, sensing Maria wanted to talk but needed a little more prodding, asked conversationally, "Do you still keep in touch with Eddie?"

"Haven't talked to him in years. I think he's working construction these days." Maria hesitated. "Always used to stop by the Deuce on South Beach for a beer after his shift ended," she finally added.

"Thank you," Rachel said quickly, scribbling down the name. "Thank you so much. I really appreciate it." She set down the receiver slowly, staring at the name she'd written: Eddie Torrino, the Deuce.

All three cats stared at the notepad with the kind of focused intensity usually reserved for can openers at dinnertime.

"Finally!" Scarlett exclaimed to her siblings. *"After all those useless calls, she actually found someone!"*

Rachel was already reaching for the phone again. The cats watched as she dialed Natalie, their earlier boredom completely forgotten.

Rachel knew she wasn't relieved of phone duty just yet. Natalie couldn't build an entire investigation around a single interview—assuming Eddie Torrino was even willing to talk to her.

But it was a start. And after so many days of nothing but dead ends, to Rachel it felt like a bona fide victory.

BY FIVE THIRTY NATALIE was at Mac's Club Deuce, the oldest bar on South Beach. She'd been there a few times over the years and, she noted, the place never seemed to change—small and dark, with a horseshoe-shaped wooden bar scarred by decades of use, pink and green neon lighting (left over from a *Miami Vice* shoot), and a jukebox that had been playing what she thought of as the "Stairway to Freebird" genre of music since the 1970s.

Natalie's only experience at the Deuce was with the late-night crowd—an exuberant mingling of drag queens, club kids, trust funders, bikers, suburbanites looking for a walk on the wild side, and an array of semi-regular barflies with no place better (or cheaper) to go.

The after-work crowd she encountered now gave off a decidedly different vibe, consisting mostly of construction workers enjoying a low-key Thursday happy hour, still dusty from jobsites. Natalie slipped a ten-dollar bill to the obliging bartender, who discreetly pointed out Eddie Torrino. The TV above the bar was playing a rerun of Sunday's Dolphins game on its VCR as Natalie pulled up a stool a few down from Eddie and ordered a beer. On the TV screen Marino got sacked, and both Natalie and Eddie groaned aloud.

"They were better when Shula was coaching," Natalie commented in Eddie's general direction.

Eddie grunted and took a long pull off his beer. "Jimmy Johnson's okay. But he lets Marino get away with too much."

"I guess it'll never be '72 again," she said, referencing the year the Dolphins had enjoyed a perfect season straight through the Super Bowl. It was a lament heard frequently from longtime fans.

Eddie looked over at Natalie for the first time. "You don't sound like you're from around here," he noted.

"Nope." Natalie took a pull on her own beer. "Queensland, Australia native, but I've been here a few years now."

"Oh, yeah? I'm from Queens, myself. Queens in New York," he added, as if unsure whether an Australian would make the connection. "Seems like everybody in this town comes from somewhere else."

"My friend Rachel says Miami Beach is a town where people occasionally die, but nobody ever seems to be born." Eddie laughed, and Natalie added, "Although she actually *is* from here, which kind of blows up her whole theory. I'm Natalie, by the way."

"Eddie." He hitched his barstool closer and held out a hand for her to shake. "What kind of work you in, Natalie, that brings you all the way from Australia?"

"I'm an investigative journalist." Natalie took another swig on her beer and kept her eyes on the TV screen. "Right now I'm looking into some wild parties out on Mercury Island back in the early Nineties."

Even though she continued to stare straight ahead, in her peripheral vision she could see Eddie stiffen—although his tone was deliberately casual as he said, "Find anything interesting?"

"Lots of interesting stories." Natalie was still watching the screen. "You know how those rich types like to party."

"Yeah, I guess." Eddie took another drink. "Though I wouldn't know personally. I've always been more of a beer-and-football guy myself."

On the TV, Marino threw an interception. They both winced.

"I've been trying to track down people who worked those parties." Natalie kept her tone light. "Security, catering, that kind of thing. Harder than you'd think after all this time."

Eddie's hand tightened on his beer bottle. "Why would you want to do that?"

"Just trying to get a picture of what that whole scene was like. The excess, the glamour." She paused. "The things that went wrong."

"Nothing good comes from digging up old dirt." Eddie's voice didn't sound casual anymore.

"Maybe not," Natalie conceded. "But sometimes people need to know what really happened."

Eddie turned to look at her fully. "You said you're a journalist?"

"That's right."

"And you just happened to sit down next to me to talk about the Dolphins?"

Natalie met his gaze steadily. "I heard you might have worked some of those parties back in the day."

Eddie's face went hard. "Whoever told you that should mind their own business." He started to stand. "I work construction now. Been doing it for years. Got nothing to do with any parties or rich people or any of that."

"Eddie, wait." Natalie kept her voice low, aware of the other patrons. "I'm not trying to cause trouble for anyone. I'm just trying to find out what happened to a young woman."

Eddie paused, still half off his stool. "What young woman?"

"He name was Alicia Rodrigue. She died after a party on Mercury Island. Back in December of '93."

For a moment, Eddie stood frozen. Something passed across his face. It was guilt, old and heavy.

"I don't know anything about that."

"I think you do," Natalie said gently. "And I think it's been bothering you."

"You know what bothers me?" Eddie's voice was low and tight. "People who show up asking questions about things that are none of their business. I'm working construction now, at that new multiplex they're building in Coacoochee. And you know who's building it? Julian Singer-Adams."

"I understand," Natalie said. "But—"

"No, you don't understand." He threw money on the bar and headed for the door.

Natalie didn't try to stop him. "I'm just trying to find out what happened to Alicia," she told Eddie's retreating back. "I think her parents deserve to know, if nothing else."

For a long moment, Eddie stood frozen at the door. When he finally spoke, he didn't turn around.

"Things got crazy that night. People were messed up on all kinds of stuff. Toward the end I saw some guy who worked for Julian with a girl who was in bad shape. Practically had to carry her. I heard him tell Julian he'd take her to the ER over at Jackson Memorial." Eddie laughed mirthlessly. "Took me a lot longer than it should have to wonder why he'd bring her all the way out there."

On the TV screen, the Dolphins scored a touchdown and the stadium crowd cheered wildly. Eddie pushed through the Deuce's front door and was gone. It swung closed behind him with a soft hiss of well-oiled hinges, leaving Natalie alone at the bar with her beer.

CHAPTER 24

THE MULTIPLEX CONSTRUCTION SITE at dusk was Samkhat's grocery store, restaurant, and hunting ground all rolled into one. She picked her way between towers of PVC pipe and pyramids of cinderblocks, her head turning in practiced sweeps to compensate for her blind left side. Years of navigating with one eye had taught her to keep walls and solid objects to her left whenever possible, protecting her vulnerability. The workers had left an hour ago—she'd watched them pile into pickup trucks and head for the causeway, their radio music fading into the distance.

She'd been hunting alone again ever since Laurie had forbidden Kotik to leave the house. Before that, the young tuxedo had taken to joining her sometimes—not every evening, but often enough that she'd grown used to his earnest questions about which restaurants had the best dumpsters, or how to creep up on a mouse so swiftly and silently, it never saw you coming.

Samkhat had enjoyed teaching him more than she'd expected. Even his moonstruck sighs whenever Vashti's name came up had become oddly endearing. Poor kid didn't stand a chance with that snow-white princess, but at least his romantic delusions kept him entertained.

Friday evenings were especially good—the site would be abandoned until Monday morning, giving the local wildlife a whole weekend to explore without interruption. No dawn arrivals of rumbling trucks to scatter her hunting. The air still held warmth from the day, tinged with sawdust and the faint sweetness of primer paint. A mockingbird called from atop a crane, announcing the change from day to evening.

Near the trailer that served as the construction office, Samkhat caught a promising scent. Tuna salad. Her whiskers quivered with interest. Someone's lunch remnant, forgotten in the day's hustle. She followed the trail, pausing at each turn to swing her head right, checking her blind side before committing to the new direction.

The scent led to a spot beneath the trailer itself—perfect. She could eat in shelter while keeping track of any activity above. She settled with her left side against one of the concrete blocks supporting the structure, positioning herself where she could monitor approaches while she ate. The sandwich lay half-wrapped in deli paper, only slightly worse for its afternoon in the heat.

She'd just started on the tuna when voices drifted down through the trailer floor. Julian Singer-Adams—she recognized him immediately. Ever since Daisy Locarro died, he'd been moving through Coacoochee like a cat walking through puddles, all careful steps and barely concealed tension. But lately he'd seemed easier in his skin again. Back to the smooth-voiced tom who knew he owned the territory.

And Dahlia Delgado, eternally cheerful, one of those humans who seemed to know everyone. She and Julian didn't always get along. Sometimes she and the rest of the Historical Society would stand outside some crumbling building, shouting to the TV cameras about how Julian Singer-Adams was destroying Coacoochee by getting rid of everything old—while Julian would calmly argue, in that smooth way he had, that the Historical Society was destroying Coacoochee by not letting him build anything new. But Dahlia only spent a few hours a week volunteering with the Historical Society; she spent her whole days working for the Department of Tourism.

This time, all sides had apparently been in agreement that tearing down the moldering old parking garage all the way down at the dead distant end of Hibiscus Road—and replacing it with a multiplex movie complex that also had room for shops and restaurants and apartments—was a wonderful idea for locals and tourists alike.

Samkhat had loved that old parking garage. Almost nobody had ever parked there, which had made it an ideal spot for rodents to multiply, and for Samkhat to hunt them while shielded from both blinding sun and pouring rain. But apparently it hadn't occurred to Julian or to anyone at the Department of Tourism to think about what would be best for Coacoochee's outdoor cats.

Her ear flicked automatically as Dahlia and Julian spoke in the trailer above her—a survival reflex that had sharpened since she'd lost her eye and hearing had become even more crucial. But she didn't pause in her meal. The tuna was good quality, not mixed with too much mayonnaise. Just the way she liked it.

"—can't thank you enough for making time." Dahlia's voice bubbled with its usual enthusiasm.

"Not at all." Julian's voice was, perhaps, a trifle ironic. "The Historical Society does important work."

"And we're incredibly grateful for the donation you plan to make from the multiplex's first-week earnings." Above her, Samkhat could hear papers rustling. "Now, about the gala," Dahlia continued. "It'll be the official kickoff to Season this year, and we're hoping you'll say a few words. Nothing elaborate—just share your vision for how the multiplex fits into Coacoochee's growth."

"Of course."

They discussed dates, times, the tedious details humans loved. Samkhat had finished half the sandwich and shifted slightly, angling her good eye toward the gaps in the trailer's undercarriage while keeping her back to the protective concrete block.

"—and of course, we'll want to highlight the Historical Society's preservation efforts in your speech. That's really what resonates with donors." Dahlia's voice had taken on a careful tone.

"Preservation is close to my heart," Julian said without even the slightest hitch in his voice, despite what sounded like a skeptical scoff from Dahlia that masqueraded as a well-timed cough. "When it's done right," he clarified. "In fact, I've been thinking lately about that whole stretch of Hibiscus Road between Sixth and Eighth. Those midcentury buildings deserve to be restored to their original glory."

"Still hoping to acquire Title Wave's building?" Dahlia's tone was gently teasing. "I don't think Dorothea's as willing to sell now as she once might have been. Rachel Baum's really turned the place around—people come all the way from South Miami just to meet those cats of hers."

"Far be it from me to root against Rachel Baum and her famous bookstore cats." There was a hint of amusement in Julian's voice.

"Such a hard worker, that one! Between running the store, planning the Halloween event—which is coming together beautifully, by the way—and now this book she's working on." Dahlia's voice warmed and Samkhat heard the shuffling sound of her stuffing papers back into her leather satchel. "Actually, you know what? You should talk to her!"

"Oh?" Julian's voice carried mild interest.

"She's researching Coacoochee's social history. I stopped by the store this afternoon to finalize Halloween details, and she was on the phone with some employment agency, trying to track down people who worked the Mercury Island party scene back in the day."

The trailer went quiet. Samkhat's ear twitched—not at the silence itself, but at its quality. She'd heard this kind of quiet before, when a feral tom near the marina spotted baby birds in a low nest.

"The party scene?" Julian's voice hadn't changed in volume, still pleasant, but something had shifted beneath it—like claws extending while the paw stayed soft.

"There was one party a few years ago during the holiday season that she was particularly interested in," Dahlia continued. "She had this yellow legal pad covered in notes, lots of crossed-out names and phone numbers."

"The holiday season? Do you remember what year?"

"December of 1993, I think. It must have been a wild one! She seemed a bit flustered when I asked about it." Dahlia laughed. "You were already living out there back then, weren't you?" Her voice brightened as she moved into her favorite territory—connecting people, building community. "Talking to you would probably save Rachel a ton of legwork."

Silence stretched between them. Instinctively, Samkhat pressed closer to the concrete block, making herself smaller.

"I know she'd be thrilled to talk to someone who was actually there," Dahlia continued, oblivious to the shift in atmosphere. "Oh, Julian, you could be such a help to her! Sometimes these projects just need that one perfect source to come alive."

"I'll consider it."

They returned to gala planning, and Dahlia chattered on happily about catering options and venue logistics, the very picture of someone pleased with a productive meeting. Julian seemed to be listening politely but didn't contribute much. Finally, Dahlia rose to leave. The trailer floor creaked with footsteps, the door opening above.

"Thank you again for everything," she called. "The Historical Society is so lucky to have your support. Oh, and Julian? Do think about reaching out to Rachel. You'd be doing her such a favor!" Samkhat could hear the smile in her voice as she added, "And I'll bet you'd enjoy talking to her about the old days."

"You may be right about that." The grin in Julian's voice was as big as Dahlia's. "I'll have to track Rachel down."

"Wonderful! She'll be so pleased. Well, I'm off—have to stop by the printer before they close. See you at the gala!"

After Dahlia's car had disappeared in a cloud of dust and exhaust, Samkhat rose and stretched, automatically checking her blind side before emerging from under the trailer back into the gathering dusk. Her mind turned over what she'd heard. Julian Singer-Adams taking that kind of focused interest in Rachel's questions—that wasn't nothing. Samkhat had survived this long with only one eye by knowing what happened when a powerful creature turned their attention on a weaker one.

The outcome was rarely good for the weaker one.

The scent of fried chicken wafted from somewhere near the dumpsters, and evening was prime hunting time. But she'd already decided—after she ate, she'd head over to Title Wave. Homer and his sisters would want to know what she'd heard. Rachel had caught the attention of someone who could squash her like a palmetto bug, if he wanted to.

Samkhat padded away from the trailer, checking left before each step into open space, leaving behind the small office where Julian Singer-Adams remained, sitting very still.

CHAPTER 25

IT WAS NEARLY ONE a.m., and the narrow hallway separating Red Room's front-of-house dining area from the "secret" VIP room in the back pounded with a bass line Rachel could feel in her sternum. She and Tommy emerged from dinner into a wall of sound and bodies, the party already in full swing.

"I ate too much," Tommy groaned, pressing a hand to his stomach. "That truffle risotto was my undoing."

"Forget the risotto—I'd like to build a summer house in that bread pudding," Rachel replied, adding with mock seriousness, "And, no, you can't visit."

Red Room on Allamanda Avenue was a two-part establishment—a nightclub that was also renowned as one of the best (and priciest) restaurants in Coacoochee. "Celebrity Club"—Red Room's weekly Saturday-night theme party and the brainchild of its promoter-in-residence, Keith Cranford—took full advantage of both components. Each week a different Coacoochee "celebrity" was selected as the party's honoree, and he or she was invited to bring a small group of friends to a comped dinner in Red Room's restaurant. After dinner there was a full-blown party in the private back room. Partiers in the know would access the room, not through the club's main entrance on Allamanda, but through the back-alley service entrance. The girl who worked this door on Saturday nights was simply called L. L was tall and lanky and speckled with a constellation of tattoos, and she had the ruthlessly appraising eye of a horse trader when it came to sizing up candidates for entry into the inner sanctum.

Tonight was Danny Elliott's Celebrity Club, and Rachel had been surprised to find herself included among his ten invited guests for dinner. "I've *told* you, darling," Tommy had said. "People know who you are now!"

Still, it was nothing short of miraculous that she'd made it at all. The cats had been absolute terrors while she was getting ready—Scarlett had somehow managed to snag her dress so badly it looked like it had been through a paper shredder, Homer had wailed so piteously it was as if his very soul was being separated from his body, and even Vashti kept winding around her ankles like she was trying to trip her. If Laurie hadn't answered her frantic phone call with the offer of a loaner from the boutique, she might have had to stay home altogether. And that, she thought—basking in the glow of a grand meal and a heady sense of belonging—would have been a real shame.

Danny had been the perfect host throughout dinner, keeping the conversation flowing with practiced ease. He and Rachel had huddled briefly before everyone had been seated to go over last-minute details for Title Wave's Halloween party—now only a week away. The music wasn't as loud in the dining room as it was in the club itself, but they'd still found it necessary to bring their heads so close together, they were practically touching—so close Rachel could feel Danny's breath on her cheek. "I know my schedule's been a nightmare this month, with the book launch and everything." His warm smile had ensured, as it so often did, that he was instantly forgiven. "Tuesday after the store closes works for me, if it works for you," she'd told him, and he'd quickly accepted. "I'll bring samples. It'll be fun!"

Now the dinner portion of the evening was over, and Danny—plus his ten guests—were trying to squeeze their way into Red Room's red-velvet jewel box of a back room, where it seemed the entirety of Coacoochee's nightlife elite were already crammed in.

Rachel and Tommy paused just inside the doorway, letting the sensory assault wash over them. The room pulsed with beautiful bodies in motion, conversations shouted over music, perfume and cologne mixing with the underlying scent of expensive liquor. Through the crowd, Rachel caught glimpses of Danny standing near the bar with Griselda and her boyfriend. He was laughing at something Griselda had said.

"He looks happy," Rachel observed. It was true—Danny seemed younger, somehow, and carefree without his customary black chef's hat.

"He should be." Tommy snagged a martini from the bar. "Griselda told me at dinner they did two hundred covers tonight before he left. Sabrosa's killing it."

Almost the first people they ran into as they attempted to cross the room were Tatiana Monster of Art and her live-in manager, Rune Solberg. Tatiana was dramatically tall, slender, and black-haired. A former fashion model, she'd moved to Coacoochee and taken up a career as a sculptor, painter, fashion designer, and classical pianist—and what was arguably the art world's most attention-grabbing moniker. Born in Milan and raised (as Coacoochee legend claimed) in a Russian monastery, Tatiana was believed to be fluent in eight or nine languages. She was always out with Rune, a six-foot-six Norwegian native with long blond hair and a full moustache and beard.

Rachel—who barely reached five-foot-one when not wearing heels—felt positively dwarfish in their presence.

Tatiana gasped loudly as Rachel and Tommy stood on tiptoe to kiss her hello. "I was just thinking of you!" she exclaimed to Tommy in her heavy Russian accent. "You will put me in your next column, yes?"

As Tommy assured Tatiana that she would soon see her name in *Palm* print, Rachel caught a glimpse of Brock Winfield standing near the bar, wearing what appeared to be a blazer made entirely from silver sequins. Standing beneath the red bulbs that lit the space, he resembled nothing so much as a giant traffic light. His eyes met Rachel's, and his lips curled into a sneer before he returned to his ineffectual attempts at getting the bartender's attention. Rachel realized she hadn't seen him lurking around Title Wave for the past couple of weeks—but she knew he was still out there, nursing his grudges like an expensive glass of scotch.

Rachel felt a twinge of uneasiness but was quickly distracted by Laurie Castillo, waving at her from a nearby banquette where she sat with Robert, her geometric print dress unmistakable even in the dim lighting. Sabine Ackermann held court a few tables away, her platinum hair glowing under the red lights like a halo.

All the usual suspects, Rachel thought, as she waved enthusiastically back to Laurie. In a deliberately oversized gesture, she swept one hand up and down over the floor-length, spaghetti-strapped black dress Laurie had lent her, mouthing: *It fits!* And Laurie laughed as she mouthed back, in an equally exaggerated way, *Of course! I'm amazing!*

There was something undeniably electric about tonight—maybe it was Danny's infectious joy, or maybe it was just the Saturday-night energy that made Coacoochee feel like the center of the universe. She and Tommy maneuvered their way to the banquette Keith Cranford had reserved for them, where a lissome waitress with a curtain of yellow hair was already arranging their complimentary champagne service. Rachel trailed behind Tommy as he paused here and there to exchange air kisses with people he knew. As she passed, Rachel caught a snippet of conversation between the good-looking twenty-something who wrote the nightlife column for the *Miami Blade*, and the pretty blonde with Alice in Wonderland hair who always seemed to be with him.

"—knew Marc was into coke," the writer was saying. "Explains every-thing."

"Right?" The pretty blonde took a sip of her cosmopolitan. "No wonder he was so aggressive at Sabrosa."

Rachel had been hearing similar whispers around the café for days now. The lie had taken root so easily, transforming Marc from victim to villain in the span of a few *sotto voce* conversations. While Rachel was happy to see Tommy restored back into Sabrosa's (and Danny's) good graces, she wondered if anyone would remember the real Marc—the meticulous journalist, the man who'd died pursuing the truth. She turned to see if Tommy had overheard as well, but he'd successfully squeezed past one last pair of gyrating bodies to arrive safely at their table. Rachel seated herself next to him and picked up one of the two glasses of champagne the waitress had poured before turning her attention to another table.

"So," Tommy said, leaning close to be heard over the music, "you never finished telling me about this afternoon."

Rachel felt her face warm, and not from the champagne. "About Evan?"

"Yes, about Evan!" Tommy regarded her with amusement. "I want all the details. Spill!"

She laughed, remembering. "We were going over his spring catalog, and suddenly he's fidgeting with this advance copy of the new Barbara Kingsolver, all nervous and everything, and he says—" she pitched her voice lower in imitation, "I don't want to seem to forward or anything, but would you maybe want to go out with me sometime? Like maybe after your Halloween party?' And I said, 'You really want our first date to be in full costume?' And he laughed and made this funny face and said, '*You'd* look great in anything, but in my case a costume could only be an improvement.'"

Tommy's face lit up with genuine delight. "Finally! I was starting to think I'd have to lock you two in the romance section until something happened."

"Stop it." But she was grinning. The champagne and the warmth of the room made her feel lighter than she had in weeks. "I said yes."

"Obviously you said yes. Where's he taking you?"

"I don't know yet." Just thinking about it sent a flutter through her stomach. "It feels weird, you know? Dating again."

"It feels perfect," Tommy corrected. "You deserve someone who brings treats for your cats and gets nervous asking you out."

Before Rachel could respond, she noticed Isabella approaching through the crowd in vintage Leonard Paris—a floor-length, form-fitting explosion of enormous pink, teal, and lavender flowers that bloomed extravagantly against a black background. Even in a room full of people trying to be seen, Isabella moved like someone who never had to try.

"Tommy, darling." She air-kissed his cheek. "Wasn't dinner divine? Keith really outdid himself."

Rachel watched Tommy's entire demeanor shift—shoulders straightening, smile becoming more eager. She knew he'd been trying all through dinner to steer the conversation toward the *Daily News* position, only to have Isabella skillfully deflect. Whether because the only news on this particular subject was bad news, or simply because she was still irritated with Tommy for having avoided her calls, was impossible to guess. Isabella's face was smooth as porcelain and gave no hint, one way or the other.

"It was incredible," Tommy agreed. "Listen, Isabella, about lunch next week—"

"Absolutely, we must." Isabella's smile was warm but impersonal. "My assistant will call you. Now, if you'll excuse me, I promised Sabine I'd say hello." She kissed Rachel's cheek. "You look wonderful tonight, my darling." Leaning in to whisper conspiratorially in her ear, Isabella added, "I know Danny thinks so!" Rachel looked at her, startled, and felt a blush creep over her cheeks. Isabella smiled and squeezed her arm. "Enjoy the party," she told them both, and disappeared back into the crowd.

And then she was gone, leaving Tommy deflated and Rachel perplexed. She cast a quick glance over to the bar where Danny still held court. He caught her eye and smiled with an impish display of dimples before turning back to Michael Tronn, who currently promoted parties at the popular nightclub Liquid.

"Isabella's definitely avoiding the subject of the *Daily News*," Tommy said glumly.

Rachel brought her attention back to him. "Maybe she's just being careful," she said soothingly. "This isn't really the place to talk business."

"Everyplace is a place to talk business in this town." Tommy drained half his glass of champagne in one gulp. "What if I really did ruin everything? What if—"

A sudden burst of laughter from Laurie Castillo's table cut him off. "Come on," Rachel said, tugging Tommy's arm. "Let's go say hi to Laurie. You can worry about Isabella later."

They made their way through the crowd, Tommy's mood visibly lifting as they navigated the familiar choreography of a Coacoochee party—the subtle sidesteps around dancing couples, the brief pauses to acknowledge acquaintances, the balancing of champagne glasses held high above the fray.

"Rachel! Tommy!" Laurie rose from her banquette as they approached, stunning in a skintight zebra-striped dress that fell to her ankles. "That dress looks *perfect* on you." She pulled Rachel into a warm hug that smelled of jasmine and champagne.

"And *you* are an angel of mercy!" Rachel returned the hug and settled onto the burgundy velvet banquette. "So how's Kotik? Has he learned his lesson?"

Robert laughed, his usually serious demeanor softened under the strobe lights. "He's been a model citizen. I think we wore him out with all the extra attention."

"I may grant him parole in a day or two," Laurie admitted, though she tried to sound stern. "He's been following me around the boutique, helping arrange displays. Well, 'helping' might be generous. Mostly he sits in the middle of whatever I'm working on and purrs."

"Speaking of the boutique," Tommy said, "that window display with the Pucci scarves is genius. Very Slim Aarons meets Miami Beach."

The conversation flowed easily, punctuated by the bass line that made the ice in their glasses tremble. They discussed the upcoming Halloween parade, Robert's latest case (carefully edited for public consumption), and whether the new sushi place on Seventh Street was worth the hype. Rachel found herself relaxing into the rhythm of Coacoochee small talk, though she noticed Tommy's eyes still tracked Isabella's movements across the room.

After about twenty minutes, during which they'd been joined briefly by Keith Cranford himself and witnessed Tatiana Monster of Art's dramatic interpretation of what might have been either dancing or performance art, Rachel felt the inevitable call of too much champagne.

"Excuse me," she said, touching Tommy's arm. "I'll be right back."

"Through the kitchen and to the left," Laurie advised, correctly guessing Rachel's destination. "The line for the main restroom is probably around the block by now."

Not for the first time, Rachel reflected that there were two types of people in Coacoochee: the people who waited in line for things, and the in-the-know types who never had to wait for anything. She was grateful for Laurie's insider knowledge as she navigated her way back through the crowd and slipped through the swinging doors into Red Room's bustling kitchen. The sudden shift from red-tinted darkness to bright fluorescent light made Rachel blink, and she hurried past the line cooks who barely glanced up from their stations.

The bathroom was mercifully empty, a small oasis of relative quiet where the bassline was muffled to a distant heartbeat. Rachel took her time, checking her reflection in the mirror and reapplying the lip gloss that had disappeared somewhere between the bread pudding and her third glass of champagne. The bathroom's art deco fixtures gleamed under soft lighting, and she allowed herself a moment to appreciate the blessed coolness after the heat of the packed party.

She was still thinking about Evan as she made her way back through the kitchen, nodding to a server who balanced an impossible number of plates, although her mind couldn't help but settle on Danny for a moment or two. Isabella's whispered comment had left her unsettled. The swinging doors to the main room loomed ahead, promising a return to the sensory assault of the party.

That was when she spotted him.

Julian Singer-Adams stood in the narrow service corridor that connected the kitchen to the VIP room.

Waiting for her.

"Rachel." Julian's voice was pitched low despite the music. She could see the tension in his jaw, smell expensive cologne underlaid with nothing—stone-cold sobriety in a club full of celebration as he stepped forward to kiss her cheek. Rachel fought the urge to step back, even as she automatically kissed his cheek in return.

"Julian." She tried to sound casual, but her heart was racing. Still, she managed to keep the tremble out of her voice as she said, "Enjoying the party?"

"Not particularly, no." A brief, ironic smile that managed to perfectly convey Julian's distaste drifted across his lips. "But I wanted to speak with you." One hand reached up to smooth out his silk tie. "About your recent curiosity."

The words hit her like cold water. *He knew.* Somehow, *he knew* what she'd been looking into.

"I don't know what you mean."

"Don't you?" His eyes bored into hers. "A word of advice, from someone who's been in this town longer than you have. Some stories are better left untold."

The music seemed to fade around them, the party noise dimming until all Rachel could hear was her own heartbeat and Julian's words.

"Especially when people have already paid too high a price for their curiosity." His gaze held hers. "I'd hate to see you become another cautionary tale."

"Is that a threat?" Her voice came out steadier than she felt.

Something flickered in Julian's expression, but he was already backing away. "Enjoy your evening," he said. And then he was gone, moving through the crowd toward the exit.

"There you are!" Tommy appeared at her elbow. "Was that Julian?"

"He—" Rachel tried to find words. "Okay," she began, "so I've been helping Natalie a little with her investigation." Tommy's face paled, and she hastily added, "Just making a few phone calls. Nothing *dangerous*." The tremble she'd successfully kept out of her voice while talking to Julian returned with a vengeance. "But now he knows. He warned me about asking questions, said he'd hate to see me become another 'cautionary tale'."

"He threatened you?" The color that had fled Tommy's face a moment earlier came back and doubled.

"I don't know." The champagne wasn't sitting well anymore. "I think I need some air. Can we get out of here?"

"Tommy!" A voice called out from near the bar. Rachel recognized the lean figure of Manny, *Palm*'s nightlife photographer, who was making his way toward them with camera equipment slung over his shoulder. "Sorry I'm late—Yucca was insane tonight."

Rachel saw the conflict play across his face. Tommy Duvall, her friend, wanted to make sure she got home safely. But "Mr. Nightlife" had professional obligations—Danny's Celebrity Club was the social event of the week, and his column about it would need accompanying visuals.

"You should stay." Rachel presented what she hoped was a reassuring smile. "This is your job."

"Rachel—"

"Really." She squeezed his hand. "Two a.m. is late for me, but your night's just getting started." It was true—if anything, the crowd had grown thicker, the energy more electric. Through the mass of bodies, she could see Danny near the DJ booth, his black silk shirt now unbuttoned at the collar, his smile incandescent under the lights. Isabella was beside him, whispering something that made him laugh.

Manny stood awkwardly to one side, clearly sensing he'd interrupted something. "I can come back later if—"

"No," Tommy said, and sighed. "No, we need to get started." He turned back to Rachel, lowering his voice. "But tomorrow—first thing—we'll talk to Natalie. Maybe even Nick Torres."

Rachel nodded. "First thing tomorrow," she agreed. "Now go do that voodoo that you do so well." She smiled reassuringly. "I'll grab a cab."

Tommy hesitated a moment longer, then pulled her into a quick hug. "Be careful getting home," he murmured against her ear. "Lock your doors. And leave a message on my machine when you get there, okay?"

"I will," she promised.

Tommy squeezed her hand one more time before turning to Manny. "Let's start with Danny by the DJ booth. The light's good there, and we can get some of the crowd in the background..."

As Tommy and Manny moved away, Rachel glanced around to make sure Keith was nowhere in sight—although her view was obscured by the thicket of partiers who still packed the room to capacity. The last thing she needed was Red Room's promoter-in-residence catching her "sneaking out" at what he'd consider an insultingly early hour. With any luck, she could slip away while he was holding court elsewhere.

The night air hit Rachel like a slap when she finally emerged outside, and her ears rang in the sudden quiet. She made her way through the back alley, waving goodbye to L and marveling at the long line of aspirants still clamoring to get in. She'd gotten all the way out to Allamanda Avenue, and had her hand on a cab-door handle, when a voice behind her said, "Excuse me, Miss Thing!" Rachel turned to see Keith Cranford's slim-hipped form approaching swiftly from the darkness of the alley. The look in his pale-green eyes—which, in better lighting, made for a striking contrast against his café au lait skin—was unmistakably determined. "Where do you think you're going?"

"I'm sorry I didn't say goodbye." Rachel's pulse was still racing from her encounter with Julian, and Keith's sudden appearance had made her heart skip another beat. She forced herself to breathe normally. "I couldn't find you," she lied. "I was just headed home."

Keith briskly tapped the roof of the cab, indicating that it should drive on. "No, you're not." He took her arm firmly. "Let's go back inside. I'll send you another bottle of champagne."

Rachel's head was spinning as she found herself deposited back at Tommy's table, where he was deep in conference with Manny. He looked up in surprise at her return, then caught a glimpse of Keith—who was already signaling to the waitress to bring them another bottle of champagne—and his brow cleared. "Keith came by and asked where you were, but I didn't think he'd actually go looking for you."

Rachel sank into the banquette, accepting the champagne flute that had appeared before her. "I'm the only person I know," she said, "who gets kicked *into* clubs."

Tommy's eyes sparkled with amusement. "I told you, darling. People know you now."

The champagne tasted expensive yet somehow bitter; the adrenaline that had flooded through her system when Keith accosted her still hadn't receded entirely.

It was flattering, Rachel realized, that her absence had been noticed. Six months ago, she'd been nobody. But as the music pounded and the beautiful people swirled around her, all she could think about was Julian.

She was trapped in this velvet box. Rachel remembered the envy she'd seen on the faces of those still waiting outside as Keith Cranford had personally escorted her past the velvet rope. He'd brought her back to rejoin her with the rest of the scenesters and personalities he'd collected—the entire cabal of gorgeous and odd-looking and eclectic and slightly outrageous Coacoochee "celebrities" who'd given this party its blinding luster.

Like she was one of them now.

Whether she wanted to be or not.

CHAPTER 26

Moonlight filtered through the plantation shutters of Julian Singer-Adams's study. He reached for the antacids again—his third dose tonight—and dry-swallowed them with practiced elegance. Even this small discomfort couldn't disturb the careful composure he'd worn like armor for more than twenty-five years.

His stomach had been in knots ever since Friday's meeting with Dahlia. Three days of churning anxiety that had grown markedly worse since dinner tonight. Perhaps he should speak with his chef about the menu, which apparently still wasn't simple enough for his increasingly sensitive digestion. Age and its laments, Julian thought wryly. Turning fifty a few years earlier had taken a toll that all his money couldn't buy him out of.

He settled back into his leather chair, the buttery soft material sighing beneath him. Through the windows, his estate stretched down to a private beach Julian hadn't set foot on in at least a decade. Once he'd imagined the wife and children who would enjoy the fruits of his labor—and when it had become clear that the schedule he kept and the time he spent traveling back and forth between Miami and Los Angeles weren't conducive to family life, the beach had become the perfect backdrop for entertaining. The silence now was almost oppressive—no preparations for weekend festivities, no caterers' trucks rumbling up the drive. His neighbors certainly didn't miss those days, nor did his accountant miss writing checks for damaged landscaping and noise complaints.

Just when he'd thought the situation with Daisy and Marc was settling—that life might return to its careful, controlled rhythms—Rachel Baum had emerged as an unexpected problem. Julian didn't miss much, but he had to admit he hadn't seen her coming. Dahlia's cheerful chatter about Rachel researching Coacoochee's "social history," tracking down people who'd worked the Mercury Island "party scene" in December 1993, had nearly knocked him off his axis.

It had taken every ounce of Julian's practiced composure not to react.

He found himself thinking about Rachel now as he sipped a glass of the cold ginger ale his housekeeper, Sofia, had arranged on his desk before retiring for the night. He'd been itching to get his hands on Dorothea Wilson's building. Although he'd bought, renovated, and sold dozens of buildings on Hibiscus Road, none had quite the appeal of the one that housed Title Wave Books, with its one-of-a-kind original terrazzo floor and that upstairs terrace dripping with potential.

The bookstore had struggled as much as one would expect in a town like Coacoochee, especially back when it had been managed by...Julian's stomach clenched again, and he found he couldn't remember the name of the unimpressive fellow who'd run it before Rachel. (Brad, maybe, or Brick.) Julian had known it was only a matter of time before he'd be able to take it off Dorothea's hands for a song—some absurdly small sum that would be a pittance for him, but nonetheless a small fortune for a retiree who didn't want the burden of running a shop fulltime and couldn't find good help to do it for her.

He remembered seeing Rachel in passing, in those early days after she'd first moved to town. All gritted teeth and grim determination to start over following some personal catastrophe, with her wild curls and three cats—one of them blind. Rachel had a kind heart, Julian supposed. He'd expected her to be even worse for the shop than the previous manager, but it hadn't worked out that way. Dahlia was right that people came to Title Wave just to see the cats, but it was more than that. Rachel had been good for the store in a way that nobody, except maybe Dorothea herself, could have foreseen. The shop was now a genuine asset to a community that its new manager hadn't even set foot in only a few months earlier.

Rachel didn't belong, yet somehow she fit. The same could be said of Coacoochee's glittering nightlife scene—hardly a hospitable environment for a bookish woman with cats. Yet people seemed to like her. Even Julian couldn't help but feel a grudging respect for her. There was something refreshing about a person who knew exactly who she was, who didn't perform for anyone.

The thought brought his father to mind, and Julian's stomach gave another painful twist. Julio Santos Sr. had been the same way—authentically himself whether he was speaking to his construction crew or the wealthy homeowners whose driveways they poured. Never modulating his voice, never hiding his Honduran accent, never understanding why his son spent money on elocution lessons.

It shamed Julian how little he'd thought about his father in the years since he'd died. There had been an empire to build and little time for sentimental reflection. But the older Julian got, the more he saw his father's face looking back at him from the mirror. *Como dos gotas de agua,* people always said. Like two drops of water. That's how alike Julian and his father had once been.

His father would have liked Rachel, Julian thought now. Would have appreciated her straightforward manner, the way she seemed comfortable in her own skin. He would have been deeply ashamed of the way his son had spoken to her at Red Room on Saturday night. Not just because his father had possessed a certain old-world chivalry that could never have countenanced threatening a woman. His father would also have been shrewd enough to see through those threats and recognize them for what they were—desperate moves by a desperate man.

Julian rose from his desk, moving to the window with the measured grace that had become second nature. Twenty-five years of practice had made the performance seamless.

The parties had been part of that performance. Back in his Gatsby phase, when he'd thought lavish entertaining would show the world how successful he'd become. He hadn't particularly enjoyed them—all those people treating his home like their personal playground, the forced conversations with politicians and models and trust fund babies, whose observations he had to pretend were clever.

But having a private chef—now that had felt like true arrival. Not just catering staff for parties, but his own personal chef, traveling between his L.A. and Coacoochee properties. Danny Elliott had been perfect for the role. At twenty-five he was young, talented, and possessed a preternatural golden-boy charm that made everything seem effortless. More than just cooking, Danny had understood the theater of it all. He could work a room like a politician, always knowing who needed attention, who was holding the best drugs—and which beautiful girls he'd ask to join him in the pool house for private festivities.

December 4th, 1993. Alicia Rodrigue arriving in her department store dress, clutching her invitation nervously. Lord knew which of the college bars or model casting calls—the ones Danny regularly trawled for "fresh talent," as he put it—he'd found her in. She'd arrived early, before all but the least fashionable of his guests.

"Your house is unbelievable," she'd said, dark eyes wide as she took in the soaring ceilings and museum-quality art.

He'd given her a tour, finding himself charmed by the sincerity of her enthusiasm. When Danny appeared with that Polaroid camera he was always carrying around—hoping to capture something titillating or compromising (or both)—Julian had posed naturally, his arm around Alicia's shoulders.

He'd left soon after for dinner downtown with the bankers who were financing the most ambitious project he'd undertaken to date—the demolition of the old Bakery Centre down in South Miami and its replacement with an extravagant new outdoor mall that, if all went to plan, would make Julian wealthier than even he had ever imagined. He'd already committed to using a portion of the funds to sponsor next year's Make-A-Wish gala, the black-tie fundraiser that was the premier annual event on Miami's social calendar. And that was just the beginning. By this time next year, Julian had reflected, he'd be one of Miami's biggest and best-known builders and philanthropists.

"Keep an eye on her," he'd told Danny, nodding in Alicia's direction as he was leaving. Danny had been nearly as comfortable playing host in Julian's home by then as Julian was himself. "She seems overwhelmed."

When he'd returned shortly after midnight, the party had shifted somehow. Julian's stomach heaved again as he remembered it now—the way Danny had met him in the garage before he could even enter the house, his ruddy California tan ashen beneath the fluorescent lights.

"We have a problem."

In the pool house, Alicia lay unconscious on a white leather sofa. Her pretty coral dress was rumpled, her breathing shallow and labored.

"What did she take?"

"Pills from my stash." Danny ran a hand through his carefully tousled hair. "She was trying to keep up with girls who party every weekend."

Julian was acutely aware of the guests whose cars were still parked outside—Commissioner Carpenter. The Mayor. A couple of state representatives and even one of Florida's two U.S. senators, back from D. C. for the holidays. Not one of them would want to be associated with something like this. And not one of them would hesitate to throw Julian under the bus, if that's what it took to preserve themselves from being tainted by scandal.

Julian was suddenly enraged by the whole thing—by the careless way this pretty young girl had been treated in his home, by the way his supposed "guests" trashed it weekend after weekend, by the unfairness of this happening *now* when he was on the brink of achieving *everything*.

Mostly, he was enraged by the fear that underlay all of it.

"*Well?!*" he'd snapped at Danny. "Why are you staring at me like an idiot? Call an ambulance, for God's sake!"

"Julian, we can't call 911 here," Danny had said. "Think about it—paramedics, police, investigations. Your name in the papers. Everything you've built. Everything you're *about* to build…"

Julio Santos Aguilar from Hialeah would have called for help without hesitation. But Julian Singer-Adams had spent too many years burying that man to give him any oxygen now.

"I'll take her," Danny had said. "Drive her over to Jackson Memorial myself. Tell them I found her outside a club."

Julian had taken a deep breath, trying to remain calm and logical. "Bring her to Coacoochee General. Jackson's all the way over the causeway."

"Exactly. Far enough that they won't connect her to Mercury Island." Danny was already lifting Alicia, her body limp as a doll. "I'll handle it. You just get everyone out of here."

Julian had let him go. He'd spent the next fifteen minutes dispersing guests with practiced calm. A gas leak, he'd said. Nothing to worry about, but naturally everyone had to evacuate the grounds while it was sorted out.

By dawn, it was as if the party had never happened.

Except Alicia Rodrigue was dead. Found abandoned outside Jackson Memorial's emergency room. Left there by someone who'd driven away without getting help.

WHEN TOMMY DUVALL'S BLIND item had appeared a week later—with its vague, salacious tale of a Mercury Island party and a girl who'd partied too hard—Julian had been certain his world would collapse. Somehow, somebody had discovered the truth and sold him out. Christmas decorations had begun to appear around town; to this day, Julian still associated the holiday season with the agony, the crushing guilt, of those final weeks of 1993.

But nothing had happened. Somehow—a miracle, that was the only way to describe it—the whole thing had blown over. Most likely, it hadn't occurred to anyone to connect the chichi parties Julian Singer-Adams hosted with the tawdry "models and bottles" gathering the blind item had alluded to. The gossip faded, and life had continued.

Later, after cautious questioning, Julian learned that Daisy Locarro had been Tommy's source. His assistant, who spent her weekdays filing his papers and scheduling his meetings, who was never invited to his weekend gatherings. But she'd lived her own wild life outside of Julian's office. She'd been to enough parties in other Mercury Island homes—and had more than enough imagination, apparently—to craft a colorful "fiction" and sell it to Tommy Duvall and *Palm* magazine in exchange for some much-needed rent money.

The cosmic joke of it—her made-up story accidentally matching reality—might have been funny if Alicia hadn't died.

Five years ago, when that blind item first appeared, Danny had come to him in a rage. "Someone knows," he'd insisted. Julian had let him believe it, had even paid him to go away—startup money for Sabrosa, enough to get Danny out of his life. Danny had thought he was blackmailing Julian, but the truth was Julian had never felt better about a single dollar he'd ever spent than he did now, in using his vast fortune to buy Danny Elliott out of his life.

And, anyway, it was better to have Danny think that some anonymous person out there really did know the truth. It kept him careful. It kept him in line.

Julian had fired Daisy, of course. Generous severance, glowing references, but he couldn't have her around anymore—despite how much he'd come to genuinely like her, with her tall tales and extravagant humor, and the way she instantly enlivened any room she walked into. Not when her "harmless" gossip had come so dangerously close to the truth.

Not when she was another pretty, vulnerable young woman who might get dragged down by the undertow of his life.

But Julian had watched over her. He'd driven out to more clubs and late-night parties to give her a ride home than he could count, not wanting her dependent on the largesse of her fellow partiers, who might or might not be prepared to look out for her safety. He'd "loaned" her money countless times when she couldn't afford this or that much-coveted bauble, or when she was having trouble making rent. Isabella didn't like it, and he understood why a publicist would think it was a bad idea. But *somebody* had to look out for Daisy.

It had been his penance for Alicia, in a way—keeping Daisy safe when he'd failed the other girl so completely.

Had his father lived to see what had happened to Alicia, and Julian's role in it, his disappointment in his son would have crushed him beyond repair. On some level, Julian was always hoping he'd be able to meet his father's eyes in the mirror again.

But then had come that morning back in late September—only a day or two before *Palm* magazine's big party at Sabrosa, celebrating their five-year anniversary—when Julian had given Daisy a ride home from some after-hours over the causeway. He'd dropped her near Title Wave, whose café was now Daisy's favorite spot for coffee, and found her unusually downbeat.

It hadn't taken much prying for her to tell him what was troubling her: some late-night confession she'd made to Marc Gottsegen—who notoriously loathed Tommy Duvall—that she'd "invented" the entire blind item that had made Tommy's career. Marc had been bothering her ever since, demanding more details, determined to expose the whole thing and show Tommy up for the fraud that Marc had convinced himself Tommy was.

Now, Julian's stomach flipped again. The light from the lamp on his desk blurred and became as haloed as the moon outside, and Julian barely made it to the bathroom before the entire contents of his stomach came up.

Daisy's words had hit him like ice water, cutting through twenty years of carefully maintained control. Marc Gottsegen was digging into December 1993. If he was thorough—and reporters looking to destroy rivals usually were—he'd track down everyone who'd worked for Julian back then. The drivers, the housekeepers, the security.

The personal chef.

A few quick calls confirmed that Marc had already started poking around, tracking down former employees and groundskeeping staff. Eventually, someone would remember the golden boy from California. Who knew what Danny would say if cornered? His planned expansion of Sabrosa into Los Angeles and Las Vegas was at stake. He had investors of his own now. There were whispered rumors that those investors were becoming concerned; that Danny occasionally treated Sabrosa's bank account as if it were his own personal fund. If that was true, then Danny couldn't have anyone looking too closely into his affairs. He'd sell Julian out in a heartbeat.

Julian had driven home after dropping Daisy off, his mind racing. He needed to make things clear to Danny. Now. He'd dialed from his study, hands unsteady.

Danny answered on the third ring, kitchen sounds clattering in the background. "Julian?" The surprise in Danny's voice was genuine. They hadn't spoken directly in years. "This is unexpected."

"We need to talk. Can you speak privately?"

A pause. The background noise faded as Danny apparently moved somewhere quieter. "What's up?"

"A reporter is digging into December 1993." The words came out harsher than intended, his usual smooth delivery cracking.

Silence on the line. Then: "How do you know this?"

Julian wasn't about to mention Daisy's name—and, fortunately, there was no reason for Danny to make the connection. "He's been calling around. Talking to people who worked for me back then." Julian heard his father's accent creeping back into his voice, the way it always did when he was rattled. "If he finds you—when he finds you—you say nothing. You know nothing. You were just hired help cooking canapés."

"Julian—"

"If you even think about talking to him, I'll bury you." The threat spilled out, unpolished, desperate. Nothing like the subtle maneuvering Julian Singer-Adams was known for. "I'll tell everyone how you got the money for Sabrosa. The drugs. The girl you left to die. Everything."

"Are you threatening me?" Danny's voice had gone cold.

"I'm telling you what happens if you talk." Julian's hand gripped the phone too tightly. "So keep your mouth shut."

The line went dead. Danny had hung up on him.

WHEN HE'D HEARD ABOUT Daisy—found dead outside Title Wave's front door of an apparent heart attack—Julian's first thought was that the timing was impossible. His second thought was to wonder why his hands were shaking.

Julian knew how much Daisy had respected Rachel. Perhaps she'd gone there when she'd begun to feel ill, thinking Rachel would know how to help her. And young people *did* have heart attacks sometimes. Julian had never known her to touch anything stronger than alcohol, but Daisy *might* have picked up new habits since the days when she'd been his personal assistant. None of it was completely implausible.

At the funeral, Julian found himself glaring at Tommy Duvall. The gossip columnist had stood a few feet in front of him, shoulders shaking with what looked like genuine grief. The rational part of Julian's mind knew Tommy wasn't really to blame—he'd just been a hungry young writer who'd bought a story five years ago.

But Julian had never liked Tommy, the blatant social climber who'd built his career on a rotten story and set this all in motion. And why should *Tommy* get to feel so obviously comfortable in his own skin—going everywhere, talking to everyone like he had nothing to hide? Why should things that had been so difficult for Julian come so easily to someone who was hardly more than a tabloid journalist?

It had always been easier to dislike Tommy than to hold himself accountable.

Julian had never once entered Sabrosa—the shrine to Danny Elliott's cooking brilliance that his money had paid for—but he broke his own rule to join Marc and Isabella there that Monday night, in the desperate hope that Isabella might be able to steer Marc toward other stories.

By Wednesday morning, Marc was dead too. Another heart attack.

And suddenly, with crystal clarity, Julian had understood.

Danny had killed them both. The man who prepared food for half of Coacoochee—who grew his own herbs and knew exactly how to mask any unusual taste—had become a poisoner. Somehow, he'd figured out Daisy was Marc's source.

The realization came with a wave of nausea that had nothing to do with his sensitive stomach. He'd threatened Danny to protect himself, and Danny had responded by killing Daisy. Julian's clumsy attempt at self-preservation had signed her death warrant.

And now Marc was dead, too. Three people dead—Alicia, Daisy, Marc. He couldn't go to the police without revealing everything. His role in Alicia's death, his threat that had triggered Daisy's murder, his failure to act when he'd suspected the first killing.

The golden boy chef with his cookbook empire and expansion plans had become a serial killer, and Julian had helped create him.

Still, Julian couldn't deny that it had been a relief when Marc died. And the Medical Examiner finding cocaine in Marc's system had been a stroke of luck. Julian knew Commissioner Carpenter had his own reasons for wanting to close the books quickly on this one—which explained why he'd invited Julian for that round of golf in the first place. It had almost been amusing, Julian thought now, to see the Commissioner working "subtly" to get Julian to do something—tip off Isabella about the cocaine rumor, let her carry the ball from there—that Julian was willing and actually eager to do, anyway.

It would be infinitely harder to bury Daisy in his heart than it had been Alicia, whom he'd barely known. But at least he was safe now—safe in every possible way. Marc was no longer digging. Rachel was an intelligent woman and, though she'd done an admirable job of maintaining her composure, Julian could see in her face that his words to her on Saturday night had hit home. Danny didn't know Rachel had picked up the investigation from Marc, and there was no reason he ever needed to know.

And as for Julian himself, Danny would never get to him. He'd never entered Sabrosa except for that night with Marc, and he carefully controlled every aspect of his life. Danny might be a killer, but he wasn't a magician. Julian's Mercury Island estate was an impregnable fortress. Danny Elliott would never set foot inside its gates again.

The pressure in Julian's chest now was just aggravation. Aggravation and too much food at dinner. He pressed a hand to his sternum, waiting for the discomfort to pass. Perhaps he should call Dr. Hirsch about adjusting his medication.

Outside, the October sun had begun to rise from the water, and Julian's study glowed in deeper shades of gold. Later today, he'd talk to Sofia and ask her to tell the chef to prepare lighter meals. Something easier on his increasingly sensitive stomach.

The day stretched before him, quiet and calm. This was the way he preferred it now. No more parties. No more chaos. Just the perfectly ordered life of Julian Singer-Adams, safe in his Mercury Island castle, cool and serene as he floated high above the hot struggles of strivers like Tommy Duvall and Danny Elliott.

He had work to do—permits to review, contracts to sign. The multiplex development wasn't going to build itself, after all. Julian turned back to his desk, pushing aside the lingering discomfort in his chest. There would be time to deal with his health concerns later.

He'd built his empire. Now it was time to run it.

CHAPTER 27

NICK TORRES WAVED HIS way past the guard gate at the end of the causeway connecting Mercury Island with the rest of Coacoochee. Late-afternoon sunlight filtered through the fronds of the royal palms lining the entry road like a double row of additional sentinels. The sea air smelled even more refreshing out here in the middle of Biscayne Bay, and Nick drew a deep breath as he drove.

He'd been off duty since Sunday, enjoying a quiet couple of days with his family. But Nick had walked right back into it Tuesday morning, when Natalie Dunbar had called and given him the lowdown on Rachel's confrontation with Julian at Red Room. He'd wanted to drive out and talk to Julian immediately, but the morning had exploded with tourists behaving badly and a five-car pileup on the Julia Tuttle, which had tied up traffic—and buried Nick in paperwork—for hours.

But here he was at last. Now all he had to do was figure out how to warn off one of Coacoochee's most powerful residents without making it seem like a threat of his own.

Julian Singer-Adams had connections that ran deep. Golf with the Commissioner, dinners with the city planners, donations to every politician and charity that mattered. You didn't confront a man like that directly. You danced around the edges. Let him know Rachel Baum also had friends.

As Nick approached the Singer-Adams estate, the gatehouse guard barely glanced up from his monitors before hitting the button. That was two guard gates in under two minutes, Nick reflected. Maybe money couldn't buy happiness, but it sure bought plenty of insulation.

The Singer-Adams estate hunkered behind its coral rock wall, bougainvillea spilling over the top in cascades of magenta. As Nick turned into the circular drive, he had to pull sharp right to avoid the ambulance heading out. No lights, no sirens.

Transport, not emergency.

The driver nodded at Nick as they passed, one uniform acknowledging another. Nick nodded back and kept driving.

The drive curved past manicured gardens toward a Mediterranean revival that sprawled like a small resort. As he parked, Nick noticed a woman in a housekeeper's uniform standing near the front door. The look on her face was stunned.

"Ma'am?" He climbed out of the cruiser. "I'm Chief Torres. I was hoping to speak with Mr. Singer-Adams."

Her face crumpled. "Oh, sir. You haven't heard." She pressed a hand to her chest. "Mr. Julian, he—we found him this afternoon. In his study. Heart attack."

It was the classic fool's errand: Nick had come to deliver a warning to a man who no longer needed one.

"I'm very sorry. When did it happen?"

"Maybe an hour ago? He'd been in his office all day." Her accent carried a soft South American lilt. "Wouldn't come out for breakfast or lunch. When he still didn't answer at four..."

"Had he been ill?"

"Since last night. After dinner, he said his stomach was bothering him." Tears tracked down cheeks crisscrossed by the lines of late middle age. "I left him ginger ale on the desk in his office before I went to bed. This morning he called through the door, said he still felt unwell. I should have insisted..."

The sinking sun beat down, and Nick could feel sweat accumulating beneath his sunglasses as he handed her a handkerchief. "You couldn't have known. Sometimes these things happen suddenly."

And they did. Fifty-something men with high-stress jobs had heart attacks all the time. Hell, stomach upset was a classic early warning sign. Everything about this made perfect sense.

Except for that persistent itch at the base of Nick's skull. Three deaths in three weeks. All heart attacks. All connected to the same story.

"Mrs.—?"

"Hernandez. Sofia Hernandez."

"Who else is here?"

"Just me and Chef Graham in the house. The security team is handling...procedures. Calling lawyers, checking the perimeter cameras. Keeping visitors away."

Of course. Death among Coacoochee's elite came with protocols. By tomorrow, this place would be wrapped in legal tape tighter than any crime scene.

"Mrs. Hernandez, would you mind if I came in? I'd like to understand Mr. Singer-Adams' last few days."

The housekeeper merely nodded, seeming too emotional to speak for the moment, and turned to walk up the drive.

"His physician came?" Nick asked, as they passed through the front door.

"Yes, Dr. Hirsch. He signed the certificate. Said with Mr. Julian's blood pressure..." Mrs. Hernandez trailed off, dabbing at her eyes.

Nick followed her into a grand foyer. The house felt like a mausoleum—all marble and shadow, their footsteps echoing off surfaces that had never known warmth. She led him through rooms that looked more like museum displays than living spaces, everything arranged for impression rather than comfort.

There were cops who couldn't handle the pressure of the job, Nick thought, as his eyes took in abstract art hanging on the walls that even he could tell were worth a small fortune. Cops who'd lost marriages and kids and any chance at peace of mind because of it. But Nick wasn't one of them. Nick was the kind of person who thrived under pressure—who actually found it calming. There was serenity in the crystal-sharp awareness a high-pressure situation forced you into. In the way everything slowed down and came into focus.

As he followed Mrs. Hernandez now, Nick could feel every ounce of awareness he possessed narrow in on one, immutable certainty:

This death would be the easiest one for the Commissioner to hand-wave. The attending physician had already signed off on the death certificate. Heart disease was the leading cause of death for men in Julian's age bracket. The thing was entirely above suspicion. And yet—

Three deaths. In three weeks. All connected to the same story.

Nick had a one-shot opportunity. Right now. It was pure chance that he even happened to be here at this precise moment—because nobody would have summoned the Chief of Police officially to "investigate" a middle-aged businessman's heart attack. So if he couldn't come up with something solid—something actionable—before he left today, he'd never get to. Nick would never be in this house again. Never get a second chance to interview any of these witnesses. The body would be buried with all due care and ceremony, and the killer—if he or she were smart—would take the win and wait a good long while before striking again. If they ever did.

The tingling feeling at the base of Nick's skull told him the answer was somewhere in this house. All he had to do was tug at every thread. Eventually, one would come loose. And then he'd pull on it and pull on it until all the rest unraveled.

Mrs. Hernandez brought him to a sitting room overlooking a pool so still it might have been glass. The air conditioning was set to arctic, as if Julian had thought he could buy his way out of the very humidity that blanketed all in Miami, rich and poor alike.

"Can I get you something? Water? Coffee?"

"No, thank you." Nick settled into a chair that was all sharp angles and expensive leather. "I know this is difficult, but I need to ask—had Mr. Singer-Adams been under any unusual stress lately?"

Mrs. Hernandez perched on the edge of a matching sofa, hands folded in her lap. "No more than always. He worked constantly. Even weekends."

"Any difficult business dealings? Problems with the multiplex project?"

"He never discussed business with me."

"Phone calls that seemed to upset him? Visitors who left him agitated?"

She shook her head to each question. "No, nothing like that. His days were very ordered, very predictable."

The word hung in the air between them. Predictable. Men like Julian Singer-Adams built their lives on predictability—same meals, same schedule, same rigid command over every variable.

Until something disrupted the pattern.

"Had his routine changed at all recently?"

"No, sir. Work in his study, meals at the same time, bed by eleven." She paused, the slight upward turn of her eyes telling Nick she'd remembered something. "Although he did go out late Saturday night. That was unusual. I'm not sure where he went, though."

Julian had been at Red Room on Saturday night, where he'd threatened Rachel Baum. Nick kept his expression neutral, just a cop taking notes. "How did he seem when he returned?"

"I was already asleep. But Sunday morning he seemed different. Not upset exactly. More like..." She searched for the word. "Watchful."

Interesting choice. Not angry or worried, but watchful. Like a man waiting for something to happen.

"Any visitors Sunday? Monday?"

"No one. He worked in his study both days. Took his meals there."

"And his health? Apart from the blood pressure?"

"He had a sensitive stomach. Very particular about his food. That's why it surprised me when dinner upset him—Chef Graham knows exactly what Mr. Julian can eat."

Nick leaned forward. "He ate dinner as usual last night?"

"At seven, like always. But by nine he was complaining of stomach pain. Asked for ginger ale."

Stomach pain. Could be stress, could be the beginning of a cardiac event. Could be a dozen things.

"Would it be possible to speak with Chef Graham?"

"Let me see if he's still here." She rose. "You sure I can't bring you anything from the kitchen?" Nick shook his head and she hurried off.

While Mrs. Hernandez was gone, Nick studied the room more closely. Everything in it screamed money and taste, but nothing personal. No photographs, no mementos, no signs of a life actually lived. Even the books on the built-in shelves looked like they'd been bought by the yard, leather spines chosen for color rather than content.

The sound of footsteps pulled him from his observations. Mrs. Hernandez returned with a younger man in chef's whites. His eyes were red-rimmed, hands clasped nervously in front of him.

"This is Tony Graham."

Tony shook Nick's hand stiffly, clearly unused to talking to the police.

"I'm just trying to understand Mr. Singer-Adams's last few days." Nick kept his tone conversational. "His state of mind, any changes in routine. Mrs. Hernandez mentioned he became ill after dinner?"

"His stomach was upset, yes." Tony's voice caught. "But that happened sometimes. He had many sensitivities."

"What did you prepare last night?"

"Pan-seared grouper with herbs. Wild rice. Roasted vegetables." He listed each item like a litany, as if the familiar recitation could somehow change the outcome. "Very simple, very light. Nothing that should have bothered him."

"And you'd made this meal before?"

"Many times. I know—knew—exactly what Mr. Singer-Adams could tolerate. Though I did try something new with the fish," Tony added. "A different herb blend."

"Oh?" Nick kept his voice casual, but his heart sped up.

"Danny Elliott gave it to me. You know, from Sabrosa? I met him at his book signing. I was waiting in line so he could autograph my book." Tony looked somewhat abashed. "When I finally got to the front of the line, I told him I work here now. We talked about spices and techniques. He said he'd give me a special blend sometime. Something Mr. Singer-Adams would love."

Danny Elliott. Marc had eaten in Danny's restaurant on Monday night. By Wednesday morning he was dead. And hadn't Nick read something about a big *Palm* magazine party at Sabrosa a night or two before Danny Elliott's book signing? It seemed like exactly the kind of event Daisy Locarro would have attended...before she was found dead only a few hours after the signing was over.

Julian had eaten a Danny Elliott "herb blend" just last night. Now he was dead, too.

"Danny used to work here," Mrs. Hernandez interjected. "This is where he got his start, right here in Mr. Julian's kitchen. Maybe five years ago? You know, Mr. Julian gave Danny the money to start that restaurant. But he never took any credit, never went there and asked for free food."

Five years ago. Right around the time of the scandal Marc had been investigating. Nick's pulse was hammering now, but he kept his voice level. "And he still sends ingredients?"

"Just the one time," Tony said hastily. "I was at Sabrosa with my girl-friend a few nights ago, and he came over to say hi to us personally." His expression was one of pride trying not to reveal itself. "He remembered my name and everything."

Nick heard a ringing in his ears. Three deaths. Three connections to Danny Elliott's food. "Do you still have the packet you used Monday night?"

Tony blinked at the urgency that had crept into Nick's voice. "It was empty and I threw it away. But it's probably still here. Trash pickup isn't until later tonight."

"Show me where the trash can is. And I'll need a baggie, if you have one to spare." Nick pulled a pair of latex gloves from his pocket. "Did you try any of the herb blend the other night when you prepared Mr. Singer-Adams's dinner?"

"He was a germophobe. Didn't like me to eat from anything he was going to eat later." Now Tony looked alarmed. "Danny told me this was Mr. Singer-Adams' favorite herb blend from back in the day."

Once Nick had the empty packet securely ziplocked, he moved toward the service entrance that led outside from the kitchen, past the perplexed faces of Mrs. Hernandez and the chef. "Thank you both for your coop-eration." His tone had softened, but he didn't break stride. "I'm sorry for your loss."

Nick jogged out to his cruiser, where he grabbed the radio handset. "Dispatch, this is Chief Torres. Patch me through to Officer Martinez."

After a moment, Jessica's voice came through. "Chief? What's up?"

"Julian Singer-Adams is dead. Heart attack after eating food prepared with an 'herb blend' that Danny Elliott made for him." Nick kept his voice steady despite his racing thoughts. "I think Danny might be connected to the Locarro and Gottsegen deaths too."

"Are you serious?"

"Dead serious. Let's pick him up for questioning. And tell everyone to use caution. We're looking at three potential murders."

"Geez." He could hear her moving, probably already heading to coordinate the response. "I'll get units rolling now."

"Check his restaurant first, then his residence."

"Copy that. I'll handle it personally."

"And, Jess? Call the morgue and tell them this is now a homicide investigation. Then call Dr. Michel and tell her I want a full tox panel. I also want the Locarro and Gottsegen samples re-tested. If the Commissioner has any questions, he can come see me personally."

Nick replaced the handset and started the engine. The dashboard clock read six fifty-two. Dinner prep time at Sabrosa. Danny should be there, orchestrating his kitchen like a maestro. They'd find him, bring him in, sort this out.

The pieces were falling into place, but the picture they formed was still unclear. Only one thing was certain:

They needed to find Danny Elliott before anyone else died.

"FINALLY!" RACHEL SAID WITH a laugh. Danny stood just outside Title Wave's door, balancing a tray of the Halloween samples he'd been promising to bring her for nearly two weeks. "Your timing is perfect. I'm just about to lock up."

"Better late than never." Danny flashed a winning smile. "And I come bearing gifts!"

Rachel returned the smile and shooed Homer away from the door as she stood aside, allowing Danny to pass. Then she shut the door behind him, flipping the *Open* sign to *Closed* as she locked it.

CHAPTER 28

IT WAS UNUSUAL FOR Rachel to lock the cats upstairs before she'd even closed Title Wave for the day. Then again, a lot of unusual things had been happening lately.

No one could deny that Coacoochee was experiencing one of its craziest Octobers on record. But even two unsolved murders masquerading as natural deaths had temporarily faded into the background noise of Rachel's mind, which was working overtime to figure out *why* all three of her cats seemed to be having simultaneous nervous breakdowns.

They'd become obsessed with her. There was no other way to describe it. Everywhere she went—the shop, the bathroom, the storeroom, behind the cash register—they went too, trailing behind her as if she were a book-selling mother duck.

When she shelved books, Homer followed so closely that if she stopped unexpectedly, his little black nose ran right into her ankle—just like it had when he'd shadowed her as a tiny kitten, trusting Rachel's footsteps to guide his own through the darkness. When she was behind the café counter, Vashti positioned herself directly beneath the bar flap—facing away from Rachel and toward the rest of the shop—which made it impossible for anyone else to get behind the counter without encountering Vashti first. (Not that anybody had ever tried to; people weren't exactly clamoring to pour their own coffee and toast their own muffins.)

It had amused Rachel at first, the way Vashti sat there as if she were the world's smallest bouncer guarding a VIP lounge. But by the third time she'd tripped over Vashti while racing to the ringing phone across the store, the charm had worn off—and she resolved to talk to Dorothea about installing an extension behind the café counter.

Even Scarlett, who typically preferred comfort to companionship, had taken to following Rachel from room to room—although she was no more interested in actual cuddling than she'd ever been. Still, she was walking *so* slowly down the stairs these days, turning her head every so often as if to ensure Rachel was still safely following behind, that Rachel had very nearly tumbled over Scarlett on her way down this morning.

She couldn't help being touched by how much her cats suddenly seemed to love being with her. But it was also exhausting. Despite their protests—Vashti's refined objections mixing with Scarlett's more colorful commentary—Rachel had finally locked them upstairs so she could get some actual work done.

Only Homer remained downstairs. The cat who was notoriously bad at hiding had successfully concealed himself among some unopened boxes from Daydouble. *"Somebody needs to stay down here with her,"* he'd hissed at Scarlett, as she attempted to push her way in and join Homer's hiding spot. *"She's already chasing you; if you come back here, she'll end up finding both of us."*

"He's right, Scarlett," an out-of-breath Vashti had interjected. She was deploying her standard "dart and weave" maneuver, which had never yet succeeded in getting her out of vet appointments or the occasional round of prescription medication. But it did keep Rachel running until her en-

ergy flagged. Maybe this time she'd get *so* tired of chasing Vashti, she'd give up and say, "Fine! Stay downstairs if it means that much to you!"

But that had never happened before, and it didn't happen today, either.

A decidedly more collected Rachel now finished ringing up the last customer of the day, who departed with a cheerful wave and a promise to return the following evening for the monthly Book Club. (This month's selection was *Dolores Claiborne*.) The sun was low and Hibiscus Road's fairy lights had begun to twinkle through the windows as Rachel walked around the store and closed the shutters.

When she reached the café, she paused to look again at the Polaroid photo of Julian and Alicia, which she'd asked Natalie to bring by earlier that morning. Something about the picture had been bugging her ever since she'd first seen it, and she hoped if she looked at it long enough, she might figure out what it was. The bell above the door chimed, and Rachel hastily propped the Polaroid against the café's cash register.

"Finally!" she said with a laugh. Danny stood with one foot inside Title Wave's door, balancing a tray of the Halloween samples he'd been promising to bring her for nearly two weeks. "Your timing is perfect. I'm just about to lock up."

"Better late than never." Danny flashed a winning smile. "And I come bearing gifts!"

Rachel returned the smile and shooed Homer away from the door as she stood aside, allowing Danny to pass. Then she shut the door behind him, flipping the *Open* sign to *Closed* as she locked it.

The click of the lock echoed in Homer's ears, yet he barely heard it. He was too busy analyzing the gust of air that had entered the shop when Danny opened the door. There was something in it, something achingly familiar. Not because Homer had smelled it so often—in fact, he'd only ever smelled it three times—but because he'd been turning it over in his mind, visiting and revisiting it endlessly, ever since the Friday when Daisy had come into Title Wave to get her morning coffee for the last time.

It was a scent Homer now associated with death.

Floral. Medicinal. Slightly bitter. The same scent that had clung to Daisy's and Marc's bodies had just re-entered Title Wave with Danny Elliott. The scent had been stronger on Daisy and Marc, as if it had come out through their skin like sweat. It was fainter on Danny—*on* him, but not *in* him. It clung to him like an invisible shroud. And in that moment, like a flash of lightning that illuminated a dark landscape, Homer understood.

Danny Elliott was the killer.

Danny had killed Daisy. Then he'd killed Marc. Homer didn't know why he'd killed them. There were only two things Homer *did* know: First, that Rachel had no idea Danny was the killer.

Second, that she'd just locked herself into the store alone with him.

The air currents around Homer's whiskers told him that Danny was about to walk past him, deeper into Title Wave. Without thinking, Homer flipped his body around so he was facing Danny, standing directly in his path. Every strand of his fur stood on end. His tail had puffed up to three times its normal size.

People always talked about how "little" Homer was, but he knew they were wrong. In this moment, Homer was as enormous as any big cat ever was. He could actually feel how much bigger his anger—that this creature would venture into *Homer's* territory, that he'd dare to come near *Homer's* person—had made him.

Homer knew he was the biggest thing in this room right now. He might even be the biggest thing in the whole world.

Homer faced Danny and planted both front legs firmly. His bristled tail stood up, and all his hackles were raised as he drew back his lips to bare his fangs. Then he hissed at Danny with a wild, vicious hiss that seemed to start at the tip of his tail and pick up strength as it rolled through his entire body before it exited his mouth.

"*Ho*mer!" Rachel exclaimed. "What on earth has gotten into you?" She moved to hold Homer back with her foot as Danny made his way past her into the café area, where he set his tray of samples down on a table. "I'm so sorry about that," Rachel added to Danny. "All three of them have been acting weird lately."

"No worries," Danny said, though he kept his distance as he angled past Rachel and the still-hissing Homer. "Cats can be temperamental."

Despair washed over Homer. He intuitively grasped that he and his sisters had lost all credibility with Rachel. They'd been acting too strangely for too many days for Rachel now to note any one odd behavior—like the way Homer continued to hiss frantically at Danny Elliott—as being somehow worthy of special attention. It was simply one more on a long list of inexplicably odd things all three cats had been doing for days.

Homer wasn't as good at figuring out solutions to problems as Vashti was. But as his mind raced, looking for something—*anything!*—he could do to protect Rachel, it occurred to him that a human who liked to cook and also liked to poison other humans could do both things very easily just by putting poison into the food he prepared.

Homer crept silently away from Rachel, who continued to chat easily with Danny. Her voice came from near the door, still apologizing. Danny's deeper tones were several feet away, preparing to describe his Halloween creations. Neither human noticed the small black cat slinking purposefully toward the café table.

Homer's whiskers brushed the table leg as he jumped up in one fluid motion. Nothing here smelled poisonous—but, Homer thought, trying to reason it out the way Vashti would, it couldn't hurt to make a clean sweep of everything.

The metal tray was cold under his paws as he gave it an experimental push. It barely moved—too heavy to knock off the table entirely. But the individual samples were another matter. His paw found what felt like a small cake near the tray's edge and sent it tumbling to the floor with a splat. A round cake pop followed, rolling across the hardwood. Homer worked quickly, methodically, his paws swiping treats off the table. A sugar ghost shattered. What looked like a chocolate book spine split open, revealing blood-red filling that oozed across the floor. A pumpkin macaron rolled away like a small orange wheel.

"HOMER! That is ENOUGH!"

Homer felt rather than heard Rachel's brisk, angry footsteps as she approached. She scooped him up before he could attack the remaining samples, one hand firmly clutching the scruff of his neck while the palm of the other supported his chest and belly. Homer hissed all the way to the back storeroom. *"Rachel, it's him! You have to listen to me!"*

Rachel assumed that Homer was hissing his displeasure with her. "I'm not especially happy with you, either," she told him. "Maybe a time-out with your sisters will cool you off."

Inside the apartment, Vashti rushed toward the door as Rachel opened it and deposited Homer inside.

"Finally!" Vashti began, her green eyes bright with relief. *"Rachel, you must—"*

But the door was already closed, Rachel's footsteps retreating down the stairs.

"The killer is downstairs!" Homer informed his startled sisters. *I smelled the poison on Danny Elliott—the same smell from Daisy and Marc! He's the murderer, not Julian!"*

"What?" Scarlett leaped to her feet.

"And Rachel's locked in the store downstairs with him!"

"Then why are we still standing here?!" For once, it was Scarlett who led the charge toward the dumbwaiter shaft, where she plunged swiftly into the darkness. Vashti and Homer were close behind. *"Careful,"* she called up to them. *"I think the wood's a little warped from that thunderstorm this weekend."*

They inched their way downward in complete silence for a few seconds. At last, frustrated with her own slow pace, Scarlett loosened her hold on the sturdy old rope and let gravity accelerate her descent. Vashti and Homer could hear the whisper of her fur against the wood of the shaft as she fell. Then there was a soft, whistling *thonk!* followed by complete silence—a silence that was quickly broken by a colorful string of unprintable feline oaths.

"What's wrong? What happened?" Vashti squinted to try to see Scarlett in the darkness below her.

"She's stuck." Homer's ears had correctly identified the sound almost instantaneously, and his matter-of-fact tone belied the swift feeling of panic that shot through him.

This dumbwaiter shaft was their only way out of the apartment and into the store—where Rachel, whether she knew it or not, desperately needed their help. Homer's voice was an octave higher than normal as he said to Vashti, *"Maybe if the two of us slide down really fast and crash into her, we can force her through?"*

Upon hearing this, Scarlett's curses raised in both volume and unprintability.

"Or we might get stuck ourselves." Vashti sighed and began climbing back up. *"Let's go,"* she said to Homer. *"We'll figure this out upstairs. And we'll find a way to get you unstuck,"* she called down to Scarlett.

"Don't you dare forget me down here!" Scarlett shouted at their retreating backsides.

"We'll figure it out!" Vashti repeated. And, to Homer, she added, in the most soothing tone she could muster, *"There's no reason for Danny to hurt Rachel. If he wanted to poison her, he could have done it plenty of times already. I'm sure she'll be fine without us for the next few minutes."*

"She'd better be." There was real menace in Homer's voice—something Vashti had never heard before. It grew even more pronounced as he repeated:

"Rachel had better be fine when we get down there."

Downstairs, Rachel surveyed the aftermath of Homer's destructive spree with embarrassment. Danny had already cleaned most of the mess, his movements efficient and untroubled.

"I'm really sorry," she said, helping wipe up what looked like raspberry coulis. "The cats have been acting strange all week."

"Already forgotten." Danny's smile lit up the café. "Most of it survived. Let me show you what I've been working on."

He'd arranged the remaining samples with an artist's eye. Even reduced in number, they were impressive—each one a tiny masterpiece.

"This one," Danny said, picking up a black sesame tombstone, "has been my biggest challenge. The cookie needs to be sturdy enough to stand but delicate enough to melt on your tongue."

His enthusiasm was contagious. Rachel leaned forward, drawn in despite her lingering embarrassment.

"The filling is matcha cream infused with yuzu. I know a guy who grows it himself out in Homestead. The bitterness of the tea plays against the citrus beautifully."

He described each creation with authentic passion—the midnight velvet cupcakes with temperature-activated color-changing frosting, delicate spiderweb cookies spun from caramelized sugar so fine they seemed to float above their chocolate base, the "poison apple" tarts hiding cardamom surprises.

"The black garlic aioli for these canapés took three attempts," Danny continued. "The first batch was too pungent—cleared out my kitchen for hours. The second was too sweet, like garlic candy, which tastes even worse than it sounds. But the third..." He kissed his fingers in an exaggerated chef's gesture that made Rachel laugh.

She watched his hands as he spoke, noticed how they moved with the fluid grace of someone who had spent years perfecting their craft. His right hand swept over the display as he explained the inspiration behind each creation.

"You've really outdone yourself," Rachel said, genuinely impressed. "These aren't just desserts, they're art."

"Wait until you try them." Danny selected a perfect miniature pumpkin, its orange shell crafted from modeling chocolate and filled with spiced cream. "This one's my favorite. The spices are all from my personal garden—"

He held the candy pumpkin out for Rachel to take it. That's when she saw it.

The ring on his left hand. Heavy silver with a Celtic knot pattern.

Her gaze darted to the café's cash register and the Polaroid propped up against it. The photographer's hand in the bottom corner, pointing toward Julian and Alicia. On that hand—

The same ring. A ring Danny always wore. One she'd seen dozens of times without taking any particular notice of it.

Until now.

Time seemed to slow as understanding crashed through her mind like dominoes falling in perfect sequence. Danny had taken that photograph. Danny had been at Julian's estate five years ago. Danny had been there the night Alicia Rodrigue died.

And now people connected to that night were dying. Daisy, who'd sold the story to Tommy. Marc, who'd been investigating.

But why would Danny have been at a party on Julian's estate? Unless...

More pieces clicked into place with sickening clarity. Danny's restaurant funded by a mysterious investor. His rapid rise from nowhere to celebrity chef. Rachel recalled now that, among the various Danny Elliott "origin stories" that had made their way through the Coacoochee rumor mill, was the one that said he'd started out as a private chef for some rich guy on Mercury Island.

"Some rich guy" had been Julian.

Daisy and Marc—both of them young and healthy—had supposedly died of heart attacks. Of *course* they'd been poisoned. And who would find it easier to poison them than someone who fed them regularly? Someone who grew his own herbs, who knew exactly how to mask unusual tastes?

She must have gasped. She felt the blood drain from her cheeks, then rush back in a burning flush. Danny caught the dramatic change in her expression, and his eyes travelled from her face in the direction of the cash register—where the photo of Julian and Alicia was still propped up. It was on the side of the register, and it was difficult to make out any details from where Rachel and Danny were sitting.

Unless you already knew what the picture showed.

The moment stretched between them like a held breath. Then, with deliberate calm, Danny brought the candy pumpkin to his lips and took a bite. He chewed thoughtfully, swallowed, dabbed his lips with a napkin. "It's not poisoned, if that's what you're thinking." His tone was cheerful as it had ever been. "It never occurred to me that *you* were the one I had to worry about."

"I don't...what are you talking about?"

"Oh, Rachel." Danny shook his head with sincere affection. "Never take up gambling. You have a terrible poker face."

The heat in her cheeks intensified. Every thought, every realization, every flash of horror—it was all written across her face.

"The last time I saw that photo," Danny continued conversationally, "it was lying on the ground in a blind alley three blocks from here. I know Marc got it from that busybody Carlos who did pool maintenance at Julian's place." His voice took on a bitter edge. "Carlos was always trying to get me to hook him up with invites. As if Julian would ever deign to party with the help. He barely let me show my face outside the pool house." The last words dripped with old resentment. "But I'd love to hear how *you* ended up with it."

Rachel leapt up so quickly that the chair she'd been sitting in toppled over backward with a loud clatter. Construction-paper bats dangling from the ceiling overhead danced merrily in the breeze it created.

Danny's hand shot out just as quickly and pinned Rachel's wrist to the table. She tried desperately to pull her arm away, but his grip only tightened.

"Why the hurry?" Danny said. This time, his smile didn't reach his eyes. "Nobody else will be here until tomorrow morning, right?"

CHAPTER 29

THE SOUND OF A chair crashing to the floor had reached Homer and Vashti just as they'd emerged from the dumbwaiter shaft. Now, pressed against the floorboards of the apartment, Homer could track every movement from the café below—the scrape of table legs against terrazzo, the sharp intake of Rachel's breath, the low murmur of Danny's voice saying something that made Homer's fur stand on end.

"Why the hurry?" The words drifted up through the old building's bones, muffled but still audible to Homer's sensitive ears. "Nobody else will be here until tomorrow morning, right?"

"Rachel figured it out." Homer pressed his ear harder against the floor, straining to catch every vibration from below. The wooden boards carried the murmur of voices—one calm and conversational, one higher with stress. *"She knows about Danny. And Danny knows she knows!"*

Vashti's fur stood on end. She was pacing the apartment in tight circles, her normally organized mind scattered by panic.

"Have you brilliant strategists figured something out yet?" Scarlett's voice carried up to them from the dumbwaiter—angry, but Vashti could also hear the fear that laced her voice. "My legs are going numb!"

"We're working on it!" Vashti called back.

Vashti knew everybody thought she was vain. She also knew they weren't entirely wrong. But the thing she'd always been secretly proudest of—far more than even her astonishing good looks—was her intelligence. It was Vashti who the other cats always turned to in a crisis, Vashti who was able to pull solutions seemingly out of thin air.

Which was made the current situation even more agonizing. Vashti already knew what neither of her siblings had yet figured out—that, this time, Vashti would fail. For the life of her, she couldn't see a single way out of their predicament—much less one that would get help to Rachel before Danny did something terrible.

If Homer was right about what he'd overheard, then they didn't have long. Every second that went by was one that put Rachel's life more at risk. And lord alone knew what would happen to the three of them—to this whole family they'd built together—if Rachel were suddenly gone.

"Think," Vashti commanded her exhausted brain. *"THINK!"*

She was so lost in her desperate calculations that she almost missed Homer's sudden alertness. His head snapped up and turned evenly from left to right, his ears at full attention. Then his whiskers twitched forward—the way they did when he was pleased.

"What is it?" Vashti asked, not daring to hope.

"Shh." Homer's whole body had gone still, focused on something beyond the apartment walls. Then he turned his face toward Vashti and announced: *"Samkhat and Kotik are coming!"*

Relief flooded through Vashti so swiftly, her legs felt weak. She rushed to the window, shoving aside the ill-fitting screen. Sure enough, the two cats had turned off of Hibiscus Road toward the side of Title Wave's building, most likely planning to walk around to the loading dock in back.

"Samkhat!" Vashti cried. *"Kotik! Up here!"*

The two cats looked up from the sidewalk. Kotik was even more startled than Samkhat; obviously, he'd counted on having a moment or two to collect himself before his reunion with Vashti.

"Vashti! I—" Kotik's prepared speech about how he'd thought of nothing but her green eyes during his captivity died in his throat. The fear written across her face was visible even from two stories down. *"I mean—what's happened? Is Rachel all right?"*

"Danny Elliott is the one who killed Marc and Daisy!" Samkhat's one eye widened. Kotik looked shocked as well. *"He has Rachel trapped downstairs! Scarlett's stuck in the dumbwaiter shaft—we can't get down!"*

Normally, the prospect of two humans fighting between themselves wouldn't have struck Samkhat as an especially urgent situation. But Rachel's cats were her friends, and the food Rachel always put out for Samkhat had saved her from more than a few cheerless, hungry days.

"What do you need us to do?" was all she said.

Vashti's mind raced, formulating strategy even as she spoke. She pushed the screen until it fell away altogether and nudged Homer toward the open window with her nose. *"Samkhat, help Homer make the jump from the windowsill to the staircase."* Vashti struggled to keep her voice calm, desperately hoping Homer wouldn't be able to hear her terror as she regarded the nearly seven-foot gap between windowsill and staircase—and the two stories of empty air below it. Vashti didn't know if any cat could make that leap—but if any cat could, that cat was Homer. *"He'll need guidance. Just talk him through it. Then get him around the building to our cat door. I'm going to work on getting Scarlett unstuck. Kotik, you have the most important job of all."*

Kotik straightened his posture and stood at attention. The orange-gold rays of the setting sun lingered on the black-and-white fur of his tuxedo coat, which had been burnished to a high gleam by Laurie's close attention over the past week and change.

"Go find Hot Mike!" Vashti told him. *"Bring him here as fast as you can!"*

"Don't worry, Vashti!" Kotik knew that staying out too late and exploring too far from home were the exact crimes for which he'd just been punished. But surely even Laurie could appreciate how badly his help was needed now. *"I'll have him here before you know it!"* With that, Kotik shot

off in the direction of Natalie Dunbar's house like a black-and-white dart, his paws barely touching the pavement.

By now, Homer had climbed out the window and was standing in precarious balance at its farthest edge. Vashti pulled her head back in, unable to watch, and turned her thoughts to Scarlett. *"I know you can do this, Homer,"* she said. *"I'm going to get Scarlett loose, and the two of us will meet you downstairs."*

At least this time she'd managed to keep *some* of the doubt out of her voice, Homer thought wryly. Then he hunkered down on the windowsill, preparing to hurl himself into space with nothing but Samkhat's voice to guide him. *"How far is it, Samkhat?"*

Samkhat thought for a moment, trying to think of the best way to explain the distance so Homer could understand it. *"Do you know the door Rachel uses to get out to the loading dock?"* At Homer's nod, Samkhat continued, *"It's about the same as the distance from there to the spot where she leaves food for me."*

That was far! Unconsciously, Homer backed away from the edge of the sill by an inch or two.

"There's also a handrail," Samkhat added helpfully. *"You'll have to give yourself some extra height to clear it."*

Homer waited to see if Samkhat was going to ask him to pull a can of tuna out of his ear, or some other obviously impossible feat. But Samkhat fell silent, and Homer inched back to the edge. He stood there, quivering, trying to gather his courage.

Homer had always prided himself on being fearless—on showing everyone who'd pitied the "poor blind kitten" exactly how wrong they were. Sometimes, though, even Homer got scared. One of his earliest memories was of being a small kitten, new to Rachel's home. He was sitting at the edge of the bed Rachel had shared with Henry, wanting desperately to leap down from it onto the floor below.

It was a jump he'd made dozens of times without hesitation. Yet suddenly, Homer had felt as if he took that leap into the dark unknown, he'd fall into something deep and endless. A chasm he'd get lost in forever. How could he know the floor was really there if he couldn't see it?

Homer had gotten stuck inside his own head. His doubts swirled and agitated until they crowded out everything else.

Rachel must have seen him trembling at the edge of the bed. She could easily have picked him up and placed him safely on the floor herself. Instead, she sat down next to him and rubbed gently behind his ears.

"Be bold," she told him, in the low-pitched near-whisper that Homer had already learned meant she was talking just to him, and nobody else. "Be bold, and mighty forces will come to your aid."

It had taken every ounce of Homer's courage. Before he could think about it—before he could think about anything other than Rachel's words—Homer had leapt. And from that day to this, he'd never been afraid to leap again.

Until now.

Homer couldn't see how high up he was. But he could tell from the way the air whistled beneath him that he was standing atop a vast emptiness. His fear of leaping from bed to floor now seemed almost humorous by comparison.

"You can do it, Homer." Samkhat's voice, calm as ever despite all the hard times she'd seen, reached him from the ground. *"I've seen what you can do. You've got this."*

Homer hadn't known at the time what Rachel meant by "mighty forces." He'd assumed that Rachel herself was the mighty force who would always come to his aid.

Teetering on the edge of the windowsill now, though, Homer realized that things had somehow reversed themselves. *He* was the mighty force. And if he didn't come to Rachel's aid, he might never hear her voice saying anything of comfort to him ever again.

Homer lowered his body into a crouch, muscles tensed in preparation. Every instinct screamed at him to back away, to find another path, to wait for help. His claws gripped the windowsill so hard they ached.

Be bold, he told himself. He took a deep breath. And then, before he could lose his courage, Homer leapt.

CHAPTER 30

Warily, Danny had loosened his hold on Rachel's wrist just enough so the two of them could right her overturned chair. Once she was seated across from him again, his grip tightened. Had any passerby on Hibiscus Road been able to peep through the closed shutters, it would have looked for all the world as if Rachel and Danny were lovers, holding hands across an elegant café table in the town's charming little bookstore.

"I don't think any woman has surprised me this much," Danny said affably, "since Daisy Locarro showed up the night of my signing."

"You didn't expect her to be here." The realization dawned as Rachel spoke. "That's why you turned so red when you saw her. You thought she'd be dead already."

"I thought it worked faster!" Danny's air was that of a man whose expensive new stereo wasn't quite living up to the hype. "Granted, I was working with homemade stuff. A little extract from the oleanders I grow in front of Sabrosa. All I had to do was sprinkle it into a few of the 'special' tidbits I told Daisy I'd made just for her, and presto!" Danny's free hand slapped the tabletop and Rachel flinched. "Heart attack the next day! Nothing to show up on a tox screening unless they already know what they're looking for."

Rachel thought about Daisy's sunny charm and quick wit. Even right after her breakup with Henry, when just getting out of bed had felt like a painful chore, Rachel would nonetheless smile as she got dressed in the morning, imagining the breathless, hilarious tales Daisy would share when she came in for coffee.

"But there Daisy was, dressed to the nines, standing next to you." Danny shook his head admiringly. "She had the constitution of an ox, our Daisy did. Still, I gave Marc a little extra." Danny winked at Rachel. "Just to be on the safe side."

After weeks of wondering, theorizing, investigating...hearing the truth now wasn't nearly as gratifying as Rachel had thought it would be. She recalled that she'd found this man *attractive* at one time and felt physically ill.

Keep him talking, a clear, cool voice inside Rachel's head instructed. *Buy yourself time to find a way out of this.*

"So Daisy told you Marc was investigating Tommy's blind items."

"No, actually." Danny seemed pleased to correct her. "Daisy was all weepy and vague the night we talked. I knew it had something to do with Marc and Tommy." He used his free hand to pluck a stray bit of lint from his black shirt. "But I didn't put the whole thing together until Julian called to threaten me about some reporter. Said he was asking about that girl..." Danny gestured vaguely in the direction of the Polaroid.

"You did it for nothing, you know," Rachel told him. "Daisy made up a crazy fake story five years ago and sold it to Tommy for rent money. Tommy always knew it was shaky. Why else would he have run it as a blind item? If he had the goods on *Julian?* Did you *honestly* believe that?" Rachel knew she should stop, that she wasn't helping herself even a tiny bit. But she couldn't. She was deriving too much pleasure in seeing the way confusion replaced the smug expression on Danny's face. "Daisy never knew anything about Alicia Rodrigue. She never knew you dumped that poor girl *outside* Jackson Memorial and left her there to die. She didn't know any of it. You did it for nothing. You killed Daisy for *nothing!*"

The room fell silent. Rachel watched various emotions flicker across Danny's face as he processed her words. Then he looked at her, and his smile was chilly. "Don't worry." Rachel's trapped wrist began to sweat beneath Danny's hand. "They won't say that about you."

KOTIK'S HEART HAMMERED SO hard he could hear it pulsing in his ears, drowning out everything but the urgent need to get there, get there, get there. Every leap over a curb sent a jolt through his legs, but he pushed harder, his bottlebrush tail whipping behind him for balance as he skidded around corners. The setting sun threw long shadows across his path, turning familiar streets into a maze of light and dark. But Kotik never paused. After all those days following Marc around to impress Vashti, he could have made the run to Marc's house—and Hot Mike's, right next door—if he was blindfolded.

Natalie's coral-colored stucco house finally came into view, and Kotik took a deep breath. Gritting his teeth, he accelerated into one last burst of speed, grateful he no longer had to worry about saving his energy. He noted Natalie's Volkswagen Beetle in the driveway as he crept around to the back yard.

"Hot Mike!" he called in a breathless loud-whisper. *"Hey! Hot Mike!"*

Kotik waited for the rubbery *woosh* and *slap!* of Hot Mike's doggy door opening. But the silence was broken only by a few cicadas and the chirps of a nearby mockingbird serenading the close of day.

Kotik gathered his nerve and squeezed through a gap in the wooden fence, splinters catching at his fur. *"Psssst! Hot Mike! Are you here?"* Although his already-knotted belly fiercely protested (what if Hot Mike mistook him for an intruder?) Kotik ventured all the way up to the house and tentatively poked at the doggy door's heavy rubber flap. Getting it to budge was easier said than done, but Kotik finally managed to get enough of his head through to loud-whisper again, *"Hot Mike?"* His voice echoed through the deserted kitchen and into the rest of the silent, clearly empty house.

Kotik wasn't as foolish as others sometimes thought he was. He was aware that he'd been sent to get Hot Mike because he was expendable. He didn't have Homer's super senses, or Samkhat's street smarts, or Vashti's keen intelligence. He could run fast and he knew exactly how to get to Hot Mike's house. It wasn't much of a resumé, but it had made him perfect for this particular job.

Except that he'd failed at getting the job done. It hadn't even occurred to him that Hot Mike might not be home. This despite the fact that just about every dog owner in Coacoochee seemed to be out walking with their dogs at this precise time of day. Kotik could have kicked himself for being so foolish.

"Well, well, if it isn't Romeo." Stewie hovered in the air about three feet above Kotik's head. *"You and Juliet have a lover's spat?"*

Kotik had opened his mouth to utter a downcast, *"Shut up, Stewie."* But a sudden inspiration closed it again.

Kotik knew how high the stakes were—that there were things on the line infinitely more important than impressing Vashti. Nevertheless, he'd indulged in a daydream or two as he'd made his desperate run to Natalie's house. Kotik had imagined himself bursting triumphantly into Title Wave on an avenging Hot Mike's back; he'd pictured Vashti bounding over to him, admiration written in the deep green of her eyes as she bunted her head against his and exclaimed, *"My hero!"*

In the end, though, it didn't really matter who got to be a hero. All that mattered was rescuing the one human Vashti couldn't live without.

Stewie still hovered, clearly puzzled his teasing hadn't produced the usual embarrassed indignation that so tickled his funny bone.

"Hey, Stewie," Kotik began tentatively. *"I need your help."* And then, sensing he'd begun on precisely the wrong foot, he hastily added, *"And Rachel's in danger! She needs your help, too."*

But Stewie had already burst out laughing. He laughed so hard, he couldn't have responded even if he'd wanted to as he turned and began to fly away.

"The cat actually asked me to help him!" Stewie chortled helplessly.

"Rachel feeds you, too!" Kotik yelled desperately. He could hear Stewie hooting and guffawing as his shape grew smaller in the darkening sky. *"What'll you do if Rachel's not around to fill your feeder anymore?"*

The image of the poinciana in front of Title Wave *without* a full bird-feeder to greet him at the break of day was so sobering, Stewie's laughter died instantly.

Oh, for crying out loud. Stewie loathed Kotik as he loathed all cats—but he couldn't dispute the logic.

Hope rose in Kotik's breast as Stewie winged a slow path back. *Hurry!* Kotik thought. *Please hurry!*

At last, Stewie reached him. Regarding Kotik with a look of deep suspicion as he stayed well beyond the range of his claws, Stewie grudgingly asked, *"What would I have to do?"*

"What's taking so long?!?" Scarlett's voice—the voice of a cat whose patience had been exhausted some time ago—drifted up to Vashti from the depths of the dumbwaiter shaft.

Vashti was using her forehead to shove a yellow-gold bottle of cooking oil from the far end of one of the pantry's shelves all the way to the other end, which was next to the dumbwaiter shaft. Her white paws trembled with each shove—not from exertion, but from the knowledge that every second she spent up here was another second Rachel was alone with...

Vashti's plan was simple: She was going to push the bottle until it was next to Rachel's small stepladder, which had fortunately been left near the opening to the dumbwaiter shaft. Then she was going to turn the bottle onto its side, roll it onto the top of the stepladder, flip open the flip-top, and spill the oil into the shaft until Scarlett was freed.

That was assuming, of course, that any one of the million things Vashti could foresee going wrong didn't happen. (What if the bottle rolled onto the floor? What if she couldn't get the flip-top open? What if got the flip-top open and *then* the bottle rolled onto the floor?)

"You did it for nothing!" Rachel's voice, sharp with anger, pierced through the floorboards. Then something else—was that a cry of pain? Vashti's heart stuttered. She shoved harder at the bottle, but her trembling

paws slipped against the smooth shelf. She stumbled, nearly sending the oil toppling the wrong way.

No, no, no. She steadied herself, claws aching from the strain of gripping the wooden shelf. Every muscle in her body screamed to abandon this plan and race downstairs, but Scarlett was trapped, and they needed everyone if they were going to save Rachel.

"I'm getting you Rachel's cooking oil," She informed Scarlett through gritted teeth. The bottle was surprisingly heavy; she had to brace her back paws and really dig in to get it to move even an inch or two. *"Then I'm going to pour it down the dumbwaiter shaft, and you'll be free in no time."*

Upon hearing that she was soon to be doused in an entire bottle of Wesson, Scarlett flung a string of un-repeatable epithets up the shaft in Vashti's direction.

"Swearing like that makes you sound like a street cat." Vashti tried not to let her irritation distract her. Push, slide, reposition. Push, slide, reposition. She knew Scarlett was as terrified as she was. Displaying anger to hide her fear was one of Scarlett's oldest tricks.

"Don't you call me 'street,'" Scarlett fired back. *"You're the one who was found literally wandering the streets!"*

"Like being found in a cardboard box with a bunch of other kittens makes you any better!" Vashti retorted. Why, why, **why** couldn't she get this wretched bottle to move any faster???

"At least I have a lineage!" Scarlett shrieked.

"Absolutely the most unbearable..." Vashti muttered under her breath as she continued to push.

Although she never said so to anyone, Scarlett often thought about how extraordinarily fortunate it was that—in a world filled with humans whose company she wouldn't have found tolerable for even half a minute—somehow she'd ended up with the one and only human whose presence she found bearable. The one human who'd learned to read and respect her moods, who never made her feel like there was something "wrong" with her just because it took her so long to warm up to new people. There weren't many humans capable of giving their whole heart to a cat, but Scarlett had known she'd had Rachel's whole heart since they day they'd met.

And Rachel had hers.

Scarlett didn't know how she'd been lucky enough to end up with someone like Rachel. But she did know she'd never get that lucky again.

"Please, Vashti." The anger had left Scarlett's voice. *"Anything could be happening down there right now."*

As if Vashti didn't already know that. Another sound from below—a scraping chair? A struggle? Vashti's usually precise movements turned jerky with panic. The bottle seemed to have gained a thousand pounds. Push, slide, reposition. Push, slide—her paw slipped again, claw catching painfully in the wood grain. She yanked it free, leaving a small tuft of white fur behind.

Her next shove was too forceful, born of desperation. The bottle rocked dangerously, and Vashti had to lunge forward to steady it, her heart hammering so hard she felt dizzy. She forced herself to take a deep breath, pausing both to calm herself and to examine her progress.

Vashti's heart began to race again when she saw how close she'd finally gotten. One more shove ought to do it...

NATALIE SAT ON HER favorite bench at the end of the boardwalk closest to Hibiscus Road, watching the ocean take on a pebbly blue tint against the darkening sky. The boardwalk hummed with evening activity—joggers getting in their laps as the heat of the day receded, couples strolling hand in hand, a group of teenagers clustered around somebody's boombox. Hot Mike sat beside her, his massive head resting on her knee.

She caught the gray and white blur descending rapidly from the sky in her peripheral vision. But Natalie didn't give it her full attention until it swooped directly at Hot Mike's head.

"What the—" Natalie jerked back as the mockingbird regrouped and once again flew straight at Hot Mike like a kamikaze pilot. The bird pulled up at the last second, circling back for another pass.

Hot Mike's head snapped up, a low growl rumbling in his chest. The mockingbird paid no attention, diving again and again, its shrill chirps growing more insistent. It fluttered around Hot Mike's head like a demented halo, dodging when he snapped his teeth at the air.

"Shoo! Get away!" Natalie waved her free hand at the bird while keeping a firm grip on Hot Mike's leash.

But the mockingbird was undeterred. He hovered in the air just in front of Hot Mike, chirping frantically. Then he flew at Hot Mike again. This time, Hot Mike cocked his head to one side inquisitively, and stood still while the bird chirped directly into his ear. He stopped growling, his whole body motionless.

The bird flew off, as inexplicably as it had first arrived. Natalie breathed a sigh of relief and rubbed Hot Mike behind the ears. He turned his head to look at her and, for a second, Natalie could have sworn she saw an apology in his expressive brown eyes.

Then Hot Mike lunged.

The force nearly yanked Natalie off the bench. She wrapped both hands around the leash, digging her heels into the boardwalk. "Hot Mike, no! Heel!"

But something had possessed him. He strained against the leash with every ounce of his considerable strength, pulling toward Hibiscus Road. The leash burned through Natalie's palms and she stood up, struggling to keep her grip. It was like when she and Hot Mike had played tug-of-war with an old rope when he was a puppy, except there was nothing playful or puppyish about Hot Mike now. Unconsciously, Natalie loosened her hold on the leash just a bit—just enough to give the collar around Hot Mike's neck a little slack so it wouldn't choke him.

With one final, powerful jerk, Hot Mike tore free.

He took off like a shot, his black-and-tan form racing down the board-walk toward Hibiscus Road.

"Hot Mike!" Natalie sprinted after him, crashing through a line of tourists waiting at the gelato stand, her sandals slapping against the wood-en boards. "Hot Mike, stop! Hot Miiiiiiike.....!"

"I KNOW WHAT YOU'RE thinking," Danny told Rachel. "You're thinking that you'll never eat anything I've prepared ever again."

It wasn't *exactly* what she was thinking, but for once, Rachel tried to manage a neutral expression, revealing nothing.

"No, I suppose you won't." Danny continued, as if she'd agreed with him, and his grip on her wrist tightened again. "But people take terrible falls every day, you know." He tilted his head, considering. "Of course, I don't have to tell *you*. With all these cats you've got running around to trip you up. I bet the blind one gets underfoot all the time."

He doesn't have a weapon, the cool voice in her head noted. That was good news—at least it evened the odds a *little* bit. She knew every inch of this store so well! Surely there was something she could find, something she could use to get the advantage and...

But it was hard to think past the image Danny had just planted—Homer's small body at the foot of the stairs, her own neck at an odd angle, and everyone nodding sadly about the inevitable danger of keeping a blind cat. Only someone with Rachel's foolish softheartedness would have taken him in the first place, they'd say.

She loathed giving Danny the satisfaction, but her eyes burned with sudden tears—not from fear for herself, but from imagining her cats separated and split apart, shipped away from each other to live with strangers, all because she had failed them. The tears blurred her vision until she could have sworn she saw Homer himself. There he was, emerging from the darkness of the bookshelves, his one funny white whisker—the only thing on his whole body that wasn't black—visible before anything else. Phantom-Homer slunk carefully around behind the café counter, and—

Wait a second. She squinted, raising her free hand to wipe her eyes so she could get a better look.

This wasn't an imaginary Homer. This was *actually Homer!* Rachel's heart slammed against her ribs—once, twice—then seemed to stop entirely. The world narrowed to Homer's small black form, and she couldn't breathe, couldn't think, could only watch in frozen horror as her blind cat prepared to take on a killer.

How was this possible? She'd locked Homer upstairs. She'd done it *herself!* It was impossible—it was *physically* impossible!—for Homer to be standing in front of her right now.

Homer was now crouched at the edge of the café counter, all four sets of claws extended. His head turned evenly from left to right, ears at full attention. Rachel knew what this stance meant. And unless Scarlett was also around here somewhere, the only one Homer could be preparing to "attack" was...

Every cell in her body screamed *NO!*—this tiny cat who trusted the world because she'd always kept it safe, who didn't know what danger looked like, who was about to—

"HOMER!" The word ripped from her throat, raw and desperate. "HOMER, *STOP!!!*"

Homer had gone airborne a split second before she'd cried out his name, so Rachel's last-moment interference didn't do any good. Homer's trajectory didn't change by a single millimeter.

Danny, on the other hand, had started to turn his head to see whatever it was behind him that Rachel was yelling about.

But by then, he was too late.

CHAPTER 31

Kotik didn't know what he'd expected to see when he let himself into Title Wave through the secret cat door. It certainly wasn't Vashti standing atop the bathroom counter on her hind legs, using her front paws to unspool the roll of paper towels hanging above it. Nor was it an oiled and wriggling Scarlett, fur sticking out in wild tufts all over her body, rolling around in the great, billowing sheets of paper towel that Vashti dispensed.

Nevertheless, this is what Kotik saw.

He'd had an urgent realization as he'd watched Stewie fly off to get Hot Mike (hopefully)—a realization *so* urgent, it had seemed to warrant the extreme step of letting himself into his friends' home when, technically, he hadn't been invited.

"They're still just talking," Vashti said in an anxious loud-whisper when she spotted him, not seeming at all surprised to see him there. *"I had to use cooking oil to get her out,"* she added, nodding at Scarlett and abandoning the paper towels, which she'd finally spun down to the cardboard roll. Vashti looked worried. She'd been hoping to find Homer waiting for them when they finally got free of the dumbwaiter shaft and didn't like to think about what his absence might mean.

"Scarlett's slipping and sliding so much she can barely walk," Vashti said. *"But we need to get in there to help Rachel now!"*

"I'm cleaning up as fast as I can!" Scarlett snapped. *"Nobody told you to use the whole bottle!"*

Vashti leapt down from the bathroom counter, skidding a bit as she landed. (She'd ended up with oily paws herself.) The swift, ecstatic hope that shone from her eyes as she looked at Kotik would live in his memory until he was an old, old man. *"Is Hot Mike on the way?"*

Kotik nodded, fervently hoping it was true. *"But somebody has to open the door for him when he gets here. That's what I came to tell you."* The image of Hot Mike barking ineffectually through Title Wave's front door, unable to gain entry and actually help anybody, had presented itself to Kotik somewhere between Natalie's house and Hibiscus Road.

"Shoot! You're right!" Why was it, Vashti wondered, that every time they solved one problem, a new one cropped up? Even if she could manage to prop Scarlett steadily on her feet long enough to get her to the front door—and even if her paws weren't too greasy to manipulate the bolt lock and door handle—there was still the problem of Scarlett's appearance. At the moment, she looked like some sort of feline/otter hybrid who'd stuck a fork in an electrical outlet. There was simply no way they could get Scarlett all the way from the back storeroom to the front door without Danny Elliott spotting her.

"We need a diversion," Vashti mused aloud.

The blood-chilling sound of a woman's agonized shriek rose up from the café to split the three cats' eardrums. They raced for the doorway connecting store and storeroom, Scarlett skitter-sliding over from her mound of paper towels, almost too afraid to look and see what terrible, terrible thing was happening to Rachel in the café.

Kotik had the best view and saw it first. He froze where he was standing. Then his mouth dropped open.

"What is it?" Scarlett nearly fell over on her oiled paws as she struggled to see what was going on.

Then Scarlett's mouth fell open, too.

Vashti strained to see from where she stood. *"Okay, somebody had better tell—"* Abruptly, she stopped talking. Whatever she'd been about to say no longer mattered.

The high-pitched screams had come from Danny Elliott, not Rachel. What had initially sounded like an incoherent stream of womanly shrieks resolved into actual words: "GET IT OFF ME! *GET IT OFF ME!!!*"

The "it" in question was Homer.

Homer was alive!

Homer was alive and he'd made the jump!

Homer was alive and kicking and he had…surrounded Danny. There was no other way of describing it. Homer was everywhere. He was on Danny's arm, digging in with his claws, and when Danny shook him loose Homer quickly attached himself to Danny's leg. When Danny bent down to pry Homer's claws loose from his leg, Homer hooked onto Danny's torso. He moved like liquid shadow, using Danny's own movements against him. Every attempt to dislodge him simply gave Homer a new angle of attack. His fur and tail stood completely on-end, his mouth frozen open in a way that bared his fangs. Each of his claws was extended from its sheath and caught the light.

Danny finally seemed to give up on trying to detach Homer and decided to outrun him—but somehow, every time Danny tried to take his first running step, Homer was right in front of him, waiting to leap again at whichever part of Danny's body he could latch himself onto the fastest.

It was as if Danny were a magnet and Homer a pile of metal shavings.

Homer's own snarls and growls had been continuous, but they were effectively drowned out by Danny's unabated screams. Samkhat—who'd refused to enter Title Wave after walking Homer to the cat door—was nearly two blocks away now, but she could hear Danny faintly, in the distance. She shook her head and smiled. *"He actually pulled it off!"*

"GET. IT. *OFF.* ME!!!!!" Danny shrieked again, and Rachel looked as if she'd like nothing better. Her wrist was free now, and she was poised to run for the phone behind the cash register on the other side of the store. But

Rachel was also terrified to leave Homer with Danny even for a moment. Danny was now aggressively grabbing at Homer—who had managed to evade Danny's hands so far while also launching his own, more successful, attacks.

Still, Rachel knew that if Danny got his hands on Homer, he could snap Homer's neck faster than she could get back across the store. So she stood transfixed, clutching the heaviest book she'd found nearby—Harold Bloom's *Shakespeare: Invention of the Human*, an enormous hardcover doorstopper—watching for an opportunity to bring eight hundred pages of hard-core scholarship into direct contact with some vulnerable part of Danny's body.

"Is this the kind of diversion you were hoping for?" Scarlett whispered to Vashti.

All three cats stood in silent, open-mouthed awe as ten seconds ticked by.

"I've never been this proud of him," Scarlett said. Which was true. Before this moment, she'd never once been proud of Homer at all.

"He can't keep it up forever," Kotik said. *"He's getting tired."*

With the eye of a natural predator, calibrated to detect the faintest signs of weakness, Vashti saw the way the barely perceptible pauses between Homer's attacks grew longer. He was definitely starting to flag.

"You have to open the door for Hot Mike," Vashti told Scarlett. *"Go now while everybody's distracted."*

"If I open that door right now, Rachel's probably going to see me—she'll know I did it." Scarlett, giving her paws one last wipe-down on the paper towels, paused to look meaningfully at Vashti.

"Rachel's going to know a lot of things when this is all over." Vashti's tone was resigned. *"It can't be helped."*

Scarlett walked forward carefully, eyeing the distance between herself and the front door. *"I'm still pretty slippery."* She placed one tentative paw onto the terrazzo, testing. Would it slide? She shifted a fraction of her weight forward, felt the paw begin to glide, and tried to pull back.

Too late! That small momentum carried her forward. Her front legs skated ahead while her back legs remained anchored in place, stretching Scarlett out like pulled taffy.

She scrabbled frantically, claws clicking uselessly against the polished floor, managing to haul herself back together just before her chin would have made contact.

Behind her, she heard Vashti's sharp intake of breath.

Another desperate attempt at forward motion sent her into an undignified spin near Mysteries. *Screw it,* Scarlett thought. She dropped to her haunches and pushed off with her hind legs, using her front paws to accelerate and steer. Walking had been slow and difficult, but *this* was amazing! Scarlett scooted across the terrazzo as smoothly as an ice skater. She careered dizzily in the direction of the front door, picking up speed as she passed Fiction and headed toward Self-Help. Danny looked up briefly and saw her gliding past—and Scarlett, unable to resist, grinned evilly at him as she went.

Danny had no idea *what* the oily creature with the crazy spiked fur actually was. But the way it bared its teeth at him as it sped past would haunt his nightmares for years to come.

Homer, of course, knew exactly who it was. Kotik, Scarlett, and Vashti had only convened in the back storeroom a couple of minutes earlier, but Homer had been aware of their presence the entire time. (More or less. His nose had picked up Kotik, Vashti, and someone else who was *probably* Scarlett...but who also inexplicably smelled like stir-fry night in Rachel's kitchen.)

Homer had heard the way all three of their hearts had begun to beat faster when they'd seen him with Danny. They were scared for him, Homer could tell, but the only thing he himself felt was a wild all-encompassing joy. *This* was what he had been made for! *This* was why he had claws and teeth and speed! Homer let out a loud whoop of delight as Danny once again tried to get past him, and Homer sank his claws into Danny's shin.

Then Homer's ears picked up something else: the distinctive four-beat cadence of a German Shepherd at full gallop, still several blocks away but closing in fast.

"Hot Mike's almost here!" Homer called out breathlessly. *"Scarlett, have you—"*

Homer's split second of distraction, combined with legs beginning to tremble with fatigue, was all Danny needed. Thick fingers finally found purchase on the loose skin at the back of Homer's neck.

The world tilted sickeningly as Homer was yanked into the air. For one terrible moment his paws clawed at nothing, his small body twisting frantically—then the ancient kitten reflex betrayed him, forcing him limp against every screaming instinct. He dangled from Danny's grip, ribs heaving. The fingers around his neck were thick as sausages, and Homer could feel his pulse hammering against them, fragile as a bird's.

Scarlett had made it to the front of the store and was standing at the furthest edge of the display window that held the vintage typewriter and Day-Glo monsters. *"Scarlett,"* Vashti whispered frantically. *"Scarlett, hurry!"*

Scarlett hastily wiped her paws on the black-velvet backdrop of the Halloween display. Then she turned her attention to the bolt above the door handle. All she had to do was flip it from left to right, then dangle herself from the door handle until her weight pulled it down, causing the door to open.

She'd done it a million times. Nothing could be simpler.

Scarlett rose on her hind legs, stretching to reach the bolt. But her right paw, still a little slick, slipped off the metal.

Now the other three cats could hear Hot Mike's approach, too.

Rachel realized Danny had stopped moving—that he'd temporarily rendered Homer immobile. In two swift steps she was upon him with the Harold Bloom, but he saw her coming in his peripheral vision and quickly swung around, holding Homer between them like a shield. He looked like he'd lost a fight with a thornbush.

Hot Mike's galloping footsteps grew louder in Scarlett's ears as she tried again to get the bolt to turn. *"Hurry, Scarlett!"* This time Vashti and Kotik yelled in unison.

Homer flailed helplessly as he dangled by the neck from Danny's hand. His claws sliced at the air and he growled in the direction of Danny's face.

"You're going to do what I say," Danny told Rachel. He was scratched up, out of breath, and clearly trying to recover his dignity. "Or else..." He gave Homer a shake, and Homer hissed wildly. Rachel's vision blurred—not with tears this time but with rage.

Hot Mike was running at the door. He announced his approach with three sharp barks.

Scarlett's whole body shook with the effort of not slipping as she rose on her hind legs once again. Homer's labored breathing filled her ears. Hot Mike's frantic barking grew closer.

If I fail, we did all this for nothing.

Scarlett threw everything she had at the bolt—every ounce of strength, every moment of love she'd never admitted feeling for her irritating little brother. Her paws burned. Her muscles screamed.

This time, the bolt moved. She felt it turn in the opposite direction, then settle with a satisfying click. She continued leaning forward, allowing the weight of her body to drag down the door handle.

A shift in air currents tickled Scarlett's whiskers as the door began to open.

CHAPTER 32

Brock Winfield stood just outside the bookshop. His left hand was thrust into his jacket pocket, where it fingered a small plastic baggie.

In his right hand was a key that unlocked Title Wave's front door.

Brock hadn't made any headway with the health department. All he'd gotten was a big runaround about how Title Wave always passed its inspections handily and how everybody in town just *loved* those "bookstore cats," so why was Brock complaining?

(As it happened, Coacoochee's only public health inspector, Phyllis Weaver, was a thirty-five-year veteran who played bridge with Dorothea

Wilson once a week and had a Russian blue of her own. Like it was news to Brock how riddled with corruption Coacoochee's local government was.)

What Brock needed was incontrovertible evidence. Something no reasonable person could dismiss. A smoking gun. And when, after days of thought, he came up with the solution, he could have kissed himself for being so brilliant. It was like a plot ripped straight from the pages of one of his very own novels.

Brock knew a few socially challenged people who kept cats. All he had to do was grab a few pinches of fur from the rug or couch of one such friend, sneak into Title Wave after hours, sprinkle the fur onto a few mugs and plates, and take pictures of it for proof. Then, *voila!* With photographic evidence right in front of them, the health department would *have* to act. And wasn't it clever of Brock to have had the foresight to hang onto his Title Wave key all these months!

(Actually, Brock had just been too lazy to bring the key back to Dorothea, despite her having asked him for it repeatedly—but making that distinction seemed like splitting hairs.)

Brock grinned as he inserted his contraband key into the lock. By this time tomorrow, pictures of the cat-fur café Rachel ran would be in Phyllis Weaver's hands.

Before Brock could turn the key, however the door slowly creaked open, seemingly of its own volition. Brock hesitated, his gut whispering sharply that this was a bad sign. But curiosity got the better of him. Brock took one tentative step in, then used his hand to open the door the rest of the way.

Fluent as he considered himself to be with his pen, even Brock Winfield couldn't have found the words to depict the tableau before him.

Rachel Baum stood only inches away from Danny Elliott, holding aloft an enormous book that she very clearly planned to brain him with. Danny himself looked as if he'd been through the wars. His shirt was torn in places, and his arms, neck, and cheek were covered in scratches. Rachel must have sicced one of her cats on him. Probably the blind one, Brock thought, watching as it twisted and dangled from Danny's right hand like an angry snake.

Books lay scattered across the floor where displays had been knocked over. The bestseller table sat at an odd angle, its neat pyramid of hardcovers now tumbled in all directions. A spinning rack of bookmarks had tipped over and disgorged its contents across the tile floor.

From the corner of one eye, Brock saw some sort of feral animal with weirdly spiky fur skim across the floor toward the back storeroom. It gave him a baleful glare as it slid past, and Brock felt the hair on his arms rise. He had absolutely no idea what that…that oily *thing*…was, but Brock knew there was only one way to account for it and the chaotic mess all around him and the way Rachel was aiming that book at Danny—apparently with every intention of inflicting serious head trauma upon Coacoochee's premiere celebrity chef.

Rachel Baum had obviously suffered a complete nervous breakdown.

Maybe it was her recent breakup. Maybe it was the stress of her job. But Rachel and sanity had parted ways, and she'd violently assaulted Danny Elliott for good measure.

Who knew what insane thing she'd do next? Unconsciously Brock backed up a step, taking care to hide the camera he was holding behind his back.

Rachel and Danny, both still panting, stopped to look at Brock, as confounded by his presence as Brock was by theirs. Even the blind cat's face turned toward his with blank incomprehension.

Before any of them had had the chance to form a single question in their minds, however, an enormous black-and-tan shape charged past Brock into the shop, nearly pushing him over. Homer caught a strong whiff on the rush of air currents the furry figure brought in, and his heart beat high.

Hot Mike's intelligent brown eyes swept the scene and locked onto Danny Elliott, still holding Homer aloft. A low rumble began deep in his chest. The growl started soft, almost conversational, but grew in volume and menace as Hot Mike took three measured steps forward.

Danny's eyes widened. Once again he attempted to shield himself with the small black cat swinging wildly in his grip. "Look! A *cat.*" He used a sing-songy voice he seemed to feel a dog might appreciate. "Mmmmmm, yummy yummy." Danny once again dangled Homer in front of Hot Mike. "If you leave me alone, I'll let you have this cat. Wouldn't that be more fun?"

Hot Mike's growl grew louder, and his lips pulled back until all his teeth were showing. *"You okay, Homer?"* he woofed. If Homer *wasn't* okay, Hot Mike might have a difficult time controlling his temper.

"I was kicking his ass until he stopped fighting fair!" Homer raged. *"The big crybaby!"* He was still writhing in Danny's grip, which loosened just a

fraction as he swung Homer at the advancing German Shepherd. Quick as a flash, Homer managed to twist his head around and sink his teeth deep into the flesh of Danny's hand.

Danny cried out in pain and dropped Homer to the ground.

Hot Mike advanced on Danny with patient inevitability. Danny stumbled backward, his legs hitting a wooden café chair. He sat down in it, hard.

The instant Danny was seated, Hot Mike's growl stopped. He lowered himself to a perfect sit three feet from Danny's knees, close enough to act, far enough to dodge. His brown eyes locked onto Danny's face with the focus of a dog who'd never lost a staring contest in his life.

Danny leaned forward slightly. This time Hot Mike bared all his teeth, a warning growl so deep it vibrated through the floor and up Danny's spine. Sweat beaded on Danny's forehead, trickling down to sting the scratches Homer had left. His hands gripped the chair arms, knuckles white.

"Nice doggy?" Danny's voice cracked.

After two more attempts to rise—each met with increasingly dramatic displays of canine dentistry—Danny Elliott slumped in defeat. He cradled his bitten hand against his chest, watching as it began to puff up.

Rachel scooped Homer up, her hands closing around his small body. He was warm and alive against her chest, his rapid heartbeat drumming on her palms. She had to sit down hard on the overturned bestseller table, Homer pressed against her as she told him, "Never do anything that stupid again. Never—do you hear me?"

Rachel's scent surrounded Homer like a fortress. He could hear her heart racing as fast as his own, could feel her hands trembling as they checked him for injuries with gentle efficiency. Homer purred and pressed his forehead against hers. Then he dragged his face down to Rachel's chin in the greeting they gave each other when they were happiest at being reunited after a long trip, or even just a long day. *I wasn't being stupid,* Homer's purrs—tired, but happy—told her. *I was saving you.*

"Sabrosa." Danny's voice was low-pitched and dejected. "Vegas, Los Angeles..." Each word came out smaller than the last. The golden boy chef who'd charmed all of Coacoochee was shrinking before their eyes, scratched and bitten, his silk shirt in tatters. "I was going to be on the Food Network."

He looked bitterly at Rachel. "All because some nobody at a party took too much—" He stopped, seeming to realize that confessing further wouldn't help.

Scarlett, Vashti, and Kotik watched from the back storeroom, peeping out carefully to avoid being sighted themselves. Vashti was actually glad to see Brock. Rachel and Homer were okay and now had him as additional backup, along with Hot Mike. Between the three of them, plus Homer, they should be able to keep Danny in line until the police arrived. Vashti could hear Rachel calling 911 now.

Vashti had always known that if their plan to rescue Rachel was successful, Rachel would almost certainly figure out a few things. That she'd find the dumbwaiter shaft, at minimum, seemed a near certainty. How else to explain tonight's odd occurrences? And who knew how hard Rachel would keep looking, once she'd started? The secret cat door could be the next thing to go.

But if one or two things could be attributed to *human* activity, maybe Rachel would be willing to overlook the rest of it.

It was worth hoping for, anyway—no matter how much Scarlett would disapprove.

"You should get home, Kotik," Vashti told him. Laurie would be furious if he stayed out all night again.

She was gratified that he didn't start or tremble or gaze at her like a mooncalf. He simply bunted her on the cheek and said quietly in her ear, *"Get a good night's sleep. You've earned it."* Vashti watched as he disappeared through the cat door, wondering whether he'd find an angry Laurie or clear passage when he got home.

The moment Kotik was gone, Vashti's legs began to shake. The adrenaline that had kept her going drained away all at once, leaving her dizzy. Beside her, Scarlett swayed on her oil-slick paws, her earlier bravado gone. They still had to clean up, had to get upstairs, but Vashti wasn't sure either of them could manage another step.

"Come on," she said wearily to Scarlett. *"I think we might actually get away with this if our luck holds. But we have to get as many of the dirty paper towels as we can into one of those big trash bags, and we have to be upstairs when Rachel gets back."*

"Just when I thought I'd already had all the fun I can possibly stand." Scarlett rolled her eyes, although secretly she was impressed that Vashti had figured out a possible way to protect their secret exits.

"This is Rachel Baum at Title Wave Books," the cats heard her tell the 911 operator, her voice shaky. "Danny Elliott attacked me. He also confessed to the murders of Daisy Locarro and Marc Gottsegen. Yes, he's still here," Rachel added, apparently in response to a question the operator had asked. "Natalie Dunbar's dog is guarding him."

Scarlett cocked one ear toward the store as she worked on shoving the soiled paper towels toward trash bags. Danny was muttering to himself under his breath—nothing Scarlett could make out, although Homer was probably getting an earful. Danny must have tested getting up, as twice Hot Mike snarled loudly before settling back into watchful silence.

Brock had been uncharacteristically quiet. It had quickly dawned on him that he *might* have initially mis-assessed the situation. And now he was in a real pickle, because how was he going to explain his appearance at Title Wave? What possible reason could he manufacture for having deliberately come by *after* the store was closed for the day, prepared to let himself in with a key he no longer had any right to carry?

It was too late to leave unnoticed, or Brock would have slunk out. Besides, from what he'd overheard in Rachel's 911 call, he'd stumbled into ringside seats for what was going to be Coacoochee's most gossiped-about event until at least the Millennium and possibly longer. It was all unfolding right in *front* of him! He was an eyewitness to history!

Maybe even more than an eyewitness? There was, after all, plenty of credit to go around in a situation like this. Surely Rachel would concede that his presence *may* have contributed a *tiny* amount to Danny's apprehension...

Brock knew he hadn't been quite as welcoming to Rachel as he might have been these past few months. He hadn't always lived up to his own standards of graciousness. But perhaps Rachel could be prevailed upon to overlook any lapses in his behavior. Especially considering how sincerely sorry he was for all of it now.

"Listen, Rachel," Brock began in a subdued tone. He moved to bring around the camera, still hidden behind his back, so Rachel could see it. But he paused, unnerved by the way she was looking at him. Agog and perplexed. As if she had never seen him before.

"You saved my life, Brock." Rachel's voice cracked with emotion. "If you hadn't opened that door when you did..."

"WHAT?!!?" Scarlett screeched from the back room—so loudly that Homer had to pretend the sound came from him, causing Rachel to eye him quizzically. Vashti hurried to Scarlett's side.

"This is how we get to keep the dumbwaiter," she told her sternly.

"Well, I..." Brock trailed off. Any minute now, Rachel was going to realize there was no logical reason for him to be there. Should he come up with some stupid explanation before she asked for one? That would probably look less suspicious. "It's funny, because the only reason I'm even here is..."

Once again Brock fell silent midsentence—this time because Rachel had walked across the room to throw herself into his arms.

"Thank you," she told him tearfully. "I wouldn't even be standing here right now if it wasn't for you!" Rachel pulled a tissue from her jeans pocket and blew her nose. "And thank you for saving Homer's life, too."

"It was...erm..." Brock awkwardly patted Rachel's back with one hand, still holding the telltale camera with the other. "It was my pleasure."

"This is SO not worth it," Scarlett grumbled in the back room. They would have to spend the next few weeks listening to Rachel call Brock a "hero"—and all because he was taking credit for something that *she,* Scarlett, had done!

Scarlett's three years of life thus far had been an endless catalog of grievances and wrongs inflicted upon her. Nevertheless, this was still the least fair thing she'd ever heard of.

CHAPTER 33

HIBISCUS ROAD HAD SURRENDERED to Halloween with characteristic excess. Fairy lights in the royal palms jostled for attention with glowing strings of plastic jack-o'-lanterns. Storefronts that usually wore their pastel colors with dignity now sported cardboard witches, inflatable ghosts, and enough fake cobwebs to suggest a year's worth of shoddy housekeeping. Music rose in all directions—"Monster Mash" on repeat from the vintage boutique, atmospheric lounge music from the 710 Bar, which was projecting *Nosferatu* in a continuous loop on its rear wall. Spooky tangos emanated from Club Yucca, and Laurie's Closet had been playing Rob Zombie all day.

The pedestrian mall grew ever more crowded as the sun set, the throngs a preview of what Hibiscus Road would look like in just a few weeks, when Season finally began. Costumed children darted between the legs of exhausted parents like schools of tropical fish—witches and zombies, two Backstreet Boys, a wailing dinosaur whose younger brother, Charlie Chaplin, had stolen his KitKat. Adults spilled in and out of bars dressed as genies, doctors, ghosts. Sonny and Cher paused to chat with three Marie Antoinettes—complete with gloves, crinolines, and skyscraper wigs—who held court over a shared cigarette outside Gallery Moda.

At nine p.m. precisely, the parade would begin on Allamanda Avenue, led by the Coacoochee High marching band dressed as skeletal mariachis. Any and all Coacoocheeans who wished to march behind the band and show off their costumes were invited to do so. Until then, Hibiscus Road was clearly the place to be, thrumming with the kind of energy that suggested everyone had agreed to be ridiculous together, just for tonight.

Photographers were out in full force to document yet another Coacoochee Halloween celebration, and a tight cluster had formed around Title Wave Books. Isabella Stuart stood in front of the store in a drop-waist Daisy Buchanan dress with Art Deco beading and a feathered headband. She had, after all, volunteered to manage publicity for Title Wave's Halloween event. And if Isabella was conscious, as she greeted reporters, that this was also the venue where one of her star clients had threatened to murder a shopkeeper—having just murdered *another* of her star clients in his own home—she gave no sign of it. Isabella's voice was calm and professional while cameras clicked around her, and she gestured at Title Wave's display windows—where the Hawaiian-shirted skeleton and spooky vintage typewriter made their farewell appearance—with poised assurance.

Rachel also stood on Hibiscus Road, watching as costumed children and their exhausted parents streamed out through Title Wave's doors to begin trick-or-treating. Standing next to her was Dahlia Delgado. "I'm going to miss him when he's gone." Dahlia regarded the plastic skeleton mournfully.

"We'll come up with something great for Thanksgiving," Rachel assured her.

"I know you will." Dahlia slung an arm around Rachel's shoulders and squeezed her in a brief side hug. "You've handled everything with such grace, *mami*," she added in a low, confidential tone. "Everybody thinks so." The Chamber of Commerce had sent Dahlia on Wednesday with an immediate offer to find a backup location for this year's pre-parade celebration. Nobody expected Rachel even to show up at Title Wave by Saturday, much less plan a full day of Halloween festivities for half the town.

Time off sounded good in theory, Rachel acknowledged, and a big part of her longed for just that. But after only one day upstairs "recuperating," she'd insisted on getting back to work.

In fact, the more work the better.

Rachel reminded herself that this was what she'd signed up for as she surveyed tables sticky with the remains of "monster brains" (raspberry Jell-O with mandarin orange segments suspended inside), crumbs from the "mummy dogs" (pigs in blankets wrapped to look bandaged, with mustard dots for eyes), and the spectacular wreckage of the "haunted graveyard cake"—chocolate sheet cake covered in crushed Oreos, with Milano cookies as tombstones and gummy worms writhing through the "dirt." Some of the moms had stepped in after Danny's arrest, and Rachel had to admit the kids seemed just as happy with Jell-O as they would have been with any of Danny's more ambitious creations.

Nick Torres and his family were among the last stragglers. Nick was due at the station before the parade started—Halloween was always a lively night in Coacoochee, especially when it fell on a Saturday—but the kids had wanted to stay at Title Wave long enough for the face painter to complete her *pièce de résistance*: clown makeup for Lucas (who was otherwise dressed as a cowboy) and "fairy princess" heart and flower designs for Hanna, who wore a pair of iridescent butterfly wings. Nick caught sight of Rachel standing outside with Dahlia, the black-velvet cat ears she wore only slightly askew in the curls of her hair. Her simple black dress and tights still looked surprisingly sharp after hours of reading spooky stories, supervising craft stations, and cleaning up spills. Hard to believe that just four days ago, she'd been fighting for her life in this same space.

Also hard to believe Hot Mike had flunked police training! Nick looked over to where he stood now, pressing against Natalie Dunbar's leg as she chatted with Dorothea Wilson. Natalie was dressed as Crocodile Dundee—leather vest, distinctive hat, the whole works—but every eye turned to the German Shepherd beside her. No costume for Hot Mike, although he might as well have been wearing a cape. The "hero dog" story had been all over the news, and people around town still pointed and stared when he and Natalie went out.

Nick caught her eye as he was leaving, and the two exchanged friendly nods. Then Nick and his family merged with the trick-or-treating multitudes swarming Hibiscus Road.

Natalie had been as perplexed as anyone when she'd finally made it to Title Wave on Tuesday night, panting and more than a little harried from having dashed into business after business on Hibiscus Road, looking fruitlessly for Hot Mike. She was no less astonished in hearing about his fortuitously timed entrance than Rachel had been to see it happen. How could Hot Mike possibly have known how desperately his help had been needed?

"Honestly, the way Danny was shrieking, I'm surprised the whole neighborhood didn't come running." Danny himself was being led out in handcuffs as Rachel made this observation, and she smiled sweetly at him as he was manhandled past her. "Hot Mike must've heard it and thought somebody was attacking an opera diva."

"I guess so…" Natalie said doubtfully. It was a nagging question, and Natalie didn't give up easily on nagging questions. Journalistic curiosity notwithstanding, however, she realized this was probably the best explanation she was ever going to get, and decided to let the matter drop.

Natalie and Hot Mike ended up spending the night in Rachel's apartment—along with Tommy, who was duly called and notified as soon as Rachel had finished giving her official statement to Jessica Martinez. A quick trip upstairs to check on Scarlett and Vashti revealed that, on top of everything else, Scarlett had somehow managed to overturn an entire bottle of Wesson Oil onto her head. "Stay with me," she'd said to Natalie. "We'll order a pizza and you can help me bathe my incredibly pissed-off cat." This was a fair description; Rachel had never seen a deeper scowl on Scarlett's face.

The three of them sat on Rachel's terrace until the sun came up, drinking from the bottle of vodka Tommy brought and picking at the remains of the pizza. Natalie claimed to be "surprised, but not *flabbergasted*" about Danny. "I always thought he was a little *too* charming."

"Thanks for the heads-up," Rachel said dryly.

"Don't get me wrong," Natalie said hastily. "End of the day, I still thought it was Julian. Next time I investigate a poisoning," she added sheepishly, "remind me to *start* with the bloke that cooks everyone's food."

Rachel laughed, but only a little. There wouldn't be any "next time" for her.

Tommy, meantime, had shared the news that he'd called Isabella and taken his name out of the running to replace her at the *Daily News*. He'd also put in his notice at *Palm*. This was a genuinely shocking development, and Rachel's mouth fell open as she regarded him.

"I've been thinking about it ever since Julian threatened you," Tommy said. "If something I wrote five years ago could lead to so much ugliness now, maybe I don't want to write things like that anymore."

Rachel thought of Julian with a twinge. Nick had told her what happened. She'd realized too late that Julian's threat had actually been a warning—that he had, in his own way, been trying to help her.

In the end, though, he couldn't even help himself. Now all his projects and properties would grind to a halt while lawyers hashed over the minutiae of his vast estate. In the days that followed, nobody in Coacoochee would be able to identify a single verifiable heir.

Vashti had laid claim to Tommy's lap the moment he'd sat down, and Hot Mike had fallen asleep on the terrace floor, his huge head resting on Natalie's feet. Homer was an immovable fixture in Rachel's lap. Between his physical exhaustion and the warm relief of Rachel's familiar scent, Homer had passed out-cold. Rachel looked down at him, still not quite able to believe they'd both gotten through the night's events alive and unharmed. The warmth of his fur beneath her tenderly stroking fingers seemed miraculous, somehow, and Rachel bent to whisper in his ear.

"Eres mucho gato," she told him, paraphrasing Ernest Hemingway in *For Whom the Bell Tolls*.

Thou art plenty of cat.

Only Scarlett remained alone, drying sulkily atop a terrycloth towel on one of the chaise lounges. "Poor Scarlett!" Rachel exclaimed as she drained the last of her vodka. "You may be the only one whose night was worse than mine."

Scarlett threw her a baleful look. *"You don't know the half of it."*

EVEN WITH THE STORE'S recent notoriety—not to mention Isabella Stuart's professional prowess—Rachel wasn't sure how many people would turn out for the "grown-ups" party on Halloween night. So it came as a heartening surprise to find the store packed to capacity (and possibly a scooch beyond) before it was even eight o'clock.

Rachel always loved the way Title Wave looked, but even she had to admit it had never looked better than it did tonight. Glittering cobwebs stretched between shelves in gossamer sheets that caught the purple and orange spotlights Rachel and Nadia had set up, creating shadows that shifted and breathed with the movement of the crowd. Paper lanterns in deep crimson and midnight black cast pools of colored light across the terrazzo floor, while vintage horror-movie posters had replaced the usual cover blowups adorning the walls. The poetry corner had become a fortune-teller's lair, complete with shimmering curtains and a crystal ball that caught the light and cast rainbows onto laughing faces.

Even the cash register had transformed into a Gothic masterpiece, draped in rich burgundy velvet and crowned with an elaborate candelabra whose electric flames flickered so realistically that guests reached out to test their heat. The entire store glowed with an otherworldly ambiance that turned familiar corners into mysterious grottos where pirates traded gossip with phantoms, and witches in couture gowns shrieked with delight.

Rachel stood behind the café counter dispensing hot apple cider in paper cups. Griselda, dressed as Morticia Addams, was helping—although finding it difficult to keep her enormous sleeves from dipping into the crockpot keeping the cider warm. Rachel was also slightly paranoid about spilling anything on her own dress; she did, after all, have her first date with Evan Kirschner later that evening.

"Have you thought about what you're going to do next?" Rachel asked Griselda when there was a lull in the action. It had only been a few days since Danny was arrested, but Rachel knew from experience that when your life falls apart, *What's Going to Happen to Me Now?* is the movie your mind plays and re-plays on an endless loop.

"I'm not sure yet." Griselda waved at her boyfriend, Paolo, who'd dressed as Gomez Addams and was now approaching the café counter. "I've almost finished up my business degree at Nova so..." She shrugged prettily and smiled at Rachel. "I guess we'll see! *Gracias, mi amor*," she added to Paolo, who'd brought her a small packet of candy corn wrapped in colorful cellophane. "These are my secret weakness," she confided in Rachel with a wink. "Don't tell anyone!"

Rachel chatted with Griselda and Paolo for a few more minutes, then let Nadia, costumed as Rosie the Riveter, take over the hot cider and headed toward the front of the store to tidy the display tables. "Mysteries To Die For" was still in decent shape, but "Gothic Romance" was a disordered mass of heaving bosoms and brooding castles. Clearly this was a popular genre, Rachel noted as she neatly restacked the books. Unlike the pristine, almost entirely undisturbed display table dedicated to *Borrowed Glory*. Rachel didn't know if it was the book itself that accounted for lackluster sales thus far or Brock's tendency to hover nearby, lying in wait to rope hapless passersby into a conversation about the way he'd saved *two* lives right here, in this very store.

Rachel was no fool. She'd seen Brock's camera and knew he probably hadn't been skulking about Title Wave after hours with the purest of intentions. But fair was fair, she told herself. Brock had saved her life. And Homer's, too! A front-of-store display table all to himself—just through Thanksgiving—seemed like the least she could offer in return.

Scarlett had already coughed up three hairballs on the *Borrowed Glory* display. Rachel was beginning to suspect it was deliberate.

The party around her was now in full swing. Dorothea, dressed as Agatha Christie in a sensible tweed skirt and oxford shoes, regaled a group of cronies over by Caribbean travel. She paused mid-anecdote to give Laurie and Robert Castillo pecks on the cheek as they made their way past her in the crowd. Laurie was a riot of color as Frida Kahlo, her costume a masterpiece of layered Mexican textiles and fresh flowers woven into her elaborate updo. Robert was pitch perfect in Diego Rivera's paint-splattered smock and wide-brimmed hat. Rachel had already told Nadia not to worry about cleanup—that she'd take care of it herself in the morning—but the grad student nevertheless moved through the crowd now, collecting discarded paper cups into a trash bag.

Tommy approached in full Ziggy Stardust regalia—a metallic silver jumpsuit that caught and reflected every colored light in the store, paired with four-inch platform boots that had him towering unsteadily above the crowd. The iconic lightning bolt blazed across his right eye in metallic red and blue paint, and he wore a red mullet wig with gravity-defying spikes. Glitter dusted his cheekbones, his face had been contoured into sharper angles, and his lips were painted deep metallic purple, completing the otherworldly transformation to glam rock alien.

He held two cups of cider, and Rachel accepted one gratefully. "Have I told you how amazing your costume is?"

Tommy killed his cider in one long swallow. "And have I told *you* how amazing your costume *isn't*." He looked pointedly at Rachel's black dress, black tights, and black ballet flats, then shook his head sadly. "I don't know why you'd even bother walking in the parade tonight. You'll never win the costume contest like this."

"You seem to have forgotten that I *won't* be walking in the parade. Remember?" Rachel felt her cheeks warm as the grin spread across her face. "I'm going out with Evan tonight. All I have to do is take off the ears, and I'm wearing a simple, tasteful black dress that just happens to look awesome on me."

Tommy stepped back and surveyed her critically. "It *does* look awesome on you," he agreed, smiling at her. "You've come a long way in six months."

From the corner of her eye, Rachel saw Evan walk in. With a start, she realized that five entire days had gone by in which she hadn't thought about Henry once. Surely that was progress. It was getting harder with each passing day to remember what her life before Coacoochee had felt like.

"I think you might be right about that," she told Tommy.

Rachel thought at first that Evan wasn't wearing a costume—although she wasn't sure why he'd opted for a suit and tie. But as he walked deeper into the store and began to look around for her, she noted his thick glasses (Evan didn't wear glasses) and the Superman t-shirt peeking out beneath his partially unbuttoned dress shirt.

"Eight-thirty!" Without warning, the music stopped playing and Dahlia Delgado's voice rose above the din of murmured conversations. "We need to start moving toward Allamanda if we want good spots for the parade."

Evan looked up just then and saw her. A smile lit up his face, and Rachel could feel her heart beat faster.

"Good luck in the costume contest!" she told Tommy, squeezing his arm as she walked away.

RACHEL'S THREE CATS HADN'T wanted to attend Title Wave's Halloween party. Homer in particular.

Rachel was in perfect agreement.

Homer had always attracted attention, but lately it had become overwhelming. Anytime he'd set one paw in the store this whole week, he'd been overwhelmed by gawkers and well-wishers and people asking (or even demanding) to have their picture taken with him.

Rachel decided it might be best for all concerned if the cats made fewer downstairs appearances until things had settled down. She seemed to have accepted that Homer had pushed the screen from the open window, jumped out, and somehow found his way back inside the building. Like Natalie, she realized more or less consciously that this was the only explanation she was ever likely to get, so she might as well make her peace with it.

Still, Rachel felt better knowing that her cats were safely tucked away upstairs.

So they observed Halloween night from above—sprawled atop the wall on Rachel's terrace that overlooked Hibiscus Road—as the exodus from Title Wave began in earnest. Pirates stumbled arm-in-arm with zombies, their plastic swords and fake wounds dramatic under the fairy lights. A group of mermaids in iridescent stilettos clicked past, shedding sequined scales as they navigated the crowded pavement.

Homer swiveled his head to track the cacophony of laughter and music drifting up from Hibiscus Road. The autumn air rose to meet him, mixing with perfume and greasepaint and the lingering sweetness of drugstore candy.

Vashti saw Brock go by. He was half-jogging to keep up with a man in a vampire costume, insisting, "*Two* lives. I saved *two* lives that night!"

Scarlett had seen him, too. *"At least we still have the dumbwaiter shaft,"* Vashti said, but Scarlett's expression remained stony.

"It could have been a lot worse," Vashti reminded her gently.

Surprisingly, Scarlett actually appeared to consider this. Her face softened, and her eyes turned in Homer's direction.

And then something astonishing happened—something that had never happened even once before:

Scarlett gave Homer a compliment.

"That was a brave thing you did." Homer could hear the sincerity in her voice—along with the struggle it had taken for Scarlett to bring herself to say it. *"For Rachel, I mean."*

Homer's chest swelled with pride. He'd been waiting for Scarlett's praise his whole life! But he was also embarrassed, somehow, and if he'd been a human, Scarlett and Vashti would have seen him blush furiously. *"Aw, that's okay,"* he managed. *"You would have done the same thing."*

Scarlett wasn't so sure about that, but she let it drop. The cats continued to watch the Halloween revelers below, now moving with determination in the direction of Allamanda Avenue. Rachel emerged from Title Wave, having shed her cat ears somewhere between the store and the street. Her black dress looked elegant in its simplicity, especially compared to the costume chaos surrounding her.

Beside her, Evan had loosened his tie further, the Superman logo now fully visible beneath his dress shirt. They paused on the sidewalk, and even from the terrace, the cats could see them laughing at something—probably Evan's attempt at adjusting his fake glasses.

"Rachel looks happy," Vashti said.

"She sounds happy too," Homer observed, able to hear the trace of laughter in Rachel's voice, even from all the way up on the terrace.

"We should go inside," Scarlett said. *"It's getting late."*

The cool fall air was too pleasant, however, for the cats to think of going in just yet. They stayed as Rachel and Evan turned down Hibiscus Road in the opposite direction from the throngs headed toward Allamanda. They stayed until Hibiscus Road had exhaled into stillness, leaving only a few bedraggled cardboard witches and mounds of candy wrappers tumbling like autumn leaves in the salt-scented breeze. They stayed until they heard the first distant chords of music from the Coacoochee High marching band as they prepared to lead the 1998 Coacoochee Halloween Parade.

Only then did the three cats stand, stretch, and move toward the comfort of their beds inside.

Heartfelt thanks and profound gratitude to my amazing Patreon patrons (and their cats!), without whom I could never have completed this book.

Special thanks to Patti, Nikolaka & Koa!

- Diane Aba
- Alyson Amsterdam (and Louie & Biggie)
- Margaret Auld-Louie (and Blossom & Phoenix)
- Julie Brandt (and Lizzy)
- Charles Brackney (and Shane & Chloe)
- Dorothy Brown (and Patrick, Camel & Sugar Maple)
- Jane Broyles
- Julie Burns
- Lisa Calarese (and Riley, Mordecai & Rigby)
- Mari Cisneros (and Tabitha)
- Dawn Cole (and Reggie)
- Maria Dallin (and Creamsicle)
- Paige Davis (and Grey Goose)
- Christina DeSalvo (and Beaver, Silver & Nugget
- Deborah Foresman (and Tinkerbell)
- Jamie Forster (and Leenda
- Paul Froiland (and Louie & Fitzy)
- Meg Galipault (and Scout, Waffles, Sisu, Dru & Huckleberry)
- Serena Rae Gallegos (and Katniss, Peeta & Primrose)
- Lee-Ann Gillian (and Nemo, Kenobi & Frodo Underfoot)
- Tracy Ginnane
- Jayne Goby (and Frankie Rotten Cat & her other feline friends!)
- Sara Goodman (and Dennis)

» Wanda Goodwin (and Lewie Stewart)
» Jill Graves (and Greyson)
» Susan Haenicke (and Bessie & Hamilton)
» Marianne Harding (and Charles Carlos Ambrose Harding)
» Sue Harsevoort (and Mac, PC & George)
» J. Eric Hoehn
» Wendie Howland (and Mikey and Ava)
» Susan Anne Kadlec (and Maggie, Sammy, Dynamo & Shelley)
» Andrew Kaplan (and Penelope)
» K. Karpet (and Simon, Fausto, Walter & Jacob)
» Connie Keith-Kerns (and Zoey, Ari, Kai & Mrf)
» Julie Kennedy
» Calvin & Eileen Keyser (and Ashes, Ninja & Snickers)
» Beth Kirby
» Ken Kistner (and Beau, Hunter, Bear, Blue, Amber, Hera, Max, Sam, Zeus, Apollo & Athena)
» Catherine Larklund
» Louisa Lee
» Carole Loftin (and Seamus, Thelma, Biscuit & Brazil)
» Julie Lowe (and Gracie, Cougar, Java, Raven, Meeko, & Bella)
» Laveda Malu (and Baby Sherlock & Ariaal Ashlie)
» Dolores Manzino (and Antigone "Tiggy")
» Angie Mason (and Mickey & Ellerbean)
» Martha Moore (and Cagney, Kelsey, Holly, Tabitha, Charlotte, Matilda, Olivia, Savannah, Emma, Ashley, Tyler, Jacob, Caleb, Logan, Duncan, & Brandon)
» TJ Murphy (and Reggie, Thomase, Jacob & Oliver)
» David Nagreski (and Smokey & Ember)
» Matthew O'Leary (and Hank)
» Melanie Paradise (and Idia)
» Teresa Pesce (and TabbyCat)
» Stephanie Peters (and Alfie, remembering Max)
» Magdalena Plewinska (and Bassie)
» D.H. Powell IV (and Bobby & Willow)
» Vanessa Ramirez
» Stephanie Reicen (and Oliver, Mickey & Helen)
» Kathryn Rigsby

» Felicia Roe (and Eurydice & Cassiopeia)
» Janice Rogenski (and Buster, Misty & Alyssa)
» Andrea Sachs (and Abby & Jimmy)
» Kathy Schlichthernlein (and Bastet, Serenity, Meowcielago & the Gang)
» Zoe Shinno (and Midnite)
» Christine Sorenson
» Andrea Sparkevicius (and Binx & Butters)
» Emily Stafford (and Randy & Pepper)
» Anne Teghtmeyer
» Margaret Tucker (and Princess & Carol)
» Anita Uotinen (and Sheldon, Mikey, Hadley, Sierra, Hope, & Little Jack Henry)
» Lenai Waite (and Cordelia Fox)
» Allison Walls (and Podo, Rue & Dom)
» Lola Whitehead
» Katie Williams
» Trisha Yost (and Ivan)
» Michele Zarichny

GWEN COOPER IS THE *New York Times* bestselling author of the memoirs *Homer's Odyssey: A Fearless Feline Tale, or How I Learned About Love and Life with a Blind Wonder Cat*; *Homer: The Ninth Life of a Blind Wonder Cat*; and *Homer Returns*, as well as the novel *Love Saves the Day*, narrated from a rescue cat's point of view. Her work has been published in more than two-dozen languages. She is a frequent speaker at shelter fundraisers across the U.S. and Europe and donates 10% of her royalties from *Homer's Odyssey* to organizations that serve abused, abandoned, and disabled animals. **You Only Live Nine Times** is her first mystery novel.

Gwen lives in New Jersey with her husband, Laurence. She also lives with her two perfect cats—Clayton "the Tripod" and his litter-mate, Fanny—who aren't impressed with any of it.

www.gwencooper.com